## THE RED LANTERNS

The Lanterns were known in mercenary circles for three things: their high contract price, their absolute ruthlessness, and the color of their airplanes: SU-27 Flankers, the big, maneuverable Russian-designed fighters that were deadly in the hands of an experienced pilot, another trait for which the Lanterns were famous.

Sent by Viktor's moneymen, there were now forty-eight of them joining the massive dogfight over the small island in the middle of the South China Sea. The Lanterns split into four waves of twelve. It was all too clear that once they hooked up with the surviving Tornados, Jags and Q-9s, they would make mincemeat out of the remaining United American airplanes, which were depleted of fuel and ammunition.

The MiG-25 Foxbat, painted all black with a hot red trim, came suddenly out of the northwest. It was huge for a fighter, long of snout, thick of wing, with a pair of high-rising tailfins. It tore through the air swiftly, laying down a constant barrage of sonic booms, before targeting each plane and shooting it down.

From the beginning there was no doubt whose side the mysterious airplane was on or who was at its controls—Hawk Hunter, the Wingman, had arrived!

# WINGMAN

## TARGET: POINT ZERO

### MACK MALONEY

**PINNACLE BOOKS**
**KENSINGTON PUBLISHING CORP.**

PINNACLE BOOKS are published by

Kensington Publishing Corp.
850 Third Avenue
New York, NY 10022

Pinnacle and the P logo Reg. U.S. Pat. & TM Off.

First Printing: August, 1996

Printed in the United States of America

10 9 8 7 6 5 4 3 2 1

# Prologue

Five years have passed since the end of the Big War.

The American continent, once fractured and steeped in anarchy, has been recivilized. A central government is now firmly in place in Washington, both coasts have been reconnected and cleanup of the country's devastated midsection has begun. Many citizens who had fled to Free Canada in the times of trouble have now returned, repopulating the cities and the countryside.

Once again, a strong military establishment is in place to protect the liberties that had been lost and then won back at great cost.

The revival of American freedom was, for the most part, the work of a small group of modern-day patriots, professional soldiers who'd planned the campaigns, fought the wars and apprehended the criminals and terrorists responsible for so much misery in postwar America. These men, and the armed forces they still command, are known as the United Americans.

But just because America is now stable and free, this doesn't mean the struggle is over. Major battles have been fought against America's enemies in the Pacific and most recently in Southeast Asia, brutal campaigns which the United Americans won through a combination of strength, cunning and the knowledge that their purpose was right and just.

Once again, a new, more dangerous menace is emerging, one that threatens the renewed America more than any other in the past five years.

One which will present the United Americans with their most serious challenge yet.

# Part One

# One

It was hot.

Broiling hot. So hot the air was thick with scorching vapors, rising and falling across the lush, devastated tropical landscape.

It was midmorning now and the sun was its usual merciless self. Off to the west was a swift-moving, high, dark bank of clouds that stretched from one horizon to the other.

In minutes, it was overhead, obscuring the sun and turning everything dark. The first rain drops began to fall and in a heartbeat, they were coming down at a steady pace. After a half minute, the rain was a torrent. In forty-five seconds, it was like a hurricane. Within a minute, it was a full-blown monsoon.

Just like that, the heat of the morning was replaced by a deluge of hot steamy water. It was amazing to see, the best Nature could offer as proof that when things changed in this haunted part of the world, they usually did so very quickly.

On the main runway of the air base, the wreck of an airplane was still burning, some forty-eight hours after it had crashed. The monsoon rains would soon put an end to that—even now the plane's hot metal was sizzling in the growing storm. Clouds of steam were rising above the burned and battered airplane, too. Like a dying breath, they ascended only a few hundred feet before fading away completely.

The airplane was a C-5—or it had been at one time. Still visible on its skeletal front section were the remains of the twenty-foot-high shark's mouth, the signature nose art of the special operations group which had called the airplane home for the past month. Only this snout had remained intact in the crash and had remained unburned in the time since. This, too, was a sign from the ethers—a cosmic tweak that sometimes good does endure, if only in repose.

In the large building at the opposite end of the five thousand, four hundred foot runway, twenty-four men were sitting around a huge table. Their names were familiar to those privy to the United American command structure: Toomey, Wa, Crunch, Kurjan, Geraci. They were ignoring the tempest which had appeared so suddenly outside. This storm, as violent as it might be, was a daily occurrence in Da Nang. The monsoon arrived with such regularity, you could set your watch to it. Still, the men inside the building had ceased to be impressed by it long ago. They had other things on their minds.

Six of the two dozen people sitting around the table were heavily bandaged, sporting broken arms, legs, and fingers, along with many bruises, cuts, and minor burns. But they were all alive—and that was the most important thing. They, and twenty-two other men, had been inside the big JAWS C-5 when it crashed at Da Nang. It had been a spectacular wreck, all fire and smoke and dust, but in the end every man aboard the big airplane had made it out alive. That shark-toothed mouth on the wreck of their airplane wasn't smiling for nothing.

The six men were Captain Jim Cook, his staff officers

Warren Maas, Mark Snyder, Sean Higgens, Clancy Miller and Jack Norton, the top echelon of the JAWS group. Formerly of upstate New York, the JAWS team had evolved from a local police force into a crack special ops outfit which specialized in everything from mountain warfare to fighting in the desert. Battered and bruised as they were, this was a happy occasion. No one else in the room believed they'd ever see these men again. But they were here, alive, and with an astonishing tale to tell.

They had been part of the first legion of C-5s dispatched to Vietnam at the height of the emergency in Southeast Asia. Of all the first group of planes sent, the JAWS crew were the only ones who didn't make it. Everyone feared they'd gone down in the South China Sea, either at the hands of enemy fighters or the harsh elements. They had been intercepted about forty miles off the coast, in the middle of a monsoon, by two fighter jets, who escorted them to a small island one hundred twenty miles away. It was only by cool piloting and massive energy conservation that the JAWS C-5 made the trip at all—its tanks were dry when it finally touched down on the island.

As it turned out, the two interceptors had done them a favor. There had been a pack of MiG-25 jets hiding in the storm, just waiting to pick off stragglers in the United Americans' C-5 fleet. The JAWS plane would have certainly fallen to them had the two mystery airplanes not shown up when they did.

But who were these benefactors? Crawling out of their empty plane that day, the JAWS team soon learned the people who ran the base on the secret island were a collection of mercenaries, tech people and strategists, all loyal to a command staff of British RAF pilots, known informally as the Tommies.

The Tommies were in Southeast Asia for the same reason the American C-5s were: to help the South Vietnamese fight off the threat of the enemy of the north, the quasi-communistic enterprise, known as CAPCOM. While literally thousands of mercenaries had helped the South Vietnamese recently prevail over the brutal CAPCOM, the Tommies and their small legion had been working behind the scenes, attacking CAPCOM ships in transit, intercepting and destroying CAPCOM aircraft and running naval covert actions.

They were a highly secret unit and they had to stay that way to be effective. This meant that, although JAWS had been saved from a certain doom, they had to stay put, on the secret island, and remain *incommunicato* until the war on the Vietnamese mainland played out.

Only when they heard that CAPCOM had lost the last key battle—more to their operations going bankrupt, than the outcome on the field—did JAWS attempt to rejoin the American Expeditionary Force. A nasty encounter with two rogue MiG-25s on the way back had resulted in a very shot-up C-5, thus the spectacular crash landing at Da Nang. But payback was a bitch—both MiGs fell to the guns sprouting out of the gigantic JAWS gunship before either fighter could deliver a killing blow.

So now JAWS was back—and the American Expeditionary Force was whole again. But they had brought with them word of an even-larger threat to the region, one that made the brutal shenanigans of CAPCOM pale by comparison. That's why this meeting was called. The battered and burned JAWS team was briefing the United American command staff on what they'd discovered while everyone else was out fighting the Second Vietnam War.

Captain Cook, the overall leader of JAWS, displayed a series of high-altitude recon pictures. The photos were all of an island located some five hundred sixty miles southeast of Tommy Island, one of the Paracel Islands. The island in the photos bore the unlikely name of "Lolita." Probably a bastardization of the name Loaita

Island, this speck was located about five hundred miles west of the Philippines, almost equidistant between the Filipino city of Balabac and the Vietnamese coast. The photos had all been taken at weeklong intervals over the past six weeks.

Cook held up the first shot. It showed the twenty-square-mile Lolita Island from a height of forty thousand feet. It looked like a postal stamp surrounded by water. It was as close to being nowhere as one could get.

"As you can see, in this first photo we have a flat piece of rock," Cook explained. "Barren. No trees. No vegetation. No people."

He held the second photo.

"Same place, a week later. Still flat. Still barren. But notice the dark spot right in the middle."

The photo was passed around. In the exact middle of the square Island, a dark shape had begun to form.

"Same place, a week later," Cook said, distributing a third photo. This one showed the dark spot had grown bigger.

"Here's four and five," Cook continued, holding up two photos which showed the dark spot now expanded to nearly half the island. "And six and seven . . ."

These last two showed the island nearly covered by the shadowy spot. Everyone agreed that it looked like vegetation had filled in the island's formerly bare terrain—but had done so in an incredibly short amount of time.

"According to the Tommies, that island hasn't sprouted vegetation in thousands of years," Cook explained. "Yet now, in less than two months, it's suddenly a jungle."

It was a rather tantalizing mystery—but then Cook revealed an even more sinister angle.

"The Tommies have noticed some Asian Cult activity in the region lately, too," he said, his voice raspy with anger.

This news did not surprise anyone around the table.

The Asian Mercenary Cult was the Number One trouble-maker in the Pacific Rim. Sailing a fleet of some three dozen battleships, they'd been terrorizing the helpless people of the islands stretching from Japan, their home base, all the way to Indonesia and beyond. The Cult had been major supporters of CAPCOM in this latest Indo-china war—until CAPCOM began losing, that is.

"The Tommies know that if the Cult is involved in this, no matter how minor their role," Cook explained, "then something foul is afoot."

There was a round of grim agreement from those gath-ered.

"So what do the Tommies want from us?" Ben Wa, one of the top United American officers asked.

Cook just shrugged. "Well, they're a small outfit," he told them. "And the trouble is, they don't have the pro-jection needed to check out what's going on on that is-land. They've got a couple Tornado jets and a converted destroyer. But their airplanes can't land there—and if the destroyer is spotted anywhere near Lolita, their cover will be blown. That would be disastrous. Their whole reason for being is their secrecy."

There was a wave of troubled looks around the table.

"So they want us to do it for them?" Ben Wa asked.

Cook nodded gravely. "If not us, who?"

A silence descended on the room. Outside the mon-soon continued to roar. Every man involved knew that in saving JAWS, the Tommies had rescued one of their own family. There was no way they could turn down their re-quest for aid. From a contingency standpoint, getting some eyes and ears on the ground on Lolita Island wouldn't be that hard. The C-5 fleet had many options to turn to for such a long-range spy mission.

The problem was that, though the men sitting around the table were well-known for the countless acts of bravery and gallantry in the name of liberty, the group was not complete. Their key member was not among them. Hawk Hunter, AKA the Wingman, had taken off, alone, from Da Nang a little more than seventy-two hours earlier—and no one had heard from him since. They didn't know where he was or even if he was still alive. This cast a disturbing pall over the proceedings.

But, like always, the group pressed on. They discussed the situation with the Tommies and Lolita Island further and decided they would lend a hand and send a spy team to the isolated island.

But in approving the mission, each man knew that this type of thing always went better when Hunter was involved.

And each man couldn't help but wonder exactly where their friend was at the moment. . . .

# Two

*Central Europe*

The huge tanker truck was out of control.

It was skidding down the winding, slippery, barely paved mountain road, tires squealing, brakes smoking, huge clouds of exhaust belching from its twin stacks. It was traveling so close to the edge of the roadway, the rear wheels were sliding out over the ledge on every turn. Trying to recover, the truck would fishtail left, slamming its undercarriage into the mountain wall on the opposite side of the road. With six thousand gallons of gasoline sloshing around in each of its two tanks, it appeared the truck would come to a fiery end at any moment.

But appearances can be deceiving.

The truck was not in trouble. In fact, its driver knew exactly how fast he could go down the steep, icy roadway, how sharp he could turn, how much deceleration he would need to counteract any skidding, all while maintaining a high rate of speed. He'd driven the truck over dozens of mountains in the past forty-eight hours, all of them in the exact same fashion: fast and with controlled abandon. This one was no different.

Hawk Hunter was behind the wheel of the big tanker. He'd been pushing the double-loaded Benz-fueler for two days now, growing colder and more tired with each mile. He'd seen no other human beings in that time; he'd passed no fuel stops, no outposts of civilization, either in the mountains or on the vast stretches of wasteland in between. This part of Europe—last known as the Austrian Free Zone—had been desolate for years. Across the bleak landscape, the gray-slate sky changed only when night fell. When he wasn't going over mountains, the road was unrelentingly straight and empty.

Good thing he didn't have to worry about running out of gas.

He'd found the tanker truck in a deserted fuel depot outside the Russian city of Baikonur the morning before last. Baikonur was the site of the old Russian government's "Star City," a socialist's version of Cape Canaveral. Many spacecraft, manned and otherwise, had been launched from Baikonur during and after the Cold War. It was the home of Soyez, the Mir and Sputnik It was where some cosmonauts spent their entire lives. The place was thought to have been abandoned shortly after the Big War.

But just seventy-two hours ago, a spacecraft had roared off the main pad at Star City. Hunter had seen it go up. It was a space shuttle, a crude but apparently workable Russian version designed to look exactly like the once-famous American craft.

The sight of it rising into space had been haunting him unmercilessly ever since.

He had been drawn to Baikonur from the recent war in Southeast Asia, arriving in a Galaxy C-5 cargoship just minutes before the Russian shuttle went up. From the little he had seen of it, he knew the spacecraft was probably a second-generation Russian design known as the Zon. Supposedly it had never gone beyond the planning stage. But obviously, at least one had been built—and from what Hunter could tell, it seemed to be a vast improvement over the original all-thumbs unmanned Russian shuttle craft known as the Buron.

The Zon's leap into space was a stunning turn of events

for Hunter and his colleagues. It had taken five years of struggle in America just for them to put together a credible air force. Now, for someone to actually launch a shuttle was a gigantic step forward, no matter who was at the controls. But here was the really bad news: Hunter had seen at least a dozen people getting on the Zon spacecraft before it went up. One of them was no less than the world's most wanted criminal, an individual going by the name of Viktor Robotov.

This in itself was very strange. Everyone thought the real Viktor Robotov was dead. In fact, Hunter, himself, had seen him die in the sands of the Saudi Arabian desert, not three years before. Or at least he *thought* he'd seen him die. This "new" Viktor not only looked and acted like the original, he was also just as bloodthirsty, cunning and savage—if indeed they were two different people. Demented and perverse, right down to the Satanic facial features and the devilish goatee, Viktor was responsible for a number of small wars that had flared up around the troubled globe, mostly in the Pacific of late. His methods were always the same: gather together a large number of unscrupulous, cultish mercenary forces, give them a wealth of military hardware and let them loose on the innocent, unsuspecting and helpless peoples of the targeted region. Distress, anguish and death would quickly follow.

Why was Viktor doing this? No one really knew. There was little to gain tactically or strategically from these actions—in fact, Hunter and the United Americans had soundly defeated two separate legions of these mercenary armies in just the past few months. Whoever the hell this Viktor was, winning in a military sense meant little to him. He seemed bent on one thing: creating havoc and misery on a planet that needed no more of either.

And now he was in space.

It was this thought alone that was driving Hunter faster

than the five hundred and two cubic-inch engine under his truck's hood. Big as the place was, he'd not been able to find any jet fuel for his C-5 anywhere in Star City—even worse, he had wasted many hours in trying. He did, however, find this truck, with all its stale gasoline, and had laid claim to it immediately. That had been two days ago. He'd been driving like a madman ever since.

He'd only been a few hundred yards away from the pad when the Zon went up—he'd emptied a clip from his M-16 into it as it rose into the heavens. But if he had caused any damage to the damn thing, he'd found no evidence of it later. The shuttle went straight up and then over, just like it was supposed to, quickly disappearing from his view. It was a flawless launch and now he had no doubt that the Zon was up there, somewhere, traveling around the earth, carrying at least one pair of eyes that were looking down on the battered planet and thinking of more insidious ways to fuck it up.

But in firing his M-16 at the launching Zon, Hunter had had more in mind than just shooting it down. By tracking the trajectory of his bullet stream against the trajectory of the rising spacecraft, he'd been able to calculate the Zon's acceleration, its rate of climb, its angle of flight and apparent attitude, and hence, its expected point of departure from Earth's atmosphere and its insertion into orbit. From this, Hunter had determined the Zon's probable orbital status and flight path. If he had added everything up correctly, the Russian shuttle was 127.550 miles above the earth, flying an orbit that brought it roughly fifty-one degrees above the equator and forty-two below.

From all this, he'd come up with a coordinate, a spot on the map he'd termed Point Zero. It was located more than two thousand miles west of Star City, somewhere deep in the Swiss Alps. From this place, he'd determined, he'd be able to see the Zon go over as many as seventeen times in one clear twenty-four-hour-period, including dusk, night or even early daylight. if he could get high enough, at the right angle and know exactly where to look. In that was born his current plan. If he could get to Point Zero, and take these observations, or even see the Zon go over just once, Hunter hoped he'd be able to learn something very important about the spacecraft: when it would be coming back down to Earth—and where.

If all this was made known to him, then he'd vowed to be on hand wherever the Zon landed, and personally deal with Viktor, once and for all.

It seemed like a fool's quest though.

The two thousand-mile dash in the beat-up Benz tanker alone qualified for some degree of madness, never mind expecting to find a near-mythical spot from which he could look into outer space.

But Hunter was always doing things like this. His intellectual capabilities were beyond quantum, his adventuresome spirit more intense than anyone who'd passed before. He was, no argument, the best fighter pilot who'd ever lived. He was possibly the best military strategist to ever come along as well. His mind was not simply some kind of an organic supercomputer: it *corrected* supercomputers. His ability, in flight, to anticipate the realities of the human-combat-flying experience was eerie. He knew trouble was coming anywhere from a few seconds to a few minutes before it actually arrived, a rather frightening talent. But most importantly, he was also a cosmically lucky man: he'd fought in nearly a dozen armed conflicts in the last five years—and had come through all of them with hardly a scratch. All the smarts in the world couldn't explain that.

But his goals were also immense. He wanted no less than a world in which every human being was able to make his own decisions and forge his own destiny, without interference from demagogues and power-mad personality freaks bent on fucking it up for everyone else. Five years of hard-fought combat and intense intrigue had finally brought a somewhat stable state of affairs to his beloved American continent. Just how long the export version of this noble cause would take was unknowable.

Two months before, after receiving an urgent call for assistance from the countries of Southeast Asia, Hunter had organized the large air fleet of C-5 Galaxy cargo jets, outfitted them into combat aircraft and had led them clear around the world to once again come to the defense of a struggling Vietnam. That war ended just a week ago. His comrades, as well as the majority of the air fleet were still there, keeping a shaky peace. When Hunter discovered a homing device that would lead him to Viktor, he'd outfitted it on one of the C-5s and hours later, found himself in Star City. After the Zon launch, anyone left on the ground got out of town real quick, because the place was deserted when Hunter began his search for jet fuel. Finding none, he intentionally wrecked the C-5 on the airport's longest runway, blowing large craters in it and leaving it fouled for some time to come. At least he knew the Zon would not be coming down there.

So now here he was—driving across the endless barren landscape, growing cold, growing tired, getting hungry, just driving towards Point Zero, from where he could plot his next move. And like many of his important journeys in the past, he was taking this one alone.

At last, the truck reached the bottom of the treacherous mountain roadway and now settled itself onto a long stretch of absolutely straight highway. If Hunter's recall of the area was correct, the road would run like this now for the next one hundred and forty-eight miles.

With this in mind, he pressed down on the accelerator

with even more gusto, raising the big truck's speed over one hundred ten mph.

He still had many miles to go before he could sleep.

Hunter thought he was dreaming when he first saw the Alps.

One moment, he was rolling along the frozen, barren plain—the next, the mountains were suddenly there, rising out of the haze on the western horizon. These peaks were much higher, much steeper than what he'd been shlepping over the past two days. Like teeth on a massive, snowcapped jigsaw, they stretched in both directions as far as the eye could see.

Hunter tried to conjure up a map of the region in his head. This was probably the *Zillershausen Alpen,* he figured, the first line of western Alps. This meant he was somewhere in central Austria, about one hundred fifty miles from the old Swiss border and more than three-quarters of the way to his destination.

But though it should have been a moment of triumph, Hunter let out a sad whistle as soon as he saw the mountains. *How things change,* he thought. Sure, he'd driven from the steppes of Russia to the foot of the Alps in one long dash, probably setting some kind of transcontinental land-speed record for heavy trucks in the process. Had he made the trip in his usual mode of transportation—his souped up F-16XL Cranked Arrow superfighter—the whole thing would have taken less than an hour.

He drove on for another thirty miles or so, wearily shifting his tired butt around in the uncomfortable seat every few seconds. The Alpine peaks gradually filled his windshield; it was scary how high and jagged they were. The road was leading right towards two peaks in particular, both of which were so immense, they'd blotted out the late afternoon sun a long time ago. The shadow caused by these monsters made it seem like it was night already.

He negotiated a long bend in the road and only then did he realize that there was a small city nestled at the base of the gigantic twin peaks. Even from five miles away, to Hunter's tired eyes, this place looked different from the dozens of other empty cities he'd passed along the way. Though just as dark and cold as they were, looking at it through the dirty windshield was almost hypnotic. He was warm inside for a moment, a sensation he didn't experience too often.

He brought the truck to a stop at the side of the road about two miles from the outskirts of the city. Finally killing the big engine for the first time in fifty-one hours, he sat inside the chilly cab, soaking in the stupendous scenery and paying close attention to the small settlement just ahead. It could have been a postcard for the Alps: a collection of chalets and quaint Alpine buildings with the twin peaks soaring dramatically in the background. It was incredible. Hunter believed he could never get tired of looking at it.

But eventually he found himself slumping down further into the cold, hard seat. He knew he would have to stay here, in the cab of the truck, for at least a little while. Night would soon be falling for real. If he was going to drive through the city, it was best he do so under the cover of darkness.

He adjusted himself in the seat yet again, lifting his feet up to the dashboard and leaning back against the driver's side door. Gradually his tired muscles began to relax. His ears heard nothing but silence—and were grateful for the change. Slowly, he began to close his eyes.

When he opened them again, the first thing he saw was a line of hundreds of lights, twinkling off in the distance.

Hunter was back up sitting straight in his seat in a flash.

The lights were coming from the city, aglow at the base of the two mountains. He rubbed his eyes, just to make sure. This was the first sign of civilization he'd seen since leaving Baikonu. The buildings appeared alive and cordial, the smoke from many fires wafting high above them. Another warm tingling sensation was building inside his chest. He rubbed his eyes again. When he listened hard enough, he thought he could hear the faint hum of voices, electricity and machines, the sounds of life were resonating from the place.

Rising out of the city, he could see a string of lights climbing up the side of the mountain towards the wide, snowy pass where the twin peaks met. They were headlights, faint and stuttering, illuminating a mountain roadway. This was good news; the road continued up and over the peaks, just as he'd hoped.

But there was something happening way up where the two great mountains converged. The glow of many fires was illuminating the pass and the night sky on both sides of the peaks. A thick cloud of ugly black smoke was rising above it all. It looked like a forest fire, even though both the mountains and the crevice in between were capped in a perpetual layer of snow and ice. Hunter rolled down the truck's window and turned his ear toward the west. He could hear the sound of explosions and gunfire, way off in the distance. He couldn't believe it, it sounded like a war going on up there.

He let his eyes fall back to the small city, getting slowly sucked in by its mysterious warm glow again. He hated to admit it, but he was cold, tired, hungry and thirsty. He was eyeing the place rather dreamily now—a shot of *bergenwhiskas,* a mug of beer and a plate of roast-beef stew would be a feast to him at this point . . .

The next thing he knew, he was climbing down out of the truck, jumping first to the running board and then to the snowy road below. It was cold out and he had only a medium-season jacket pulled over his flight regs. Strangely though, it seemed warm enough. Strapping his trusty M-16F2 over his left shoulder, he pulled his ball cap down over his head as far as he could, stuck his hands in his pockets and started walking.

After a while, his feet felt so light, they hardly touched the ground.

# Three

The name of the place was the *Rootentootzen*.

Located near the south end of the city just below the twin massive peaks, it was a tavern in the very best old Alpine tradition. Built of stone, wood and mud, the structure had stood in this place for more than ten thousand years. Not much had changed inside in that time. A huge fire was roaring in the hearth that dominated the west wall of the place. A massive slab of roast beef was slowly rotating above it, spattering its juices onto the flames below. A half dozen kettles surrounded the spit as well, all of them full of steaming beef stew.

The tavern was packed with a few hundred armed men, all of them wearing some variation of a mountain combat uniform. Everyone was drinking beer, everyone was eating stew. Buxom blond waitresses with blouses cut so low, their ample breasts were more exposed than not, literally flew above the crowd, trays full of food and ale balanced in front of them. Providing a soundtrack for all this, a battered CD player was pounding out the computerized bleats of an oom-pah band. Like the music, the mood inside the tavern was lusty and festive.

Suddenly the doors to the place came flying open. A squad of enormous heavily armed soldiers walked in. They were dressed in bright-white combat fatigues, wearing Alpine-style fritz helmets and carrying Heckler & Koch MP5A3 submachine guns. The place came to a dead stop. Even the roaring hearth fire quieted down. Rock-jawed and cold, the soldiers eyed the crowd cautiously. The patrons stared right back.

The man at the head of the column took one step forward. He was at least seven feet tall and sported an enormous white mustache. He gave the room a quick once-over then shouted: "Service papers . . . *please!*"

In one oddly choreographed movement, every man in the place pulled a bright blue slip of paper out of his left breast pocket and held it at eye level. The massive white soldiers quickly began checking these slips. Vital information was written on them: the bearer's name, his last rank, his weapons specialty, and how many hours of combat he'd seen in the past thirty days. Anyone bearing a card indicating less-than-expected service up on the line risked the humiliation of being dragged out of the bar and rushed back to the front.

It was called a muster check. They were a nightly occurrence in the *Rootentootzen*. This particular evening everyone on hand passed the test.

The mood in the tavern eased considerably as the last of the blue slips was checked. The gigantic officer with the white mustache signed off on the final one himself. Then, with an almost casual wave of his hand, the *Rootentootzen* came alive once more. The officer barked an order and his soldiers marched back out into the cold night, singing as they went. Down the street and into the tavern next door, the soldiers had more than a hundred and twenty-five of these places to check before their night was through.

Drinking heartily from a mammoth beer stein, his face just inches above in a plate of beef stew, Hawk Hunter had watched the incident in a state of bemused amazement. He was sitting at the table in the corner, next to the antique CD machine. When the muster soldiers reached him, not only did they ignore him, they seemed to be looking right through him. Between his mouthfuls of stew, he'd simply stared up at them and very quickly they went away.

Hunter had found the muster drill somewhat fascinating. The whole thing had played out like a ritual. It was obvious the huge white soldiers were looking for deserters and malingerers—the most interesting thing was they didn't find any. Nor did it look like they ever did. It was clear to Hunter that great dishonor would have been felt on both sides should anyone be found out of order.

He'd relied on his extraordinary pickpocketing talents to get the funds to purchase the bowl of beef stew and the huge stein of thick, sweet beer. All of it was going down extremely easily. He'd been at it for quite a while now, eating, drinking, studying the people and he'd learned much in this time. Though everyone was armed and obviously combat-hardened, they were a civilized lot. Many were drunk, but no one was rowdy. Many were horned up, yet no one was harassing the airborne waitresses. This was a very strange thing: a well-behaved, almost polite army.

He'd also learned that a war—a small but brutal one— was being fought way up on the mountain, near the pass where the twin peaks converged. The glow of fire, the pall of smoke and the explosions he'd heard earlier were all coming from this nasty little conflict.

The people in this city were fighting the people in another city that lay on the other side of the peaks. Hunter had heard many disparaging curses describing the *alpineoberlanders*—"the people over the mountains." He'd noticed that a number of soldiers inside the tavern were missing fingers, ears, tips of the noses, bits of lips and chin. Others were limping noticeably. These fighters had been victims not of bullets but frostbite. Hunter shivered at the thought of it: mountain warfare was probably the worst way to fight; the worst way to die. If the guy shooting at you didn't kill you, then the cold and the snow would, even if it did happen one digit at a time.

After a trip to the head, he pinched some more money—weird-looking purple notes, splattered with portraits of apes, monkeys and chimps. He lifted enough to buy another bowl of stew and a refill for his stein. He'd shot down one of the waitresses, and during a moist session on his lap, she'd told him much about the cold little war up on the peaks. The city on the other side of the mountain was attempting to invade its neighbors. The city's defenders had stopped them at the mountain pass. A frozen-form of trench warfare had been going on for six months now—and getting worse by the week. More casualties, and more deaths, were being reported every day. Supplies on this side of the mountain were running very low. No one in the city felt safe anymore—and everyone was expecting some kind of a larger, surprise attack at any moment.

Hunter really didn't want to hear any of this. It said a lot about the world these days: the first place with any signs of life in two thousand five hundred miles had a war going on close by. But even worse, he was still at least one hundred fifty miles away from Point Zero, the magical place he had to climb in order to get a good look at the Zon. It most certainly lay over this mountain and a few dozen more.

So what should he do? Attempt to drive over the peaks anyway? Could he somehow avoid all the shooting and get to the other side to continue his journey?

Probably not.

But going around the conflict and searching for another way through the mountains would take much too long. This left a very short list of options, none of which he knew could be acted upon in here in the tavern. Reluctantly, he let the waitress go, scraped his bowl clean and then drained his stein.

It was time to tell someone he was here.

\* \* \*

The official name of the city was *Clochenspieltz.*

It had served as an exclusive ski resort for Europe's rich and famous for centuries; even swells from the Bronze Age came here for the scenery. These days, everybody in the region knew it by the nickname: "Clocks."

There was a huge pyramid in the middle of Clocks. It was made of solid gold and was lit on all sides by huge halogen lamps. This imposing, magnificent building was actually the main headquarters of the *Volksdefensfuhr,* the city's Home Defense Forces. Within it, a command staff of five hundred people ran operations against the army hired by the people on the other side of the mountains. The enemy city was just as big, just as isolated and oddly, just as picturesque as Clocks. Its official name was *Werkenhausen.* Everyone called it "Works."

On the top floor of the pyramid was the combat command center itself. It was a large, spare place, filled with radios and computers to assist the humans in the war effort. Next to the war room were the private quarters of the man responsible for running the defense of the city. Part-defense minister, part-mayor, part-dictator, he was known throughout Clocks as the *Wehrenluftmeister.*

It was almost midnight when the *Wehrenluftmeister* came through the door of the war room; he'd just arrived back from the front. He found most of his command staff were asleep; the others were masturbating quietly in the corner. The *Wehrenluftmeister* dismissed his bodyguards, breezed through the command room and wearily unlocked the door to his private quarters. It had been a very long day; he was absolutely dead on his feet.

He slipped inside, closing the door softly so as not to disturb anybody. He had barely enough energy to flip on the light—and he wasn't surprised when it did not come up to full power right away. Electric flow was fluctuating throughout the city this night, just like every other night this week.

It was just another problem the *Wehrenluftmeister* had to worry about; the city had experienced a major blackout two nights before, and the lights had been flickering then, too. Soon, he might have to order all electrical devices shut off during certain hours, if only to rest the city's already-ragged power-generating turbines.

He threw his helmet and gun on the floor and walked deeper into his spacious, but spartan room. A lighted planning table dominated the middle of the compartment; the *Wehrenluftmeister* collapsed into the overstuffed chair next to it. He was an enormous individual, tall and hefty—and the chair bent mightily against his weight. It would have been very easy for him to fall asleep at that moment—and be out cold for hours. But sleep was not an option for him now; indeed, it was no more than a sinful temptation. He had so much work to do, it would be hours before he could consider even taking a short nap.

So, reluctantly, he dragged the chair up to the blinking light table and retrieved a leather packet from his uniform pocket. Emptying out its contents, he was soon looking at three dozen photo negatives with a magnifying glass. To his dismay, more than half of them were solid black, either from bad development or bad imaging. Disgusted, he swept these off the table.

But when he began examining images that he could actually see, he felt his heart sink even further. They were pictures from the front. Most of them showed the same two ragged set of battle trenches dug deep into the snow and ice at the top of the mountain. Both trenchworks were three kilometers long and they ran almost exactly parallel to one another. In between were blotches of smoky fires and bomb craters, many more in front of the eastern line, the one occupied by Clocks' Home Guard.

This alone was a stark reminder of which side was getting bested in the high-altitude, frozen war.

In fact, close-up photos revealed many breaches had been cut in the *Volksdefensfuhr's* lines in the past twenty-four hours. The enemy had brought up more heavy guns during the previous night. They'd been blowing bigger holes in his defenses ever since. Now in a pique, the *Wehrenluftmeister* swept all the photos away from him—each one had brought more bad news than the one before. Disheartened, he slumped back in his chair. At this rate, his army could not hold out very much longer. Maybe two weeks, maybe three at the most.

But after that . . .

The *Wehrenluftmeister* closed his eyes—he was praying to go to sleep now, if only to get away from this highly disturbing situation for a few hours. But no sooner had he drifted off when he felt compelled to open his eyes again. When he did, there was a rifle snout hovering just two inches from his nose. A man was standing right in front of him, holding a rifle on him. It seemed impossible. How had he so suddenly and so quietly crept into this heavily guarded room?

The *Wehrenluftmeister* began to stand up, but the point of the cold rifle forced him back down again. The figure took a step forward; the bare light from the plotting table finally illuminated his face. The *Wehrenluftmeister* gasped. The sharp, handsome features, the grown-out mane, the hawkish face. He knew this man—he'd seen his photograph many times over the years, even before the Big War.

"You're . . . you're . . ." he began stammering in perfect English.

"Never mind who I am," the voice behind the rifle said. "Who the hell are you?"

The *Wehrenluftmeister* gulped hard.

"I am the commanding officer of the defense forces

of this city," he said quickly. "I was hired to protect it from invasion. I have a ten thousand man regular army division at my disposal, plus another ten thousand militia and mercenaries. My command staff numbers five hundred and one."

The rifle moved every so slightly towards him. "Are you the good guys or the bad guys?" the voice said.

The question momentarily stumped the *Wehrenluftmeister.*

"We're the *good guys,*" he finally replied. "The people who hired me are honorable individuals. This city, *their* city, was in danger of being invaded. I came to their assistance . . ."

"That's what Hitler said before he stomped Poland," the voice interrupted.

The comment exploded in the *Wehrenluftmeister's* ears. His face instantly turned crimson red with anger.

"We are *not* Nazis, sir!" he shouted, even though the rifle snout was now but an inch from his nose. "Though I can assure you you'll find plenty of that ilk on the other side of the mountain!"

A short silence descended on the darkened room. The *Wehrenluftmeister* shifted nervously in his chair. The rifle moved in again.

"You're not an American, are you?"

"Free Canadian," the *Wehrenluftmeister* replied. "My name is Orr. Major Stanley, P. Central European Liberation Forces, Inc."

"How much you getting paid?" the voice asked.

Orr hesitated a moment. "Nothing but food and shelter," he revealed at last. "For the time being, at least . . ."

Only then did the rifle barrel move, its snout disappearing back into the shadows. Then its owner stepped forward again. The *Wehrenluftmeister* looked up, and saw the face once more.

He gulped. "So . . . it is *really* you?"

Hunter lowered the gun completely, then casually took a seat on the edge of the plotting table.

"Yeah," he said finally, "it's really me."

The *Wehrenluftmeister* took a shaky glass of water. He still couldn't believe it. Hunter snapped his fingers and suddenly all the lights came back on.

"Not going too well up top?" he asked Orr.

The *Wehrenluftmeister* pushed what was left of the pile of recon photos Hunter's way.

"You're an expert," he said. "You tell me."

Hunter leaned over the lighting table and began studying the pile of photos himself.

He had to agree with the *Wehrenluftmeister.* The images did show a rapidly deteriorating situation. Clocks' defense forces were getting pounded by heavy artillery the enemy had stacked in the mountain crevices high above the trenchworks. Larger, higher gun emplacements were being worked on as well, even as the battle raged on in the pass below. Once these bigger guns were operational, there would be no defense against them. The troops holding the eastern trenches would be quickly finished. It would be a very cold, very brutal way to die.

"We'd been holding them off before these big guns appeared," Orr told him. "But now . . ."

Hunter studied another set of photos, these showing the enemy's trenchworks. The fortifications appeared full, sturdy and heavily reinforced, with plenty of reserve stocks lying in the rear areas.

"Who are these guys you're fighting?" he asked Orr. "Are they really Nazis? Or just fake ones?"

Orr just shrugged.

"Many of them are German," he replied. "But many are not. They're part of a larger army which has been steadily moving east for about a year now, taking over large chunks of the Continent in the process. We've been able to slow them down, here, but only because of the mountain. They are despicably patient, which tells me they are being paid handsomely. But if they get through us, there'll be nothing to stop them between here and Siberia . . ."

Hunter continued studying the photos. "I assume from your title that you have aircraft at your disposal too?"

Orr laughed bitterly.

"Well, that's actually a joke in these parts," he replied. "We took delivery on an attack squadron about two months ago. We were sure then that with air support, our troops would be able to throw the invaders back over the mountain. But a cruel ruse had been played on us, I'm afraid. Or perhaps it was of some nefarious design . . ."

Hunter looked up at him. "What happened? The planes come with no engines?"

Orr laughed again. "If only that was the problem."

He walked over to a file cabinet, retrieved a large brown envelope and tossed it onto the light table. A spread of photos came out. They were pictures of biplanes. Vintage stuff, from World War One and even earlier.

"What the hell is this?" Hunter asked, almost laughing himself. "You didn't actually buy these things, did you?"

"My superiors hired agents who did," Orr replied soberly. "You're looking at what was bought for one hundred and sixty pounds of pure gold."

Hunter quickly studied all the photos. They showed six Fokker triplanes, two Spads and a Sopwith Camel, ancient flying machines which had fought in the Great War. The pictures themselves looked almost as old as the airplanes.

"Who sold these to you?" he finally asked Orr.

The *Wehrenluftmeister* smiled again, though grimly. He held up a smaller five by five photo; faded and blurry, it looked like it belonged on a wanted poster.

"This man did," he said to him, adding, "and if you are who you say you are, you know him, too."

Hunter took a long look. He knew him all right. The

36 *Mack Maloney*

furrowed brow, the roadmap of a nose, the glint in his eyes revealing a born salesman.

His name was Roy from Troy.

# Four

One hour later, Hunter and Orr arrived at a small airfield outside the city.

They had made the short trip from Clocks in Orr's specially armored Rolls Royce Silver Shadow. Now the *Wehrenluftmeister* led Hunter to an unguarded warehouse located on the edge of the airfield's single grass airstrip. It was a dark imposing building with a load of fake snow camouflage on the roof and about six feet of the real stuff on top of it. Orr unlocked the two huge doors and they walked inside. The place was unlit, deathly quiet—and clean. There was no smell of oil, grease or hydraulic fluid, no signs that any work, either maintenance or repair, had taken place inside the place in a long time, if ever.

In the shadows, Hunter could see nine biplanes, lined up perfectly in a row. A gag insignia painted on the wall above them showed a circus-type pachyderm, standing on two legs waving a flag which read: *Witen Proboscidietz-Platz Staffelizen*. Almost literally: The White Elephant Squadron.

Though there was hardly a reason to, Hunter was feeling guilty to a degree. He was quite familiar with Roy from Troy. He'd purchased a number of warplanes from the used airplane salesman just a few weeks ago, during the pivotal battle of Southeast Asia. Hunter knew Roy's selling operations had spread around the world, but he was amazed they had made it all the way to this snowy little part of the planet. And while Roy had always done right by him, his methods were certainly "unorthodox"— now and in the past. It wasn't beyond him to sell a bunch of seventy-year-old airplanes to a dot on the map called *Clochenspieltz.*

But something inside Hunter was telling him there had to be more to it than that.

Orr had dug out the contracts surrounding the airplane purchase. One thing in Roy's defense, the agreement did call for "light aircraft to be used in strafing, scouting and recon operations, capable of operation from rough airfields, low on maintenance and good on gas." The shadowy line of airplanes Hunter saw before him did appear to fit those qualifications, at least technically. Trouble was, they fit them better almost a century ago.

Hunter approached the first six planes in line. They were Fokker Dr. Is, the famous triplanes. Stubby yet oddly sleek, they were said to go up like an elevator in flight. These airplanes boasted the distinctive, triple wingspan, thick struts and a heavy-duty undercarriage. Hunter pressed down on the wing fabric; and found little give at all. He gave the wing a tap, it came back as metallic. Suddenly his opinion of Roy's shady deal got slightly brighter. The wings in this airplane had obviously been reinforced with lightweight metal, probably aluminum. The fuselage had been similarly strengthened, too.

He walked around to the front of the airplane. If memory served him, the Fokker's two hundred-plus horsepower engine had been a powerhouse in its day. But now Hunter's eyes nearly popped when he saw the airplane's present engine. Sitting in a reinforced basket sunk into the slightly elongated nose was a fifteen hundred-horsepower Packard-built Merlin! This was impossible—the Merlin was the same engine that powered the famous P-51 Mustang. How the hell had Roy's men put such a big engine into such a small airframe? Hunter was stumped—

he just didn't know. But there it was. Hunter peeked through the engine cowling and saw the motor was in excellent condition. With its bright blue paint and well-oiled components, it looked almost new.

He had to stop and think about this concept for a moment. A Mustang engine in a Fokker triplane? If it didn't tear the fuselage apart, this plane could haul some serious butt. Again he grudgingly had to give Roy some credit: the airplane's redesign was bordering on masterfully improbable.

He next studied the airplane's armament. Instead of a pair of rinky-dink .50 caliber machine guns, this baby was boasting a small twenty-millimeter cannon attached by pod to the center of the middle wing. The ammunition load was limited to two hundred ten rounds, but for such an elderly airplane, it still packed an incredible punch.

His mind spinning, Hunter walked farther up the line; Orr following silently behind. The next five Fokkers were like the first: reinforced, reengined, and rearmed. Three had been further rigged with munition hardpoints under the bottom wing. With the big engine and the light air frame, Hunter estimated the planes could lift at least five hundred pounds in bombs apiece, probably more.

When they reached the last Fokker, Orr fished a certificate out of a pocket behind the servicing door. It gave very extensive schematics and maintenance instructions, right down to the amount of lubrication suggested for the hinges in the canopy. Rarely had Hunter seen such specific care information for a used bird. Most warplanes these days, old and new, came with little more than how to start the engine and fire the gun. Everything else the owner had to figure out himself.

The next two airplanes were the Spads, two-winged planes that were similar in size and performance to the Fokker. They, too, had reinforced skeletons and were carrying big Merlin engines. They'd also been outfitted as

light bombers, their underwings fitted with five hardpoints each, plus two pylons for small weapons pods on
the fuselage itself.

Like the Fokkers, the Spads looked like extremely well-
preserved museum pieces—or better yet, exact recrea-
tions of the long-gone fighter plane. Hunter was
beginning to get the feeling that Clocks actually got a
deal on this sale—if they'd been in the market for col-
lectors pieces.

Aircraft Number 9 was actually a two-seat Sopwith
Camel. It was bigger and wider than the other airplanes,
with a large radial engine mounted between the two elevated wings. Though obviously intended as a recon platform, this airplane looked to be lovingly reconditioned,
too, right down to the brilliant red, white and blue color
scheme.

Hunter was starting to suspect that Roy had raided an
aircraft museum somewhere, and then turned over the
booty to some master craftsmen who updated the airplanes for sale.

They looked great, but what could they do for Clocks
in their fight against the enemy over the mountain?

Hunter had turned to ask Orr that very question, when
suddenly an oddly familiar sensation washed over him.

He had to stand there for a moment and think about
it: It'd been a long time since he'd felt like this.

Then, just like that, he knew: *Aircraft. From over the
mountain. Coming right towards us.*

A second later he was running. Out of the hangar, out
on to the small airstrip. A very surprised Orr was fast on
his heels. They reached the center of the field just as the
first wave of lights came over the top of the twin peaks;
two more were right behind them. Twelve airplanes appeared in all, flying in three chevrons of four apiece.

It was classic preattack formation.

"You have *air raids* here, too?" Hunter yelled over to Orr.

But the *Wehrenluftmeister* could hardly speak. His jaw hanging wide open.

"No, never . . ." he finally gasped.

"Well," Hunter told him, "you're about to have one now."

The bombs started falling on Clocks just two minutes later.

They came down in strings of twelve, hitting the buildings and the streets and causing huge explosions of red and green as they fell. Bombs from the first wave of attackers leveled the city's water supply house, its auxiliary electrical plant, a fuel storage facility and one of its banks. The second wave dropped its bomb loads on the heavily populated eastern side of the city. A number of the elegant apartment houses were destroyed instantly, including many shared by militiamen and their families. There were some incendiary bombs dropped in this mix, and now, even as the second wave of bombers departed, many fires were breaking out in the eastern district.

Greatly lightened of their bomb loads, these four airplanes began a wide turn to the north, one which would bring them right over the airfield. By this time, Hunter had flown up to the top of the field's dormant control tower, alighting on the roof of the place, his M-16 and a pair of high-powered electronic binoculars in hand. Orr was right beside him, furious that Works had stooped to the barbarism of bombing civilian targets inside Clocks.

Hunter held his anger—he was concentrating on getting a good look at the culprits first. It was a very dark night, overcast and moonless, and he'd yet to see any of the attacking airplanes up close. Still, he could tell by the drone of the approaching engine noise that the enemy bombers were not much newer than the gallery of an-

tiques he'd just inspected inside the hangar. Even above
the roar of bombs exploding and buildings collapsing inside Clocks a mile away, Hunter could detect the sounds
of engine backfiring and fuel overloading on some of the
oncoming bombers. They were definitely prop-driven, two
engines per aircraft. The planes were not going much
faster than ninety miles per hour when they released their
loads. And their bombs had made a distinctive whine as
they fell out of the sky. Quick calculations of all these
factors led Hunter to one conclusion: the airplanes had
to be something built back in the 1940s.

One went overhead about twenty seconds later. It flew
right into Hunter's electronic sights—and at last he had
a clear frame of the offending aircraft. He'd been right.
The planes were reconditioned He-111 Heinkel medium
bombers, a mainstay of the old Nazi Luftwaffe.

In an instant the airplane was gone, its pilot yanking
back on the control column and turning back towards
the crotch between the twin mountains. Back in Clocks,
Hunter could hear fire bells ringing, secondary bombs
exploding, even the cries of many people, all running at
once. And above all this, the rumbling of the third wave
of bombers approaching the city. Just like the aircraft before them, their flight path would bring them right over
the airfield as well.

With this in mind, Hunter slapped a tracer clip into
his M-16F2 and adjusted the electronic sight.

It was time to go hunting.


The noise inside the Heinkel was incredible.

Everything that was not tied down was rattling mightily—and a lot of things weren't tied down. It was all the
pilot could do to scream instructions over to the copilot,
who in turn would scream them down into the bombar-

dier's bay and hope that somehow the man down there would hear him. The noise was that loud.

What's more, the bomber crew was being tossed around inside the airplane as if they were dolls. The air currents here on the eastern side of the mountain were not what they had expected. They'd assumed the night air above Clocks would be calm, smooth, and even helpful in their low-level bombing raid. But just the opposite was true. The turbulence was ferocious—obviously the winds sweeping over from the west side of the mountain turned convex once they'd reached the other side. Instead of a smooth ride, flying low over Clocks was a very scary proposition.

Still the bomber crew pressed on. They were the lead ship in the last wave. They had waited slightly north of the city, circling while the first two waves went in and did their work. Seeing the initial explosions, they had sent an enthusiastic report back to Works. "Clocks on fire," it had said. "All bombs hitting targets . . ."

This was not true, though. Clocks was hardly on fire, in fact, many of the bombs dropped by the first two waves had missed their designated targets by as much as three city blocks. Some large fires could be seen, and some primary targets had been damaged—but Clocks had hardly turned into Dresden. Not yet anyway.

It was now time for the third wave to go in. The one thing they hadn't seen was any substantial groundfire rising out of Clocks. This was a good sign. The bombing raid's first objective—to conduct a surprise attack—had worked perfectly. The city of Clocks had been caught completely unaware and no one was firing back. This, too, was good—the last thing the Heinkel crew wanted to worry about was getting shot down.

The pilot, a Captain named Heinz Franz, put the He-111 into a long, slow sweep towards the south. They would go over the center of Clocks in an east-to-west direction.

Once they'd dropped their bombs, they would pull up quickly and gain altitude for the return dash over the mountain. If all went well, they'd be landing back in Works less than five minutes later.

Franz yelled over to the copilot who yelled down to the bombardier to get ready. The Heinkel was down to five hundred feet now, and the winds above Clocks were throwing it all over the sky. There were four other crewmen on the plane—gunners stationed at midfuselage. They'd been battered around so much, one had been completely knocked out. Franz gripped the steering column of the He-111 even tighter. This was his first time flying a Heinkel in combat. It was becoming a little more than he'd bargained for.

It will be all over in a matter of seconds, he told himself. Just stay low and steady and unload the bombs when you're supposed to. They were now about three quarters of a mile from the drop point; Franz brought the Heinkel down to three hundred feet, the prescribed bombing altitude. Once again he yelled over to the copilot who yelled down to the bombardier. Twenty seconds to drop. They were right over the city now, the Alpine-style homes and buildings passing below them in a blur of fire and smoke.

Fifteen seconds to go. The old Heinkel was rattling down to every screw and bolt now, the engines were backfiring and smoking badly—the rich fuel mix and the thick, wild air above Clocks made for a bad combination.

Ten seconds. One last shout over to the copilot, who loudly began screaming out a countdown. ". . . Ninzen . . . eightzen . . . sevenzen . . ."

They were flying so low now, Franz could see people running on the street below. Some were looking up at them and shaking their fists. Five seconds . . . they were over the city's main power plant. Four . . . now through the smoke from the burning waterworks. Three . . . the main target, the city's military headquarters loomed right off the Heinkel's nose. Two . . . One . . .

"Bombs away!" Franz yelled.

"Drop now!" the copilot screamed out.

"Dropping . . . *now!*" came the muffled response from the bombardier.

Instantly, they all heard the clanging of the bombs falling off their racks, and the response from the engines as the airplane got progressively lighter.

"Weapons gone!" the bombardier yelled up, but already Franz was cranking the Heinkel to the left, trying to aim its nose towards the split in the mountains and the safety of Works beyond. But suddenly, the cockpit exploded in a rush of fire, glass and smoke. In that first instant, Franz thought they'd run into their own bomb load—so quick and violent came the blast. But then the copilot fell forward, and in the horror of the next second, Franz realized that incredibly, the man had been shot six times through the head. His body was now pressing down on the steering column, causing the He-111 to go into a catastrophic dive. Franz was screaming for someone to get up to the cockpit and pull the dead man off the controls, but it was too late for that. The bomber's engines coughed once, twice, then three times, all inside of a few seconds. The strain was too much—they both burst into flames a moment later. Franz ruptured blood vessels in his arms and hands trying to pull the plane out of its death plunge—but he wasn't that strong. No one was.

They were going to crash and he knew it. Water and oil spilling onto his face, smoke filling his unprotected lungs, he somehow managed to yank the plane once more to the right, towards the only open area in sight. With the last of his strength, he succeeded in killing both engines. Then he shouted back to the rest of the crew to get ready.

The Heinkel plowed into the open field ten seconds later.


The fires had gone out by the time Hunter and Orr reached the downed Heinkel.

They'd made the fifteen-minute dash from the airfield to the crash site in Orr's Rolls, nearly blowing out all the tires on the rough, snow-encrusted ground. Now leaving the car a safe distance away, they approached the airplane wreck slowly, weapons up, watchful for any armed survivors who might be hiding in the battered fuselage or in the patches of woods nearby.

Like the elderly flying machines back in the warehouse, this airplane, too, looked like it had just fallen out of a history book. Hunter reached out and touched the still-smoldering tail, as if to check that the airplane was indeed real. Obviously, the city of Works had gone shopping in a time warp for its warplanes, too. Hunter's perfect shot from the roof of the control tower had reduced its air force by one.

"I'm no expert," Orr said, contemplating the vintage bomber himself. "But didn't these things go out of style about fifty years ago?"

"More like sixty," Hunter told him.

Making their way along the crumpled airframe and up to the shorn-off wing, they pulled a section of the airframe away from the skeleton and examined it. Oddly the gray-green paint was still wet in some places. A lot of the wiring looked new, too, though heavily taped. There were even a few microprocessor units taking the place of the older, heavier original equipment. Obviously the Heinkel had just been refinished, too—but the work was nowhere near the craftsmanship displayed in Clocks' WWI fighters.

They finally reached the shattered cockpit. The copilot

was still there, slumped over the controls, bleeding heavily from a multitude of wounds. The rest of the airplane was empty however—there were no bodies, no sign of the other six crewmen. Not even any footprints in the blackened, thick snow.

They took another long look around. The crash site wasn't really near anywhere else. The base of the twin mountains was just a mile away; the airfield was about two miles in the other direction. There was some thin forest to the east, a wide chilly river to the south, neither of which was a good place to hide.

This meant only one thing. If the rest of the bomber crew got away in one piece and if they were nowhere in sight, the only other place they would have gone was into the city of Clocks itself.


Hunter and Orr spent the next two hours patrolling the streets of the city, looking for any sign of the escaped aviators.

More than a hundred military police had already been called out to search for the escapees, but many of them were being redirected to help in the aftermath of the aerial bombing. Making a short broadcast over the city's *Volksradio,* Orr had appealed to citizens to join the hunt for the enemy fliers. Hundreds responded.

But the search so far had been fruitless. The city of Clocks was a great place to hide. It was honeycombed with narrow streets and alleys, centuries-old buildings and an extensive ornamental canal system. The shadows alone could conceal a good-sized army. What's more, nearly half of Clocks' current population was made up of strangers—mercenaries, wearing many different kinds of combat uniforms and known only to themselves. It would be a hard job indeed to find six men in all this.

The manhunt did give Hunter an opportunity to see

the city close up for the first time. Most of the shadowy streets looked like sets from a 1930s Expressionist movie, but Clocks had also retained a lot of its look from its high-flying fancy resort days. Many of the residences were chalet-like, and there was an overabundance of inns, taverns and gambling parlors, especially on the south side of town.

The city itself was laid out in a circle; the pyramid housing the military HQ being at the center. The western districts were taken up mostly by military installations and mustering houses. The eastern edge was mostly residential. To the south, the Sodom-like sin palaces, and to the north, the city's formidable academic and cultural establishments.

Orr revealed to him that learning the ins and outs of the various neighborhoods had taken him quite a while himself. He brought Hunter to a very strange place located just on the outskirts of the eastern edge of the city. A small village had once stood here, but now all its houses were wrecked, snow-filled and abandoned. Many appeared to have been crushed by some giant force.

"A monster came down from the mountains about this time last year," Orr told Hunter as they surveyed the eerily empty settlement. "A dinosaur—maybe a Tyrannosaurus Rex, I don't know. Anyway, it came here and started stomping houses before the police and soldiers arrived and chased it away. Killed about fifty people or so before it was driven off. No one wanted to live here after that . . ."

Hunter took a good long look at the abandoned village and the huge footprints still evident in the frozen-over ground.

"I don't blame them," he said.

# Five

Hunter spent the next three hours upside down inside the Sopwith biplane's beautifully reconditioned Wycoming engine.

He was intent on getting the biplane airworthy. To do so, many things had to be checked: connecting rods, struts, wires, flaps, plugs, and magnetos. Unlike a modern jet fighter, there was no computer that could diagnose any potential problems with the push of a button. Everything had to be done by hands, eyes, and ears.

As it turned out, prepping the Sopwith for flight had been the easy part—getting the damn thing out the door was another. The hangar was one in name only. It was really a big, empty storage facility that'd originally housed an Olympic-sized ice rink. When Clocks took delivery on the squadron of elderly airplanes, they'd come in crates, packed and disassembled. A freelance Polish aeronautical team had expertly put them back together again without realizing the doors of the building were too narrow to get the planes out. It took Hunter and six other people nearly an hour to manipulate the Sopwith an inch at a time and finally get it out of the building without ruining its fragile wings and tail.

By the time they did this, the sun was rising over the miles of flat plains east of Clocks. Just as Hunter and the makeshift ground crew finally got the biplane out onto the only runway, a rare streak of sunlight made its way through a thinning bank of clouds. It had been a long time since the Wingman had seen the sun—he took a moment and allowed it to warm his face. Then he climbed into the Sopwith's front seat.

The engine grumbled to life on the second try. Orr strapped himself into the rear gunner's seat—there never was any question as to who would be going along with Hunter on this, the first aerial recon flight of the Clocks Air Force. On his lap, the *Wehrenluftmeister* had two large cameras, a box of mice and a fully clipped M-16 rifle.

The overall defense of Clocks had many problems, but one of the most serious was the lack of battlefield reconnaissance. Previous recon photos had been taken by intrepid militiamen who had climbed the peaks *above* the battle zone and pointed their cameras down. This was a brave, but rarely successful means of gathering usable intelligence. There was really only one good way to take pictures of a battlefield—that was to fly over it.

And that's exactly what Hunter had in mind.

He took about ten seconds to familiarize himself with the plane's controls, not that there were more than five of them. Then, with the engine up to peak, the oil pressure zooming and Orr buckled up in back, he gunned the plane's oversized powerplant and started rolling down the frozen-hard airstrip. With the cheers of a dozen Clocks soldiers urging them on, the old airplane roared off into the frigid morning.

At last, the White Elephant Squadron was in the air.

Up they flew, almost straight up. Past the morning mist, through the pall of smoke still hanging over the city and into the low, wintry clouds. One thousand feet, two thousand. Three . . . Hunter was pouring the rpms into the big Wycoming and it was responding without so much as a cough. The Sopwith was old, but it flew neat, powerful and clean. By the time they broke through the top cloud layer forty-five seconds later, Hunter was in love with the reconditioned airplane.

He turned it over and they were soon looking up at the massive twin mountains. It was an illusion of flight that things appeared smaller from the air than from the ground. But not now. The twin Matterhorns looked tremendously big and impossibly high. Hunter pulled back on the plane's stick and sought to climb even higher. The engine began screaming, the cold air rushing madly against his face as they rose another one thousand feet. Still, the peaks seemed miles above them.

Then the wind whipping between the mountains caught the bottom of the biplane. Suddenly they were going straight up and twice as fast. It was all Hunter could do to keep the twin wings level; he finally resorted to steering the plane *with* the wind, back and forth, like a gyrocopter. Yet even with their enhanced speed, it still took another minute to reach the top of the mountains.

When they finally did clear them, it was like climbing out of a dark hole. The sky above the peaks was bright, clear—and cold. *Damned* cold. The air temperature had plummeted by more than fifty degrees Fahrenheit during the wild ascent. The Sopwith was still performing like a dream, but Hunter and Orr, sitting in open cockpits, were very quickly freezing up. The plane's heater was working, and waves of irradiated air were washing through the cockpit, but they did little good. Within thirty seconds, both Hunter and Orr began to collect rows of long, sparkling icicles on their hair, noses and beards.

He banked again, putting the Sopwith's nose slightly off true south. Below them now were the trenchlines that made up the craggy, Alpine battlefield. It was amazing. Looking up from Clocks, the mountain conflict appeared troublesome but remote, a perpetual stream of flame with a cloud of smoke hovering above it. But from this height, looking down onto the trenches, it was easy to see just how nasty this little war had become.

There'd been so much bombardment going on between the two sides, the snowcap in the pass between the mountains had actually melted in some places. Much of the frigid, two-mile-long battlefield was now covered with a layer of soot, rock and dislodged dirt. The whole area had become distinctly lunar—if it snowed on the Moon, this is what it would look like.

As they approached from five hundred feet, Hunter could clearly see the lines of riflemen and machine gunners on both sides firing madly at each other. The combined fusillade was solid and continuous. So, too, the flare from mortars, small cannons and multiple-rocket launchers. From this altitude, Hunter could tell it was crowded in ditches, on both sides. To his eyes, it seemed like every last one of the ten thousand men currently fighting for Clocks was jammed into the front line of trenchworks someplace. The combined body heat was enough to cause a fine mist to rise above the ditch.

He swung the biplane back to the north, edging closer to the enemy lines. Just as Orr's blurry recon photos had revealed earlier, the trenches dug by the Works army were larger, longer, more elaborate and more interconnected than those built by Clocks. Orr had been right—the invaders *were* taking their time executing this battle. Their network of ditches alone must have taken months to create.

Hunter steered the Sopwith into a huge updraft, it carried them up another five hundred feet in just a matter of seconds. His attention was drawn away from the battlefield and to the valley on the other side of the mountain. It was strange—he'd assumed Works was just like Clocks: a collection of Alpine-style houses and buildings, surrounded by grand snowcapped mountains. But Works was hardly like Clocks. Rather it looked like a city that had been transported from another, more industrial part of Europe and plopped down in the middle of the Alps. A handful of slate gray buildings dominated its center; they were surrounded by stalks of thin, spiraling skyscrapers. An extensive network of walkways and people-trams connected these buildings, giving the impression that the city was enshrouded in a gigantic spider's web. Swarms of small helicopters were flying around everywhere, keeping an eye on things.

*Metropolis*—that's what it looked like. Not the home of Superman, but the city in the movie of the same name by Fritz Lang. Eerie, stark and mechanical. There was nothing warm or inviting about this place.

"Where Nazis go to die," Hunter thought.

He banked back left and returned to the business below. Orr was snapping away madly with his cameras now, delighted that for the first time, Clocks was getting an accurate assessment of the enemy's disposition of forces, weaponry and supplies. But just from what Hunter had seen, it was obvious that the invaders had twice the men, twice the weapons and apparently all the time in the world to wear down their enemies.

This was not a good situation.

Giving in to a rare temptation, Hunter decided to shake things up a bit. He suddenly dropped the Sopwith into a screaming dive, plunging towards the Works lines. Much to his pleasure, many enemy soldiers began scrambling out of their trenches, so sure they were that he was going to open up on them. Instead, Hunter yanked the plane's choke lever, causing the big engine to backfire, further terrifying the Works soldiers. It was almost comical to see them running in every direction. Hunter was glad that Orr was capturing the whole thing on film.

He finally pulled up from the prank, banked left and found himself clear on the other side of the mountain, very low over the rear area of the enemy line. The roads leading up the peaks on the Works side were packed with supply trucks and fresh troops. Hunter put the biplane into another steep dive. The enemy soldiers on the roads scattered just as quickly as their comrades had in the trenches. Though they'd seen him coming, not one of them attempted to fire back at him. Everyone on the Works side of the mountain seemed to be more interested in finding cover than fighting back.

Hunter looped around and was soon back over the Works army trenches again. Orr had depleted two-thirds of his film load by this time; there was just enough for one final photo pass. But just as Hunter was banking to do this, the hair on the back of his head suddenly began to curl. Instantly his eyes became fixed on a point halfway up the southern peak, about two miles from the end of the Clocks left flank. It was a large cave, possibly man-made, and located in such a way that everything within was bathed in perpetual shadow, except its precipice. Poking out from this darkness, Hunter could see the long metallic snout of something big, something mean.

A cloud of vapor poured out of his mouth. *Jessuzz,* he breathed. Is that really a gun?

It *was* a gun. Actually a huge cannon, the tip of its wide barrel giving only a hint of its massive size. It had to be at least a 205-millimeter barrel, a gargantuan piece of long-range artillery. Yet from its semihidden position, it was all but invisible to the Clocks troops in the trenches. Hunter jinked the plane closer towards the opening—he could see much evidence of construction going on deeper inside the cave. He pointed the gun out to Orr who, slack-jawed and frigid, used the very last of his film shooting the big emplacement.

The gun was not yet operational, thank God. But when it was, Hunter had no doubt it would be able to easily lob shells not only onto the unprotected soldiers but onto the city of Clocks itself. Combined with the enemy's heavy aerial bombardment capability and its stronger position in the trenches, it seemed like only a matter of time before they overwhelmed the defenders.

With this chilly thought in mind, Hunter finally turned the Sopwith over and began going down again, back towards the embattled city of Clocks.

# Six

They lit the evening fires early that day in the *Rooten-tootzen*.

A large calf had been partially butchered around noon. It was now cooking slowly over the spit inside the tavern's enormous hearth.

There had been a change-out of units up on the mountain just after dawn. Seven hundred fresh soldiers and militiamen had reached the trenches, relieving a similar number of cold, hard, battle-weary troops. They now had forty-eight hours of warmth, food, drink—and if they were lucky, sex—waiting for them before they had to climb back up the peak again.

Many of these soldiers were now just arriving back in Clocks, having endured the long, slippery six-hour trip down the mountain. At one time, earlier in the war, returning troops would first report to the muster halls on the west end of town, where they would be formally released for their forty-eight-hour liberty. Not anymore. Some soldiers leapt from their troop trucks just as soon as they came in sight of the notorious southside of the city, intent on storming their favorite beer hall, chow palace or brothel. Many others dropped off further along the way, too. For most of the remaining soldiers though, the only slightly less disreputable *Rootentootzen* was the tavern of choice.

It was now three in the afternoon, but thick clouds and

heavy snow had turned the early afternoon as dark as dusk. Even the streetlights had blinked on—not that it made any impression on the patrons crowded inside the *Rootentootzen*. The *faux*-oompah music was blaring, the stew was crackling and the beer was flowing. Soldiers returning from the fight heard tales of the harrowing air raid the night before, and most especially, about the wreck of the He-111 out on the northern plain. The downed airplane had been the object of study and inspection by many of the townspeople this day. The rumors said the *Wehrenluftmeister*, Colonel Orr himself, had shot down the enemy bomber; others claimed it fell to the guns of a "super-mercenary" who'd just recently come to town. Some lips, those most doused by ale, dared to breathe that this helpful stranger was none other than Hawk Hunter himself.

But few people believed this—why would the Wingman come to little old Clocks? Still the talk of Hunter perked up at least some ears inside the bar, especially those belonging to the half dozen men sitting at the far corner table. Eating from a single cauldron of stew and nursing a small pitcher of beer, they'd been inside the beer hall since early morning, talking quietly and keeping to themselves. Such behavior was not unusual for the *Rootentootzen;* with so many hired guns in town, the sight of six strangers spending all day in a bar was more the norm than the exception. These men *were* mercenaries—but not for Clocks. They were airmen for the Works *Luftstaffel;* they'd arrived rather ungraciously in the Heinkel bomber now sitting wrecked out on the city's north plain.

The six aviators had escaped their crash with remarkably few wounds—cuts, bumps and bruises, mostly. It was a tribute to the skill of Franz, the bomber's pilot and senior officer. It was his idea to come here, to one of the most popular taverns in the city, in order to hide out. With the police still scouring the backstreets and the surrounding countryside looking for them, he believed their best plan was to conceal themselves in plain sight. There was no better place to do that than the *Rootentootzen*.

A few gold coins found in the pocket of the dead co-pilot had bought them their meal and the precious pitcher of beer, and they were keeping warm. But they had many problems facing them. They desperately had to get back to Works, though this desire came not from any sense of patriotism or loyalty. The air crew were all Germans, but they were also paycheck warriors. They'd been promised a half pound of gold apiece to take part in the bombing raid on Clocks. That substantial bounty still lay on the other side of the peaks.

And now this talk of Hawk Hunter was upsetting them. Three of the airmen had fought in America with the Fourth Reich XX Corps two years before. During the first few months of that conflict, it was taken for granted that Hawk Hunter had been killed in the opening battle of the war. That assumption came back to haunt the Fourth Reich in spades. When Hunter eventually showed up and began leading the American effort, it was the beginning of the end for the Nazis' Amerika adventure. In the series of battles that followed, the Fourth Reich was soundly defeated by resurgent American forces. So many Fourth Reich soldiers had been taken prisoner, the Americans had no choice but to ship them all back home in disgrace, adding yet another inglorious chapter to German military history.

It was no surprise then, that the mere mention of the Wingman would make the three airmen nervous.

Franz, too, was unsettled by the blabbering about the American superpilot. In his typically Prussian way of thinking, he knew if Hawk Hunter *was* in the area then it could mean only one thing: Works would eventually lose this fight, too. All the more reason to get back over the mountain and get paid before the next boot fell. But how to do it? He and his men had spent much of the time inside the beer hall trying to devise the next step of their escape. They'd quickly discovered they really had few options to get out. They had no guns, no warm clothing, no maps, no radio, and now, little money. Other than sprouting wings and flying over the top of the mountain, there really was no way out.

The few coins they had left bought another bowl of stew and a mug each of ale. As the bar became more crowded, and more festive, a strange thing happened: the enemy fliers found themselves getting caught up in the rowdy atmosphere of the *Rootentootzen.* There were many, many pretty girls, and they all seemed enamored of anyone who walked through the door in a uniform. Several had already made passes by the air crew's table, eyes darting this way and that, just hoping to be invited to join the six rugged aviators. The men from Works had been able to resist temptation, but just barely.

They did, however, get swept up in one of the many sing alongs that periodically washed through the well-oiled crowd. The song, "Ferme le Pook," was a favorite on both sides of the mountain, and the strong ale gave the Works aviators the courage to take a chorus by themselves. This brought several rounds of complimentary drinks to their table, which they drained heartily. This, in turn, led to further singing, and more free ale, and soon, the enemy fliers were standing on their chairs belting out old favorites like "Under-handen der Fräulein" with lusty abandon. Very quickly, their table was close to toppling over, so full it was with steins of gratis beer.

But then, just as the enemy aviators had taken their sixteenth round of free ale, the door to the bar suddenly burst open and a dozen soldiers marched in. Dressed in Alpine-white camouflage suits and carrying submachine guns, the city's muster squad was raising soldiers for the next deployment up the mountain.

"Papers, please!" the officer at the head of the squad announced loudly—and with just as much verve, the dozens of soldiers crammed into the beer hall quickly complied. Some had just come down off the mountain and resented the so-soon intrusion on their liberty. But most simply held out their blue cards and let the soldiers take their cursory look. It took about five minutes in all. The last table the muster soldiers came to was the one bearing the six escapees.

It was Franz who smashed the stein of beer in the officer's face. The man went over backwards, tripping on his own feet as he fell. Franz was on top of him in a flash, digging the jagged edge of the broken cup into the officer's neck. He found the jugular quickly, slashing it open and releasing a massive stream of blood all over the muster soldiers and the patrons.

Suddenly tables were being knocked over and chairs were flying through the air. Everyone dove for cover. One of Franz's men grabbed the dying officer's rifle and began firing it around the beer hall with ruthless abandon, killing and wounding several people. With this as cover, the six escapees made their way towards the front door, picking up more weapons as they went. Women were screaming, men were shouting. But through it all, no one fired back at the enemy fliers.

Finally Franz and his men fell out onto the snowy street. Each one had a weapon now and they were ready to shoot anything that moved. The street was empty—and deathly quiet. No one came out of the beer hall to chase them; no one raised an alarm. The only sound they could hear was the murderous wind, rushing off the mountain.

They started walking, briskly, not running as that would draw too much attention. They ducked down a back alley, and headed east. It was now about five in the evening and Clocks was as dark as midnight, providing the escapees with even more cover. Still, only after they'd moved several blocks away from the *Rootentootzen* did they start to relax.

They reached a particularly dark district—one that was still smoldering from the bombing raid the night before. Franz ordered his men to stop, if only to catch their breaths for a moment. Leaning up against the side of an abandoned building, the crewmen suddenly broke out into a chorus of "Ferme le Pook."

Franz did not join in—he couldn't. A bright light had appeared overhead, and he was now paralyzed by the damn thing. It suddenly began dropping out of the sky, heading right towards them. It grew so bright as it approached, it hurt Franz's eyes to look at it. His men continued their singing, somehow unaware of the terrifying light.

It finally pulled up in a hover, not thirty feet right above Franz's head. It was tremendous in size, saucer-shaped, and giving off a loud mechanical hum. Bursts of light and color were sparkling all around it. When Franz looked closely, he could see it was revolving at an impossibly high rate of speed.

Suddenly, a searing beam of bright light flashed out of the bottom of the object, hitting two of Franz's men in their chests. They lit up instantly—Franz was astonished that he could see the bones moving around inside their skin. There was a sound akin to a crack of thunder and then, the two men simply disappeared.

With that, the craft shuddered once, and in a great burst of power and speed, shot straight up into the night sky. Horrified, Franz watched it quickly disappear among the stars overhead. Throughout the whole episode, his other three men never stopped singing.

Shaken and confused, Franz somehow recovered long enough to bark out an order. His men jumped to their feet on the first syllable and wordlessly retrieved the weapons dropped by their disintegrated colleagues.

Still drunk, the remaining escapees began running. Down the street, across a small square, through a children's park; Franz was in the lead, running without his pants on.

They soon found another darkened alley, and quickly turning into it, vanished in the snowy night.

Hunter was clear on the other side of town when he heard about the shootout at the *Rootentootzen.*

He was inside the golden pyramid, sitting at a table in Orr's war room that was so large, it could hold up to one hundred twenty seats. Just over a dozen of them were occupied at the moment.

The mood around this table was understandably grim. The presence of the huge enemy gun up on the south mountain was catastrophic for Clocks. Fighting a cold, trench war way up in the clouds was one thing; living under the barrel of a weapon that could lob a one ton shell up to ten miles was quite another. No sooner had Hunter and Orr returned from their photo recon flight when they agreed that the big gun would have to be attacked immediately.

Before them now were twelve men—freelance pilots hired by Clocks before the city took delivery on its triplane air force. The pilots had been living inside the pyramid for the past six weeks, staying out of the public eye, content to collect their pay though they'd yet to fly a single mission. At first glance, the conflict between Clocks and Works meant little to them. It was simply business.

The twelve pilots were all Russian. Only about a third could speak English, and not very clearly. One man spoke English fairly well. His name was Alexander Ivanov and he was the commander of the mercenary air unit. He'd flown just about every airplane in the old Russian Air

Force, he'd told Hunter, from MiG-25s to the giant Antonov cargo plane. The Wingman was impressed by Ivanov's knowledge of airplanes and aeronautics. With his sharp eyes and quick wit, Ivanov seemed a natural for the fighter pilot game.

His pilots, known collectively as the *Sturmoviks*, had been together for three years now. They were warriors-for-hire true, but all had avowed hatred for the notorious Red Star group, the clique of renegade Russian militarists who'd started the Big War in the first place. As a collective unit, the *Sturmoviks'* reputation was impeccable; they'd fought in many of the conflicts that had raged throughout Central Europe in recent times, and boasted an impressive record of always winding up on the winning side. But like most mercenary groups, Hunter knew the true test of their mettle could only be proven in combat.

The past few weeks had been easy for the *Sturmoviks*—or "Stormers" as Orr called them. This was not because they didn't know how to fly the antique collection of airplanes in Clocks Air Force—Orr had told them to sit tight until he could locate some more-modern airplanes for them. But now, with the discovery of the big gun, time was quickly running out on the city. The Russians were told they would have to take to the air in the refurbished World War I planes. In the end, it didn't seem to faze them one way or the other.

Spread out on the big planning table before them, were the three dozen blow ups of photographs Hunter and Orr had taken earlier. These included the clearest views they had of the big 205-millimeter gun sticking out the south peak. The Russian pilots' eyes went wide when they saw the size of the cannon and its substantial cavernous emplacement. No translation was needed here: the gun would be the first target for their first mission for Clocks.

Hunter had left it up to the Stormers on how best to attack the big gun. Though Clocks aerial force was all outfitted with weapons pods, they had no real blockbuster bombs at their disposal. It was foolish to think they could actually destroy the gun itself. Rather they would have to go after the big weapon's ancillaries—its controls, its ammunition and the people who ran it.

The timing for all this would be critical. Though it was impossible to see just how close the big gun was to becoming operational, Hunter's gut was telling him the weapon could start lobbing shells into Clocks at any time. The air strike would have to be carried out as soon as possible. Ivanov assured him his men could familiarize themselves with the Fokkers and Spads inside of an hour. Loading up weapons, fuel and getting the damn things out of the so-called hangar would take at least several hours more. It was now close to midevening. Hunter suggested that they go up at dawn. The Stormers quickly agreed.

They had just settled down to iron out the dozens of details when the first report reached them about the *Rootentootzen*. Orr went pale when he heard the news, brought to him by his top defense officer, a man who was wearing a bright red clown's suit. Fourteen people had been killed, many more wounded, some very seriously. The *Wehrenluftmeister* took the loss of every man in his command personally—an endearing human trait, which nevertheless was a quick path to lunacy for any military leader. Details about the bloodbath were sketchy—at first everyone had assumed the perpetrators were mercenaries who did not want to return to the war at the top of the mountain. But Hunter knew better. He suspected the culprits to be the escaped Heinkel crewmen from the start— the brutality of the incident alone was enough to convince him.

Orr was quickly on the phone, once again rounding up the city's police forces and militia to begin a hunt for the killers. Leaving the Russian pilots to continue planning the attack on the big gun, Hunter loaded up his M-16F2 and told Orr he would join him on the dragnet.

He wanted to see just how desperate these men from Works could be.

# Seven

There was a long line of armored vehicles waiting outside the golden pyramid when Hunter and Orr emerged.

The ACs were brimming with the *Volkspolizi,* the city's combination police force and Home Guard. Many of these soldiers were mercenaries, too. Any able-bodied man who was a citizen of Clocks was more likely to wind up on the front line, leaving the rear area duties to the paid help. The Clocks' *Volkspolizi* was made up mostly of Czechs and Free Canadians, many of whom had come over with Orr a few years back. There were a number of Italians and Scots as well.

The *Volkspolizi* had a reputation for being tough but fair, but with reports that some of their brethren had been killed in the shootout at the *Rootentootzen,* these men were now visibly agitated. Hunter could see it in their eyes—they couldn't wait to start looking for the escaped enemy pilots. They would have their work cut out for them though—finding someone in the darkened corners of Clocks would not be easy. Every ounce of adrenaline would be needed to aid them in the long night ahead.

Hunter and Orr climbed into the first armored car. It was a twenty-year-old RPX 3000, complete with a Milan antitank gun on top. The vehicles behind them were Dutch YP-408s, each with its trademark Browning M2HB side-mounted heavy-machine gun on the turret. Orr checked the line of vehicles, then gave the start-up sign.

With a tremendous roar, a dozen diesel engines came to life and the column moved out.

The search of the city had begun.


Clocks was laid out in a roughly circular pattern.

The northern part of the city was an area thick with bunkers, warehouses and storage buildings, all great places to hide. The eastern streets, the mostly academic and residential section known as *Volkshamlet* also afforded a lot of invisibility; so, too, the western end, though this was where most of the city's troops were quartered. When the *Volkspolizi* column reached the middle of town, two ACs each split off to patrol the north, east and west.

The six remaining vehicles, including the one containing Hunter and Orr, would tackle the southern end of town, the tough area beyond mildly bawdy establishments like the *Rootentootzen*. Officially, this part of Clocks was known as *Seutendenzen*. But the place was so notorious, so dangerous, everyone called it *Badentown*, or simply, "Badtown."

Hunter had seen many seedy places in his travels, but *Badentown* managed to astound even him. It was the kind of place that, no matter what the weather, the road pavement always seemed wet, dark and grimy. There was little need for streetlights here; the glow from all the neon provided more than enough illumination, creating many shadow-filled and darkened areas.

Once inside the district, it was evident there were three main kinds of establishments in Badtown: beer halls, gambling dens and whorehouses. There was so much loud music blaring from these places, it all seemed to meld into one, crazed symphony. Many faces—either tough and broken-nosed or young, painted and innocent—peeked out of the shadowy doorways as the column passed by. Somewhere Hunter could hear a woman screaming. Or was she laughing? He couldn't tell. That seemed apropos. Badtown was Las Vegas divided by Amsterdam, then multiplied by Bangkok, he decided. It oozed danger, lust and intrigue.

All the music stopped as the column of armored cars pulled onto the main street. The number of eyes staring out from the shadows increased a hundredfold. You could almost hear the sound of a few thousand bullets being slipped into a few thousand gun chambers. Hunter was beginning to think a half dozen ACs might not be enough.

But he had to give Orr credit—the guy knew how to make an entrance. The *Wehrenluftmeister* called the column to a halt in front of what Hunter understood to be the most dangerous, most disreputable beer hall in the city, a place called the *Shitzenhouzen*. It was a grand, rundown saloon built in the best American Wild West style, complete with bar girls, hustlers, shelves of cheap booze and of course, all kinds of weaponry.

Orr leapt out of the AC, waved his machine pistol around and had the *Volkspolizi* unit dismount. Each AC was carrying six troops plus the driver and gunner. Now this small army was assembling on the sidewalk outside the *Shitzenhouzen*. It was an impressive show of force—a large firearm and a uniform went a long way down here in Badtown. Hunter climbed out of the AC and cranked his own M-16F2 to life. Suddenly he wished he'd brought a pair of shades. The glare from the neon lights on the moist streets was that bright.

Orr went through the door to the *Shitzenhouzen* like a man shot out of a cannon. Hunter was right on his heels, along with twelve *Volkspolizi*. There were at least two hundred people in the place, many sitting around gambling tables, others lounging along the bar rail itself. There were many women around, too—all of them scantily clad, some even topless, in the best European tradition. Hunter followed Orr right up to the main bar, the sullen crowd parting reluctantly as they moved through. Most of the *Volkspolizi* were wearing regulation ski masks, for identity purposes. Orr, too, was wearing a face guard. Hunter, dressed in his black flights, a bandolier of ammo slung over his left shoulder, had his baseball cap pulled low to his eyes. He really didn't want anyone recognizing him at the moment either.

Orr reached the bar and without missing a beat, dove across it, grabbed the biggest, toughest-looking bartender by the collar and dragged him right across the wet, beer-sticky top. The place gasped as the man fell to the floor only to be hauled to his feet again by Orr. The bartender started to say something, but Orr slapped his words away. The place closed in on them; Hunter raised his rifle slightly, purely on instinct. But Orr had the crowd in the palm of his hands.

The *Wehrenluftmeister* let go a stream of some language close to the bartender's ruptured face. Part-German, part-Swiss, and part-Old English vulgarity, the bartender's features dropped with every word. It was clear he wanted no part of Orr and the *Volkspolizi*. Obviously Orr was questioning the man about the escaped Works aviators but the bartender just kept shaking his head. He didn't know where the hell these guys were.

"We're tossing this place anyway," Orr told him, first in loud and clear English, and then German, then Swiss. "We don't want any problems. Neither do you . . ."

The bartender raised his hands as if to say: go right ahead. But Orr smashed his head into the bar anyway, knocking him out cold. Then with great flourish, he turned and barked an order to his men. In seconds, half the *Volkspolizi* were stomping up the stairs to the *Shitzen-houzen's* second floor, while the other half was climbing down into its bunker-like basement-*cum*-gambling-hall.

Hunter turned back to Orr who was now coolly pouring a draft of beer into his kit tin, courtesy of a nearby spigot.

"All that yelling gets your throat a bit dry," he told Hunter with a straight face.

They decided to split up. While Orr joined his men in the basement, Hunter went up the stairs; something was drawing him to the second floor of this place.

On reaching the top of the stairs, he found an extensive network of small hallways containing dozens of doors. The six *Volkspolizi* ahead of him were systematically pounding on each one of them, kicking it in if they didn't get a response after two knocks. Hunter glanced into each of these open rooms, finding just about every sexual combination possible: man-woman; man-girl; man-woman-girl, woman-girl, girl-girl, etc. Each client looked drunker than the next, each *demimondaine* cuter and younger. None of them seemed too surprised to find a bunch of ski-masked men with huge rifles poking in on them—this sort of thing went on all the time in the *Shitzenhouzen*.

The search quickly become tedious. Hunter's instincts were telling him the escaped airmen were not up here; yet his gut was pushing him towards something that might be helpful in the search. He found himself climbing up a third set of steps, and after passing through a dark attic used to store liquor, ammunition and cocaine, stepping out onto the roof itself.

The *Shitzenhouzen* was hardly the tallest building in Badtown, but even from this height, the view was startling. The south district looked like an outline of neon, hellishly carved out of the deceptively peaceful circle of Clocks. It seemed the natural place for the escapees to hide. Beyond it lay the military bases, then the road out of town and finally the grand, twin-peaked mountain itself. It appeared huge from here, seemingly towering into the night sky by ten miles or more. It was so close, Hunter imagined he could reach out and touch it.

At its summit was the permanent glow from the non-stop battle, with a cloud of mist, blowing snow and smoke enshrouding the peaks themselves. The fighting seemed particularly intense on this calm, clear night. He was sure the light could be seen for hundreds of miles.

He drew his eyes from the terrifying beauty of the landscape and back to the matter at hand.

There were obviously no fire codes enforced in this part of Clocks. Hunter could practically step over onto the roof of the next building, and then to the one after that, and the one after that. The whole neighborhood was a clutter of old wooden structures, bedecked with brightly lit signs and enclosed in a maddening web of fire escapes and rickety ladders. Even someone with normal vision had no trouble seeing into any one of a dozen windows nearby, every one of them a Peeping Tom's dream. Hunter's extraordinary sight allowed him to pick up faces, eye color and even positions as far as three blocks away.

But right now he was looking down at the gravel roof around his boots. He gave the air a mighty sniff. What was that smell? He crouched down and saw a drop of dark red liquid; beside it was another, larger drop and beside that one, another. He concentrated his powerful vision on the still-wet fluid and took another deep sniff. His instincts had been right. It was blood.

Orr was suddenly beside him, his flashlight illuminating a crimson trail that stretched halfway across the roof.

"Could it be from an animal of some kind?" he asked Hunter. "A cat? Or a rat?"

Hunter took off his flight gloves and put his hand down close to a particularly large pool of blood. A half inch away from making contact, he could feel its heat.

"No, it's human," he confirmed. "Been here only two minutes, tops."

Using Orr's flashlight, he looked even closer. He could

see hundreds of tiny swastikas swimming around in the
small crimson drops. He pointed them out to Orr.

"So they *were* here," the *Wehrenluftmeister* said. "They
must have left when they heard us drive up."

Hunter was suddenly back on his feet again. Without
another word he checked the wind direction, then leapt
over to the roof of the next building. Orr signaled two
of his men to stay put, then he and three others jumped
to the next building as well.

The hunt was on.

They followed the trail of blood for the next ten minutes—running full-out over the rooftops and up and
down fire escapes. The blood became more voluminous
the further they went. By the time they reached the twen-
tieth or so building, the blood was so thick, it was covering
most of the rooftop. Still they pressed on. Hunter always
seemed to be three steps ahead of Orr and his men. They
had only their eyes to guide them; Hunter had his eyes,
plus his nose and ears working for him.

Finally they reached an alley that was just off the busiest
intersection in Badtown, the convergence of *Buuster-
strausse* and *Wolkthyss* Way. There was so much blood here
it looked as if it had been applied by a thick paintbrush.
A large old hotel dominated one side of the alley; a number of ladders led to its roof. Every one of them was
absolutely coated with fresh, warm blood.

"Not a lot of people roaming around this part of town
bleeding like this," Orr told Hunter, still out of breath
from their dash across the rooftops. "Someone gets cut
down here every night, either that or goes home wearing
a bullet. But I don't think they'd be bleeding by the gallon . . ."

Hunter moved to the corner of the building and took
a look out onto the main street. It was filled with hookers,
gamblers and pimps. The hotel was the biggest structure
around. The surrounding buildings were connected to its

top by ladders and walkways, though most of these were twenty feet long or more.

His instincts were telling him that if these were the enemy aviators they were chasing, then they were hiding somewhere inside the hotel. He slipped back into the alley for a quick confab with Orr. The *Wehrenluftmeister* and his men would attempt to get in by the front door to the place. Hunter would try the back.

He moved even deeper into the alley and quickly located a fire escape that led all the way up the hotel's seventeen floors. He began climbing, past many uncurtained, brightly lit rooms, all of them containing even more acts of unspeakable sex and/or perversion within, and soon gaining the top of the building. It was here he found the first aviator.

The man was lying face down in an ocean of his own blood, his legs and feet covered with mud and oil. His throat had been slashed—by his fellow airmen, Hunter suspected. He held his unprotected hand over the fresh corpse. It had shaken its mortal coil some time ago, he guessed, and had been dragged this long way just so Hunter and the others would follow.

A distinctly disturbing chill ran through him now. He checked his M-16's ammo load—as always it was filled with tracer rounds. Making his way to the rooftop door, his spine began tingling—warning him that he had to be careful. Strange things lay ahead. He nudged the door open with the snout of his gun and peered inside. A long dark hallway stretched before him.

He stepped inside, closed the door and began feeling his way along the corridor, a formation of crows flying strange maneuvers just above his head. Unlike the rest of the building, the top floor was not rocking and rolling. The silence up here was almost eerie. He reached one door; it was locked and dark inside. He tried the next one—it, too, was locked but its door knob was warm and sticky. The third door was a quarter of the way open. A thin shaft of candlelight was falling out of it.

Hunter opened this door all the way. Inside he found one of the most beautiful females he'd ever set eyes on.

She was sitting on the edge of a large bed, wearing a skimpy negligee. She was blond, probably not yet twenty, maybe not yet eighteen. Her face was simply radiant, almost angelic. It seemed to be glowing in the darkened room. She smiled slightly when she first saw him, as if she couldn't help herself. Her nipples, fully visible through the skimpy clothing, immediately went hard, too.

Hunter had no more blood trail to follow, but that wasn't important anymore. He knew the surviving aviators were close by—possibly right behind the partially opened door. But first things first. He was still studying the beautiful girl.

"What's your name?" he asked in a whisper.

"You mean you don't recognize me, Hawk?" she replied.

Her question caught him off guard. He took an even closer look. Those eyes, those lips, those breasts, those legs. Yes, he *had* seen them all before—a long time ago, in the cramped cabin of an aircraft carrier. Push-pull. Push-pull. He remembered now—her name was Emma.

What happened next Hunter had only experienced a couple of times before in his life. It sounded like such a tired expression, but time did indeed stand still. His eyes locked on the young girl, his mind flashed in reverse. Three years ago, nearly four. He was in the Med, tracking the first super-criminal to go by the name of Viktor. A major war was imminent in the Middle East and Viktor's hand was in every aspect of the coming battle. Hunter joined a bunch of British adventurers and helped them tow the disabled aircraft carrier USS *Saratoga* to the Suez Canal where jets launched from its deck halted the advance of Viktor's invading armies. Along the way they'd saved a group of young call girls who wound up staying with them for the entire voyage east. One of them was Emma, a dead ringer for his true love, the beautiful, elusive, Dominique. Emma and Hunter had been close. *Real* close.

And now she was here, back in his life. But under such strange circumstances!

Suddenly his entire body began vibrating; jolts of electricity were running up and down his spine. Danger was all around him—he could *feel* it. And now, he had to get ready to stop it.

It took some doing, but Hunter forced things to start moving again. Time sped up. Emma was still smiling at him, but in a slightly different way. It was a signal; he knew what it meant. He took a step to the right and ducked—a stream of bullets passed over his head a microsecond later. Falling to one knee, Hunter raised his M-16F2 precisely sixty-two degrees from the floor and squeezed off two shots. Both went through the head of the armed man who'd shot at him from the shadows. His body fell heavily right in front of Hunter. There was no doubt he was one of the Works aviators.

At that moment, there was a great crash of glass. Three ghosts were going out the window, smashing through the panes, guns raised and dragging Emma with them. Hunter was across the room and out the shattered window in a shot, landing feet-first on a very rickety fire escape. There was another building across the alley—it was a twenty-foot leap away. The silhouettes of the escaped aviators were double-timing it across the roof, pulling Emma along with them. Overhead, a pterodactyl suddenly appeared, screeched, then disappeared. A makeshift wooden ladder, probably placed between the two buildings centuries ago, now lay broken in the alley seventeen stories below him. The escaped fliers had used it to go across to the next roof and then kicked it away.

Hunter didn't hesitate a moment. With one great push of power, he leapt out from the fire escape and flew across the great divide and onto the next roof. He landed with a grunt, his rifle up and cocked. One of the aviators spun around, a look of utter astonishment on his face. He clumsily pointed his pistol back at him, but Hunter shot it out of his hand. Eleven degrees to the left, he fired a burst into the feet of the man who was dragging Emma. He stumbled badly, a total of five toes blown off. Emma went flying through the air, flapping her arms. Hunter rushed forward and caught her before she went off the roof completely.

Covering her body with his, he rolled again, avoiding a stream of gunfire from the lead aviator. The enemy fliers made the leap to the next building and started firing even before their feet hit the roof. Not a second later, a counter-fusillade of gunfire erupted from the windows of the hotel. It was Orr and his men. They had spotted the Works aviators and were now shooting wildly at them. Taking advantage of this cover, Hunter managed to carry Emma to a protected corner of the flat roof, out of harm's way. His intent was to leave her there and join the battle—but suddenly his senses began tingling again.

He quickly turned to the west, towards the immense, twin-peaked mountain.

Something was coming over the top . . .

First one, then two, then six, then twelve dark forms were emerging from the starry murk on the other side of the peaks. Their combined roar was all too familiar—a sound Hunter would never forget. It was a flight of Heinkels, coming over the alp to bomb Clocks again.

But now, unlike the night before, streams of AA fire began rising above Clocks. It was coming from the northern district of Clocks, the place where the military was quartered. The Heinkels were drawing even closer, but now heavy weapons fire was coming up from the eastern edge of the city, and from the center of town, too. Where the hell did Clocks suddenly get all this antiaircraft weaponry? Hunter didn't know, but it seemed like anyone who had a large gun in the city was now firing at the approaching bombers. Suddenly the night sky was lit as bright as day. Red, orange, yellow, even some greenish-blue tracers, all converging into an area above the city through which the bombers were passing.

The airplanes' sudden appearance did little to dampen the rooftop gun battle. The Works aviators were slowly moving across the top of the next building, still firing their weapons. Suddenly the air was cut with another sound, this one sharp and thunderous. Hunter scanned the smoky skies—then he saw it. Off to the west, a flying object, bright and fiery. It was moving quickly through the smoke and clouds—and heading right for the roof of the next building, where the Works aviators were. The lights on the bottom of the craft grew incredibly bright as it approached.

*What the hell is this?* Hunter heard himself scream into the howling wind.

Then, in the next instant, he knew. It was a helicopter—a big one—coming down out of the clouds to pick up the escaped aviators.

The men from Works saw the copter, too. It went into a hover above the far northeast corner of the next roof. An ancient set of stairs no more than twenty-five feet from Hunter connected the two buildings. Obviously, this was the enemy airmen's intended route of escape. They could go across to the next building, jump into the helicopter and be gone.

Hunter couldn't let that happen.

Emma was crying and shaking now, both from fright and the cold. She was squeezing Hunter so hard, it felt like she'd already cracked one of his ribs. He finally disengaged himself from her and moved her even further into the corner. Then he scrambled over to the edge of the roof, his gun cocked and ready. The enemy aviators were slowly making their way along a short, metal railing, ducking and dodging the furious gunfire coming from Orr and his men. Meanwhile the nearby helicopter was stirring up a tornado of wind with its massive rotor blades. Hunter let the enemy airmen continue—his best shot would come once they reached the steps. He brought his gun up and began to set the laser-sighter. But once more, he was distracted, his body suddenly vibrating with his built-in warning system.

*Now what?* he thought.

He spun around to see the main force of Heinkels had penetrated the box of furious antiaircraft fire—they were now letting loose streams of bombs onto the center of Clocks. Three of the bombers had broken away from the main group and they were now over Badtown itself. They, too, had opened their bomb bays and were dropping their weapon loads. As Hunter watched in shock, at least a dozen bombs went crashing into the *Shitzenhouzen,* three blocks away. A stream of red and yellow fire erupted from the streets below. It was Orr's *Volkspolizi* firing at the Heinkels as they roared overhead. One stream of bullets hit the underbelly of the middle airplane. There was a huge midair explosion—a lucky shot had found one of the airplane's bombs just as it was falling out of its weapons' bay. The Heinkel was instantly swallowed up in a ball of flame and smoke. There was another explosion—a frightful screech filled the air. Then the Heinkel began coming down.

Hunter quickly flipped over and made it back to Emma just as the huge burning fuselage went over his head and slammed into the building next door. The resulting explosion was so violent, it lifted them high into the air, tossing and turning them over like dolls. They fell, together, still embraced, towards a huge hole in the side of their building. At the very last instant, Hunter managed to snag a thick pipe with his right arm. Still holding the terrified Emma with his left, his quick action prevented them from being blown off the building altogether. The shock wave from the crash hit an instant later—it was tremendously powerful. Hunter did what he did best—he hung on and closed his eyes. Chaos completely engulfed them—explosions, screams, the roar of flames filled his ears. It finally passed over them. The firewind died down and the great ball of smoke went right by them and ascended mushroom-like into the night.

When Hunter looked up again, there was nothing left of the building next door—no aviators, no helicopter, nothing.

All that remained was a massive hole in the ground with the long crumpled tail of the burning He-111 sticking out of it.

The next thing Hunter knew, he was falling again.

Down past the seventeen floors of the hotel, past all the windows with all the freakish acts still going on within. Emma was in his arms, laughing wildly as they fell. The conflagration caused by the downed Heinkel had been spectacular and so close—but Hunter could not feel it. The flames coming from the crash looked real but the heat felt fake.

Interesting . . .

They came to rest very gently on the sidewalk outside the front of the hotel. The streets were still crowded with pimps, hookers and assorted denizens, but now fire apparatus was speeding through the narrow thoroughfares and firemen running everywhere, adding greatly to the clutter. Alarms were going off—bells, klaxons, sirens. Explosions could be heard in the distance. Two more Heinkels had been shot down in the center of Clocks, another had gone down in the east and two more had plowed into the side of the mountain to the west. The

remainder had quickly fled back over the peaks, dogged
by AA fire the entire way.

Emma was leading Hunter now, through the crowded
streets, past one group of firefighters who were directing
hoses filled with milk at the wall of flames. They ducked
down one alley that was crowded with a flock of nuns,
another was thick with ducks. They ran past the *Shitzenhouzen,* supposedly obliterated in the bombing raid. But
half the building was still standing and at the moment,
some kind of religious service seemed to be taking place
inside.

They finally made their way away from the madness
that had gripped Badtown, to a section of Clocks not too
far from the *Rootentootzen.* Hunter had a million things
he wanted to ask Emma, most importantly how she came
to wind up here, in Clocks. But every time he tried to
say something, she just put her finger to his lips and giggled. *There will be plenty of time to talk later,* he supposed.

She finally led him into a building that seemed too
ornate and out of place for this part of town. It was an
apartment house of some kind. They went immediately
to the second floor, stopping in front of a door marked
number thirteen.

"I hope you like my place," Emma cooed, fishing
around in her skimpy outfit and somehow finding a key.

She handed it to Hunter who put it into the lock and
began to turn it. She laid her hand on his and directed
his eyes back towards her. Her negligee was gone now—
Hunter found himself staring at her lovely naked body.

"Looking is just as good as doing," she said with a
mischievous shiver.

Hunter couldn't help himself—he reached out to
touch her. But quite suddenly, she was soaking wet, as if
she'd just stepped out of a bath.

"I just came from a swim," she explained mysteriously.

"I go to a favorite spot of mine, down at the lake, where it's really cold."

Hunter just shrugged and tried to turn the key again. But then Emma bent down and attempted to look into the keyhole.

He asked her what she was doing. She just smiled again, suddenly dried, suddenly back in her flimsy outfit.

"I said sometimes it's more fun to watch," she replied inexplicably. "Don't you think?"

Again Hunter shrugged and turned the key—finally the door opened. He was shivering a bit now, too, anticipating what he and Emma were about to do.

As the door swung open he was astonished to find the dozen pilots of the *Sturmoviks* squadron waiting inside. They were all wearing their green flight uniforms, including helmets and goggles, and lounging about the small apartment as if they'd been there for some time.

Hunter was very surprised to see them.

"What . . . what are you guys doing here?" he gasped.

The leader of the Russian mercs, the man named Alexander Ivanov, stepped forward and smiled broadly.

"Major Hunter, my friend," he said. "Have you forgotten about the big gun we must take out?"

# Eight

It was suddenly five-thirty in the morning.

The sun was not up yet, and many stars and planets could still be seen in the crystal clear sky overhead. In the background, the nightmarish peaks soared many miles into the sky. A pall of smoke was rising above them, too. It was glowing, as always, lit by the perpetual exchange of gunfire coming from the embattled trenches below.

Suddenly, the air was shocked by the roar of nine powerful piston engines being cranked to life. Nine plumes of smoke mixed with the early fog to create a blue shroud above the tiny airport outside Clocks. Very quickly, nine airplanes—six Fokkers, two Spads and the two-seat Sopwith—began making their way towards the airfield's only runway. Beneath their wings were fully loaded cannon pods, weapons dispensers and five hundred-pound ironhead bombs. In their cockpits, a total of ten men, each one determined to change the face of battle high up on the mountaintops.

The Spads took off first. Side by side, they jumped into the air with the deft touch of their Russian pilots. Behind them, three Fokkers roared away, the unique triwings rising very quickly into the early morning air. No sooner were they gone when the second trio was off. Behind them, came the Sopwith two-seater. Once again, Hunter was in the pilot's seat; Orr was strapped into the back.

The *Sturmoviks* did not hesitate in their approach to the lofty battleground. While another batch of aviators might have taken time to form up and collect their thoughts, the Russians went right to work. Once they were all airborne, they put their airplanes into screaming climbs and were soon rushing through the clouds and towards the opening between the two mountains. Being last in line, Hunter slammed the Sopwith's throttles forward in an effort to catch up to the smaller fighters. But it was no contest. Already, they were out of sight of him.

Pressing the throttle ahead full gear, the Sopwith's engine screamed in response and began climbing very rapidly. Through the overcast they went, the wind sounding like a woman's screams as it roared off the twin wings. By the time Hunter broke through the clouds at five thousand feet, the Spads were already turning on the south mountain, and the great gun emplacement halfway up its slope.

Their cannons and weapon-pods erupting in brilliant flashes of yellow and gold, the tiny biplanes brazenly dove on the gun opening, covering it with a flourish of small but lethal explosions. It seemed like they were going to crash right into the mountain themselves—they came that close to the snowy ledge. But they pulled up and then out, their oversized engines screaming as they rose even further into the cold morning air.

The Spads left just in time for the first pair of Fokkers to come in. These two triplanes were outfitted with mighty-midget weapons dispensers; powerful weapons, but not exactly ideal in attacking a rocky enclave. The hundred or so submunitions contained in the dispensers were better adapted for attacks against troops and equipment spread out on level ground. But the Stormers had never read the user's manual. Their huge engines burning full-out, both triplanes swooped up the cave opening, let their ordnance go at the precisely same instant and then rolled over in a heart-stopping acrobatic loop. The death-defying maneuever served to fling their submunitions loads right into the cave opening, like two bananas going through a hoop. Suddenly the cave mouth was awash in explosions, blue flames and clouds of smoke, punctured by thousands of bits of flying rock. Hunter was astounded. He couldn't imagine anyone within one hundred yards of the cave opening living through such a vicious barrage.

No sooner had these two Stormers cleared the scene when a second pair of Fokkers arrived. Perfectly mimicking their predecessors, these two also sent a storm of bomblets into the opening, pulling up, tails straight, at the very last instant. Another wave of explosions engulfed the cave's opening. Once again, Hunter was astonished at the Stormers' violent but highly successful maneuvering.

Now the trailing pair of Fokkers appeared. Each one was lugging a five hundred-pound bomb. They roared in, one behind the other, their engines screaming like banshees. The first triplane unleashed its bomb high—it slammed into the mountain fifty feet above the cave opening. A grand miss! Or so it seemed.

The second Fokker went in and delivered its bomb in the exact same place. Suddenly it seemed as if the whole mountain was moving. An instant later, a huge flood of snow, ice, rocks and dirt dislodged itself from the peak and came crashing down the side of the alp. Even above his airplane's noisy engine, Hunter could hear the frightening rumble as the avalanche slammed into the cave opening—and kept right on going. Gathering snow, debris, bodies and pieces of wreckage from inside the gun emplacement with it, the landslide left a trail of smoke and snow so thick, it totally obscured the mountain for ten long seconds.

When this cloud finally cleared, the western side of the southern peak had redefined itself. It was now steeper, cleaner, whiter. Hunter turned his Sopwith over and flew close to where the cave had once been. The area was now as smooth and pristine as a ski trail—all evidence that the huge gun emplacement that had once marred its face was gone. He shivered at the horror of those entombed inside. Cold, dark and airless—it was an awful way to die.

Without missing a beat, the Stormers formed up into a V high above the twin mountains. As one, they banked hard to the right and were suddenly diving on the Works trenchline, cannons opened up on full. Chaos broke out inside the invaders' ditch. This was the first true air attack on their positions, and it was evident they were woefully unprepared for it. As with Hunter's dry run the day before, many of the hapless Works soldiers jumped out of the trenches and began running away—a foolish thing to do. The lead Russians bore down on these fleeing troops first, perforating them with dizzyingly accurate gunfire.

Though the enemy line was nearly two miles long, the Stormers went to work on tearing up its entire length. Flying little more than fifty feet off the snowy top, their blazing guns found dozens of targets, both human and mechanical. They seemed to be causing an explosion every few feet or so as their rounds not only ate through human flesh, but ammunition stores and fuel tanks as well. Trailing behind the action, Hunter could see the snow on the eastern edge of the mountain actually turning red with blood.

At the end of the trench, the six Fokkers and two Spads pulled up, looped and then swooped in for a second strafing run. This time the Spads concentrated solely on the fleeing, terrified soldiers, while the Fokkers continued attacking the trenches themselves. Even though return fire was now rising up from the Works position, it didn't affect the Russians one bit. They stayed steady, straight and true, mercilessly gunning down enemy soldiers and destroying any weapons they found along the two-mile fortifications.

Hunter turned the Sopwith over again and found himself riding two hundred fifty feet above the Clocks positions. The friendly soldiers in the eastern trenches were hunkered down and holding on for dear life as the enemy soldiers they'd been trying to kill, one at a time for the past three months, were being slaughtered by the *Sturmoviks* just a few feet away.

It went on for ten full minutes—wave after wave after wave of Stormers swooping down, their Merlins smoking mightily in the frigid air, their cannons strafing the Works trenches mercilessly from one end to the other. Hunter went in on the tail end of one strafing pass made by the three Fokkers and was astounded at the number of casualties lying in the snow. The sun was rising now and its first rays clearly revealed the destruction the Stormers were wreaking. There were thousands of dead and dying Works soldiers staining the icy landscape, froths of blood all around them. Any major weapons systems the invading army had employed—from heavy mortars to rocket launchers—also lay in smoldering ruins. Smoke and huge fires were flaring up everywhere.

Never before had the Wingman seen such quick and complete destruction.

After a while it seemed as if there were no more targets for the *Sturmoviks* to shoot at. Still they formed up once again and as one pounced on the enemy trenches.

The Clocks Air Force had no radios; there was no way at all to communicate between pilots. Had there been, Hunter would have called off the air assault at this point. Destroying an enemy's war-making capability was one thing—firing on helpless, wounded and obviously defeated soldiers was another.

But now, all he could do was watch with growing repulsion as the Stormers once more opened up on the men fleeing the Works trenches. Hunter realized just what a shitty business he was in. Superheroics aside, he was, in the end, a practitioner in the art of making war, and war only led to suffering, misery and death. Had he the ability at that moment to throw a switch and turn it all off, he would have done so gladly. What he was witnessing wasn't really a battle now—it was one-sided butchery. He was almost beginning to feel pity for the routed Works soldiers.

Still, the *Sturmoviks* continued attacking. They were concentrating on troops in the rear areas of the Works positions now, gunning down unarmed supply troops and civilian support people. Soon the entire eastern side of the enormous mountain was running red with blood, giving the whole thing a distinctly surreal edge. Just when would the Stormers run out of ammunition? Or fuel? Or targets to shoot at?

Finally it got to the point where Hunter knew he had to call a halt to the action, in whatever way possible. He flipped the Sopwith over and made a beeline for the far end of the Works trenches. Two Fokkers were just completing yet another strafing run. As they flashed by, Hunter began giving them the cut signal, emphatically drawing his finger across his throat. But whether the Russian fliers saw him or not, he couldn't tell. The Fokkers pulled straight up and began climbing madly, a maneuver Hunter took to be the prelude to a loop and yet another attack.

Two more triplanes came off the shooting gallery—Hunter gave them the kill sign, too. But just like the first pair, they either didn't see him or they chose to ignore him. They, too, put their triplanes on their tails and began climbing straight up. The last two Fokkers arrived next, but they pulled tails-up even before Hunter could attempt to signal them. The trailing pair of Spads did the same thing. Before he knew it, all of the Russians were heading straight up, climbing so high, they quickly passed out of sight.

*What is going on here?* Hunter thought madly.

At that moment, he felt a mighty pounding on his left shoulder. He turned to see Orr grabbing him, a look of absolute horror etched across his face. He'd long ago dropped his cameras and was pointing straight up with his free hand. Oddly, Hunter could even see some of the Clocks soldiers glaring up into the early morning sky. Even some of the surviving enemy troops on the Works side were gazing heavenward.

Finally Hunter looked up, curious to know what the hell everyone was looking at. An instant later, his jaw dropped open as well.

There was a huge shadow passing over them—it was so big, it blocked out all light from the rising sun. All Hunter could see at first was black—squares of it, they seemed scorched and burned. Then he saw the huge wing, then the gigantic nose, then the trio of monstrous tailpipes and finally the massive tail itself. The sound of a woman screaming filled his ears again. It quickly turned into a screech.

Only then did he see it full view.

Flying right over them, slower than possible and coming in for a landing, was the Zon space shuttle.

Hunter could not believe it. The thing looked like an enormous flying battleship, filling up the sky. His blood began to boil. His muscles tensed to the point of bursting his flight suit. So this was how it was going to be? The mountain was coming to Mohammed? Well, okay, that was fine with him. He had no idea why the Zon was coming down here, at Clocks, but it didn't make much difference, did it?

In fact, the cosmos had just made his job a lot easier.

A second later he, too, was flying straight up, at the same moment, screaming back at Orr to get the Sopwith's machine gun ready. The *Sturmoviks* were already firing on the great spaceship, their guns blazing as they flew rings around its nose and tail. Two Stormers were pouring fire into the Zon's cockpit windows, two more were firing directly into its exposed underbelly. The other four were strafing it up and down and every which way. They were showing even less mercy with the spacecraft than they had with the enemy troops below.

Soon enough, streams of flame and smoke were breaking out all over the shuttle. Still the huge spaceship continued floating towards the ground, its nose pointing towards the insanely short runway just outside Clocks.

Hunter madly was pouring on the rpms now, seeking with all his might to climb and join the strange battle. But it seemed the faster he went, the more distance he found between himself and the smoking, flaming Zon. What was this? Were the instruments in his open cockpit reading wrong? Were the winds screaming between the twin peaks counteracting his attempts to close in on the shuttle? Or was it something else?

He pushed his throttle forward all the way and then some. Still, it seemed like he could not quite catch up with the falling spaceship. He turned back towards Orr, who was now incomprehensibly wearing a swami's turban and playing a long ebony flute. Hunter turned back to see the Zon was suddenly below him, the *Sturmoviks* still buzzing around it, firing their massive cannons and pouring fire into dozens of already smoking wounds.

It was time for a change of tactics.

Hunter laid on the throttle as heavy as possible and soon the Sopwith was plummeting back to earth. Down the side of the mountain they went, quickly gaining speed and getting below the floating shuttle once again. In seconds, he was able to bring the biplane in for a short, quick, almost violent landing. He didn't even bother to kill the engine—once it had stopped, he simply jumped out and ran, full tilt, towards the end of the small runway.

The Zon was just coming in, trailing hundreds of

streams of smoke and fire behind it. The *Sturmoviks* kept firing on the shuttle even as it touched down with a cloud of dust, smoke and snow. It roared by Hunter, its rear chutes deploying and somehow slowing it down in an amazingly short amount of distance. The massive shuttle came to a halt in a mere five seconds.

Suddenly the tiny airfield seemed very crowded. It was as if the entire population of Clocks had turned out for this strange arrival, soldiers and civilians alike. An oom-pah band—a real one—was lined up near the nose of the smoking spacecraft, belting out its lustiest tune. Soldiers were firing their guns into the air—Hunter couldn't tell whether it was in anger or celebration. He ran up to the front of the shuttle, his M-16F2 gun suddenly appearing in his hands. A ramp was lowered from the front door of the spacecraft and Hunter bounded up its steps, taking three at a time. Then the door to the shuttle itself began to open, very slowly. Hunter reached the top and put his M-16 on full auto—he was intent on killing the first person to come out of the Zon and everyone behind them as well.

Finally the hatch was swung back all the way. Hunter raised his weapon, took a bead on a dark figure emerging from within the shuttle. His fingers began to squeeze the trigger just as this person walked out into the suddenly brilliant sunshine. It was a man, tall, wearing enormous sunglasses, with long hair, sideburns, a dark collarless suit, tight pants and high-heeled black boots. He was carrying a banjo with him and was plucking a tune on its strings.

Hunter's next breath caught in his throat—*Jessuz*, was it really . . .

"Who are you?" he asked incredulously.

The man looked back at him, lowered his sunglasses, and laughed.

"C'mon boy . . ." he said, through a curled upper lip. "Don't you recognize the *King*?"

Hunter stared back at him *"Elvis?"*

A moment later, he sat straight up—and smashed his head on the steering wheel of the tanker truck. His legs were instantly entangled; his hands, feet and fingers were numb. He closed his eyes, counted to three and then opened them again.

And that's when it began to sink in. He was still inside the cab of the cold Benz trailer truck, parked along the side of the road leading up to the twin mountains.

He had fallen asleep.


Fifteen minutes later, Hunter was driving up to the base of the twin peaks.

There was a city nestled in here all right—large, cluttered and charmingly Alpine. But it was dead and empty, just like all the other cities he'd seen in his trip across the barren continent. Its streets were bare, its houses either boarded-up, flattened or slowly surrendering to the mercy of the elements. No one had lived here in many years, he knew. No light had burned, no fire had been struck in a very long time.

He pulled the big rig onto the mountain road and began the long slippery climb up. It was no different than a dozen other mountain roads he'd traveled in the past two days; if anything, it was maddeningly familiar. He reached the summit after a while and stared off to the west to find more mountains, with more barren, slippery roads in between.

He stopped the truck at the peak and stared back down at the deserted city for a moment. Though fully awake now, it was still hard for him to believe. There was no Clocks, no Orr, no *Volkspolizi*, no *Rootentootzen*, Badtown, biplanes or *Sturmoviks*. *How strange it was*. Frozen wars, UFOs, Nazis and free men, pyramids, space shuttles, dinosaurs, Emma and Elvis—these were the things the Wingman dreamed of.

That is, when he dreamed at all . . .

# Part Two

# Nine

*Vietnam*

It was twelve hundred hours, high noon, when the trio of C-5 Galaxy gunships began taking off from Da Nang air base.

The first to go was "Football One," one of three C-5s operated by the United American Football City Special Forces. The enormous red, white and blue-striped airplane was known as a "shooter." It contained two dozen antiaircraft missile ports along both sides of its vast fuselage. Specifically these were locked-down Stinger missile platforms. The airplane also had a dozen Sidewinder air-to-air missiles hanging beneath its wings. Sophisticated air defense radar installed in the airplane's cargo bay had the capability to pick up enemy fighters from as far as one hundred miles away. Any unfriendly airplane coming within twenty-five miles of Football One would be shot out of the sky almost immediately.

The second Galaxy to launch was called "Black Eyes." It was operated by an aerial intelligence unit attached to the United American Armed Forces Command Section. Its bay contained tons of high tech navigation and detection equipment; poking out of the top of its fuselage was a huge revolving radar dish more commonly seen on AWACS aircraft. A recent transient to Southeast Asia, the equipment contained inside *Black Eyes* was so advanced, even some members of its eighteen-person crew didn't know the true capabilities. The rumors said the plane could see up to five hundred miles away, on land or sea.

In contrast to the first two, the third C-5 to take off was nondescript. It had no intriguing nickname, no fancy paint job. It was simply covered with dull sea-camo gray and had very few attachments sticking out of its body or wings. This C-5 simply was a cargo ship; oddly though, it was the most important airplane of this mission.

Once aloft, the three huge planes turned out over the South China Sea and headed east. Ten minutes later, they were picked up by their fighter escorts, two F-20s of the Football City Air Force. Once connected, the five-ship formation immediately went into radio silence. They climbed to twenty thousand feet and turned south.

Though the communist capitalists of CAPCOM had been soundly defeated, there was always a chance that fighters hired by forces unfriendly to the United Americans might be about. Even a stray force of air pirates, still plentiful around the troubled planet, would relish the chance to shoot down a United American aircraft; there were huge bounties offered by many despots around the world that would pay an unsavory pilot to do just that.

But this flight turned out to be uneventful and routine. The five airplanes maintained their altitude and three hundred fifty knot speed for one hour. Two blips appeared on the radar screens within the *Black Eyes* intelligence craft. The radar indications turned into a pair of medium-sized fighters, appearing out of the south. The five airplanes went up to high alert, but this, too, was just procedure. They'd been expecting the two fighters at this coordinate. They were Panavia Tornados, the entire complement of the Tommies' Air Force.

The Tornados took over escort duties for the F-20s, who turned with a wave and then accelerated back to-

wards Da Nang. Now covered by the Tommies, the three
C-5s altered their heading slightly, pointing southeast
now. They flew along like this for another hour and a
half. At precisely fourteen thirty, a terrain search and
guidance radar aboard *Black Eyes* picked up a speck of
land in the middle of the vast, empty sea.

It was Lolita Island.


Preparations for the second phase of this secret mission
had been going full-steam in the back of the non-descript
C-5 since takeoff from Da Nang.

Any C-5's original claim to fame was its vast cargo bay.
It could carry one hundred fifty tons inside this maw,
whether that load be made of men, material or weapons.
The package inside this C-5's hold weighed less than eight
hundred pounds however.

It was one of the rarest aircraft in the world. Called a
FW-1 Flex Wing, it was half ultralight, half hang glider.
Fifteen feet long, barely five feet wide, it was a favorite
of U.S. special operations groups in the 1970s. It could
carry two crewmen and up to one hundred fifty pounds
of equipment. Though basically a ferry craft, it still carried admirable capabilities for maneuver and speed. This
was due to its flexible kite-shaped wing. The batlike affair
could be raised and lowered by the pilot at will, allowing
the aircraft to either hover for long periods of time or
dash ahead at a respectable eighty knots.

The FlexWing inside the C-5 hold was attached to a
system of winches and rollers, the same used for loading
and unloading cargo pallets aboard the airplane. Two
men were already strapped into its seats. Ben Wa would
be piloting the airplane; his colleague and friend, J. T.
"Socket" Toomey was riding in back.

Below them now was the island of Lolita. It was almost
perfectly square, about five miles on each side and sur-

rounded by rings of glittering coral reefs. As in the recent recon photos, the island appeared completely covered with vegetation—shrubs, trees, and grass. Yet now, seeing it live, the people inside the C-5s couldn't help but feel the jungle below them was a little too green, too cluttered to be real.

And it really was out in the middle of nowhere. There was not a surface ship or airplane anywhere within a two hundred fifty-mile radius of Lolita, a fact confirmed by the gizmo-packed *Black Eyes*. The island was about to have a couple of visitors—in the FlexWing.

The three C-5s now went into a wide orbit above Lolita, the protective Tornados following in their wake. On cue, the huge clam shell doors at the rear of the gray C-5 opened up. The hold was struck by a fierce whirlwind, everyone inside had been strapped onto long tethers, so great was the danger of being sucked out the back of the airplane.

The trio of C-5s descended to fifteen thousand feet, then ten thousand. At this point, Ben Wa started the Flex-Wing's souped up two hundred ten-horsepower engine. The racket from the small engine filled the already chaotic cargo hold. Its nose pointed backward, the fumes from the engine were vented by the vacuum created by the large open doors.

The C-5s then went down to five thousand feet and adjusted their course slightly to the north. This side of the island had a small beach about a quarter mile long. With the suddenly enveloping foliage, it was the only clear area of any consequence on Lolita. If all went well, it would provide the FlexWing with a suitable landing strip.

The unmarked C-5 broke away from the others and descended to a heart-stopping altitude of fifteen hundred feet. The huge airship slowed its speed down to two hundred ten knots and banked even sharper over the north side of the island. The tethered cargo hands in the back of the airplane did a last check on the FlexWing, then with a thumbs-up from both Ben Wa and Toomey, they kicked away the FlexWing's undercarriage restraints. With a whoosh and the snap of metal, the diminutive aircraft went right out the back of the plane.

Ben Wa gunned the Flex's engine as soon as they were free of the C-5. It sputtered once, then easily went up to full rev. Ben did a quick visual of the plane and its controls, then pointed the nose of the Flex towards the north end of the island.

In seconds, he and JT were spiraling downward, shifting their weight this way and that, positioning the motorized kite for the best attitude for landing. Even as they rode this breathless controlled plunge, they couldn't help but notice just how damn green everything seemed on the island below them. The closer they got to *terra firma*, the more dazzlingly emerald everything became. By the time Ben was putting the kite into its final approach, both he and Toomey knew the jungle that had so suddenly swallowed up Lolita Island was anything but ordinary.

They set down with a bang and bump, Ben steering the bucking aircraft towards the hardened edge of the narrow beach, kicking up clumps of wet sand and sea-spray in the process. They rolled to a stop in about forty-five feet, a perfect landing. The circling C-5s began drifting away, slowly moving towards the east, where they would wait while Ben and Toomey did their work. Likewise the covering Tornados zoomed up to thirty-five thousand feet. They would watch over everything from this height.

It took about a minute for Ben and Toomey to pull the Flex up out of the lapping shoreline to the drier part of the beach. They did a quick check of both their primary and backup radios—the comm techs on *Black Eyes* responded in kind. Then Ben and Toomey checked their personal weapons, both M-16F2s. They, too, were in good order.

They began moving towards the jungle.

They reached the top of the sandline, climbed a coral rock and stared out at the vast swatch of foliage. The prevailing wind, providing little relief on the hot sun baking down on the vegetation, was blowing with a familiar but vague odor—and herein lay the answer to the mystery of Lolita Island.

Ben and Toomey climbed down off the rock and walked to the edge of the jungle itself. Toomey reached out and grabbed the longest branch of the first tree he came to. It literally came apart in his hand, covering his fingers with a hot, oozing substance. Ben did the same thing, grabbing a long piece of what looked like elephant grass. It, too, quickly turned into a greenish slime. They began pulling up everything they could get their hands on. Each time, the foliage practically melted away at their touch.

They finally stopped, looked at each other and began laughing. It was funny, in a very strange kind of way. Mother Nature hadn't suddenly bestowed the green life on the isolated island; this covering was hardly natural. It was plastic—thin, delicate and extremely real-looking. The foliage, the trees, the bushes, and the fields of grass, were all fake.

They walked about ten feet into the plastic jungle, the highest plants no more than five feet above their heads. Toomey bent down and began hauling up some of the *faux*-plants by the roots. It took some doing; unlike their branches, the fake plants were literally cemented into the ground. The fake jungle was standing on a vast platform of recently poured concrete.

Wa and Toomey weren't laughing anymore—they were just staring at each other now. The scope of what they were looking at was almost mind-boggling. Somebody—or something—had actually gone through the trouble of lugging thousands of square feet of concrete to the small island, had laid it out in a huge twenty-square-mile pattern, and had taken care to drill literally hundreds of thousands of tiny holes in the drying concrete into which each fake plastic piece of vegetation was placed.

It was an incredible notion, but after twenty minutes of wading through the stuff, Ben and Toomey were convinced that the whole island was covered this way. Lolita was a huge concrete platform in disguise. The concept was rather frightening.

They continued walking through the fake jungle, taking pictures and retrieving samples. By the time they returned to the FlexWing on the beach one hour after landing, they were pondering only two questions. One: who had the capability and the resources to build such a massive slab? It was a construction project of enormous proportions.

The second question was even more intriguing: *Why* in the world would anyone want to do such a thing?

# Ten

As luck would have it, the first living, breathing human being Hawk Hunter came upon after three days of driving turned out to be a naked woman.

It was midmorning. Six hours had passed since he'd crossed the twin peaks. It had been one mountain road after another until, suddenly, a huge crystalline lake appeared between the Alps. About three miles up its shoreline, rising out of the morning mist, there was a city—a real one this time. The map in his head told him he was nearing St. Moritz, the famous Swiss resort. If so, he was no more than a hundred miles from Point Zero itself.

He'd driven about a half mile along the lake's shoreline road when he got *the feeling*—there was at least one person up ahead, and probably many more. Did this mean the city itself was populated? If so, he would have to deal with its residents very discreetly. He didn't come all this way just to blow the mission on the wrong word said to the wrong person.

He parked the tanker trucker in a shielded wood and made his way along the edge of the shimmering, pristine lake. Staying deep in the underbrush, while keeping in sight of the road, he soon found himself climbing to the top of a massive outcrop of rock. Fifteen feet below was a small, snow-encrusted beach. And there she was. Swimming, alone, in the frigid waters of an Alpine lake, a beautiful, naked girl.

She was blond, slight, and doing a languid backstroke about twenty feet out from the shore, totally unaware of his presence. Hunter was distracted for a few seconds, unable to take his eyes off her gently moving form. She was gliding so smoothly through the placid waters, it was exhilarating just to watch her. Her hair was flowing behind her as if in slow motion, her body wet, silky, pert, and hairless. Hunter felt his heart deliver three massive beats. In that one, quick, strange moment, he realized that she might be the most beautiful woman he'd ever seen.

He quickly shook himself back to the matter at hand; he really had no time for this. He could see the city finally emerging from the thick morning mist about two miles up the shoreline and exuding many signs of civilization. The place was alive, populated—he was sure of that now. But more than warm bodies and naked flesh lay up ahead of him. There was the barest trace of aviation fuel in the air. One sniff and Hunter knew that an airplane of some kind was also close by.

His attention drifted back to the naked girl—and, still hidden, he found himself taking the outrageous luxury of the next two minutes just to watch her. At first, he tried to tell himself that this "recon" was necessary; after all, shouldn't he learn everything about her, so he would have some kind of idea exactly what kind of people were up ahead? But in the next breath, he was laughing to himself, not in humor but in surprise. This was not intelligence gathering he was engaging in here—it was blatant voyeurism. He'd seen a million naked women in his time and just about all of them had made him shake. But he usually knew when to turn it off and get his big head thinking again.

So what was it about this particular girl that was so hypnotic?

It took him another minute of spying on her before

he was able to slap his libido back under control. Obviously he'd been driving too long—this was not like him at all. He had to get closer to the speck of civilization a few miles down the road, *that* was the important thing. Finally tearing his eyes away from the beautiful vision in the lake, he began climbing back down the small cliff, intent on returning immediately to the tanker truck.

He'd walked about one hundred yards when something froze him in his tracks.

He never really heard the shriek—he felt it, just like in his dream. It was high-pitched and so unusual. Even now, he couldn't tell whether it was in fact a scream or a laugh. But whatever it was, it had come from the direction of the swimming girl. Hunter had to assume she was in trouble.

He was back up the shoreline and climbing the rock in a flash. Two men had come up in back of the girl just as she'd been getting out of the water. They had forced her to the ground. One was holding her hands and trying to kiss her; the other had jerked his pants off.

Hunter's weapon was up in an instant, his laser-sighter pinpointing the pantless man's left ear. It would have been a clear head shot—but Hunter did not squeeze the trigger. His instincts were telling him this was not the thing to do. Instead, he flew off the high rock, hit the pantless man in midair and kicked him away from the woman. Then he hit the ground, rolled once and managed to deliver a massive punch to the head of the man holding the girl down.

Both assailants went sprawling. The man without his pants landed ten feet out into the water; the holder had bounced off the base of the rock, cracking his head open in two places. It was over in less than two seconds.

The woman, still naked, was lying on the ground, astonishment washing across her face. Her eyes locked onto Hunter's—again he felt his heart deliver three massive beats. She was absolutely stunning. But then, in the course of a microsecond, her face changed from surprise to bafflement. Suddenly, her eyes were not so much emitting relief and gratitude, as trying to ask Hunter: *who the hell are you?*

In the meantime, the man thrashing about in the water had regained his footing and was coming back to shore. He was spitting and sputtering, trying to simultaneously hold his aching head, his stomach and his scrotum.

Hunter grabbed him by the collar, held him straight out in front of him, and perfectly lined him up for another boilermaker punch. But he felt someone pulling on his shoulder. It was the girl. She was right beside him, restraining his arm.

"Please, mister, don't," she pleaded in lightly accented English. "It's okay. They weren't doing anything wrong . . ."


It was cold in St. Moritz. Too cold.

The resort city itself was nearly frozen over. It looked like one gigantic glass palace. Every building was covered with ice, snow, or some combination of both. The streets were especially thick with it, dirty but amenable to traction. The sidewalks, too, were encased in ice, though no one had seen them in a while. So much frozen precipitation had fallen on the city, the people got around town through tunnels carved beneath the fifteen-foot perma-layer. Even the rudimentary thermal-power generating plant on the edge of the city was covered in ice.

Nevertheless, the place was still elegant. Supremely so. If anything, all the ice made the city dazzle—literally. The main streets and those along the lakeshore were lined with old hotels, gambling parlors and eateries. Snakelike tunnels led in and out of their grand black-oak, hand-carved doorways. Yellow-halogen streetlights—they looked like huge candelabras—lit the entire scene.

And then there was the lake itself. It provided a perfect mirror for the city. It was long and wide—and bottomless. It was so deep, it refused to ice over even in the worst of winter. It, too, looked alive, the clouds of rising condensation mimicking breath. Vain and beautiful, there was no way the lake was going to hide its charm up here. Not with all these lights.

Hunter was surprised to see so many automobiles making their way around the outskirts of the city. You never really saw cars anymore, he thought. Anyone driving around these days was more likely to be piloting a military vehicle or a truck. But there were some fancy wheels here in St. Moritz: Mercedes, BMWs, some Jags and a few Rolls—they were the chariots of the postwar rich, come back to life in the frozen wonderland. This cheered him to a small degree. If people were back to tooling around in these babies—and getting them fixed and serviced and fueled—well, then that was one more indication, tiny as it might be, that the world was swinging back to normal.

The streets were filled with people; none of whom appeared to have missed any meals lately. They were robust, healthy, well-clothed in furs and heavy wool, and acting disturbingly happy. Though their eyes went slightly wide at the sight of the big, dirty, double-duty tanker making its way towards their little outpost, many of the citizens nevertheless let out a friendly whoop and a wave as the truck rumbled by. Everyone looked a bit in the cups, too—slightly drunk but enjoyably so.

The two-mile drive into town was enlightening for Hunter; almost to the point of dismissing the fact that there were three more people squeezed into the cab with him: the beautiful girl and her two would-be assailants. While the perceptive left side of Hunter's brain was appreciating the beauty and civilization of the frozen city, the cold, analytical right side had continued skewing the three other occupants. Who were they? And what the hell had happened back there?

The two guys, of course, were getting most of Hunter's intense, invisible scrutiny. It was a rare day that he misread a situation. *Any* situation. Something in his neurons almost always prevented this from happening. It was hardly a subtle thing he thought he'd seen developing back on the small beach. It had looked like nothing less than an impending sexual attack.

But after dramatically breaking the whole thing up, he was simply flabbergasted by the girl's request that he not beat her two attackers to a pulp—indeed, she insisted that not only were they not doing anything wrong, but that she'd been expecting it, and yes, even *asking* for it.

Hunter wasn't sure exactly what to make of it all—sometimes the wildest truths were the slowest in coming. But as he understood it, he'd stumbled upon an elaborate sexual psychodrama. The girl, beautiful, and naked, swimming alone in the isolated part of the lake, is taken by two sex-starved Nordic types. Not too wild as far as these kinds of fantasies went, he supposed. But still, it was such an odd thing to see acted out, live, in color—and in the frigid outdoors.

After getting a first pass at the story, he'd kept his mouth shut. He pretended to buy the bizarre explantion for only one reason: the girl. He was even more dazzled by her now. She was frighteningly lovely; eyes, nose, mouth, and cheeks arranged in an unusual yet perfect way on her face, which seemed slightly hidden by cascades of flowing blond hair at all times. Her body—and he had seen all of it up close—would keep a legion of painters employed for a century or two. The breasts were just a little too big for the curvy, trim hourglass frame, her nipples pink and erotically tiny. Her toes and fingers were delicate in their painted pink nails; her grooming habits especially erotic. The whole package was so *ne plus ultra*, Hunter lost his breath for a moment any time he thought about it.

She was so gorgeous, he was becoming very concerned, frightened almost of all the time he might now spend thinking about her when he should be concentrating on other things. But who could blame him? Now wrapped in a lambskin jumpsuit and fur-lined boots, she was nuzzled up so close against him, it was all he could do to keep the tanker on the road. He felt like he was dreaming again—except that his dreams, wild as they were, were never *this* good.

They finally pulled into the middle of the city where the two hunky wanna-bes departed, each with a sullen kiss to the girl's cheek and a mumbled promise to see her later. Most of the trip had been silent, but as soon as the mooks left, the girl finally opened up.

Her name was Chloe. She spoke perfect English, with a lilt of a British accent. She lived in St. Moritz along with a few thousand other privileged souls, most of them the grown children of Europe's pre-Big War rich and famous. When the conflict started and the world order began to collapse, they had been sent to a secret, exclusively appointed shelter blasted into the side of a nearby mountain years before by the old Swiss government. Here they stayed, in comfort and luxury, until two years ago, when they emerged, found the conditions outside tainted but not deadly, and repopulated the dazzling city. In other words, everyone here was wealthy, incredibly wealthy. And safe. Supply shipments were frequent, there was no lack of water or booze and they were protected by a handful of unseen, highly paid armies deployed in the mountains around them.

The whole concept fascinated Hunter in a perverse kind of way. It gave new meaning to the word extravagance. He had entered a place that seemingly had no worries. The people had five divisions watching over them, plenty of food, fuel, and creature comforts, plus startling views, and a postcard environment. What a way to spend the time while the still-chaotic world tried to get its act back together.

As it turned out, Chloe was actually more interested in Hunter than in talking about herself. Who was he? What was he doing here? Where was he staying? And what was with the big, dirty truck?

He found himself stumbling over the simplest answers—it had been a long time since he'd been so tongue-tied. She was genuinely friendly, warm, and just oozing with sensuality. Without even having to ask, she volunteered to get him fed, lubricated and into a warm room. Hunter found himself accepting everything she offered, without thinking twice about it. *How things change,* he thought. He hadn't any intention of stopping anywhere along the way to Point Zero. If the city had been abandoned or if it hadn't existed, he would have kept right on driving. After all, he was racing the clock to a certain extent.

But whenever she spoke, he could resist none of what she said. So under her direction, he parked the truck behind a large chalet he would come to learn was hers and they went inside. The place was monstrous—multi-windowed, with a breathless Alpine setting at each turn. A fire was already roaring in the huge hearth; a bottle of wine was already chilling. Chloe excused herself momentarily, only to reappear after changing into a fresh snow-suit. It was so tight, with a neckline so dramatically plunging, Hunter didn't have to look twice to capture the whole effect.

*Yes, this is trouble,* he thought as she led him to the couch located next to the largest, most impressive window and poured him his first glass of wine.

Big trouble.

* * *

A mile downtown, in a huge, ornate lodge which over-
looked St. Moritz's crystal lake, a grand celebration was
just beginning.

Nearly a thousand people were on hand, dispersed in
small groups over the lodge's seven floors, drinking, talking, eating, flirting. Two-thirds of them were women, all
of them no less than gorgeous. No one looked over thirty;
no one really looked over twenty. Everyone was expen-
sively dressed and extensively bejeweled. Champagne was
flowing like the Alpine rivers in springtime.

The celebration was for the New Moon. It was now
nearly eight in the evening and the lunar sphere, big, fat,
and orange, was just peeking over the jagged Matterhorns
to the east. Everyone stopped what were doing for
a moment and gazed upon the ascending ball. Then a
few words were said, and a short neo-New Age song was
performed and after that, everyone went back to party-
ing. This was a monthly event, and just one of several
parties held in the lodge during the lunar month. The
quarter-moon and the half-moon were also celebrated
with luxurious and intoxicating gatherings.

High-stakes gambling always provided the centerpiece
for these events and no one took the art of wagering
more seriously than the two men presently sitting at the
main poker table on the second floor of the lodge. They
tried to make it into St. Moritz every New Moon, providing they could talk their way through one of the many
heavily armed security checkposts. Like the hundred or
so other lucky out-of-towners on hand, they enjoyed mixing with the natives, getting good food, good booze and
maybe good sex. But mostly these two were anxious to
win some money at the tables.

As always, the two men had chosen the largest, most
prominent card game in the lodge to amass their fortune.

It was here that they had first witnessed a strange phe-
nonema which they jokingly called FRPE, or the "filthy-
rich-people-effect." Simply put, many of the St. Moritz
locals had so much money to dispose of, some had come
to *like* losing at the gaming tables. If the conditions were
right, these odd moneyed types could get into drunken
contests to see who could lose the most. Even better,
whenever anyone, usually an outsider, actually tried to
*win*, the locals would double or triple-up on their bets,
just to set up situations in which they could lose even
more.

Whenever the two travelers saw conditions approaching
a FRPE—booze, open drug-use and a bevy of distractingly
beautiful women were essential ingredients—they would
go into a little act. They would make a great display of
plotting and planning each poker bet, verbally taking into
account all possible permutations of a loss, and then
banking on those hands most likely to win. This approach
would almost always fascinate the local players, who, as if
on cue, would start throwing down wildly daring call bets
the other way, just to see the strangers do their stuff. More
plotting went into how many cards they should pick up,
and this led to even more outrageous counterbets. The
travelers would even stiff a few hands, in order to crank
up the excitement level before laying down a string of
winners. Then they would buy drinks for everyone involved with a small part of their winnings, thus fueling
the fire and the promise of even larger payoffs. They had
it all down to a science. It was, in effect, like taking candy
from babies.

The two men had been up to their analytical hijinks
for the past two hours, and they had won themselves a
lot of money. Two mountain peaks of gold chips had
grown before them—each chip being worth a *guldenmark*,
a coin roughly equivalent to an old U.S. one hundred
dollar bill. As the piles grew, so did the number of avail-

able girls who began orbiting the travelers. They soon had one on each lap, another draped over each shoulder. With each win, these beauties drew closer to the men and each other. The travelers were well-acquainted with St. Moritz's rather peculiar approach to sex. That was another reason they tried to get into the city as often as they could.

Though they were not natives, the travelers didn't look out of the ordinary, not at first anyway. They dressed well, spoke well and in several languages, and they knew what kind of champagne to order and when. But there was something different about these two. Both had a certain look to them, an almost imperceptive swagger in their step that set them apart from everyone else. And their eyes, though capable of coldness and downright cruelty, had a twinkle to them as well, as if they were keeping a deep, dark, but most pleasant secret.

The truth was, the two travelers *were* different, though only a vastly perceptive person could figure out why. Once the answer was at hand, it would always remain very obvious to the observer. It was a simple secret really: the two men had been somewhere few people had ever been before, certainly no one at the gambling table, or in the lodge, or in all of St. Moritz itself. These two had been to a place so big, so spectacular, so unlike any other place else, the glow it brought to them would never really leave.

The two men appeared different because they had both traveled in outer space. And once that happened to a person, they were never the same again, no matter how many sins they went on to commit.

The New Moon had fully risen over the mountains by the time Hunter and Chloe arrived at the lodge.

The place was packed by this time—all seven floors were crowded with the beautiful people, eating, drinking, getting high, and making time. It was so congested, the last refuge with any semblance of quiet and privacy was a small dark lounge located on the sixth floor of the place and tucked in the back. This is where Chloe chose to bring him, guiding him by hand through the crowd, the fact that he was wearing a black flight suit, though cleaned and pressed, hardly raising an eyebrow.

He had fallen completely for her by this time. Love, lust, whatever—he had it bad. They'd spent the last five hours sitting on the couch in her living room, looking out at the jagged peaks of the Alps, drinking wine, nibbling apple slices, and talking. There had been no physical contact, save for the occasional touch of her hand on his knee, or the very pleasant brush with her breasts whenever they would lean forward for a fruit slice at precisely the same time.

She'd told him everything, about herself and this strange settlement at St. Moritz. She was fifteen at the time of the Reemergence. Her family, still wealthy, still prosperous, decided it was better that she remain in St. Moritz for a while, until things in the less-civilized world settled down more. They sent her stipends of gold with each season and visited occasionally. To her credit, Chloe had spent much of the time both inside the mountain and now out in the air, working at self-education. She'd studied so much, that when she was allowed to take a college equivalency exam at what was once the University of Zurich, she scored so high, they gave her a master's degree in both philosophy and the arts.

Best of all though, Chloe had no idea who Hunter was, no concept of the Wingman, or what he had done, or the cult of celebrity that had grown up around him in some parts of the globe. She'd told him that she'd sensed he was famous right away, but such things had little impact on her. Undeniably, this had added immensely to his attraction of her. It had been a long time since Hunter had met someone who didn't know him or care who he was. It was the most pleasant of changes.

So they had sat and talked and laughed and drank and went over nearly every topic of their lives—except what had happened down at the lake earlier in the day. Expert at self-control though he was, Hunter had to catch himself a couple of times, just moments before he was about to blurt out the big question. His gut was telling him he would learn all about it soon enough.

Still, it was hard to keep the words inside.

He couldn't resist when she asked him to accompany her to the New Moon celebration—and now, here they were. Planting themselves at the corner table of the dark cafe, they continued their conversation. Chloe had already consumed a half bottle of *Monchere Blanc* 1986, and was showing signs of tipsy sexiness. As for Hunter, he was beyond getting drunk by now. Every fiber of his being had been standing at attention since the moment he'd set eyes on her. It would have taken a case of grape to distract his hormones at the moment.

Still, there was a benefit in just going with the spirits, so soon enough he was relaxed enough to slip his hand around hers. She gripped his fingers tightly—yet her touch was amazingly warm and soft. That's when the conversation took a distinctly sexual turn.

They had just taken delivery on their third set of drinks—brandy for her now, scotch for him—when she slid over very close and briefly rested her head on his shoulder. At the same moment, Hunter was half-watching a tiny scene play out at the table next to them. A well-conditioned middle-aged man was seated there, accompanied by a glamorous woman, apparently his wife. A much younger woman suddenly appeared and whispered something into the woman's ear. The woman smiled and then began nodding eagerly. With that, the young woman—she was brunette, poured into a snow-bunny suit and drop-dead pretty—squeezed in between the woman and the man and began paying extraordinary attention to the husband's genital area. After about a minute of this, they all got up and departed for a more private location, each one smiling more broadly than the next.

Now Hunter could see similar things taking place at the bar, too. Young women working their way into conversations between slightly older couples. Again, Hunter really couldn't get a handle on what was going on. There was no doubt though that everyone involved was enjoying themselves.

Chloe was watching all this, too. After a minute or so, she looked up at him and giggled.

"When's the last time you saw any, Hawk?"

The question was so direct, so blatant, Hunter once again stumbled on his reply.

"I can't remember back that far," he said finally.

She laughed again, then took a sip of his drink.

"I'll bet someone like you really gets turned on at this kind of thing," she asked, pressing herself even harder against his beating chest.

Hunter could hardly speak.

"Who wouldn't be?" he finally replied.

She smiled deliriously now. "That's exactly what I want to hear."

She got up, kissed him lightly on the cheek and then pointed towards the darkened hallway at the rear of the lounge.

"Down there, last door on the left, in five minutes," she whispered to him. "I promise you'll get more of it than you'll ever need."

With that, she left the table. Throwing a mischievous glance over her shoulder, she had a quick conversation with the man behind the bar, then she disappeared down the hallway and through the last door.

Hunter, frozen to the spot, watched her go, a volcano

erupting from the pit of his stomach. He might have been a hero to many people in the world, but this didn't automatically make him a saint. He'd seen his share. And done his share. And what was happening to him here definitely qualified as "something else." It was so strange, so mysterious, so erotic. He knew the curiosity alone would kill him if he didn't take the next giant step.

Predictably then, the next five minutes went by slower than the ice melt around St. Moritz. Hunter needed no watch to mark the passing of those three hundred seconds; his heart was keeping perfect double time. By 4:10, he was anxiously on his feet, paying their tab with two gold coins. He took another fifteen seconds to collect his thoughts, run the options through his head and make that one last decision to yes, proceed. Oddly the fact that this might be some kind of an elaborate trap, and that Chloe might be some kind of nefarious agent, never really came into his consideration of the unfolding events.

Had that been the case, his own internal, early warning system would have blown a gasket a long time ago.

Finally, he left the bar and turned down the short corridor. It seemed a couple miles in length now, long enough for every thought possible, both good and bad, to run through his mind. The next thing he knew, he was before the last door on the left, his hand on the warm brass knob. He turned it, slowly. It gave with no resistance. He took a deep breath and went inside.

He found himself looking into a small, dark bedroom, done in deep crimson and lit by many candles. In the middle of the room was a large throne-like chair and on this chair sat a naked man. On his lap sat Chloe. She was naked, too. Her eyes were glued on Hunter. Sleepily, she smiled at him.

Numb by now, Hunter closed the door behind him. At that moment, the man thrust himself mightily inside of Chloe, causing her to yelp with delight. He started pumping her, slowly at first, but quickly rising in volume and frequency. Chloe began groaning in delight, and soon, she began pumping back. All the while she was gasping for breath, and battling to keep her eyes open and locked on Hunter's.

He stood there like a statue, not quite believing what he was seeing. He'd had a hint that things were a little kinky, here in this postwar playground of the rich. But seeing this beautiful girl that he'd fallen for getting so vigorously nailed, was, in a word, breathtaking. His psyche had been right: it'd told him he would learn all about this strange thing soon enough. Now here he was, getting a grand and graphic education. The incident down near the lake, the overt friendliness of Chloe and everyone in St. Moritz, the little dramas playing out in the barroom—they all made sense to him now.

The young and cool in St. Moritz had grown bored with just the act of sex itself. So they had taken it all in a giant step sideways. They had added a third element, another dimension. Not only would they have sex, they would have it while a significant other was watching.

"You like it, don't you?" Chloe called out to him as she urged the young man further into her jiggling, hairless body. "Please tell me you do?"

But Hawk Hunter, the Wingman, fighter pilot and champion for causes supreme, did not reply.

For the first time in his life, he really didn't know what to say.

Meanwhile, down in the gambling area, the two travelers had again doubled their fortune.

There was a mountain range of chips sitting in front of them now, the winnings from an hour of high-stakes poker with a table full of drunken, filthy rich kids. Between the free drinks and rubdowns from a squadron of lusty females, the two men had amassed nearly two million dollars.

This was actually an embarrassment of riches for them—there wasn't very much they could do with the money where they had to go back to. Just carrying the two million would be an extra burden for them, as essentially it would be just a big bag of coins. But this did not deter them. They had done this sort of thing several times before, each time leaving St. Moritz richer than when they had first arrived. But this time, they had fallen into the super-lucky groove. The New Moon had indeed taken a shine to them.

To the people around them, the travelers had provided endless entertainment during the FRPE. This is why a groan went through the lascivious gathering when the two men finally announced that it was time for them to cash out and leave. A barrage of free drinks had changed their minds once before, but it would not happen again. Nothing lasts forever. The two men had their millions—now they had to get out.

They were just consolidating their piles when another, louder gasp went through the room. Up until this moment, the two men had been playing the poker table exclusively against members of the inebriated, well-heeled crowd. But when that wave went through the gathering, the two men knew someone who might actually try to beat them had arrived on the scene. It was an unofficial rule of all gambling halls that the big winners had to at least take on a newcomer, someone who might have a shot at winning back some of what others had lost. The two men began to panic. They had lingered too long! Now it was coming back to haunt them.

A shadowy figure was indeed making his way through the awed crowd. A few people recognized him right away—and they found themselves shaking with amazement that he had suddenly turned up among them, here in out-of-the-way St. Moritz.

It was Hunter, of course. He cut through the quickly parted crowd like a jet plane through cirrus. Chloe was on his arm, glowing, still short of breath, still slightly drunk. How strong was Hunter's psychic ability to perceive danger or opportunity? Strong enough to pull him out of the small, crimson bedroom at the end of the sixth floor hallway and bring him down here, where the two men who'd walked in space were winning the motherlode. His gut was telling him these two could help him immensely in his quest to find Point Zero.

He sat down at the far end of the card table and simply nodded to the pair. Hunter sensed both men were heavily-armed, and not reluctant to shoot up the place if pressed to do so. Hunter's only weaponry at the moment was the .357 Magnum he kept in his boot holster. He was silently praying he would not have to use it.

The room became stone cold quiet now, all the drunken chit-chat coming to a screeching halt. The patrons were pressed into two formations, like townsfolk lined up to see a shootout at High Noon. Hunter took a single two-ounce American gold coin from his pocket and flipped it on the table. On a good day, it was worth about two hundred dollars.

"My choice?" he asked the two men.

They had to say yes.

"High card," Hunter declared.

Both men gulped. Again, they had to agree.

"Two against one?" one asked, slightly confused.

Hunter smiled, but only for a moment. "Why not?"

The men looked at each other, and then they smiled, too. This guy, this famous pilot or whoever he was, was apparently drunk. No one would sanely play high-stakes high-card draw with the odds stacked two-to-one against them.

Or would they?

The travelers moved quickly. They loaded up on Hunter's two-hundred dollar bet, each plopping down two hundred, then two hundred more.

Hunter turned to the astonished card dealer. "Flip 'em," he said.

Flip them, he did. He dealt a king to the first man, a queen to the other.

He threw Hunter a card—down, the challenger's prerogative. Hunter didn't even look at it. He flipped it over to reveal the Ace of Spades.

The crowd gasped. The croupier slid the chips Hunter's way and he let Chloe stack them one by one. The Wingman tripled the bet. The two men reluctantly did the same.

"Deal them," Hunter told the pit boss. Another king to the first man; another queen to his partner.

Again, Hunter didn't even look at his card. He flipped over the Ace of Clubs.

Another pile of chips came his way and once again Chloe breathlessly stacked them. Hunter guided the stack to the appropriate felt-lined square in front of him. He'd double-tripled the bet. The crowd gasped once more. Again, the men had no choice.

Two more cards came out, face up. King of Clubs for the first guy, Queen of Diamonds for his colleague. Hunter got his card and let Chloe turn it over this time. It was the Ace of Hearts.

The two men turned pale. Both instinctively reached down to their belt buckles, feeling for the huge hand guns they had hidden there. It was a less than subtle hint that they should not be trifled with.

But Hunter only grinned when he saw them do this.

"Shame on you," he told them, piling his latest winnings with his old and now racking the bet up to an exponentially mushrooming twenty-six thousand dollars.

Both men withdrew their hands from their weapons. The truth was, they were so devastated by what they had gotten themselves into, both hardly had the gumption to start a gunfight.

Hunter took note of this reaction, too. *This won't take long,* he thought.

He pushed the growing pile of chips back in front of him again, then motioned to a nearby credit man. This man hastily scribbled something down on a piece of paper and placed it carefully on the edge of the table. Hunter's line of credit now stood at a half million dollars.

He doubled the bet again—now he had fifty-two thousand dollars on the line. The two men had to put up twice that much. Two more cards were dealt up to them. Predictably, one was the King of Spades, the other the Queen of Hearts. Hunter flipped his card over even before it hit the table. Another louder gasp went through the crowd. It was the Ace of Diamonds.

He leaned back, took a healthy swig from a recently delivered scotch-and-water, and lit up a proffered cigar.

Then he turned back to the pair of disheartened, demoralized, angry spacemen. There was little evidence of a twinkle in their eyes now.

"Shall we double it again, gentlemen?" he asked.

It was all over not ten minutes later.

Through two deck shuffles, Hunter won the next six hands. One and a half million dollars in gold chips was now sitting before him.

It was strange how money affected people—the two spacemen still had a half million dollars left, a lot more than either one of them had ever possessed before. But still, they were miserable. They had, up until a half hour ago, two million in near-cash. At this point, they would have done just about anything to get it back.

And that's exactly what Hunter wanted.

So he eased up on them, calling a halt to his streak at $1.5, and distributing twenty thousand dollars of that to the various dealers, credit men and waitresses who'd hitched themselves to his star.

The two men, both of them scowling and suddenly looking in need of a bath, knew another unofficial rule of the house. Now Hunter would have to give *them* a chance at winning back their lost fortune. They had a hasty conversation with the pit boss, who hustled down the length of the table and whispered the proposal in Hunter's ear.

It was simple: "Same time, tomorrow night, game of our choice."

Hunter was nodding even before the man had completed the message.

"I'm looking forward to it," he told them.

# Eleven

That night, or what was left of it, Hunter slept on the couch in Chloe's chalet.

She was there with him, wrapped up in his arms, snoring softly. Actually, he'd napped for only ninety minutes or so, a short charge-up for the busy day he knew lay ahead.

The weirdness of the night before was beginning to fade as he stared out at the sun, rising over the peaks, lighting up the lake and casting the first shadows on the sleeping city of St. Moritz. Despite the twists and turns, he'd learned much. He knew what was up with the two men at the gambling table—he'd met people who'd gone to space before. Once you saw the look, you never forgot it.

If these guys had walked in space then they could only belong to one of three very exclusive groups: astronauts, cosmonauts or part of Viktor's space cadet club. One look at the men told Hunter they belonged behind door number three. He was sure that Viktor had been launching the Zon shuttle for some time now, and that somewhere along the line, these two guys had taken a ride—though why Viktor felt the need to include the two gorillas was beyond him.

But that was immaterial. The real question was this: what were two of Viktor's go-boys doing here in St. Moritz? They didn't live here, that was obvious from the buzz in the crowd. So they were just visiting. But from where? After all, they were twenty-five hundred miles east of Star City, the center of Viktor's space ops.

But that's what gave them away.

Hunter's quest was to find that one spot on earth where the Zon could be plotted and tracked with the highest accuracy. It was no surprise that Viktor's minions knew this location, too. If Hunter really was a betting man, he would have laid a hundred-to-one that there was some kind of a tracking station located at Point Zero. If this was true, the job of looking for the damn thing would be that much easier.

Everything else fell into place after that: the two men were in town for a little lubrication and a dream of leaving with a barrel of gold. He couldn't imagine them wanting to stray too far from their post, so, just as he had guessed, Point Zero must be somewhere in the neighborhood, no more than a hundred miles away. This, too, was good news. Hunter was getting tired of driving over the humps. At last, he was closing in on his quest.

Hunter knew his encounter with the two men was an opportunity to push his trip into higher gear. While most of the gray matter in his head was busy soaking in Chloe, what was left still retained that feeling that somewhere nearby, certainly within St. Moritz, there was an airplane, one he was sure would be able to assist him from this point on.

Trouble was, he didn't know where the airplane was exactly; there was still the faintest smell of aviation fuel in the air, especially now, early in the morning. But he would have to find its source soon, as he was getting a vibe that the airplane might not be up to snuff exactly. Something was telling him he was about to get his hands dirty in a few hours.

He also had to start gearing up for his rematch against the space travelers that night. Nailing ten aces, in a row, in perfect order of suit, was an old trick; he'd have to change his tactics tonight. Blackjack maybe, or even three-card stud. Whatever the game might be, it would have to go off for big stakes in a short amount of time.

His thoughts drifted back to Chloe, still snuggled tightly against him. He was almost ashamed of himself by now—about the way he'd gone nuts for her, about the way she'd sent a shiver right through him by her actions inside the red bedroom. There always seemed to be a romantic angle to his adventures, at least in the early days. But he usually dealt with the phenomena quickly or not at all—the mission always had to take precedence. But now, with this beautiful girl and her strange, sexual ways—well, he was just thinking too much about it.

The truth of the matter was this: The last thing he wanted to do today was find the airplane he knew would carry him away from her.

He gulped again. Suddenly the first direct ray of sunshine hit him right between the eyes.

Yes, this whole Chloe thing was getting serious.

She finally awoke, and after a few rounds of passionate good mornings, she was off to take her daily bath in the cold waters of the lake just outside of town.

She invited Hunter to come along and looked genuinely hurt when he turned her down. He was the first to admit it: what he'd peeked in on the day before, he wanted to see again. But once more he had to yank his brain out of his pants and get it back up to the top of his head where it belonged.

So Chloe went off alone, to bathe in the nude and partake in God-knows-what else. Hunter went through his morning ritual in the emptiness of her bathroom. Then, with a newly pressed suit and an extra clip for his Magnum in hand, he set out in search of his ride out of this strange, frozen paradise.

\* \* \*

St. Moritz had no airport. Not one that was working anyway.

Hunter drove out to the place, more out of curiosity than anything else. It was located about two miles outside of the city, a twenty-minute ride in the rumbling, bumbling tanker truck. The field had three runways, two of them long enough to handle the largest of airplanes. It wasn't a stretch for Hunter to close his eyes and see squadrons of private jets of all sizes landing and taking off from the place way back in its go-go heyday. Sheiks, kings, queens and movie stars used to crowd this airport—now it was covered with snow, its buildings abandoned, its control tower battered and leaning, slowly surrendering to the years of wind and weather.

He did a cursory search of the place, but he knew there was no airplane here. He would have felt it by now. Jumping back in the truck, he set off to his next stop: a military base located five miles east of the desolate airport. Operated by one of the city's private security armies, it was a huge installation with a heavily guarded checkpoint. He'd raised a few eyebrows approaching in the battered tanker truck. He didn't try to get inside—he didn't have to. The airplane wasn't here, either. However, the place looked tight, alert and professional. This told him the security troops deployed in the mountains surrounding St. Moritz were probably the same way.

He drove back to town, parked the tanker next to Chloe's, then headed down to the lakeside. A quick recon of all the roadways around the city told him that while some of them were indeed flat, and straight—the Swiss Air Force was famous for using its highway system as emergency runways—he found none that had any evidence of recent use.

This left only one place from which an airplane could operate: the crystal lake.

There were only about a million boathouses ringing the long shoreline north of town—Hunter wound up looking inside of half of them before he finally found what he was searching for.

It was almost an airplane from a dream—*his* dream, the one he'd had while stuffed behind the wheel of the big tanker truck. He found it locked away in one of the larger houses, a place originally built for a yacht of some size. The airplane was a Macchi MC.72, a rather famous type of flying machine. A racer that was also a seaplane, it broke a lot of speed endurance records back in the 1930s, and probably still held a few to this day.

Hunter cased the place, found no one around, and quickly picked the lock on the back door. All he could hear inside the dark, dingy boathouse was the lapping of the waves echoing throughout the cavernous structure. The airplane was tied up to the enclosed dock with a legion of chains and heavy rope. There was some buildup of algae and water crud along the bottom of its pontoons, but not as much as he would have expected. One sniff of the air told him that this was what he'd been detecting since arriving in St. Moritz. Now the fuel smelled stale, as did the oil. His premonition that some work would have to be done to peak out the airplane had been correct.

Still, odd as it seemed, a seaplane was exactly what he needed up here, high in the Alps. The chances of any serviceable runway being located anywhere near Point Zero was remote, or at least any airstrip he could simply drop down onto. However, the whole area was dotted with lakes, and with a seaplane, each one could provide a runway for him. Once again, the cosmos had directed him to exactly what he needed.

He climbed out onto the wing, and after much dusting, was able to recover an ancient FOR SALE sign. There was no price mentioned. Next he crawled into the cockpit, quickly hot-wired the ignition and finger-snapped the control panel to life. Just like the pea-shooters in his dream, the Macchi's controls were quaint and rudimentary. He twisted the wires and pulled on the choke switch and, damn it if the thing didn't spring to life right away.

He gunned the engine once, then gradually cut back on the fuel mix. The motor was rough—there was no miracle happening here—and the control surfaces a little tight. But the airplane was flyable.

He climbed out, took a small bag of gold from his boot, and placed it atop the FOR SALE sign next to the head of the dock.

Then he opened the boathouse doors, climbed back into the plane and puttered away.

Ten minutes later, he was two miles north of the city's shoreline.

Hugging the nap of the lake and getting the engine in trim, he found there was about fifty gallons of gas sloshing around inside the airplane's wing tanks, and another fifteen or so in the reserves. The petro was at least a year old, maybe two, or even three. Still, Hunter was fairly sure the cold climate had preserved it somewhat and it was still usable.

The oil, too, was crappy—it had taken forever for the oil pressure gauge to start moving. Even now it was reading only halfway up to what was considered safe for take-off. But Hunter was getting impatient; he still had many things to do. With one last check of the airframe and surfaces, he gunned the engine. A few seconds later he was skimming along the mirrorlike surface of the lake.

The plane ran great—on the water. But what would

happen when he took to the air? He got it to seventy miles per hour, gave the throttle a pull and the wheel a push and an instant later, the spiffy little aquaplane rose confidently off the lake.

Big clown-feet pontoons and all, the Macchi cut through the air in a manner that impressed even him. He told himself that he shouldn't be surprised. The seaplane looked like it was going one hundred mph even when it was standing still. And usually, good looks translated into superb handling in the air.

He took it low and to the north, away from St. Moritz and any unwanted prying eyes. He put it through a series of wild gyrations for the next two minutes, a quick test to see if all the bolts were tight and the lock washers fastened. Apparently they were. Next, he pulled back on the throttle and slowed the plane down to near-stall speed—it was easier to read an aircraft's deficiencies this way. Once again, his ears were able to provide him the diagnosis: the engine was for the most part intact—about three hours of work would get it to where he wanted it.

He proceeded to the third phase of the flight. He started climbing. Past five thousand feet, then ten, then twelve. The Macchi probably never topped this high, but Hunter was sure it could take twenty-flat, if he could. Still, he played it safe and leveled out at twelve thousand, five hundred. As could be predicted, the view was spectacular. There were mountains surrounding mountains surrounding more mountains—each one snowcapped and majestic, each one beautiful yet eerie in its own way.

Checking the pretty sights was not the priority though. This was recon. He looked off at the northwestern horizon, still dark in the growing morning. Point Zero was out there somewhere. He didn't expect to see it—he was looking for the means of access to reach the place.

He found three mountain highways and a half dozen backroads that all flowed off to the northwest—mission accomplished. When the two travelers finally did leave town, Hunter was sure they would take one of these paths back to Point Zero.

With all this locked firmly in his brain, he slowly turned wing over and headed back in the direction of St. Moritz. There was no real reason to overfly the city, other than curiosity. And there was always the chance that he might spark a panic or at least a call to the outlying security forces by flying over the city. An airplane in the sky over the fun and sex capital was probably still a very unusual event.

But oddly, none of this deterred him. By the time he was over the frozen settlement, high up in the morning clouds, more hidden than not, he knew he'd headed in this direction for another reason—if he kept going for another mile or two he would be right over the place he knew Chloe would be bathing.

If he flew lower and quieter, he might even be able to take a peek in. And if he shut off the engine and just kind of glided by, then maybe he could see . . .

Suddenly he felt the airplane veer sharply to the right— a whine of protest from the engine filling his ears. He looked down and saw that it had been his own hand that had put the airplane into the violent, one hundred eighty-degree maneuver. In a flash, he was thinking with his big head again.

*What the hell was he doing? What was happening to him? Jeopardizing the mission like this, just to catch a peek at what kind of sex Chloe was having at the moment?* A wave of embarrassment washed over him, thick and draining, right to the core.

*This Chloe thing,* he thought, heading back towards the airplane's dock housing, *really* was *getting serious.*

# Twelve

It was getting dark by the time Hunter returned to Chloe's chalet.

He'd spent the afternoon inside the seaplane's hangar, working with tools three times as old as he was, fixing an engine first designed in 1929.

Despite the advanced age of just about everything he touched, the Macchi's engine was a breeze to tune-up; he'd had the thing running at one hundred ten-percent of recommended power inside ninety minutes. More tinkering got it up to one hundred twenty-percent. The rest of the plane's mechanics—the flaps, the steering, the big clown's feet, plus all the cables and wires connecting one to another—also checked out. Only a few bolts had to be tightened and a few strands unkinked.

He left it just as dusk was falling, confident that the Macchi would get him where he was supposed to go—and with a completely free conscience: the bag of gold he'd left behind before taking off on his trial run was gone by the time he'd returned.

Now he could see a soft stream of smoke rising from the chimney atop Chloe's place, and he could only wonder how warm and perfect it was inside. Fixing the engine and getting the seaplane in shape had been a distraction, true—but only a partial one. Many times during the tune-up he caught his mind wandering off the spark plugs and generators and back to Chloe's lovely face. Whenever he closed his eyes he could see her, inside the red bedroom, having sex in that strange, erotic way. As the afternoon progressed, and the day grew longer, it became impossible to keep her out of his mind. She was haunting him. More than once, he cursed himself for not overflying her bathing spot. This only inflamed his passions more.

Now, walking up the path to her house, the streams of condensed breath coming from his mouth rivaled his ROB during the hairiest of dogfights. The back door was unlocked, not all that unusual in crime-free St. Moritz. He let himself in, scanning the big main room and feeling the plunge when he realized Chloe was nowhere to be seen.

He walked over to the huge fireplace, kicked the smoldering logs over and reignited the inferno in a matter of seconds. He stood there, facing the flames for a long time. The warmth penetrated his clothes, his skin, his bones. The only bad thing about St. Moritz was that it was always so damn cold outside. It took him a few minutes to shake out the last of the chill, his eyes mesmerized by the growing, glowing fire.

He was glad she was not around—or at least that's what he was telling himself. Tonight's mission in the gambling hall was an important one. He had to perform a triple-cross on the space travelers and needed the fullest of concentration.

Still, he could not shake the feeling that he would never see her again. That he would complete his duty tonight, sleep on her couch and get up to leave the next morning without her ever coming home, without ever being able to say goodbye. He shivered at that thought, despite the warmth of the flames in front of him. There was more than just the smell of aviation fuel going around this town. Whatever the hell it was in the air, Hunter had caught it and now he had it bad.

He finally sat on the couch, giving his eyes a rest from

the hypnotic flames and gazing instead out on the mountains. The peaks were taking on a warmish glow as the city of St. Moritz began to light up, a thousand reflections bouncing off the centuries-old snowpack. He'd been many places in his travels and up until now, had thought he preferred his climate to be just a tad warmer. But here in the frozen bosom of the Alps, he'd found something very alluring, very intriguing.

Cold, but mystifying. Glacial yet . . .

He felt his heart take another plunge. *Why wasn't she here when he came back? Didn't she want to see him?*

He shrugged off that last thought and almost unconsciously, removed his bandolier of rifle ammo and set it on the masterfully carved solid oak table in front of him. Retrieving his knife from his boot holster, he pulled a handful of bullets from the ammo ring and began dislodging the tracer rounds from their shells. Behind each cap was a small quantity of phosphorescent powder, the kick that made Hunter's personalized tracer bullets fire so bright and frightening.

But this powder could do more than just light up the night. When coming in contact with certain types of metal—aluminum, silver, gold—the molecules reacted in such a way as to heat up several degrees Kelvin. This warmth, though minute, was still enough to show up on a FLIR-sight or a pair of NightVision goggles, both of which Hunter was carrying with him—that is, if one knew what he was looking for. It was imperative that he bring at least a couple grams of the bright stuff with him when he met the fellow travelers at the casino tonight.

So he sat, pulling his bullets apart, gathering together the precious compound, perched on the edge of the couch hoping that at any moment he would hear her coming in.

But as it turned out, Chloe was already home.

It was very surprising that he hadn't heard her when he first came in.

The chalet was big, and some of its bedrooms were way up top, and way in the back, and the sound didn't travel all that well throughout. But he was extremely surprised that somehow his extrasensory receptors hadn't felt her presence *somewhere* in the house. It was a disturbing indication of just how much time he'd spent dwelling on her.

He'd just emptied out the last of twelve tracer rounds when a very strange, yet familiar sound came to his ears. It was like loud purring, coming from somewhere at the back end of the chalet.

He was on his feet in an instant, all thoughts of tracer powder and gambling casinos quickly fleeing his mind. Leaving his gun behind, he went to investigate.

The stairs leading to the second floor rear were rustic and old and extremely creaky. Hunter went up them without making a sound. The second floor rear was an area used primarily for guests who'd come to ski. The floor was understandably marked up, the walls scraped by hundreds of ski pole impacts. Still, Hunter moved down the hallway with the grace of a cat; the loudest sound coming from him was the beating of his heart. It felt like it was trying to leap right out of his chest.

The purring got louder as he approached the end of the hallway. He'd been doing a lot of this thing lately, both awake and in his dreams, walking down darkened corridors, wondering what would be behind the door he chose to open. He was sure a psychoanalyst could tell him the reason for all this recent skulking. But at the moment he wasn't too sure he wanted to know the answer.

No surprise the purring was coming from the last bedroom door on the left. His heart was now racing with his brain as to which one was making the most noise—shivers of curiosity, lust, excitement and shame were running through him at the speed of light. He felt like a bomb was about to go off inside his pants.

He finally reached the door and touched the knob. It was warm. The purring was coming from inside and had now risen to a soft growl. He stopped and listened for a moment. *Whoever said that the brain was a human's most sexual organ was certainly on the mark here,* he thought with a gulp. It was all he could do to turn the knob and open the door.

But open it he did . . .

It was Chloe doing all the purring. She was naked, lying on her stomach in the middle of an enormous bed, one faceless Nordic type roasting her from the back, while she did another from the front. She saw Hunter—and smiled with delight. This had been a plan all along. She knew he'd come back eventually, she knew that eventually he would find her here. She'd reeled him in like an expert.

Hunter stood there, shocked, but more excited than ever. *What the hell was all this?* He felt like he was caught in a bad porno movie. *Was watching almost as good as doing it? Was it better?* At that precise instant in time, he just didn't know.

For the next five minutes, Chloe and her companions moved from position to position, without missing a beat. Her eyes remained locked on his throughout, though there were times when the bombastic lust of it all demanded she close them and get lost in it.

To say he had a photographic memory was drastically understating the case; his mind was like four separate cameras running at once, with perfect visual and auditory reception. He was drinking this scene in by the gallon. Very quickly, he lost track of how much time had passed. *Was it really just five minutes? Or ten? Or more?* Hunter had no idea.

Finally, he did take a step backwards, toeing the door

with him. There was a limit to everything—and an art in knowing when to go. He went as quietly as he came, turning the knob softly and finally shutting the door again. He stood there, staring at it, fighting the urge to take just one more peek.

That's when Chloe's purr-turned-growl became a scream. Or was it a laugh? Hunter pressed his ear back to the door—he'd been hearing this sound for days now, both awake and in his dream.

When he heard it again—the last chorus in a symphony of erotica coming from behind that closed door—he knew at last that it was indeed a laugh.

That's when he turned on his heel and quickly hurried away.

At least that question had been answered.

# Thirteen

The casino was packed by the time Hunter arrived.

It was hard for him to avoid making a grand entrance. Even though he came in through a side door, he was immediately mobbed by a legion of admiring, well-dressed drunks. They quickly swept him towards the same poker table that had been the center of the action the night before.

A crowd four times as large was on hand for the sequel. The two spacemen were there, too. They were sitting in the same seats, the same confused scowls etched across their faces. It was almost like they'd never left, like they'd been waiting here all day, guarding what was left of their money, anticipating Hunter's return.

He nodded in their direction then dramatically dropped his own heavy bag of coins on the table. The large felt-lined platform nearly buckled, the $1.5 million weighed that much.

The travelers' eyes went wide; a gasp went through the crowd. The tuxedoed pit boss snapped his fingers and a gigantic scotch-and-ginger miraculously appeared in front of Hunter. He drank it in two gulps.

"So what's the game, boys?" he asked them finally.

They both smiled—but nervously. They'd been planning for this moment all day. They *had* to get it right.

"One hand, draw poker," one replied in a deep European accent. "Winner take all . . ."

Hunter laughed—he was authentically amused.

"I'm in for a million and a half," he told them, "And you're in for point-five. That's a little uneven, isn't it?"

The two men never stopped smiling. One reached into his pocket and withdrew a thin piece of metal about the size of a pocket calculator. It was polished so brightly it shimmered as he threw it on the table. Meanwhile his partner let loose with a long stream of unvoweled words, spoken in some obscure European dialect.

The pit boss was immediately in Hunter's ear, but he didn't need any translation. The thin piece of shiny metal was a platinum draftnote, a rare but acceptable form of currency in post-war Europe. All Hunter wanted to know was how much it was worth.

"Approximately one and three quarters of a million," the pit boss informed him, "As of our daily call to the Zurich Central Bank this morning."

Hunter looked back up at the two men. Obviously they'd been carrying the platinum note as a backup for credit all along. Now they were willing to risk it, plus what was left of their gold chips. It was strange—he hadn't counted on them being this greedy. What was their real motive then? To *bluff* him out of his winnings?

"Well, now the disadvantage is my way," he told them. "I thought you wanted this to be even."

"We do," the second man said. "We want something else of yours as well."

Again Hunter laughed. The two men were at least getting points for sheer *chutzpah*. Maybe that was another advantage of walking in space. Maybe the weightlessness made your balls grow bigger. But the question remained: what else could these guys possibly want of his?

"I've got a two-piece tank truck sitting outside, about a thousand gallons of gasoline in it," he told them. "Will that do?"

The men laughed, a little louder now. The crowd

around them laughed, too. Suddenly Hunter felt like he was the only one not in on the joke.

"Okay, what *do* you want?" he demanded of them.

As one, the crowd turned and looked to a spot just over Hunter's left shoulder. Both travelers nodded in that direction, too.

Hunter turned and suddenly found a graceful, blond catwoman had silently crept up beside him and was now standing, chest heaving, at the center of attention.

It was Chloe.

"We want her . . ." one of the men said.

Hunter looked up at her for a moment, then back at the men.

"No way," he said, starting to pull his bag of coins away. But then he felt a soft hand touch his shoulder—it froze him from head to toe.

"Do it," Chloe whispered to him—her voice was husky with excitement. The crowd, too, began shivering with erotic delight. It was suddenly very obvious to Hunter that this type of thing went on here in St. Moritz all the time.

His mind quickly switched into overdrive, weighing the ramifications of this unexpected twist. One thing was certain: it was not likely that he would have another crack at these two characters. He would have to deal with them here and now. The sudden inclusion of the Chloe factor was not catastrophic, simply complicating. And somewhere, deep down in that part of his mind he'd been visiting recently, something was telling him this is what he'd wanted all along.

He took one last look at her—and saw her eyes were actually tearing up, so much she wanted to be part of the stake. He turned back to the travelers and then dropped the bag of gold back on the table. The crowd ooohed with excitement once again. This was how the rich and famous amused themselves these crazy days.

"Okay, one hand, draw poker," Hunter finally said. "Deal them out."

The croupier did so, slowly, making sure each card fell precisely on top of the next, with the precise angle and drop time.

The first traveler picked up his cards, scanned them, suppressed a smile, and placed them back on the table.

"I'll stay," he declared, waving away the croupier's offer of draw cards.

The second man picked up his hand, looked at it, and smiled even more broadly than the first.

"I'm good, too . . ." he said.

The crowd gasped on cue. Neither man wanted nor required a draw card. All eyes turned back to Hunter. He looked at his hand and paused for a moment. Then drawing off four cards, he placed them aside and took four new ones from the relieved dealer.

"Check to you," he told the men.

The first man cautiously laid down his hand. He had four Queens. The second man was a bit faster. He held four Kings. Hunter reached down and flipped his hand over. The crowd let out a long, mournful groan.

He'd drawn four Jacks.

The two men were so surprised, they weren't sure what to do next. The pit boss, too, was shocked. He stepped forward and in a very graceful, workmanlike manner, moved Hunter's bag of gold coins across the table, placing it in front of the two men.

Then he looked up at Chloe. She was as surprised as anyone. With very tentative steps, he escorted her over to the other side of the table as well.

The two travelers knew it was essential they get out quickly now. They stood up, loaded on their winnings, including the platinum draft, and then took Chloe by the arm.

"Nice playing with you," one leered at Hunter. "We must have a rematch—the next time we're in town."

The next instant they were gone, lugging the weighty treasure with them, and hastily moving Chloe along. She managed a look over her shoulder as she was led away. Once again her eyes locked on to Hunter's.

He was not surprised in the least to see her break into a wide, devilish smile.

It took only a few minutes for the crowd to drift away from the card table. The contest they'd been anticipating all day had indeed taken a strange twist. A fortune and one of the city's most desirable females had been won by the two unshaven men with the spring in their step and the twinkle in their eyes.

In the end it was just Hunter and croupier, the man standing station with Hunter like a priest at a burial.

"Gambling is like that, sir," he said to Hunter, offering words of solace.

Hunter just shrugged and got to his feet. "You're right about that, my friend."

With that, Hunter quickly walked away, down some steps and out the side door he'd come in.

Only then did the croupier reach down and gather up the cards Hunter had thrown away before drawing the Jacks. One by one, the croupier flipped them over.

All four of them were Aces.

Not many people saw the fellow travelers leave town.

It was about 4 A.M. Two-thirds of the citizenry was still crowded into the casino; everyone else was either sleeping or passed out. The men had packed up their means of transport, a small Audi truck, and were now in the process of fueling it via a dozen containers of gasoline they'd purchased downtown.

Sitting in the cab of the truck was Chloe, suitcases

packed, and wearing a stunning black traveling suit. They had so far refused to talk to her—and she had not tried to communicate with them either. It was a tough call as to what the men were most concerned about: their regained treasure or the beautiful young girl. In truth, never in their dreams did they think they would actually win all their money back, never mind getting this blond vision as well. They really weren't too sure what they were supposed to do with her.

Their vehicle finally fueled, they quickly brought its engine to life and were off. Tires squealing, leaving a cloud of smoke and ice in their wake, they wheeled out onto the main road and immediately turned northeast.

The major highway out of town was called the Albula Span, a road which ran up one side of the local range, and then right through one of its mountains, via a tunnel known as the Albula Pass. Once they made it through the six-mile long passage, they would be more than halfway home.

They saw no one on the main street, no one on the approach to the highway. The sound of their noisy, anxious engine echoed off the ice-encased buildings and the snow piles alike. From all appearances, the two men had made a successful getaway.

But no one saw the long line of ripples disrupting the water on the northside of the great lake either, nor the small legion of waves that lapped up against the shore a few moments later. The speedy Macchi had taken off with barely the burp of the engine and the slightly eerie whooshing sound it made as its pontoons left the water.

Climbing straight up as quickly as the clown's feet floats would allow, Hunter had stolen silently into the air.

He was quickly up and over the small mountains to the north end of St. Moritz, the unnaturally straightened road of the Albula Span stretching before him. There were a few vehicles transversing the Alpine highway in this, the last hour before dawn. Military trucks in small convoys mostly, change-outs between the private armies guarding the north and west. Many were running with the headlights on—some were not.

This made no difference to Hunter. One glance into his FLIR goggles told him the precise location of the Audi truck, along with its direction and speed. The tracer powder, which he'd first sprinkled onto his gold coins, was now all over the small truck, being transferred there just as he'd hoped by the travelers themselves, after they'd run their greedy little hands through the big bag of money.

The Audi was glowing like a spark plug, its outline on the FLIR coming across as almost bluish on the field of green. Hunter positioned himself about one mile high and two miles behind the speeding truck, staying there by kicking in the engine only every thirty seconds or so and thus maintaining a slow, seventy-five-knot power glide. This tactic also cut down on some of the noise the airplane was making—and this was very important.

The last thing he wanted now was for the two men to think they were being followed.


Point Zero wasn't that hard a place to find.

It was located approximately one hundred thirty-five kilometers northwest of St. Moritz, at the top of a peak known as the *Niedencastel.* It was a strange little place, a domed structure surrounded by a gaggle of antennas and satellite dishes. Everything on the outside was painted white, this in a land where just about everything was white, except the large, crystalline lake nearby, which was deep blue. The bloodless paint job was a crude, but effective attempt at camouflage. From the ground looking up, it was almost impossible to see the small tracking station.

But from the air—well, that was another story.

The Audi truck bearing the two men and Chloe arrived at the top of the mountain just after 5 A.M. Climbing to the peak alone took forty-five minutes. When they finally pulled up to the igloo, they were shocked to find the front door unlocked and wide open. Quickly hustling Chloe out of the truck, they stormed into the small passageway which held another door which led into the bubble-top building itself. This was wide open, too.

The men drew their guns. They were massive .357 Magnums; the very sight of them shook Chloe. No one carried weapons in St. Moritz, never mind hand cannons like these. And what did the men plan to do with them? They coolly pushed the hatchway open to find the interior of the station frozen over and partially covered with snow. Sitting in the middle of this, frozen to the chair in front of the station's main display screen was a third colleague, a man they'd left behind. He looked dead.

The two men yanked Chloe inside, then quickly closed the door behind them. One leapt for the thermostat and cranked it up to high. Somewhere deep below the structure, a small squadron of thermal-heaters kicked in. At least *they* were still working. The men next dislodged some ice from the main diagnostic panel and began frantically pushing buttons. Many things came back as blinking red—not a good sign.

Furious, one of the men gave the main console chair a mighty kick, dislodging its frosted and encrusted occupant and about a million ice particles from the seat. The man was not dead—he was drunk. He rolled stiffly across the room, whacking his head on the main console. The two men cornered him and began kicking him viciously about the groin and stomach. Terrified and confused, the victim began squealing. But his cries were drowned out by the thudding of boots to his skull and body.

Only after Chloe let out a scream did the beating stop.

Exhausted and drained, the two men continued mercilessly cursing at the man. It was obvious by now that this type of thing had happened before.

They were a strange lot, these three. True, they were somewhat educated; each had more than a passing knowledge of both astrophysics and engineering. All three had also ridden aboard the Zon into space. But they were rather crude intellects, freelance space workers left over from the old, *old* Soviet Empire. They had nary a thought of loyalty or devotion to their jobs or one another. In fact, all three frequently took advantage of their isolated station, abusing alcohol and cocaine, both of which were readily available by air-drop delivery from any one of a dozen drug cartels operating in the region.

But by agreement, this practice was supposed to stop whenever the two of them struck out for St. Moritz and left the third man behind. In reality, the loneliness only increased the temptation to get blitzed. So the third man had thrown a two-day party for himself. He'd injested an overload of intoxicants, had probably wanted to get some air and then passed out with the door wide open. Had the other two not returned when they did, the man would have frozen to death in another two hours. Soon after that, the interior of the station would have iced-over beyond repair.

This was why they were so angry with him. Letting the station fall into such a state had been not only foolish—it had been extremely dangerous. If the people who were paying them to sit here and watch TV all day ever found out how badly they actually ran the place, losing the frigid gig on top of the *Niedencastel* would be the least of their problems. Quite simply, their employers would have them tracked down and killed.

They poured a bucket of freezing water over the third man's head, reviving him somewhat, though not to the point where he had the strength to get to his feet. The dome was heating up quickly now and many of the systems automatically shut down during the freeze-out were coming back on line and blinking green. Another diagnostic check revealed no large-scale damage had been done. And apparently nothing out of the ordinary had happened with the orbiting Zon while they were away. The two travelers breathed a sigh of relief—they'd dodged a huge bullet. But an exchange of angry scowls reaffirmed an agreement they'd made long before: the third man would not get a penny of the hard-won monetary gains they'd picked up in St. Moritz. In fact, he'd just made himself very dispensable.

Chloe was leaning over this man now, cooing about his welts and injuries. To the reawakened technician, this was all like a dream. One moment he was unconscious, the next he was being beaten and kicked, and now he was looking into the face of an angel—one who was wearing a low-cut, ebony ski-bunny suit.

"Let me help you up," she said, gently pulling him to his feet. She began kissing his wounds passionately, stunning all three of them. The third man especially couldn't believe what was happening—but then it began to sink in. The other two had brought back a hooker with them. An unbelievably gorgeous one.

"So *this* is what you won in town?" he asked them between Chloe's tongue-lashing kisses.

The two men quickly eyed each other. One winked; the other displayed a sinister smile.

"It is," he replied. "At the poker table. She's better than money. As you'll soon find out."

The third man, soaking wet, bleeding slightly and massively hung over, just shook his head. Chloe was practically wrapping herself around him now. Her warm body instantly dissipated the chill from his. *Maybe he was dead,* he thought, *and this was Heaven. Or maybe he was still dreaming. Or maybe he was just still high.*

But he was also very suspicious.

"What do you mean I'll soon find out?" he asked the other two.

"We mean you can have her first," one of his colleagues replied. "With our compliments."

He eyed both of them cautiously, his eyes watering with distrust.

"Really? I can go first?"

"Yes, take her," the second man insisted, "Pave the way for us, so to speak . . ."

The two men eyed each other again. Yes, it was time for this clown to go. Slowly and painfully. And when that happened, the girl would have to go, too.

But, first they wanted to count their money.

"Take her to your room and warm yourself up," they told him. "Tell us how she is . . ."

As excited as he was, the third man just couldn't believe all this. He was suddenly very frightened of the other two. But then he looked at Chloe and she at him and he realized that she was so fucking beautiful, it would be worth the risk, whatever the other two were planning.

So he foolishly began leading her towards his sleeping quarters. Ever-so-willing to please, Chloe went without a hint of resistance.

"See you in a couple of hours," he told the other two warily.

"Sure thing," one of them replied. "Take your time."

The top of the Point Zero tracking station's dome was exactly 15,835 feet above sea level, just five feet short of three miles up.

But the peak of the mountain called *Niedencastel* was actually thirty-two feet higher than that, due to a crag that jutted out just above the northwest corner of the building's bubble-top.

This outcrop protected the dome somewhat from the fierce winds blowing out of the north. It was so blustery on the peak there was no snow—the wind had been blowing it away for eons, gradually wearing down the rocks in the process as well.

All in all it was a very inhospitable place. Still, it was about as close as you could get to the stars in this part of the world, and here, tucked into a crevice at the top of the crag, was Hawk Hunter, battling the wind and the cold, his eyes lifted heavenward.

It was now about 0545 hours—quarter to six in the morning, and about twenty-five minutes away from sunrise. Despite the harsh, arctic-like conditions, Hunter felt a faint throb of warm satisfaction beating in his chest. His calculations had told him that there must be a tracking facility at Point Zero, and here it was. Because of the angles, it was undoubtedly the best place in Europe, if not the world, to see the Zon go over and to view it for the longest time. So his long drive, and the adventures he'd experienced both awake and asleep, had been worth it. Thus, the spark of heat radiating from his rib cage. At last, it was time to turn the page and get on with the rest of the story.

He did have some idea of the last time the Zon had passed over. Computing back from when he watched it lift off, then factoring in its speed and a number of projected daily orbits, he guessed it had gone over Point Zero about sixty-eight minutes ago. This meant it should be passing overhead again inside the next quarter hour. He intended to stay right where he was until it did.

Following the two mooks to Point Zero had been easy. Fueled by greed, distracted by lust, they had taken no care at all to check if they were being followed. By alternately gliding and reviving his plane's engine every few seconds or so, Hunter had tracked them without incident all the way to the top of the mountain. He had spotted the dome and its antenna headdress as far as twenty-five miles away.

The nearby lake had provided the perfect landing area for the Macchi seaplane as a large portion of its center was essentially ice-free. Hunter set the racer down like he was landing on glass, taxiing into a conveniently hidden cove, one which would render the airplane practically invisible from all directions.

It had taken him less than thirty minutes to scale the remaining one thousand feet to the top of the mountain, an amazingly easy ascent. There was a reason for this though: the mountain was lousy with work roads and pathways to the summit, the result of their fairly recent construction. Hunter simply picked the most direct one, and double-timed it to the top.

Now he was here, a snowball's throw away from the front door of the dome, his ears peeled for any sound of Chloe coming from inside, his eyes staring up at the awesome array of stars and planets floating over his head.

He couldn't help but get contemplative—staring out at the Universe did that to him. Though he had led a dangerous and complicated life, Hunter had to admit he'd completed many of the lofty goals he'd set out for himself. He'd helped free the American continent finally—and in this he took the greatest personal satisfaction. He'd put together a team of loyal, professional and astute soldiers to secure that peace, and a well-armed, well-trained army and air force to protect it. These, too, were proud accomplishments.

But there was one mad dream he had yet to fulfill, one that up until the moment a few days ago when he saw the Zon go up, he'd considered impossible in this chaotic, confused world.

This was his dream to one day fly in space. He had come damned close once. Just months before the Big War broke out, he'd been selected for space shuttle training. He'd been just days away from his first shuttle flight when the balloon went up. In the ensuing years of anarchy and combat in America, he'd all but given up on ever going up—it seemed like the technology curve would just take too long to regain the point of launching shuttles again.

So it was one of the supreme ironies of his life that his most-despised enemy—or at least someone using his name and personage—would get him dreaming about going into space again. Seeing the Zon go up, knowing it held Viktor and a band of his cohorts had been a disheartening moment—but the Wingman was nothing if not resilient. He was an expert at finding the tiniest sliver of silver lying behind the greatest, blackest cloud. This time it came to him very simply: If Viktor could fly in space, why couldn't he? If Viktor's minions were smart enough—or was it *dumb* enough?—to light a shuttle, then certainly Hunter and his gang could do it, too, even if they had to steal Viktor's spaceship to do it.

He laughed out loud now anytime he thought back to the crazy dream he'd had back in the cab of the tanker truck. Biplanes against a shuttle? Now there was a vision for the cover of a cheap paperback. But maybe there was a message in there, too. Just like the Nazis were responsible for putting NASA on the moon, maybe Viktor would lead the democratic forces in America back into space.

But there was still a long road to go.

Hunter checked the western horizon and figured he still had about twelve minutes before the Zon would pass over. But it would prove to be eleven minutes and fifty-five seconds too long, for Hunter found his thoughts plunging from their dizzying heights and landing smack dab and hard on top of the big dome before him.

It was, of course, the Chloe problem again. If he stared long enough at the tracking station's ivory, spherical shape, he believed he would be able to see right through it, maybe into a room directly below him where Chloe was on her knees performing every gyration of the world's second-most popular sex act. It was more than a bit difficult for him to think about what she might be doing in there. Sure, her sudden inclusion in the high-stakes game had actually worked to his advantage. She certainly provided a distraction for the two men as they drove back to the mountain—and she was probably keeping them quite busy now, again all the better for him. But he felt his mouth going dry at the very thought of it. What he had seen. What he had heard. He feared he would never get it out of his mind. Not even if he wanted to.

He turned away from the dome and into the wind and let the frigid gale blow him back to reality. He would have to take in a lot of things in the amount of time that the Zon was in view. Once it was gone, he would have an ever-shrinking time span figuring out exactly what this data told him. Hopefully what he saw would be enough to guide him further towards the twin holy grails of this trip: where the shuttle would be coming down and when.

Only then could he think about rescuing Chloe—if she needed to be rescued, that is.

Five minutes to go. He bundled up against the howling wind. *Just where would the shuttle be coming down?* He really didn't have a clue at this point. He had already influenced its landing site to a degree by so thoroughly fouling the runway at Star City. But how big of an effect would this have? Like all shuttle flights, he was sure the Zon had a number of back-up sites at which to land in an emergency. All you really needed was a runway that was at least twelve thousand, five hundred feet long.

While flying around in orbit might not be as much of a tricky business as it seemed, coming back down certainly was. Once the people inside the Zon realized that the runway at Star City was not an option, they would have to find an alternate landing area that was still in their reentry path, with no more than a fifteen-degree swing either way. Now there were probably a half dozen airports somewhere in a band stretching from the immediate European neighborhood all the way to Asia and the Pacific with the extra-long runway needed to land the Zon. But who was controlling these bases? Were they all loyal to Viktor, either by money or fear?

Hunter was banking that they were not—and if this was true, it meant that once the emergency landing site *was* selected, Viktor would probably have to buy some mercenary forces on the QT and dash them to the landing place so they could secure it before the Zon came down.

But if Hunter arrived first, then . . .

Two minutes to go. He stepped back out into the roaring wind and began adjusting his eyes to the deep black sky and the massive carousel of stars above. It wouldn't be easy picking out a reflection in all that starlight—he would have to let it all burn into his retinas, memorizing it, so something moving through the field of burning specks would be evident right away.

One minute to go. He pulled his collar closer to his neck, and yanked his helmet further down on his head. Though his flight suit was minimally heated via a battery pack, it was just enough to prevent him from freezing to death and nothing more. Thirty seconds to go. A huge gust of wind nearly sent him flying down the side of the cliff. Despite the freezing bluster, he couldn't deny that there was still a warm feeling welling up inside him. Space, baby. The Final Frontier. It was inhabited by human beings again, as despicable as they were.

And now he wanted to go there more than ever.

Ten seconds. He squinted now, locking his eyes on the northwestern horizon. Suddenly he could feel it. A wave of psychic energy washed right through him. At that instant he knew all his calculations had indeed been right.

He saw it a second later.

It was just a faint light at first. Bluish in the haze at the far edge of the horizon, growing white as it approached. His breath caught in his throat as it came more clearly into his view. He had to take a moment to admire the damn thing. There was a certain amount of credit to be given to Viktor's blow boys in all this. After all, they were up there and Hunter was still down here.

Another gust of wind yanked him back to reality again. Now the wheels in his head began turning in earnest. He glued his eyes on to the thin point of light as it rose twenty degrees above the azimuth. Speed, angle of flight, even its luminosity were all taken in by his brain and absorbed, filling his short-term memory banks with more numbers than could be spun out on a small computer.

It was heading right for him, moving swift and silently through the starry ocean. *Son-of-a-bitch,* he thought, *that must be a gas.* He began craning his neck as it raced to a point right over his head. Preliminary stuff was coming in now: the Zon was one hundred and fifteen and three-tenths miles straight up. Velocity was 15,672 miles per hour. Its mean orbital path was deteriorating at a constant rate equal to $(x = y (b))$ and it was most definitely heading towards the southeast. It was all just as Hunter thought. The thing had reached space all right, but had found itself in a rather clumsy orbit. It was, in effect, wobbling through space, as opposed to speeding through it. This was the last piece of evidence Hunter needed to figure out along what reentry corridor the spaceship would be coming down.

Suddenly a huge strobe light located beneath the crown of the dome came to life. Its mad flickering gave everything within sight a bizarre fractured look. The light was so intense, Hunter could hardly look at it. He knew at that moment, the characters in the Zon were looking down at Point Zero, perhaps comforted by its nonverbal message that everything was still okay here, down on earth, as misleading as that message might be at the moment.

Hunter looked back up, instantly picking up the Zon's reflection again. It was going away from him now, a last second stutter in its path telling him that it would be coming down soon—maybe within the next twenty-four hours, and certainly no more than forty-eight. He felt another surge of excitement run through him. Part Two of this little jaunt was soon to start. As the Zon disappeared over the southeastern horizon, he knew that he'd been able to capture more than enough data to figure out along what path it was most likely to attempt an emergency landing.

As he'd previously promised himself, he'd try like mad to be there when it did.

Then, just like that it was gone—disappearing over the edge of the world, continuing its five-miles-a-second journey.

Buzzing now, Hunter stepped back out of the wind and shivered once. One mission complete—now another had to begin.

He turned his attention back to the dome again and let out a long, frosty, troubled breath.

It was time to rescue Chloe.

The door to the igloo was wide open when Hunter got there.

He checked the clip in his M-16F2; as always it was full of tracer rounds. He checked his boot pistol; it, too, was fully loaded. Slowly, surely, he made his way into the entrance chamber and up to the interior hatchway. It, too, was wide open, its hinges squeaking as the high winds outside roared into the entry tunnel.

He stopped and listened. There was static bouncing around in there, somewhere, and he could just barely hear the sound of warning lights blinking on a control panel. He also heard someone sobbing. But in an instant, he knew it wasn't Chloe.

He toed the hatch open, and immediately his laser sight finder illuminated the sleeping quarters of the man who had stayed behind. He was lying on the bed, stark naked and quite dead. His face was as white as a ghost, his body ashen and stiffening. His eyes were still open. They were dilated beyond description. Oddly, he was still smiling.

Hunter swept the red laser light to the right. It quickly fell upon the head of one of the two fellow travelers, the men he'd played cards against the night before. This guy was dead, too, the handle of a bayonet-type knife protruding from his Adam's apple. On the snowy, wet floor beside him, was the second would-be cardshark. He was the one who'd been the one crying; but he'd stopped by now. There was a blade sticking out of his gut that made the bayonet look like a jackknife. The first man's hand was holding the end of this enormous sword; it was evident that he'd just plunged it into his comrade's stomach, a thrust cut short by his own quick bloody death.

The two men had killed each other.

*But why?* Hunter took two more steps inside. Beside the pair of fresh corpses was the money he'd lost to them just hours before. It was stacked neatly, in two exact piles, each bearing more than $1.5 million each; the gold coins were sparkling in the green VDT light of the main console.

Though he wasn't sure why, Hunter's senses were telling him the deadly fight had not been over the winnings.

He found Chloe behind the main console, rolled up in a heap, sniffling quietly. She was unhurt, at least in a physical sense; her ski-bunny suit only slightly mussed and damp, not one hair on her head was out of place. Hunter lifted her gently to her feet, then took another look around the main suite. It was beginning to make sense now. The two men had killed each other not over the millions in gold but over Chloe. It took them a while, but they, too, had fallen under her spell—and mutual death had been the result.

And the man lying dead and paralyzed in his living quarters? He'd died of a heart attack—caused by over-stimulation and overexertion.

Hunter let out a long, low breath. With hardly a bat of the eye, Chloe had done more damage than a twelve-second burst from an AK-47.

Without a word, he put his arms around her frail, shaking shoulders and led her from the tracking station.

No sooner were they clear of the dome when Hunter's sixth sense began buzzing again.

He suddenly stopped in his tracks, pulling Chloe back towards him. There was an airplane circling nearby, possibly right above the lake. Hunter couldn't see it—it was hidden by the low thickening clouds. But he could tell it had four engines, probably top-mounted, piston-driven props, and that they were powering something so big and bulky it drove through the air like a truck. *So what kind of plane was it?* Hunter wasn't exactly sure. But from the sounds of it, he guessed a seaplane was up there, one that was much bigger, and much newer, than the antique that had brought him here.

He immediately pulled Chloe into the thick forest and together they began making their way back down the path Hunter had taken to the top. As they moved through the cold, covering shadows, the sounds of more engines and more planes filled their ears. By the time they reached an outcrop of rock that looked out onto the northern end of the lake itself, the sound above them was deafening. Wedging themselves into a slim crack in the rocks, they hunkered down and waited.

They had picked a perfect place to hide. Not only was

it protected, it also had a perfect view of the lake. But Hunter's eyes were actually fixed on the thick clouds hovering five hundred feet above the surface of the water at the moment. It sounded like a squadron of big airplanes droning around up there now. *Who the hell did they belong to? And why had they come here?*

The first airplane dropped down out of the misty cover a few seconds later. It did a quick fly-by of the lake, then climbed back up again. This confirmed one thing: it *was* a seaplane, a big one. In fact, it was a UF-1 Grumman Albatross, an old but rugged mainstay of the air-sea rescue game. This one had obviously come down to look for the best place on the lake to land.

Another minute went by. Then suddenly all four UF-1s dropped out of the clouds, and one right after the other, set down onto the clear waters in the middle of the lake. Hunter was impressed. It was no easy task bringing such a large airframe in on such a relatively small body of water. Yet each pilot did so effortlessly. Hunter had his powered up binocs out now, using them to scan the length of each big seaplane. None of the flying boats was carrying any national emblem or insignia or hardly any markings at all. This was a sure sign that they were part of some mercenary outfit.

Once down, the airplanes turned one hundred eighty and headed directly towards the western shore. Vast doors in the nose and rear end of each plane slowly opened up. As Hunter and Chloe watched in amazement, heavily armed troops began jumping out of these doorways, hitting the shallow water and quickly sloshing their way to the bank. Now Hunter was mildly astounded—this was a rather unique little operation they were witnessing. Landing a load of quick response troops, in a remote mountainous area, by seaplane . . .

*Not bad,* he thought.

No sooner had the troops gained the shore than they

formed up and began a double time march towards the summit of the mountain. Now it was beginning to make sense to Hunter. Chloe had told him of the mess the tracking station was in when she returned with the two travelers, and how the third man had been found drunk and blacked out. Someone must have tried to contact the station during that time, he figured, and after getting no reply, they had pulled a switch somewhere indicating that something was wrong at Point Zero. This unit had been sent to see what was up. They were an on call, for hire, rapid deployment force. A very enterprising idea.

Just who had employed them, or from where, was still a mystery. But those details were actually irrelevant. Whether they knew it or not, in the end, their paycheck was coming from Viktor and his blood money.

*And that was a shame,* Hunter thought.

"There seems to be so many of them," Chloe said. "Will they search for us?"

Hunter hesitated in his answer—was it his imagination or did he really just detect a tinge of excitement in her voice at the thought of all these guys looking for her?

"They might come looking," he finally replied, helping her down from their hiding place and then leading her back under the thick canopy of trees. "But it won't do them any good."


As a matter of policy, each flying boat left one man behind to watch the airplane while the assault troops it carried did their thing.

The man who happened to be watching Flying Boat 4 was an Austrian, and at one time, an airline pilot for Lufthansa. He'd been flying the seaplane mercs around these parts for a year now. The pay was good, the big seaplane was kept up to trim, and he never had to involve himself in any of the fighting. It was a sweet deal all around.

He was now seated in the cockpit, doing a quick run through of his diagnostics while the rest of the flight crew stretched their legs on land. His mind was already imagining what he'd do once this drill was over and they returned to their base in Venice. A dinner. A good cigar. Some brandy, maybe buy a couple bimbs and . . .

Suddenly he sensed someone standing behind him. He turned expecting to see his copilot or the flight engineer. Instead, he found himself looking into the eyes of the most beautiful young girl he could have ever imagined. She was standing in the short passageway between the flight deck and the rest of the ship. It was as if she had materialized out of nowhere.

*"Fräulein?"* he gasped, equally shocked by her sudden appearance and her stunning, rather bewildering beauty. "What are you doing here?"

She did not reply. Instead, she reached up and began unzipping the front of her form-fitting snow outfit.

*"What is this?"* he demanded, his breath catching in his throat. *"Who are you?"*

Still, she said nothing. She slid the zipper all the way down and then dramatically pulled both sides back. Suddenly the pilot was looking at two incredibly luscious breasts. It was enough to bring him out of his seat.

He never saw the fist that hit him. It seemed to come out of nowhere, as if it was launched from some other dimension. It hit him square on the jaw, fracturing it slightly and knocking him back on his ass. He hit his head on his seat console and landed in a heap on the cockpit floor.

Dazed but still conscious, he looked up to see a man was now hovering over him, pulling his gun from his holster and the ammunition from his belt. Now this man was lifting him by the shoulders and dragging him to the back of the boat. All the while the girl was standing over him, too—the front of her suit still unzipped, her breasts still mesmerizing him as they swayed.

He was pulled to the rear door of the flying boat and rather unglamorously thrown into the lake. The frigid water quickly revived the pilot, at least long enough for him to swim like mad to one of the plane's wing-mounted floats. In the short time it took him to do this, the strange individual who'd dumped him into the water had already climbed into the cockpit of the seaplane and had started the plane's two inner engines.

The Austrian pilot began screaming from his perch on the float, but the noise of the big propellers was already drowning out his cries. It became very obvious very quickly that this guy and this girl were stealing Boat #4 and there was little he could do about it. That's when he let go of the float and began swimming to shore.

It took him fifteen seconds to reach dry land. When he finally stopped, he took a deep breath, then turned around. The big seaplane was already out in the middle of the lake and beginning its takeoff run. The Austrian pilot couldn't believe it—everything had happened so fast. Barely a minute had gone by since he was sitting peacefully in his seat, dreaming of good food and Venice. Now he was wet, angry, with a sore jaw and without his plane.

He watched with building fury as the Albatross lurched forward, and with a great burst of power and spray, roared into the sky. It banked sharply the moment it was airborne, the mysterious pilot gunning the engines and pointing the nose away from the mountain.

Then, still climbing, it turned again and quickly disappeared over the southern horizon.

# Part Three

Part Three

# Fourteen

The sun finally peeked over the hazy, bluish edge of the Earth, its rays once again bathing the Zon space shuttle in much-needed warmth.

It was cold inside the orbiting spacecraft—too cold actually. The shuttle was now passing over Central America; it had been in the dark of the Earth's shadow for nearly ninety minutes. In that time, it had become so frigid inside, small beads of frozen condensation, caused by nothing more than human oxygen exhalations, had begun to appear on some of the critical control elements on the flight deck.

Now that the Zon was back in the sunshine, the warmth would melt these frozen bubbles and aid in bringing up other crucial components which had been shut down because of the falling temperatures; of course, they all had to be shut down again once the shuttle went back behind the Earth.

This endless freezing, reheating and refreezing was doing none of the components any good. Like a lightbulb that's being constantly turned on and off, the elements inside these criticals were wearing out quickly. There was no telling when one of them would pop, and what trouble it would lead to when it did.

The fluctuating temperature problem on the Zon's control deck was not the way it was supposed to be. During a normal flight, the environment inside the spacecraft was supposed to be tightly regulated. But this was hardly a normal flight for the Zon. In fact, in the orbital craft's short history, it had yet to make what would be considered a "normal flight."

There were many other things wrong with it as well. The guidance and navigation systems were only running at seventy-percent, this due directly to the wild changes between heat and cold. Seventy-percent nav operation meant seventy-percent accuracy in the steering of the shuttle, it was as simple as that. At any moment, the craft could be as many as a hundred miles off its intended orbital path.

The spacecraft's air circulation system was also breaking down; the filters in the purification elements had not been changed in three flights. This meant the prevailing smell inside the spaceship was that of body odor. There was no clean water to speak of; again a malfunction in the cabin environment filtering system. The simple electricals—lights, switches, intercoms—were becoming unreliable as power throughout the craft was also fluctuating badly. Even some of the doors and component panels were sticking shut—this due to thousands of tiny, solid contaminating particles floating freely around the interior of the ship, lodging into places unattainable in all but a gravity-free environment.

This was no way to run a spacecraft—especially one that was hurling along at five miles per second. The only reason the ship was still intact was because its engines and propulsion systems were up to snuff, though just barely, and its main computers were still fully on line. But then, it was only a matter of time before the gremlins began crawling around inside some of them, too. Then, only disaster could follow.

As it was, the Zon was breaking some kind of endurance records—though not necessarily ones to be proud of. This was the spacecraft's third flight in as many months; back in the days of regular shuttle launches, if one orbiter went up twice in a year it was a rare occurrence, and then only after extensive reconditioning. But even though each time the Zon blasted off from Star City, every bolt, weld and adhesion agent inside got that much weaker, it was still somehow holding together.

The spacecraft was also hauling a lot more weight than would be considered normal, or, better put, sane. There were no less than fifteen people currently riding the Zon, more than twice the maximum human load. The spacecraft was built to handle five comfortably; triple that number introduced a lot of problems, fouled toilets being the first of them. There was also the matter of feeding such a horde—the Zon had taken off with only enough spacefood for five people, eating three times a day for five days. It had been in orbit now for barely one hundred hours and already, almost all the food was gone.

But even this had a beneficial angle: once the food intake dropped, at least the toilet problem would stabilize.

Though the majority of space inside the Zon was unkempt and getting dirty very quickly, two areas were not.

First was the flight deck itself. Even though it bore the brunt of the constantly changing temperatures, the sole pilot occupying the spacecraft's cockpit had worked very diligently making sure the area was kept clean. This was as much an exercise in keeping his sanity as it was for concern of the shuttle's flight worthiness. The pilot was the only person onboard the Zon who was qualified to be here, and he, just barely. He'd had some of the basics of shuttle flight years before and he was a top-notch fighter pilot. If the Zon's overall operation wasn't so completely computerized, it would never be able to get off the ground. But because it did, it fell to him to fly it.

This was a strange situation as well, because the pilot

was also a prisoner. He'd been kept under duress by Viktor's forces for nearly two years. The circumstances of his captivity were as outlandish as the notion that a battered, worn-out space shuttle could actually fly in orbit. He was a member of the top echelon of the United American Armed Forces, a friend of Hawk Hunter, Commander-in-Chief General Seth Jones, Crunch O'Malley, Wa, Toomey, and the others. He'd fought in many of the early battles of American liberation; and conducted many successful covert operations towards that eventual aim.

It was during one of these secret missions that he'd been lost in action, his airplane shot down by a SAM over an obscure mid-Pacific atoll. The island turned out to be a huge staging area for the Asian Mercenary Cult, an army financed directly from Viktor's coffers. He'd lived on this island for months before being captured while trying to steal an airplane in an attempt to escape. He was nearly executed several times before one of the Cult overlords, a man who had direct connections to Viktor, recognized who he was, and how his piloting skills could be utilized.

For the next year, the Zon pilot had been subjected to incredibly intense brainwashing, including the forced injection of psychosis-inducing drugs. Viktor's underlings had made a special project of him, carting him to a secret location deep inside Russia and importing some of the most hideous of brainwashing experts from North Korea. At the end of the twelve horrible months, the pilot emerged depleted, shaken and suffering from many psychological maladies.

His piloting skills remained intact, however. And when Viktor's minions located the Zon hidden in a vast underground shelter near Star City and realized it could fly if the right man was behind the controls, the pilot was nursed back to physical health and then ordered to learn everything he could about the Russian shuttle. He'd first taken it up seven months before—this was his fifth flight.

Keeping the flight deck spotless was part of his own, self-prescribed therapy. It was, quite literally, his way of keeping what was left of his sanity. Something deep inside told him that if he kept the flight deck clean and proper while the rest of the Zon deteriorated, it would somehow prevent him from going nuts altogether. Just why he felt like this, he didn't know. That was probably his biggest problem—he had little or no memory retention these days in matters other than the technical aspects of keeping the Zon flying. The brainwashers had done their job well, almost surgically removing all aspects of his previous personality while leaving his ability to fly and understand things aeronautical completely intact.

The worst thing he'd suffered during his year in hell was the loss of his long-term memory. He was a victim of nearly total amnesia—despite all his talent and daring, the Zon pilot, an American, a true hero, a friend of the Wingman among others, simply didn't know who he was.

Not exactly anyway.


The other part of the Zon space shuttle that was not in a state of complete disarray was the ICEM, the independently controlled environmental module.

This cylindrical container was about twenty-four feet long, ten feet around, and was located inside the Zon's expansive cargo bay. As its acronym indicated, it was a self-supporting unit, a spacecraft within a spacecraft. Though it had no propulsive power of its own, it did boast its own life-support systems, including electricity, water filtration, air circulation and other essentials, all totally apart from the Zon itself.

There was no bad smell inside the ICEM, no water shortage, no temperature fluctuations, no clogged toilets.

There was only one permanent occupant within, and he was not hungry, thirsty or uncomfortable in any way, save for the nasty habit he'd developed of letting his cocaine spoon float away from his grasp, forcing him to unbuckle his safety harness and drift across the interior of the ICEM to retrieve it. This had happened to him at least ten times in the past hour, and at least a hundred times in the past twenty-four.

Being weightless in space was indeed a euphoric feeling. But being without gravity while under the influence of drugs was another thing completely. It made a weird sensation even weirder—and very unpredictable. Simple intoxicants like coke or morphine or speed could become like LSD, hallucinogenics that had the tendency to stay active in the bloodstream for longer periods of time. Many times nausea would result after injesting, or long bouts of cramping or hyperventilation. Floating while high wasn't as much fun as it sounded.

The solution to all this would have seemed simple enough—either give up the nose candy or stop flying in space. But that was the big dilemma for the sole occupant of the ICEM: He was hooked on both.

Oddly, he had much in common with the pilot sitting alone up front in the Zon's flight compartment. Like him, the man in the ICEM was something of a technical genius, an accomplished mathematician, a pilot and a professional soldier, all at one time. Or more accurately, he *believed* he'd been all those things. That he was also a KGB agent many years before was a little less certain. That he deserved the mantle as being the world's most feared criminal and superterrorist was also very unclear.

Just like the Zon pilot, as far as he knew, he had no past, no family, no history at all. He wasn't even sure what his name was. Everyone called him "Viktor" though, and after a while, he'd come to believe that was indeed his name.

At the moment, he was amusing himself by watching a pair of naked teenage girls float around the inside of the ICEM. They were trying to conduct a gravity-free forced-love session on each other, but hardly doing a good job of it. It was almost laughable to see them attempt to grasp and grope one another, all while trying their best to avoid coming anywhere near his vicinity—they knew anything could happen should they float too close to him.

So they flew about the cabin module, occasionally grabbing onto each other and performing several seconds of perfunctory lesbian sex before the uncertainties of weightlessness forced them apart to begin the whole display all over again. Viktor sat, strapped down, trying his best to pick the individual grains of cocaine out of the air with his tongue as he followed the bizarre zero-g kink show. This was usually how he passed the time during these flights; this and trying to come up with new, more efficient ways to snort his drug of choice while in orbit.

Occasionally, he used some rare energy to twist around and look out the ICEM's only porthole. He did this now and saw that they had once again emerged from behind the Earth's shadow. Somewhere in his drug-addled brain, he had the fleeting thought things were probably heating up inside the shuttle proper. Not that this made any difference to him. Shuttle operations bored him frankly— there were too many details, too many things to attend to. In many, many ways, he was just along for the ride.

Still, he was familiar with what his shuttle crew had to do while they were up here: since breaking into orbit three days ago, they'd been gathering up a series of satellites known as SDS-14s. These satellites, shot into space secretly by the United States nearly two decades before, were actually orbiting test stations, components of the so-called "Star Wars" system that had been designed to direct laser beams at enemy ICBMs, scrambling their guidance systems and their warhead targeting abilities even as they rose from their launchers.

Somehow, somewhere along the way, Viktor's technical elite had discovered these small but lethal packages could be adapted for use back on Earth, and most conveniently, from aircraft. With very little tinkering, the SDS-14s could be mounted on an airplane of just about any size and used to either destroy enemy fighters in flight or to attack ground targets. The Zon had retrieved sixteen of these packages from space so far. There was thought to be another dozen or so still floating around in orbit.

The second half of the Zon's current mission was to once again attempt a linkup with the old Soviet Mir space station. The Mir, abandoned years before, was still remarkably intact and operational. The mission of the first Zon launch several months before was to board it and replace the space station's old, dead fuel cells. Since then, two of Viktor's minions had been living inside the Mir, getting some of its systems back on line and taking out those that didn't work.

Roughly the size of two city buses, the Mir was actually designed many years before with only one purpose in mind: to serve as a high-flying spy platform. The famous endurance records set inside the Soviet space station before it was abandoned were more suited to the annals of pre-Big War intelligence-gathering than any space achievements book. It was a poorly kept secret that the Mir had been used to peek in on many NATO operations which fell below its orbital path, and especially military developments in the U.S. It was a crude, expensive way to spy, but in the end, a highly effective one. Some of the cameras secreted on the Mir boasted the often-denied ability to photograph a pack of cigarettes in a person's pocket on Earth so closely, the brand name was easily read. These cameras, designs stolen directly from the

U.S., were still operational, much to the delight of Viktor's technical corps. By using them, the two men inside the Mir could literally look in on just about any operation currently taking place in North America, Europe and the Far East. All without anyone on the ground suspecting a thing.

The problem with all this though, was locating the Mir once the Zon was up in orbit, and then docking with it once it was found. With the shuttle navigation system not being at one hundred-percent, just tracking the space station was a major chore. Once it was located, the Zon had to catch up to it, raising or lowering in its already shaky orbital path to do so. Then, if this was accomplished, the docking procedure would pose major complications. Because the Zon's flight was skewed from the beginning, its tendency to wobble as it sped around the Earth at fifteen thousand, five hundred-plus mph increased with each orbit. This meant the two spacecraft could never actually link up. The whole idea was to get the Zon close enough to the Mir to allow someone to walk in space from one spacecraft to the other.

This was not always a successful procedure—they'd lost two men on the last flight trying to go from the Zon to the Mir. One had a tether line snap at the wrong moment; the other was killed by an electrical shock once he touched the main docking attachment on the space station. His death was due to incompetence however: the men inside the space station had forgotten to negative-ground everything before the transfer took place.

But it was very important that they link up with the Mir this time though—the two men inside had been cooped up for sixty-two days, with little water, food or personal comforts. Viktor and his technical people weren't so concerned about the Mir crewmen as for the photographs they'd been taking while marooned inside the space station. That was another problem with Viktor's low tech space program. The only way they could benefit from the high-flying spy station was to retrieve the photographs firsthand.

Viktor wasn't sure exactly when he got the message that someone in the main section of the Zon wanted to come over to the ICEM.

He was bent over his seat, trying again to guide a wavering line of individual cocaine crystals up into his nostrils, when his intercom buzzed twice. It was more luck than anything that he was able to reach the return intercom button. He just happened to be floating nearby when it went off.

He was his usual gruff self dealing with the man on the other end. Viktor did not allow his minions to speak to him directly in matters that weren't of the upmost urgency. Even when direct conversation was allowed, his underlings could not look him in the eye or speak more than three sentences without stopping and asking for permission to continue.

But he usually did talk to them on the radio. This one was telling him he had an urgent message which had to be delivered directly.

Viktor told him to come on over.

The act of transferring from the Zon, through the open cargo bay to the airlock on the ICEM was a ten-minute procedure. The person coming over had to climb into a spacesuit, get powered up, checked out, etc., then enter the egress chamber, where he would have to depressurize, open the hatch, crawl out into space, go hand over hand along sixteen supports, before reaching the ICEM hatchway. He would then have to go inside, pressurize the lock, depressurize his spacesuit and finally, step inside. One wrong move, anywhere along the line, would almost always prove fatal.

The man from the Zon went through these gyrations slowly but perfectly. He came through the ICEM airlock within twelve minutes of getting permission to come over. The first thing he saw when he removed his space helmet were a pair of tiny breasts floating by. He looked away almost immediately, a wise decision.

Viktor was strapped into his seat at the far end of the ICEM capsule, his long hair and beard rising almost surrealistically above his head. He was dressed as always, in a long flowing black gown topped by a flaming-red, knee-length vest. His face was heavily made-up. He looked particularly foolish, yet sinister at the same time. No surprise then that even among the lowest of his legions, Viktor's attire was described as a cross between an especially "colorful" bishop and a drag queen.

Viktor had somehow managed to corral another long line of floating cocaine and manipulate it up his nose. The two girls came wafting by him, they were locked in a breast-to-breast embrace now. He gave them the slightest push and they went spinning off again, arms and legs seemingly going in all directions at once.

Finally Viktor turned towards the man in the spacesuit. He was breathing very heavily, both from his long arduous, sixteen foot journey and from the fear anyone got when coming in direct contact with the devil himself.

Viktor sensed this right away, and put the appropriate scowl on his face: "Come forward and report!" he screamed at the man.

Shaking, the man immediately went to his knees and gave himself a little push. He quickly shot across the ICEM, arriving just three feet from Viktor's satin-slippered feet still in his kneeling position. It was a maneuver perfected by all of the men on the Zon, just in case they had to meet with the boss one on one.

But this particular crewman could barely breathe now—he had bad news to deliver, probably the worst circumstance in which to meet with his leader.

"Disturbing news, sir," the crewman began, his eyes zeroed in on Viktor's red shoes.

Viktor never looked at him—he was too busy watching the two girls fly right above his head, their crotches fused together.

"Continue . . ." he said finally.

"We have discovered the primary landing site at Star City has been fouled, sir," the crewman said, not moving a bit from his subservient position.

This did give Viktor a pause—though only a short one.

"Fouled?" he asked, authentically puzzled. "In what way?"

"An airplane has been scuttled at its center," the terrified crewman reported. "A large one—possibly an American cargo craft. Several large holes have also been blown into the middle of the strip. We cannot land under those conditions . . ."

The two young girls bounced off the top of the ICEM and came down right in front of Viktor's face. He tickled them both and sent them on their way again.

Then he turned his attention back to the prone crewman.

"So, get someone to repair the strip," he said simply.

The man bowed lower. "We cannot, sir," he whispered, absolutely petrified now. "The damage to the runway is so severe, we cannot fix it in time for our return. Plus . . ."

The man would stumble over the next few words—badly.

". . . plus, there is no one on hand to do the repairs,"

he finally spit out. "We know of the damage only through a routine photo pass. In fact we have not had any contact with anyone at Star City in nearly three days."

Again Viktor was forced to pay attention to the man.

"No contact?" he asked. "For three days?"

"It's true, sir," the man replied. "Apparently everyone left the city right after we launched, because . . ."

Viktor's foot suddenly came up under the crewman's jaw, kicking him hard. The next thing he knew, the crewman was face to face with Viktor, so close he could smell the man's perfume-like body odor.

". . . because?" Viktor sneered at him.

The crewman gulped hard. His life was beginning to flash before his eyes. "Because, according to the last confirmed radio transmission, there was a rumor . . . a story, really, or some kind of panicked intelligence report . . . that . . ."

Viktor's devilish grin turned to a scowl.

"Speak!" he shouted at the man.

"Because there was talk that . . . well, Hawk Hunter was seen in the area . . ."

The crewman was floating nose to nose with Viktor now. He was so frightened he believed he could feel the heat rising off Viktor's face.

"*Hawk Hunter?*" he asked in a whisper. "In Star City?"

"Yes, sir," the crewman croaked.

Viktor began to say something but stopped short.

Instead he pulled the girls close to him again, nibbled on their breasts and then let them go. This was his way of thinking.

"Well, if the runway is fouled," he whispered to the man finally. "Let us set down at one of the alternate sites. How many are available?"

Still shaking, the man reached inside his suit and handed Viktor a list.

"These are the secondary bases we can secure quickly," he told him. "I can leave this with you, and you can select."

Viktor took the list from the crewman and finally released him from the tip of his toe. The crewman immediately floated back down to the bottom of the ICEM.

After a few short moments, he looked up and gulped. "Will that be all, my lord?"

Viktor looked down at him, then up at the spinning girls.

"Not quite," he said.

With the wave of his hand, he brought the two girls down towards them. He whispered something into one girl's ear and then let them go again.

They both swam the length of the ICEM and descended before the mystified crewman. Soon they were running their hands up and down his neck, shoulders and pelvis. With Viktor's approving nod, they began unzipping the crewman's spacesuit, taking extra care to unleash the fasteners around his crotch area.

It took about three minutes to get it off him completely, the crewman being totally confused as to what was actually going on. Now standing in nothing more than a spaceman's version of long underwear, the girls began plunging their hands down his PHFP, the "personal hygiene flap panel." The crewman found himself floating backwards as their knowing fingers reached and squeezed his most sensitive of areas.

He'd heard much about sex in space—how it was supposed to be ten times as intense as back on Earth, a secret kept well hidden by NASA during the American shuttles' heyday. He was beginning to believe this was all true, when suddenly he saw Viktor raise his right hand. The girls immediately stopped squeezing him and slowly floated away. The crewman looked at Viktor, who was smiling devilishly.

"All right, that will be all," he told the man.

The crewman bowed deeply. "Yes, sir . . ." he said, still confused, but anxiously pulling himself towards his floating spacesuit.

"I said, *dismissed* . . ." Viktor roared at him.

The crewman froze in place—and gently floated to the ceiling.

"But sir . . . I must get into my . . ."

Viktor just stared at him.

The crewman's eyes grew wide with fear.

"Sir . . . I need my suit to go back out . . ."

Viktor was slowly shaking his head side to side. The girls both let out a gasp.

"Dismissed . . ." Viktor said again.

The man began to cry. Slowly he drifted back to the airlock. With trembling hands, he yanked the hatch back and put one foot inside.

Then he turned back to Viktor—tears flowing off his face and into the perfume-saturated cabin atmosphere.

"Mercy, sir?" he asked, all life gone out of his voice. "I am needed to run things in the main ship . . ."

Viktor never stopped smiling. "Yes, well, just call me when you get back over there . . ."

With that he began spinning the girls again.

Having no other choice, the man stepped fully into the airlock now and with his last living movements, pulled the door shut and soiled himself at the same time. A moment later, Viktor and the girls heard a huge whooshing sound as the forward airlock door was opened and the crewman was sucked out unprotected into the airless void of space. Oddly the sound was very reminiscent of a toilet being flushed.

Viktor sat back and spun the two girls away from him again.

"Sounds like they've finally corrected their plumbing problem over there," he said, with a laugh.

# Fifteen

*The Island Of Malta*

It was just after dusk had fallen when the air raid sirens began wailing again above the city of Valletta.

The citizens of the small capital city of Malta almost routinely scrambled for the nearest bomb shelters now. As always, the women were frightened and the children crying. Members of the Malta Self-Defense Forces were racing through the streets, hustling stray civilians into the dozens of safety dugouts lining the main streets of the city, then pressing on to their battle stations along the ring of AA sites surrounding the embattled capital.

The bombers appeared overhead about a minute later. This was the fifth raid today and still, the Maltese military didn't know who these attackers were, where they were coming from, or why they were bombing their small, island-state. Sheer location had put Malta in harm's way for literally thousands of years; its population had endured bombings of all types and sizes over the millennium, but usually they knew who wanted to kill them and why.

This time though, they didn't have any idea.

The bombers themselves offered few clues as to the identity of the people flying them. There were twelve aerial attackers this time. They were Tu-95 Bears, old Soviet-built monsters whose sole claim to fame was endurance;

more than anything else, Bears were known for their ability to stay in the air for up to sixteen hours at a time, without refueling.

Spread out into chevrons of three each, six of them flew right over the center of Valletta itself, dropping tons of high explosive and incendiary bombs indiscriminately on military and civilian targets alike. The return fire from the network of AA guns located throughout the city were quickly at full-roar—but a combination of the Tu-95s' speed and height made it almost impossible to draw a bead on them. Even worse, the six other bombers taking part in the attack had fired a spread of AA-56 radar-homing missiles at the main AA defense battery just south of the city, destroying it utterly and killing most of its crew.

The first six bombers were thus able to dump their weapons loads and get away scot-free. No sooner had they departed over the southern horizon, when the second wave turned towards the city. At this point, Valletta's air defense unit took to the sky. Roaring mightily off Valletta airport's extra-long runway, they rose for the fifth time of the day to meet the mysterious attackers head-on. The problem was the city's meager air force totaled exactly three airplanes, none of which was built to perform as a jet fighter. Two were CASA C-101 Aviojets, airplanes actually built as unarmed trainers. The third plane was an ancient A-7 Corsair, a reliable little machine that was nevertheless designed as a ground attack bomber, not an interceptor.

Rising high over the airport, the three jets valiantly made a straight line for the oncoming Bears. Each plane was armed, but just barely. The A-7 was carrying a nose-mounted cannon, normally used for ground strafing; the trouble was, it had taken part in four previous interceptions today and was so low on cannon rounds, it had enough for one pass, no more. Even worse, the Avio trainers were sprouting lowly .35 caliber machine guns, the likes of which hadn't been seen on any airplane of import since the 1950s.

Though outgunned, the three jets attacked the formation of Bears with ruthless, almost insane abandon. The trainers went in first, trying to force their relatively weak shells into some crucial part of one of the bombers, hoping a lucky hit might damage the attacker, kill its pilots and even bring it down.

But this was wishful thinking—and everyone involved, from the fighter pilots, to the people inside the bombers to the people watching it from the ground knew it. The Bears were going way too fast for any of the puny machine gun fire to do any good. The trainers both made one long pass, but by the time they'd pulled up to roll over to start another, the second wave of Bears was already dropping its bombs.

This was when the A-7 arrived. With its more powerful but nearly depleted gun, its pilot, an Italian mercenary, aimed for the lead bomber, opening up with his cannon at less than one hundred yards. It was a brave but ultimately fatal thing for him to do. The cannon shells—all thirty-five of them—found a target in the cockpit of the Bear, they killed the airplane's copilot outright, and mortally wounded two of the gunners. But in keeping his plane steady in order to make every shot count, the A-7 pilot dangerously exposed himself to the lethal rear guns of the Bears flanking the leader.

These weapons were cannons, too, and they had no shortage of ammunition. Two converging streams of fire caught the A-7 right across its tail, blowing off its pipe and rear stabilizers. The little jet went nose over, half its fuselage blown away. It came down right in the middle of the city, plowing into a building that moments before had been hit with a string of bombs from the attackers. The A-7's explosion only added to the growing carnage. The bomber, less its copilot and two gunners, continued on its bombing run, then banked hard left and quickly flew away.

Within two minutes, all twelve attackers had disappeared over the horizon.

The all-clear sirens blared about five minutes later, and once again, the citizens of Valletta emerged from their shelters to see their beautiful city had been further reduced to rubble by the brutal, mysterious enemy. It was clear almost immediately that this bombing had been particularly devastating: the city's main market place had simply vanished. The main power station had also been hit, as had the island's desalinization plant, a place where nearly eighty-percent of the fresh water on Malta was processed. The main road heading into the city had also been cut in a dozen places, and the main fire station was itself ablaze.

The weary citizens stood in shock and horror as they watched the flames above their city rise higher into the night, knowing they had no means of fighting them anymore. The proud city could not withstand much more of this. In one day, nearly two-thirds of Valletta had been reduced to ruins.

Now, as the Maltese made their way back to their houses, praying that they were still standing, they heard the blare of air raid sirens again. Many thought it was some kind of malfunction at first. The bombing raids had been interspersed by at least two hours throughout this long, tragic day. No one could believe the bombers were coming back again so soon.

But they were. Way out on the western horizon, another half dozen Bears appeared. Their engines going full out, their noses were aimed right for the heart of the burning city. The remaining two airplanes of the city's air force had already landed—they were both low on fuel and there was no way they could gas up and take off to counter this new threat. Even the exhausted AA teams were nearly too weary to load and fire their guns again.

It appeared that this raid might deal the killing blow to the crippled city.

But then, appearances could be deceiving.

All the city's civilians were quickly shoved back inside their bomb shelters, so only the remaining defense forces saw what happened next.

The six Tu-95s were painted in dark blue sea camouflage this time. They were coming out of the west, right out of the last of the setting sun, the shiny tips of the forward nacelles gleaming in the fading, golden light. As always they were flying in two chevrons of three apiece. As always, their bomb bays were filled with HE and incendiaries.

No one saw anything strange at first. The AA crews on the western edge of town, those protecting the airport, were the closest to the action—and they saw only a single, bright flash. The next thing they knew, one of the Bear bombers was going down. Its engines screamed wildly all the way to the ground—one mile, straight down, ending with a mighty crash on the city airport's main runway about two thousand meters from the forward AA position.

The gun crews had no idea what had happened. It was almost as if they had shot down the huge bomber themselves, yet they had not fired their gun. Nor had any of the AA batteries in the area. Maybe one of the bomber's weapons went off prematurely inside the bomb bay.

Or maybe it was something else.

The five remaining Bears continued on, slowing their speed to two hundred knots and assuming their predrop profiles. Suddenly, there was another flash; the air rumbled with another huge shock wave a second later. At that instant, the Bears were passing through a particularly thick pall of smoke rising from previous bomb damage. It was as high and dense as thundercloud cumulus. Many witnesses saw all five Bears go into this man-made over-cast—only four came out.

The second huge Bear fell out of the sky five seconds later, crashing into the center of the airport's longest airstrip, its west-to-east runway, skidding along the ground and slamming into a large nearby docking facility. The resulting explosion was so tremendous, it threw a mushroom cloud of both smoke and steam high above Valletta's west beaches.

Now the AA batteries all around the city opened up. The four remaining bombers pressed on; their only reaction to losing two of their monstrous colleagues was to spread out their formation slightly. The rear gunners on two of them were firing their weapons—the tracer rounds lit up the darkening sky. But what were they shooting at? As far as anyone on the ground could tell, the sky was empty except for the four oncoming bombers.

The lead Bear was crossing over the last beach and was now pointed straight towards the center of the city, the last major section that had yet to be burned. Suddenly this airplane veered sharply to the right; again the turbulent air was filled with the screams of four huge turboprop engines. The Bear nearly tipped over; only at the last moment did the bomber's pilot somehow recover flight and yank the big plane back to level.

But just as quickly, it began to go over again—and this time the pilot could not recover. The plane flipped on to its right wing, blowing out both engines and hideously bending the tail. It skidded about a half mile to its right before inverting and plunging into the sea. There was no explosion this time, no violent eruption of smoke or steam. The airplane simply went into the sea and sank, a quick, frightening death.

A few seconds later, fire crews in the middle of town saw a very strange airplane pass over. It was very low and both its engines were smoking mightily. Its tail section was in tatters, not from being shot out, but from the effects of the incredible strain put on the airframe. The plane itself was almost unidentifiable; strange things were hanging from beneath its wings; they, too, were broken and in pieces. But those who saw it best—an AA crew situated on top of Valletta's city hall—would later say they were sure the strange aircraft was actually a large seaplane.

There were only three bombers left now—and they turned away, abandoning their bombing runs and passing over the burning city without dropping anything except their extra fuel in order to make an even faster getaway.

Not a minute later, everything was quiet again. The skies above Valletta were empty and only the smoke and flames from below were blocking out what was left of the brilliant sunset.


The commander of the Malta Self-Defense Forces was a man named Doomsa Baldi.

A large individual with an all-black camo suit and a wild head of hair stuffed underneath an antique-looking World War One helmet, he was sifting through the wreckage of what was left of his headquarters when he got the message that a strange plane had landed nearby.

It was just a few minutes after the aborted bombing raid and Baldi's first thought was that one of the attackers had landed at the city's huge airport, perhaps to surrender. But two of the bombers had crashed at the airport—its extra-long runway was now quite unusable.

"An airplane has landed?" he asked the young officer who'd brought him the report. "Where? How?"

"Down on the west beach," the officer replied. "The pilot says he's an old friend of yours."

Baldi was out of the wreckage and into the officer's jeep in a matter of seconds. They drove like madmen through the chaotic burning streets, passing many knots of confused citizens, who were both relieved and curious as to why no bombs fell onto their city this time. By the time they reached the beach, there was already a crowd of soldiers, medical personnel and civilians mulling around by the shoreline.

Baldi's driver practically drove a wedge into them. Quickly, he pulled up to the edge of the water.

That's when Baldi saw the seaplane.

It was bobbing around about thirty-five meters offshore. It appeared to be in such bad shape, he couldn't believe the thing had ever been airborne, never mind landed here. Its wings were bent and broken, its tail section was all but gone. The engines had taken so much strain and had run so hot, they looked like they were melting. Every window in the plane was either shattered or blown out completely.

A small door at the rear of the airplane had popped open and eventually two figures climbed out. The tide was going out and it was an easy walk for the two to make to the shore. Baldi was out in front of the crowd now, squinting through the rising night fog and the leftover smoke, trying to see just who was claiming to be an old friend of his.

Oddly the crowd recognized Hunter before Baldi did. First there was a collective gasp from both soldiers and civilians. Then the crowd broke out into a spontaneous cheer. This was no ordinary pilot who had taken on the force of bombers with the battered seaplane—this was the best pilot in the world.

The Wingman himself had saved their city from further destruction.

And he was an old friend of Commander Baldi. Three years before, Hunter and the crew of the disabled aircraft carrier USS *Saratoga* had stopped over at Malta on their way to the Suez Canal to thwart Viktor's planned invasion of the eastern Mediterranean.

Now they greeted each other warmly, Baldi putting a bone-crushing hug on Hunter. The Maltese commander couldn't believe he was really here, in the flesh. He pointed at the seaplane and then towards the airport where two of the enemy bombers were still burning fiercely.

"You?" Baldi gasped. *"How . . . ?"*

Hunter just shrugged and offered a quick explanation of what happens when one airplane disrupts the airflow in front of another. If the turbulence catches the second airplane just right, that airplane will go into a stall and most likely crash.

"It's simple, when you really get down to it," he concluded.

But Baldi wasn't listening—not really anyway. Neither was anyone in the crowd of civilians or the band of soldiers standing at the water's edge. Bombers, bombing, and why planes crash were suddenly secondary to them now.

They were all too busy looking at Chloe.

# Sixteen

Night fell somewhat peacefully on the burning city of Valletta.

Most of the major fires were out by eight P.M.; most of the injured were attended to by nine. Soup lines had been set up in the middle of the main square, an almost-festive attempt to get a hot meal into the battered civilians and weary defenders before the deepest chill of night arrived. Extra ammunition was dispersed to the outlying AA batteries; fresh crews were moved up, too.

Inside a tavern next to the bombed-out headquarters of the Malta Defense Forces, Hunter sat with Baldi and several officers and guards from his command staff. They were all slurping from vast bowls of soup, taken right off the line just outside. The only executive privilege Baldi was able to finagle was a flask of red wine. Each man had a huge cup of this *vino* in front of him.

Hunter and Baldi reminisced about their brief, but adventurous meeting several years before. Then Hunter spoke about what he'd been up to since they'd last met. Many of his exploits were known to Baldi already; tales of the Wingman still went around the world on a regular basis. Still the Maltese commander enjoyed listening to the inside dope right from the lips of the man himself.

Of course, they were all curious as to what had brought Hunter back to Malta.

Though he trusted Baldi and his men completely,

Hunter gave them an intentionally obscure explanation as to how he came to find himself on the picturesque Mediterranean island via the Swiss Alps. "A secret mission to St. Moritz" was the extent to what he told them. His aim was not to mislead, rather he didn't want to jinx the plan he'd started conjuring up on top of Point Zero. It was much too early for him to reveal all its elements, even to himself.

"It's been a very peaceful time here, surprisingly," Baldi told him of the last three years on Malta. "Lots of stuff has been going on around us. Big civil war in Italy. Fighting up around Palermo. And then there's a situation down in Tunisia. But here, they leave us alone. Thanks to you and your British friends, that is. Your reputation remained behind long after you sailed away. It's protected us, ever since . . ."

Hunter nearly snorted in his soup. He eyed the smoldering buildings right outside.

"Well, it ran out damn quick, didn't it?"

Baldi just shook his head. "This is a complete mystery to us," he said. "The bombers showed up at six in the morning and came over four more times after that. We knew they were mercenaries right away—we just didn't know who they were working for. And still don't. They didn't seem so intent on destroying the city as they were at making it burn. There was a real terror element to it."

"Any other suspicious activity around lately?" he asked Baldi. "Any spy planes flying over? Black ships offshore?"

Baldi shook his head firmly no.

"Our air force is weak but they do an excellent job watching everything around us," he said. "If someone was sizing us up, for invasion or whatever, we would have known about it. This, this firebombing, came right out of the blue."

Hunter put his soup and wine aside, and using the dust recently settled on the table, drew a crude but exactly scaled map of the region. He drew a series of faint concentric circles emanating out from Valletta, the center of this dusty universe.

"There's only a finite number of places they could have come from," Hunter told the soldiers as they gathered around. "Those Bears can fly halfway around the world, but not if they're carrying bomb loads as big as those planes were. Plus, I saw them dumping fuel up there—they wouldn't do that if they had to fly anywhere a long distance from here."

Baldi studied the map. "Maybe they came down from Sicily," he offered. "From Syracuse or Gela. There are huge merc bases up there, or so they say. Or maybe they came from the east, from Greece. I hear that a number of freelancers are also working out of Zakinthos these days. But even if we knew where they came from—we still don't know why . . ."

Hunter returned to his soup, his mind flashing options at the speed of light. He had a theory as to why the Bears had been hired to bomb Malta. They weren't looking to invade, or extract some kind of retribution or blood money from the tiny island-state.

He believed they wanted something else, and that's exactly why he'd headed straight for Malta in the first place.

He finished his soup and then drained his cup of wine. Then he looked up at Baldi and his men.

"I think we should go over and look at the airport," he told them.

Two blocks away, inside one of the few buildings that had not been damaged in the bombing raids, Chloe was sipping a cup of minestrone.

The house belonged to a girl named Gin. She was Baldi's niece, the daughter of his younger brother. As soon as Chloe arrived down on the beach, Baldi suggested that she be brought to Gin's, where she could wash up, get some new clothes and recover from her grueling day. Chloe gratefully accepted the invitation. As an additional gesture, the Maltese commander also assigned a squad of his best troops to escort her to his niece's house and watch over her while she was there.

These soldiers were now loosely dispersed around the outside of the building. Chloe was up on the second floor, sitting in Gin's kitchen, nursing the mug of cold soup. Gin had been very sweet to her so far. She was friendly and possessed a deep Mediterranean beauty. They were both about the same age and same build, though Gin's breasts were slightly smaller than Chloe's. She had lent Chloe a white cotton dress. It was homemade and fit perfectly, except around the bodice where Chloe's ample breasts tended to pop through the top.

Even though Gin had been put off at first after hearing about all the attention Chloe had received when she arrived down on the beach, they'd become instant friends, as all girls their age seemed to have an ability to do. They'd talked while Chloe bathed and climbed into her borrowed clothes, and the chat had continued nonstop as they ate the spare but nutritious meal.

Still, Chloe knew that Gin was terribly worried—her fiancé was one of the city's defenders, an officer assigned to an outlying AA crew. Gin had not heard from him since the bombing raids started early that morning. She *had* heard reports that some of the AA crews had been hit with antiradar missiles and that there were casualties at some of the posts. She was terrified that her boyfriend might have been among those killed.

So it was a joyous occasion when he suddenly walked through the door, slightly burned, dirty and sporting a large bump on his head, but all in all in good shape.

Gin was immediately reduced to tears as she leaped into his arms and flooded him with kisses. He responded in kind—he'd been worried all day that she, too, had been killed in the bombing raids. Now they were together again.

Still embracing, still kissing, they moved across the kitchen and onto the small couch just off the pantry. Gin's boyfriend, Gozo, was overcome with relief now. He was pleading with Gin to marry him, quickly, tonight even, so they could at last be joined for eternity. Gin was much too emotional to reply; she was still sobbing and hugging him tightly even as her dress was slipping off her shoulders.

Somewhere an explosion went off—it came from a few blocks away, probably a previously unexploded bomb. It shook the building slightly, but made absolutely no impression on Gozo and Gin. They continued kissing each other lustily, shouting declarations of love back and forth with increasing gusto. Quite quickly these professions of love turned amorous. Gozo ripped away what was left of Gin's blouse; she pulled his service shirt from him. Gozo undid her belt and tossed her skirt aside; Gin yanked Gozo's trousers to his ankles.

Both of them were panting now, rocking back and forth on the couch, completely caught up in their happy, sexual moment. Gin was now pleading with Gozo to make love to her even as he was asking her permission to do so.

"I don't know how I could love you more!" Gozo shouted to her.

"No, I don't know how *I* could show *you!*" she groaned in reply.

With that, they both tore away what was left of their underwear and began the final approach. But suddenly, they were aware of someone standing over them.

It was Chloe. She was naked and panting, too.

"Excuse me," she said breathlessly. "May I make a suggestion?"

\* \* \*

Both Bear bombers were still aflame by the time Hunter, Baldi and a contingent of MDF security troops reached the airport.

The expansive field, once operated by the RAF, had been cordoned off shortly after the two enemy airplanes came down. Hunter, Baldi and six special policemen would be the first then to examine the wreckage.

It was not a small part of his dream that came back to Hunter as he stepped from Baldi's jeep and walked slowly towards the crumpled back of the first Bear bomber. He almost had to laugh. The Bear had been designed in the late forties; the Heinkel 111 of his dream in the mid-to-late-thirties.

Only off by a decade or so, he thought.

The rear gunner was still inside his weapons capsule, strapped in and bleeding, his neck broken. The midsection of the monstrous airplane had all but burned away. Through its skeleton, Hunter could see a rack full of unexploded bombs and two more horribly burned bodies. He climbed over the twisted left wing, taking special note of the buckled jet-prop blades—this was evidence of the strain put on the massive engines as they unsuccessfully tried to regain level flight after Hunter had flown the seaplane so close to them he'd disrupted their forward airflow.

He climbed down from the wing and up to the crumpled cockpit. Both pilots were still strapped into their seats, huge fatal gashes cut out of their chests. The bodies of the four remaining crewmen were all lying on the runway nearby. They, too, were burned and horribly wounded, but they had all managed to get out of the airplane before expiring. The way they were lined up, it appeared as if they'd tried to crawl off towards the lights of the city, as if they believed they'd be able to find refuge there. Very odd. . . .

The front of the blue Tu-95 was painted in a garish

application of nose art. It was practically impossible to understand what all the graffiti-like swirls and nonsensical lettering meant, but below this Day-Glo mess was one word written in decipherable English. It was the plane's nickname: *Pterodactyl.*

Baldi threw up a security ring around the downed bomber, then walked up beside Hunter.

"So, where did it come from, Hawk?"

Hunter shrugged a little, then said: "Let's try to find out."

They walked over to the right outboard engine. Of the four, this one had been damaged the least. He reached deep inside its cowling and took a finger's worth of grease from the back of the lower turbo-charger. Pulling it out, he examined it briefly by the light of the smoldering fire and then put it to his tongue.

"This plane flew about an hour to get here," he declared. "Seventy minutes tops. I'd say, taking into account time to take off, form up, and then fly here, they came from about a hundred miles away."

Baldi was shaking his head.

"That proves it," he said. "They came down from Sicily. From Syracuse."

They drove up to the second wreck and did another quick but thorough inspection.

Hunter's findings here only confirmed his previous guess. The planes were definitely mercenary craft and they had definitely come from someplace nearby. This was very important information for him—and for the plan he was formulating.

"So, now we know where," Baldi said as they finished looking over the second crashed jet. "But what about the 'why'?"

"I think I know why," Hunter told him starkly.

He stepped away from the wrecked jet and looked down the extra-long runway. If his memory served him,

Malta at one time had served as an RAF refueling base as well as one for heavy bombers. As such, its runways were extra long—the main one was nearly three miles in length, with a vast expanse of flat, hard, sand and rock bordering both ends. It was certainly big enough to handle the heaviest bombers the RAF ever employed.

It was also big enough to land a space shuttle.

That's when he pulled Baldi aside and told him everything. Star City. St. Moritz. Point Zero. The Zon going over—and his guess as to when it would be coming down.

"They wanted to land here," he told Baldi. "They wanted to burn you out first, and then come in and take over."

Baldi stared back at him, his expression turning from one of astonishment, to confusion, and finally anger.

"They wanted to kill all my people just so they could land their spaceship here?"

Hunter nodded solemnly. "They'd bring it down, hold the city until a heavy-lift aircraft could get in here, and then take it out piggyback. They would have probably come and gone in forty-eight hours, maybe less."

Baldi was absolutely fuming.

"Those bastards," he cursed, angrily taking off his helmet. It attacked all of his sensibilities that he, his people and his country, would be used, abused and wiped out simply so some madman could land his trophy spacecraft.

He looked back towards the city of Valletta, columns of smoke still rising above it.

"I will find the person responsible for this and kill him," he vowed, his teeth clenched, his words seething.

Hunter clapped him on the back, calming him down a bit.

"We'll both find him, my friend," he said.

* * *

The first place Hunter went when he returned to town was the house belonging to Gin, Baldi's niece.

He was surprised when they rolled up in front of the place and found the squad of soldiers left behind were nowhere in sight. Sitting behind the wheel of the jeep, Baldi's weapon was out in a flash—he suspected something was afoul.

But Hunter indicated the MDF leader could put his weapon away. There was trouble, all right—but not the kind that Baldi suspected.

Hunter asked his friend to remain in the jeep while he climbed out and bounced up the stairs to Gin's second floor living area. He came upon three of the guards sitting on the steps, casually smoking cigarettes and jiving with each other.

They froze at the sight of him, like kids caught playing hooky. He dispelled their concerns with one wave of his hand. He had no complaint with them. If what he suspected was actually going on, well, he couldn't really blame them for leaving their posts.

He climbed up the last set of stairs where he found three more of the guards standing next to a recently painted green door. They were not smoking, nor were they joshing with each other. They were obviously waiting to go inside the apartment, the place where Gin, Gozo and Chloe were. All soldiers seemed tense, though not in an uncomfortable way. *Anxious* was more like it.

Like their colleagues, they, too, froze at the sight of Hunter bounding up the creaky wooden steps. One look at him and they knew that *he* knew exactly what was going on behind the green door. A wave of disappointment washed across all three of them. It was like a large bubble had burst. Sullenly but quickly, they left, slinking down the stairs, grumbling at the bad timing of the situation.

Hunter went through the green door a moment later—and found exactly what he thought he would find.

The other four guards were inside; as was Gin, her boy-friend and, of course, Chloe. She was lying on the couch near the pantry, naked and sweaty. Gin was sitting beside her, clinging to her exhausted Gozo, both collapsed into a deep sleep.

The four soldiers were all in some sort of undress. One was completely pantless, the three others were wearing underwear, moist though it was. Chloe looked simply en-raptured. She was writhing around on the couch, alter-nately hugging Gin and the guards. The smell of the place told of heavy, recent lovemaking.

Everyone turned towards Hunter as he came in through the door. At first they all greeted him loudly—but again, one look in his eyes and they all very quickly knew it was time to go. The soldiers departed, one at a time, all of them waiting until they were outside to climb back into their clothes.

Once they were gone, Hunter slowly walked over to the couch and took a long gaze at Chloe. She was upside down, smiling innocently up at him. On the floor in front of her was a battalion of used condoms. Gin was awake and looking up at Hunter, too, but she could see he was less than approving of what he'd walked in on.

With much effort, she was able to rouse Gozo and drag him from the room, closing the green door behind them.

Now it was just Hunter and Chloe.

She turned right side up and giggled.

"Well, what do you think of all this? Cool, huh?"

Hunter started to say something but caught himself at the last moment. Once again, he was tongue-tied. *What could he say to her?*

He took off his helmet, unstrapped his ammo belt and rifle. Then he sat down next to her and ran his hands over his suddenly tired face and head.

"What's the matter?" she asked him, authentically puz-zled. "Did I do something wrong?"

He looked over at her—the beautiful face, the naked wet body. But still, he remained silent.

She was growing concerned now. She reached up and grabbed him tightly.

"Tell me, please, Hawk," she pleaded with him. "What's the matter? *Did I do something wrong?*"

But all Hunter could do was stare back at her.

"I don't know," he finally managed to croak. "I *really* don't know . . ."

# Seventeen

These days it was called *Siracusa*.

Located on the southeast coast of Sicily, it was an opulent, seaside paradise, lorded over by members of the most prominent crime families in postwar Europe.

These characters had turned Siracusa into a mercenary's dream. An entire city filled with barrooms, eateries, gambling halls, and brothels. Everyone had money, and anyone who didn't, could earn some real quick. No less than seven armies—a total of twenty-one divisions—of hired soldiers were encamped around the city, most of them up in the hills to the north. A large, ever-changing mercenary fleet of warships—destroyers, minesweepers, fast-attack boats—were crowded inside the protected harbor. The officer corps for all this lived in the villas and grand hotels lining the main boulevards of the city.

The centerpiece of this corporate-warrior heaven was located ten miles to the west, in a place known appropriately enough as *Vallo del Mazzio Corleone*. To say this place was an airport was like saying the Mediterranean was a puddle. There were no less than thirty-two runways, six control towers, fifty miles of taxiways and more than two hundred hangars and maintenance barns, both big and small. The fuel depot alone covered nearly a half-mile square. The ammunition bunker was nearly as big.

The business at Vallo del Mazzio Corleone was aerial bombardment. Strategic, tactical, sneak attack, fire bombing—the planes at Vallo del Mazzio Corleone, or more simply "Vallo Mazz," could do it all. There were more than eight hundred bombers operating out of Vallo Mazz at any given moment. The main fleet line was made up of two hundred thirty reconditioned Tu-95 Bear bombers, the same prop-jet powerhouses that had bombed Malta the day before. Second-of-the-line were one hundred slightly smaller Bison bombers, they, like the Bears, being of early-Soviet design, There was also a similar number of Xian H-6s, Chinese-built rip-offs of the Russian Tu-16 bomber.

For special high-priority operations, the corporation at Vallo Mazz had fifty-five high tech, swing-wing Backfire bombers, backed up by twice as many Mirage IVAs. The rest of the fleet consisted of Tu-22 Blinders, several old South African Vulcans, and three squadrons of old prop medium-size attack bombers, including B-25s, B-26s and a handful of Transail C-160s, converted into gunships.

Getting into this monstrous air facility meant running a gauntlet of guardposts and checkpoints. A sign at the main access gate, written in more than a dozen languages, blared the official name of the place: WORLDWIDE LONG DISTANCE BOMBING, INC. Underneath this was scrolled: ASK ABOUT OUR ONE-WAY PACKAGES. Below that a disclaimer which read: NUCLEAR WEAPONS NOT ALLOWED BEYOND THIS POINT. As a joke, someone had faintly painted over the word "not." Those in the know would tell you it was the more accurate interpretation of the caveat.

In the middle of the air base was a large, conical-shaped building which served as both the main operations center and a debauchery palace. There was a party of some sort going on here pretty much nonstop, the ebb and flow of which depended on the time of day. Usually the later the hour, the more intense the party.

It was no different this night. The sin palace was lit up

from top to bottom, packed with aerial mercs, officers, businessmen and hookers. The occasion this evening was the more or less surprise appearance by the despot who ran this vast aerial kingdom. He was a man of indeterminate national origin, big, fat, slobby, a drunkard, and totally disrespectful of human life. He was known to all simply as the *Aero Commandante,* "the Wing Commander."

The immense-bellied individual wore the uniform of an air force brigadier general, but just like everything he did, the uniform was a fraud. The Wing Commander had never piloted an airplane; he didn't even like riding in them. They were simply tools to provide him with the gorging of his gross existence: the bombers brought him immense pots of revenue, the cargo planes brought him drug shipments, crates of pornographic films and, when the mood struck him, young hookers.

But of all the Wing Commander's bad traits, he was most noted for, and hated because, he was a thief. The majority of what had made him rich had been stolen from others; he'd much rather steal something than buy it. It was easier, cheaper and in the end, more enjoyable that way. But the Wing Commander was petty, too, some would say pathologically so.

Though a billionaire several times over, he was known to steal change off the palace bar, the pittance of money left behind as tips for the help.

The party was reaching its peak just around midnight when she walked through the door.

Everything stopped.

There were several hundred of the Wing Commander's closest friends in attendance, with twice as many call girls, and every one of them fell silent when the girl appeared.

She was dressed in a skintight red minidress, white high heels, and nothing more. Her blond hair was teased madly in the style of the moment. Pink lipstick, pink nails, pink blush on her bosom. She was a vision of *au courant* beauty. Anyone's best guess would put her age at barely eighteen.

She walked through the crowd of awed men and women, every last one of them wondering what it would be like to get her in bed. Past the main dining table, past the massive bar, right up into the slightly raised "private" section where the Wing Commander entertained his most-special guests. There was hardly a word spoken, hardly a sound at all, except for the roar of bombers taking off in the distance.

The beautiful young girl walked right up to the Wing Commander himself, stopped, looked at him, shook her body a little and then smiled.

"Hello," she said. "My name is Chloe."

More than four miles away, at the other end of the vast air base, a Tu-95 Bear was being readied for a bombing job up in the Spanish Pyrenees.

As usual, the huge, swept-wing, prop-jet bomber was loaded with ten thousand pounds of fuel and fifteen thousand pounds of bombs. The target for tonight was an anonymous military staging area and a town nearby, so the mix of weapons ranged from heavy iron bombs to incendiaries.

As part of the prep process, the Bear was washed down thoroughly. This was done to remove its thin layer of salt dust, but also to allow the bomber's wild paint scheme to shine through. This particular plane was done in a somber black fuselage, wing and tail, with a horrendously realistic painting of the Grim Reaper on its belly and nose, the arms of which extended all the way back to the tips of its wings. The message of the mural was clear—anyone looking up at this airplane would more often than not be meeting his death very soon thereafter. Indeed this was the last thing literally hundreds of people had seen in their lifetimes. Men, women, children, bombed by a painted-up airplane, driven by a crew who valued money over life and were confused by people who didn't.

The ground crew consisted of more than twenty individuals, including weapons specialists, fuelers, washers and avionic masters. They completed their work in under thirty minutes. Once the plane was ready, it was left to the hands of its crew, two pilots, a bombardier, and three gunners. They strapped in without incident and began taxiing the huge bomber across the tarmac towards the east-west junction of runways, where eighteen more bombers were also forming up for takeoff.

As soon as the Bear was wheeled out of the prep area, a low-level Bison attack bomber was rolled in. Therefore, no one in the ground crew saw the big Bear stop momentarily about a half mile away from the prep area; nor did anyone see the six unconscious bodies drop out of the forward belly access hatch to the hard runway below. Though seemingly empty at this point, the Bear nevertheless jerked forward a few moments later, its huge wheels just missing the heads of the knocked-out crew members.

It continued down the taxiway, joining even more bombers getting ready to launch for missions all over Europe, Asia and northern Africa. It finally came to a halt about a quarter mile away from the east-west junction, taking its place at the end of a long line of bombers waiting to take off.

Because of the jam-up, it would take the Tu-95 known as *Death From Above* more than ten minutes to reach the runway it had been assigned to this night.

Meanwhile, back at the sin palace, the Wing Commander had just ordered ten crates of his best champagne opened.

To the party regulars, this was an almost frightening occasion. For the WC to so openly share his purloined bottles of *Château de la Feete* 1985 defied reality. This was not like him. A man who stole from his servants would hardly pass around bottles of such rare and high-priced bubbly if he was thinking rationally.

But that was just it—the Wing Commander wasn't thinking rationally; in fact he wasn't thinking at all. He was hypnotized, mesmerized, fallen deeply under the spell of the young girl in the red minidress who claimed her name was Chloe.

It was the Wing Commander's personal bodyguards who were most alarmed at this strange turn of events. They'd steered their boss clear of many a harlot in recent times, but even they had to admit that this one was different. They could hardly take their eyes off her themselves. This all translated into trouble; they suspected the woman's sudden appearance was a prelude to something catastrophic. To a man, each one checked his weapon's ammo load. They expected trouble was not too far ahead.

Still, fearless as they were, no one in the squad of hired goons dared suggest to the Wing Commander that he might turn a blind eye towards the enrapturing female. She was now ensconced so tightly on his lap that it would have taken a platoon of them to wrench her free. She was whispering nonstop into the WC's ear, and when he was able to catch enough breath to do so, he was whispering back into hers. This would always be followed by a round of giggling and snorting.

It was a grand embarrassing display for the man who ran the largest aerial bombardment company in history, but the witnesses didn't really care: they were drinking great champagne and watching the patron saint of all strumpets do her stuff. In their world, it was all damn entertaining.

It went on like this for about twenty minutes or so.

Then the girl began a long, nonstop whisper in the WC's ear, one that had him rising off his seat an inch at a time. Just what she was promising him, no one but she and the WC knew. But it was enough for the Boss to snap his fingers twice.

He wanted his car brought around immediately.

Meanwhile, the traffic jam of bombers lined up around the east-west junction had doubled.

It was certainly a popular place. Any airplane leaving for a target east and south of Vallo Mazz was usually directed here for the most efficient takeoff. No less than four dozen bombers were waiting for takeoff clearances now, mostly Bears and Bisons, but with a handful of Backfires and Mirages mixed in, too. All of them were sitting stone-still, practically wingtip-to-wingtip, their engines screaming angrily, a cloud of exhaust rising above.

Some kind of congestion resulted here most every night; but tonight, the jam-up was worse than usual. This was because a report had just been flashed to all waiting bombers that the WC was on the field, an unusual condition known as "Zebra-Flat." No airplane could take off or land while the WC was about, due to an old order demanded by his security forces, and supposedly reserved only in cases of "extreme egress emergencies." In other words, if a nuclear missile was incoming, then the WC had to be the first one in line to get out.

Now some of the pilots in some of the waiting bombers wondered if in fact a nuke strike was on its way. It wasn't like the operations at Vallo Mazz hadn't made any enemies. But others, those with an unofficial ear into the sin palace, knew better. They knew that the WC and his latest female conquest were out riding in his staff car. The WC was very drunk and the girl was very beautiful. This kind of episode was not new, though rarely did the inside report comment on the attractiveness of the WC's current victim.

So the four squadrons of heavy jet bombers waited, falling behind their schedules with each passing minute. Some had to adjust their flight plans; others were already taking on extra fuel as they waited, preferring, as all pilots do, to have their gas tanks topped off upon launch. For the crews waiting in planes contracted to bomb some unknown target thousands of miles away, the delay added unneeded minutes to what were already ball-bustingly long missions. If bad vibes and engine noise could kill, the WC would have been microroasted by now.

At the moment though he was anything but. He was sitting in the back of his Benz 414SL, a four-door special sedan of Germany's Shickelgruber Era. The WC's trusted driver, a man named Lars, was piloting the ostentatious vehicle. Chloe was painted into the WC's substantial belly, giving him every indication that she'd be diving even lower very soon.

They were going for a plane ride—that's what Chloe wanted and that's what she was going to get. She wanted to go high and fast and stay up there for a long time—practically the opening paragraph of a Bear bomber's operations manual. Once they reached the traffic jam of bombers, the WC reluctantly allowed her to lift her head and pick out exactly which Bear she and he were going to take on their supersonic skylark.

Typically, it took her a while to shop—or so it seemed. She had Lars slow down in front of any Tu-95 that had a wild type of nose art or overall paint scheme. She discounted many as being too gaudy; others as simply too dark. She paused in front of several which featured realistically painted naked women on their noses, only telling Lars to continue on once she'd been able to drink the whole picture in.

After five minutes of this, the pilots of the waiting jets began gunning their engines, the only form of protest they could possibly commit with the WC flitting close by.

They wanted to get off the ground and get to work; the last thing they needed was a prolonged delay while the Boss's latest young twinkie was trying to decide between sea camo blue and off-camo red.

Finally, she gave Lars a slap on the head, indicating he should turn towards one particular Bear located near the end of the pack. It was nearly all black with a hideously detailed portrait of the Grim Reaper on its nose.

"This one!" she yelped, plunging her hand into the WC's quickly rehardening genital area. "This one is so *cool . . .*"

The WC was on his phone in an instant. He ordered one of the control towers to quick-prep and taxi out a replacement Bear—the one nicknamed *Death From Above*—was going to be his for the night.

There was more growling from the pack of bombers now—a blast of hot exhaust in celebration that the WC's scupper had finally picked her pleasure and that they could now get to the business of bombing. They watched as the WC and the young girl in the red dress alighted from the Benz, strolled over to the black Bear and waited for the hatch ladder to descend. The WC went up the stairs first, the girl right behind him. Those that were paying attention thought they might have seen the WC trip, or stumble or somehow make a clumsy entrance into the bomber itself. It was almost as if someone had grabbed him and shoved him to the floor. The girl went in right over him, and then the door closed, swallowing both of them up inside.

Now the Bear quickly moved out of the pack of waiting aircraft and sped to the head of the line. The plane turned onto the idle east-west runway and never stopped—its pilot hit its engines full blast, and off it went, rumbling away for a noisy, smoky, takeoff. The control tower waited a full minute for the WC's plane to clear the area before it began renewing takeoff clearances for the anxious pack of bombers.

They eventually began launching, one right after another, for the next twelve and a half minutes. The last one, a big delta-winged Mirage being sent to attack a target in the Azores, left the ground at exactly 11:59 hours.

A security patrol found the six unconscious crewmen from the plane called *Death From Above* two minutes later.

Hunter had flown many different aircraft designs in his time, from fighters, to bombers, to recon craft and everything in between.

But never, ever, had he seen a cockpit like the one inside the Tu-95 Bear bomber nicknamed *Death From Above*.

The Bear had been originally designed in the 1950s. Over the years, many adaptations and upgrades had been shoehorned into the huge airplane, to help it keep pace with advancements in technology. But two things were never changed on the Bear. One was the powerplant design; the other was the cockpit.

It looked like something designed by a mad scientist back in the thirties. There were still knobs, push buttons, turn-wheels, levers, analog computers—and dials. Thousands of dials, none of which seemed to make very much sense to anyone, even the world's best fighter pilot. Hunter had never been inside the cockpit of a Tu-95 before, but always wanted to. When he finally did, it was quite a shock.

Still it took him only a few moments to figure out how all the important stuff worked. The takeoff from Vallo Mazz had been as smooth as could be expected. Now that he was airborne it would give him some time to figure out what everything else did.

Baldi was sitting beside him, trembling as the huge

bomber cut through the turbulent air above the Mediterranean. He was no fan of airplanes, bombers or otherwise. He had shook all the way up from Malta to Syracuse,
both frightened and astounded at Hunter's ability to fly
the dilapidated seaplane barely ten feet above the surface
of the water without killing them all. Baldi was so happy
when they finally landed about a mile offshore from
Siracusa, he got down on his knees and prayed for a full
minute.

Now he was praying again.

Getting into Vallo Mazz had been easier than Hunter
could have ever imagined. Sure, the place was wrapped
a few thousand times in barbed wire and antipersonnel
mines, but they didn't cover the main gate of the place—
and that's exactly how they got in. Through the front
door, driving a stolen jeep and allowing Chloe to do the
talking. They casually dumped the car at the back of the
sin palace parking lot, and when Chloe went one way,
Hunter and Baldi went the other.

Trying to pick which Bear to steal turned out to be the
hardest thing. There were many to choose from sitting
idle on the parking apron, getting only cursory attention
from the nearby maintenance teams. Hunter and Baldi
picked the all-black, garishly nosed-up Bear simply because sneaking onto a black jet in nighttime was easier
to do than attempting to get on one bathed in Day-Glo.
The *DFA* was the blackest plane in the darkest shadow,
so Hunter and Baldi stole aboard her, hiding in the rear
bomb bay until the crew arrived and brought the airplane
to the prep shop.

Only then did they reveal themselves, knocking out the
gunners and the technicians with silent thrusts to the
throat, and then clobbering the pilots over the head with
the butts of their rifles. Chloe's timing couldn't have been
better; no sooner had Hunter and Baldi joined the back

end of the parking jam when she appeared, stringing along the WC like a mackeral to chum.

Now Hunter turned the big plane out over the Tyrrhenian Sea and pointed it due south, back towards the Straits of Sicily.

Chloe had climbed up into the copilot's seat—and she was enjoying the fast, high ride. Even when she didn't realize it, she still got what she wanted. Hunter was busying himself with the Bear's antique controls, and tried his best not to pay attention to her—but it was impossible to do. Even though his mind should have been consumed with making their grand-theft bomber caper a successful escape, he couldn't help himself from looking over at her, still clad in the tight miniskirt, her blond goddess looks clashing wildly with the dull, dial-crazy cockpit.

She was leaning all the way forward, nose pressed up against the cockpit glass, feeling her body sway as Hunter poured on the power and they gradually built up speed. She glanced over at him, began to smile—but stopped. They had hardly said a word to each other in the past few hours. The scene in Gin's kitchen had been an eye-opener—for both of them. Up to that point, Chloe thought Hunter was like everyone else she'd grown up with—into sex, both the doing and the watching. Now she was beginning to think that he was interested in only one of those. It had cast a pall over the adventurous time they'd already spent together.

Then came the plan to steal the Bear—and Chloe's surprise when Hunter gave her such a crucial part in it. She'd enjoyed using her sex into fooling the WC; she'd enjoyed the excitement of stealing the bomber. But how did Hunter feel about all that? She didn't know—and any time it seemed like the question was going to come up—he always shut up.

How then was she supposed to know what the hell he was thinking?

"You did a great job," he finally told her, quickly smiling and then turning back to the Bear's myriad of controls. "Thanks . . . I appreciate it."

She stared back at him, her eyes burning a pair of holes in his.

"I can't wait to tell my father about it," she said innocently. "He'd get a really big kick out of all this."

Hunter leaned back and then gazed out at the vast night sky above them. The stars seemed brighter up here, around forty-five thousand feet, and closer. There was a full moon, and many planets and constellations were visible overhead.

Again, uncharacteristically, Hunter found himself taking time from the mission to admire them through the bubble-topped canopy.

Suddenly, he felt Chloe's hand slip around his.

"Isn't it beautiful?" she asked, looking up at the Milky Way, seemingly just a hand grasp away from them.

"It sure is," Hunter replied finally, finding his eyes not on the stars but resting on her instead.


The Wing Commander of Vallo Mazz airfield woke up to find a knife pushing up against his throat.

He was still drunk, still stoned, and still somewhat under the spell of the young woman who'd hooked him earlier in the night. At first he thought he was taking a joyride in the sky with her, and that he had simply passed out once the plane started to take off.

This would have made sense—if it wasn't for the blade pressing into his gullet.

He finally opened his eyes and looked up to see a very large, very angry, unshaven, heavily mustached man staring down at him. He was the owner of the huge knife now drawing across his Adam's apple.

The Wing Commander instantly panicked. Something was definitely wrong here. *Very* wrong.

"You killed a lot of my people," the man with the knife was spitting at him. "For nothing. For money. You will die a very painful death for that, sir . . ."

The Wing Commander was listening to the man—but his attention was actually distracted elsewhere. He was laying on the deck directly below the forward observation hatch. From here he could see into the cockpit. And sitting there, illuminated only by the dull green of the cockpit lights, was the girl named Chloe.

She was enough to make him forget about the razor-sharp blade pressing against his neck. Momentarily anyway. But one thing had become abundantly clear: he was being kidnapped.

The Wing Commander tried to sit up but Baldi shoved him back down. Growing foolishly defiant, the WC suddenly pushed Baldi's blade away from his throat.

"You're not about to slit my throat," he told the infuriated Baldi. "What good would that do you? Once they realize that I'm gone, they'll send people out to get you. Don't you think we've been prepared for this? I'm one of the most important people in the world. We have contingencies for these types of things. They'll shoot you down if I tell them to."

At that moment, the Wing Commander heard a voice from the cockpit call back to Baldi: "Get him ready . . ."

The Wing Commander stared up at Baldi, confused. Then he leaned forward and for the first time saw the man who was driving the airplane.

*"You?* . . . The Wingman? You are real?"

"For now . . ." Hunter replied sullenly. "After this party, maybe not . . ."

He turned back to his controls. "Get him ready," he repeated to Baldi.

Once again, the WC began stuttering. "Ready? . . . for what?"

Baldi did not reply. He stood the WC up and roughly began removing his clothes.

"What . . . what the hell is this?"

Baldi had him down to his boots inside ten seconds.

"I said you have killed many of my people," he growled in the Wing Commander's face. "I said you will pay for it."

With that, he pushed the WC to the forward hatch. The airplane was now descending so steeply, Baldi and the WC were momentarily weightless. Then the plane leveled out and the Wing Commander could see they were about a mile high, over water, but approaching a small island off the eastern horizon.

Baldi pushed him even closer to the open hatch. The WC couldn't speak. This Wingman—this wasn't how he operated, was it? He and his gang weren't really going to kill him—were they?

"About twenty seconds . . ." Hunter called back to Baldi. "Fifteen . . ."

The Wing Commander was standing buck naked in the open hatch now, all of his extremities quickly freezing up. They were getting closer to the land mass: he could see waves crashing on the beaches below. And people, lining the shoreline, shaking their fists up at him. The Wing Commander realized that they were flying over the island of Malta.

"Ten seconds . . ." Hunter yelled back.

Baldi turned back to the WC. His knife was gone; he was holding a green bundle instead.

"You can't kill me!" the Wing Commander screamed as Baldi drew closer.

"We don't have to," Baldi said.

He shoved the bundle into the WC's hands, pulled its rip cord and then kicked him out the open hatchway.

The WC fell head over heels, nearly entangling himself in the unfurling parachute. Somehow, the fabric billowed and caught the air, jerking the Wing Commander to a violent midair stop. He'd voided his bladder and thrown up during this short freefall, but now he was floating and still alive—for the moment anyway.

He quickly looked down to see he was heading right for a crowd of people gathered in the main square of the city he knew from his bombing maps must be Valletta. These people were armed with guns, knives, clubs, and pitchforks. He could also feel the heat of their anger rising up to meet him. Heart-pounding, he wet himself again. He knew there was no way he'd be able to live through this reception.

Panic-stricken, he looked up at the Tu-95 as it slowly moved away from him. The last thing he would ever see was the blurry image of the girl with the red dress looking back out at him from the cockpit window.

She was waving goodbye.

# Eighteen

Da Nang
South Vietnam

The RF-4X Phantom recon jet lifted off cleanly from Da Nang's longest runway and immediately turned out over the South China Sea.

The "X" was an unusual aircraft. Formerly a fighter-bomber/ground attack plane, it had been converted into an armed reconnaissance platform about a year before. Its already-ugly nose had been extended by fifteen feet, providing room for a twelve-lens detachable SLAR/TEREC camera pod. Beneath its wings was a clutter of FLIR pods, TACAN and LANTIRN modules—and four Sidewinder missiles. The airplane was painted in a sheer black; the gold scrolling running back from the cockpit to the tail read: ACE WRECKING COMPANY.

Behind the controls of the unusual airplane was Captain John C. "Crunch" O'Malley. A gifted pilot and tactician, at thirty-six, O'Malley was the old man of the United American gang. Though originally hired on as a freelancer, he'd been flying exclusively for the UAAF for three years now. He'd been flying solo for just about that long, too. The Ace Wrecking Company was at one time a two-man operation, but he'd lost his partner twenty-eight months ago, on an operation over the mid-Pacific. Since then he'd downsized. The rear seat where his partner used to ride was now crammed with recon and intelligence-gathering gear. The Ace Wrecking Company hadn't really wrecked anything in a while, and it wasn't really a company anymore either. Now it specialized in long, *really* long, recon flights. Crunch had gotten to the point where he could do a fourteen-hour hump without breaking a sweat. In his opinion, it was a good way to spend his old age.

He had several photo targets today. He would first do a high-fly over Lolita Island, the site of the mysterious plastic forest. From there he would head east, towards the Palawan Passages, an area just west of the Philippines. This was a favorite hiding spot for the battleships of the Asian Mercenary Cult, the prime troublemakers in this vast region. From the United Americans' point of view, it was always a good idea to keep an eye out for any of their movements.

After taking a wide-sweep of Palawan, Crunch would return to Lolita, reaching there some two hours after nightfall for a series of FLIR, heat-trace and Nightvision photography. Then he would head home.

In all, the mission would last about seven hours, a short hop compared to some of his flights.

If he hurried, he'd be back in Da Nang before the moon came up.

It was fourteen hundred hours on the nose when Crunch first picked up Lolita Island on his Forward Looking Infra-Red scope.

It was still some distance away, off on the southern horizon. But just from what he could see on the IF scope, Crunch could tell something was very queer about the island. The jungle looked too damn perfect—every tree was the exact same height, every blade of grass was leaning the exact same way. The heat signature alone was enough to scramble his screen. The island had been baking in the height of hazy sunshine for two hours and its plastic foliage was giving off tremendous amounts of heat. It was so hot on the greenish world of the FLIR eye, it looked to Crunch like the island was actually engulfed in flames.

He immediately pulled back on his crank, booted the throttles and climbed nearly straight up to 63,360 feet. Once at this height—exactly eleven miles above the earth—he throttled back, turned the plane on its left wing and opened his camera pods. For thirty seconds he maintained this attitude, long enough for four of the cameras inside the pod to run through one can of film.

Then he leveled out, shut everything off and did a time and position check: fourteen hundred and five hours, just about eleven-degrees by one hundred fourteen. For his voice-activated cockpit reporter, he mentioned the heat coming off of Lolita and his own impressions of the bizarre, faultless jungle growth.

Then he punched his next destination into the flight computer and felt the airplane jerk to the left.

His nose now pointed at the eastern horizon, he pushed the throttles forward again and was off.

The crew of the huge Antonov An-124 "Condor" had been circling for hours.

They'd been holding in a ten-mile orbital pattern off the Filipino island of Tatota since before zero six hundred hours that morning; it was now almost three in the afternoon. They'd already refueled in the air twice, and as the prospect for yet another gassing was coming up, the airplane's radio man was trying frantically to contact one of the several freelance flying gas stations known to serve this part of the globe.

The problem was the price went up with each minute the giant cargo ship drew nearer to empty. These days, negotiations for an aerial drink skyrocketed the closer the fuel-starved plane got to a bingo situation. The in-flight refueling bandits were in no hurry to answer the Condor's calls; they preferred to make their customers sweat a little first, a brutal fact of supply and demand at thirty-five thousand feet.

The Antonov crew were themselves freelancers; this particular Condor was outfitted to carry a SEXX, a special-external/extra, as in extra-heavy payloads. The Condor was essentially a gigantic aerial tow truck. Its specialty was picking up broken or damaged warplanes, bombers mostly, strapping them on to its back and flying them to a destination for repair.

They'd been contracted for this particular mission around 11 P.M. the night before. Leaving their island base off Brunei, they'd reached this coordinate as instructed just after sunrise, to await further instructions. They'd been going around in circles ever since.

They had no idea if there was a problem or what was causing the delay—they'd received nothing other than a single radio message two hours back telling them to hold their position. They didn't know who had hired them—the deal had gone through an Indonesian middleman—or what they were expected to carry. All they knew was they'd get paid the minimum whether the mission was brought to the second stage or not.

It was now growing on fifteen hundred hours, and the big Soviet-designed cargo plane was nearing its bingo point once again. Once the gas light flashed red, the cargo plane would have just enough fuel left to get back to its base. If that happened, everyone onboard knew it would be a bitch to get paid at all. Contractors could always wiggle-out of a no-show bingo clause. They could always say, hey, we showed up, with a lot of gas for you and you were gone.

So the crew of the Condor were torn: should they buy some more fuel from one of the robber gas merchants and hang around a little longer? Or should they just say fuck it and go home?

In the end, they decided to stay. The contract had called for a ten-percent overpayment for a timely mission; this told the eleven crewmen that their employer had deep pockets, someone who could afford to have the largest airplane in the world circle endlessly around an isolated patch of ocean, chewing up time at more than ten thousand dollars an hour.

Finally, they made a deal with a refueling outfit out of Mindoro. Ten minutes later an ancient British-built Handley-Page Victor K.Mk2 showed up, leaking gas from all three hoses. The midair fuel-up went anything but smoothly—the tanker crew was probably drunk—but eventually the Condor took on another ten thousand pounds of fuel, good for another few hours.

After that, they would have to make the decision to stay or go, once again.

Unknown to heavy lifters in the Condor, an interloper had witnessed the whole refueling episode.

It was Crunch. He was flying ten miles directly above the Condor, watching the SEXX plane go round and round and round.

This in itself was not unusual. Many times, SEXX planes were hired prior to the opening of a battle or a military attack, and left on call, like an ambulance, ready to pick up any ailing airplanes. But this was a An-12 extra-large external lifter—a plane outfitted to carry the largest piggyback loads possible. The plane was so big, it could probably carry a small airliner on its back, even a F-111 or a Backfire bomber. So what the hell was it doing, circling around this part of the empty ocean? There were no conflicts about to break out anywhere nearby—the United American intelligence services knew these things. And certainly not one that would require the services of this flying monster.

So, what the hell was it doing out here? And exactly what had the people who'd hired it expected to carry on its back?

Crunch didn't know—and didn't hazard a guess.

Instead, he did the next best thing. He took a couple hundred pictures of the dizzily circling Condor, then turned west and headed back home to Da Nang.

This, he thought, was more important than going back and shooting Lolita again.

# Nineteen

Night had disappeared by the time the Tu-95 passed over the coastline of the country once known as Lebanon.

Hunter was steering the big airplane with his knees now, head back, resting his eyes. Chloe was asleep in his lap. Baldi was strapped into the radio engineer's seat behind him, crash helmet on, two parachutes clutched to his chest. He was a sailor; he'd yelled forward to Hunter many times during their high-altitude trans-Mediterranean flight. He belonged in a boat, on the sea, not in the belly of a monster, flying at sixty-five thousand feet.

There were many other places Hunter wanted to be at that moment, too. Chloe's warm chalet was his first choice; sleeping in the front seat of the long-gone tanker truck was his second. But he knew now was not the time to start dreaming about unattainable things. He had to keep his eyes on the prize, and his brain on the matter at hand.

The nose of the huge Bear was laid exactly on an unwavering southeasterly course. This heading was the result of a very simple navigation plot Hunter had made earlier, before they'd left Malta for the air base in Siracusa. He was sure that the people operating the Zon had attempted to bomb Valletta to its knees just so they could use the city's extra-long runway. Combining this with what he'd culled from his observations when the shuttle went over Point Zero, he'd determined that this course, which stretched all the way to below the equator before it began a loop around the world again, was a retracing of the Zon's orbital path and hence, its reentry track. In other words, the way the shuttle was flying, it had to come down somewhere along this line eventually.

Hunter's plan—and it was not a modest one—was to locate every air base sporting an extra-long runway along this course and fuck it up, just as he'd done at Star City, and on Malta. If he was able to somehow accomplish this, then possibly he could close the gap on just where the shuttle could land and further ensure his being there when it finally did come down.

But he'd have to hurry. He was sure the Zon would be reentering sometime within the next twenty-four hours. In that time, he knew he might wind up having to fly more than halfway around the globe, all in less than a day. The good news was the Bear bomber was well-suited for this quest. It was fast, somewhat fuel-efficient, and carrying all of the rudimentary navigation devices he needed to aid in his search. Also its weapons bay was filled to the brim with a variety of bombardment devices.

But how far could they actually go? Of this he was a little uncertain. Bad weather, enemy opposition and a million other things could arise and make him eat fuel and thus cut down on his range. But if he was careful, and if everything worked right, he figured he'd be able to fly all the way to the Fiji Islands and beyond, if he had to.

They were now passing over what was once the city of Beirut. These days it was little more than a burned out hole surrounded by encroaching olive groves and grapevines. They used to call it the Jewel of the Middle East. Now, like so many cities in this part of the world, it was vanishing, slowly but surely, being reclaimed by the earth and the olive groves.

They skirted the airspace around Damascus a few minutes later. Hunter noted a couple of search-radar emissions rising from SAM sites below, but nothing ever came of them. The Bear was too high to be hit with most SAMs anyway, and if a nuclear-capable strategic bomber was flying over your turf, it was good foreign policy not to piss them off. With so many different kinds of warplanes plying the skies these days, you never knew which one might return to drop a big one on you—"accidentally," of course.

They did meet up with a couple of interceptors once they'd passed out of Syrian airspace and found themselves above the relatively new country of El Alanbar. The interceptors were laughably old Mirage-1s though, planes that were obsolete before Hunter was born. They couldn't climb any higher than forty-five-angels, so their pilots could do little more than look up and watch as the turbocharged high-flying Bear passed four miles over their heads.

Chloe woke up momentarily, readjusted herself in Hunter's lap and then went back to sleep again. They passed over into airspace controlled by what used to be called Iraq, now known as Trans-Mesopotamia. Instantly a dozen SAM radars locked onto them. But again, Hunter was not concerned. He was flying so high, so fast, it would take a one-in-a-million shot to knock them down.

About one minute into Mesop airspace, he felt a jolt of electricity run up his spine. It went through his neck, around his ears and into his brain. Suddenly, a taut vibration began singing deep inside him. His neurons, all sixteen billion of them, were suddenly heating up.

"Chloe, wake up," he whispered, failing to avoid the temptation of stroking her hair lightly. She sat up sleepily.

"Are we there yet?" she asked sweetly.

Hunter shook his head and began pushing buttons and throwing levers. Suddenly the plane began losing altitude. Somewhere down there on the Iraqi desert, something was beckoning to him. Something important to this mission; critical even.

He had to go down and take a look.

The place was called Qum and it was very near a place known as Uruk.

Both cities were located in the southern portion of old Iraq, near the convergence of the Tigris and Euphrates rivers. To say that Uruk was an old city was a colossal understatement. There was good evidence that Uruk was the *first* city in human history, the place where language began, where things were first written down and where the notion of mathematical thinking was born. Forty thousand years before, the people of Uruk tended wheatfields the size of the state of Kansas. A huge lake situated nearby was thought to be the planet's only ocean. Everyone who lived there was healthy, wealthy and wise.

No surprise then that many scholars also believed that Uruk was the place that the people who wrote the Bible referred to as "Ed'n" or Eden. As translated through the twists and turns of the Old Testament, Uruk was where Adam and Eve had lived.

But it was a desert now, and had been for thousands of years. And its boast about being the birthplace of modern civilization hadn't spared it a whit from the worst that monster had created: the area had seen an unusually high number of battles, and wars in its long, ancient history. One could push a shovel into the sand and find artifacts from any number of conflicts fought in the region over the past forty thousand years. The first layer would house relics from the Gulf War; the layer below that the effects from various Arab-Israeli conflicts. Before that, World War II; before that, actions associated with World War I, and on down through the centuries, until at about one hundred and fifty feet you'd start to find the spears and rock-hurling weapons of the people who eventually conquered the first city of Uruk.

Nothing had changed over four centuries. There was a war going on right now between Uruk and Qum, its sister city that exulted in almost forty thousand years of existence as well. The cities had clashed sixteen times in the past two months, sending men, missiles, tanks and terror bombs against each other with wild abandon, killing many but making no significant gains on either side.

The two cities had much to fight over. Qum had little water; Uruk had plenty. Qum needed food for its people; Uruk had warehouses full of barley, rice, and cooking oil. Qum needed gasoline and aviation fuel; Uruk had underground tanks full of both. The people of Qum were pissed that their neighbors wouldn't share any of their wealth with them; the people of Uruk couldn't believe the freeloading audacity of their rivals over the hill.

But the battle that was going on at this moment had nothing to do with food, water or airplane gas.

The battle today was over something else Uruk had that Qum didn't: a fifteen thousand-foot runway.

It had been a strange turn of events for the military officers in charge of defending Uruk. Up until that day, the troops from Qum had always attacked through the pass in the middle of the mountain range that separated the two cities. A huge artillery barrage would give way to howitzer and missile fire, and then, an armed charge by infantry and mechanized units. The Uruk defenders usually managed to stop the invaders at the edge of the al Furat wadi, a natural formation that was now heavily fortified and bristling with weapons. Occasionally, the Qum troops would break through and run wild in the streets of Uruk. But they were always hunted down and shot like dogs, their bodies dismembered and shipped back to Qum for burial. On the rare occasions that Uruk attacked Qum, the opening artillery barrage could last up to ten hours, followed by air strikes, rocket attacks and then, maybe, special operations teams infiltrating the city and blowing up key targets before getting airlifted out.

But this day, the troops from Qum had suddenly switched tactics. Instead of coming over the mountain pass and flowing into the valley of Uruk, they climbed over the southern end of the peaks and launched a massive surprise attack on Uruk's vast military airport. In less than two hours they'd been able to seize the base's control tower, its fuel supply and half the long runway. Uruk security forces had somehow established a line that split the landing strip completely in two, and had held off the attackers until regular troops from the city arrived.

All that had happened about an hour ago. Now the fight was growing fiercer as each side closed within sight of each other, even within earshot. Weapons that had been previously used to lob weapons and artillery over distances of thousands of yards were now squared off evenly against each other, their turrets down to level, blasting away at ranges of less than one hundred meters. Meanwhile, both sides were firing tactical battlefield missiles onto the bloody runway fight, killing friendly and enemy soldiers alike. Each side also possessed a tiny number of small, battlefield nuclear weapons, mostly in the form of artillery shells. The commanders on both sides were now discussing whether these weapons should be brought into play, the first time since the latest war between the two cities began.

It was brutal, grinding, high tech warfare at its worst, and all of it was taking place near the first real city on the planet, on top of the sands which had long ago buried the Garden of Eden.

It might have seemed like an odd thing then, that all of the soldiers on both sides of this hellish battle were fanatically religious. In all their previous clashes, they had stopped fighting at precisely 4 P.M. to take a ten-minute, bow-and-prayer break. Each side believed dying in battle was a sure way to heaven, and that to run from a fight meant a one-way ticket into hell. Each side also believed that the only entity that could call a halt to a religious war was God Himself—and this they took very seriously. During each battle, special officers on both sides would simply observe the fighting as it was taking place, looking for signs that the Almighty wanted the hostilities to stop. It was called a *quar'wey*—the sign from above. Of course, these heavenly things weren't spotted very often. In the forty thousand-year history of Qum and Uruk, a *quar'wey* had been spotted only once, and that, scholars believed, was at the end of the war which ultimately destroyed the first city of Uruk.

Still, in between loading their weapons and slaughtering their neighbors, the soldiers on both sides of the battle lines were babbling prayers, beseeching God to produce the sign and end the fighting. To be fair, some of the soldiers did this little ritual rather routinely; but many others took it very gravely. Yet no matter how deep their faith, everyone knew the likelihood of anything like a *quar'wey* happening was just about nil and all this religious stuff was probably just a way to keep everyone praying and thereby *focused* during a battle.

But then, everything changes eventually—even if it takes forty thousand years to do so.

No one on the Uruk side of the line knew exactly why their enemies from Qum decided to attack the city's air base.

True, the runway was nearly three miles long, being built in secret shortly after the first Gulf War by the American CIA in anticipation of a second conflict.

The people at Uruk utilized the long airstrip certainly—they had several medium-sized bombers and fighters that found the fifteen thousand foot-runway a dream to operate from. But Qum had no aircraft, and even if it had, it would be hard pressed to find anyone to fly them. The people of Qum were called *neyetah,* people of the earth. Airplanes, rockets and things of this nature held no interest for them.

So why then were they trying to take over Uruk's airport?

Some would later say, that Qum was actually hired to do it; paid off by some mysterious people to the east. Others would say the whole thing was a mistake and that the Qum forces were simply attacking Uruk proper and faced unusually stiff opposition at the airport. Still others would say that many of the fighters for Qum had become convinced that God himself was going to come out of the sky in a huge flaming chariot to support them in their cause—but he needed a really long runway on which to land.

In the end though, it didn't matter much. In this battle, something so important was about to happen, all questions of why the Qum chose this day to try and capture the big airport would be lost.

For on this day, for the first time since the pivotal Battle of Shajk-ree forty thousand years before, both sides witnessed a *quar'wey*—the sign from above.

It happened shortly after dawn, just as the battle at the airport was moving into its third hour. Already more than three thousand men had been killed on each side, twice that many wounded or missing. In the tiny confines of the airport's taxiways, the fighting had turned to bayonets and sharpened swords, all while massive pieces of mobile artillery battered each other from three hundred feet away. Suddenly a screech was heard—the sound of many women screaming at once, was how someone would later put it. It was so loud, men on both sides stopped what they were doing and gazed upwards.

That's when everyone saw it. A huge flying machine, diving down out of the clear morning sky, its wings and tail and body shimmering in the bright, newly risen sun. It looked gigantic, terrifying. Unreal.

And it was heading right for the airport.

This was a frightening sight to see for many of the troops, on both sides. Never had they beheld such a large aircraft before. Whether the soldiers for Qum thought the beast was on the side of Uruk and vice versa, no one would ever really know. As soon as the flying monster screeched again and dropped even more steeply towards the airport, many soldiers on both sides threw down their weapons and ran away.

Was this God? Coming down out of the heavens as the rumors said He would? Was this why the soldiers from Qum had been so determined to take the airport on this, of all days? Was this an authentic *quar'wey?*

No, not really. But in the end, that didn't make any difference either.

The huge flying monster drew closer, its color scheme was so black, it was actually shiny. It had huge swept-back wings and four prop-jet engines that were smoking so badly they appeared to be on fire. The great aircraft swooped down on the airport and dropped fifteen bombs, one right after another, in a perfect row along the entire length of the long runway—all from a heartstopping height of three hundred fifty feet. There followed a string of fifteen near-simultaneous explosions, mixed with the unearthly shriek of the plane's engines as it pulled up and roared away over the horizon.

Then, strangely, everything went silent on the battlefield. When the smoke cleared, troops on both sides saw the three-mile long runway had been cratered right down its middle. Huge chunks of rock and dirt now covered it from beginning to end. The combined impact of the fifteen bombs dropping from such a short height had been so intense, it had even ignited the asphalt itself in places.

One look at the bombed-out airstrip told them it would never ever be used again.

To the religious people on both sides, this was indeed their *quar'wey*, the indication from God that they should stop fighting now, as it had finally come to displease Him. Commanders on both sides looked to their religious officers who called it a miracle, an official legitimate "sign from above."

Trumpets on both sides began blaring and men who could still walk and talk let out a great cheer of celebration. Almost immediately the mobile artillery on both sides began backing up and leaving the field. Joyous troops followed them. A war that had been fought off and on over the last four hundred centuries had finally been called a draw by the Almighty himself.

There was no longer any need to fight each other, ever again. At last, everyone could throw down their weapons and go home.

# Twenty

It was getting cold again up on the flight compartment of the Zon shuttle.

They had just passed back into the Earth's shadow, and now, all the brilliant direct sunshine they'd been relishing gave way to a bitter, metallic cold. There was no gradual warming or cooling up here in space. One second you could be blazing hot—the next, you're frozen solid. Once you were off the planet, very few things actually fell in between.

The Zon's captive pilot pulled the collar of his flight suit further up around his neck and shook off the creeping chill. The doom and gloom of the Earth's shadow would last only ninety minutes or so. But each time it happened, his cockpit got a little colder, just as the wait for the sun seemed to get a little longer.

He'd long ago begun to curse these ninety-minute retreats into the darkness; cursed the frigidity they brought with them. He'd come to believe, whether it was rational or not, that if he was just left alone in the sun for any length of time, he would begin to regain the mental faculties he'd lost during the two years of brutal mindwashing. If only he could lay out on the beach with a bucket of suds, some food and some girls—just like he used to do. Then, he was sure he would start to remember things, like who he was, and his name, and how the hell he'd gotten into this strange predicament in the first place.

But now it was cold and dark again and he had many problems literally floating in front of his face. Despite his best efforts to keep the flight compartment clean and contaminant-free, he'd been corraling tiny droplets and weightless specks of unhealthy materials all morning long. Just what these things were floating up from the disgust of the crew compartment, he didn't know. There were certainly pieces of cocaine drifting about, and the yellow drops he had to assume were urine. But other strange black things that didn't quite appear solid or liquid were besieging him in vast numbers. It was all he could do to keep vacuuming them out of the air, knowing that just one tiny piece of something could gum up the works for all of them.

But keeping the flight deck clean was actually the least of the pilot's worries. He had two potential crises looming that made his orbital housecleaning compulsions pale by comparison.

The first had to do with the Mir space station. He had successfully maneuvered the Zon close to the Mir's rear receiving ring about six hours ago. As these things go, it had been an uneventful rendezvous. Only one crewman from the Zon died in the attempt, again from electrical shock when he first made contact with the Mir while putting the universal communications tether in place. Previous attempts at such linkings had cost the lives of as many as seven crewmen, as well as some people living on the Mir. To lose just one life this time made some people in both orbiting crafts think that they were actually getting good at this type of thing.

But not the pilot—he knew they'd just been lucky and that getting entangled with the Mir would always be a deadly operation. His problem now was how to disengage from the space station when it was time, and try not to cause heavy damage to either the shuttle or the Mir. The problem was that the universal wire snigger tended to freeze up in the cold of space; when it was time to unlink it was usually stuck to the point that only the pulling away of both spacecraft could break the seal. This was highly dangerous as the Zon could easily rip away a section of the Mir, or vice versa while unlinking. All it would take was the slightest crack in the skin of either and everyone aboard the unlucky craft would die horribly in the vacuum of space about twelve seconds later.

But there was an even bigger crisis looming ahead for the pilot—one that he, nor anyone else aboard the Zon had any control over whatsoever. This problem was of earthly origin—where were they going to land once it was time to go back down? The pilot had been receiving with increasing frequency, near-hysterical reports from the Zon's communications section that all the alternate landing sites previously thought to be either "secure" or "securable" were now anything but.

First the Star City landing strip had been fouled, and then the primary backup strip on the island of Malta. Now the pilot had just received a message saying that another location, a midorbital secondary site located in the desert of old Iraq, had just been destroyed as well.

*What was going on here?* the pilot asked himself over and over again. Were these just coincidences? Not unlikely events considering the state of the planet Earth these days? Or was someone down there determined not to let them land?

The pilot pondered this last possibility for the longest time. It would have to be a very clever person, or a group of such, to actually find and destroy every available landing site the Zon could use while locked into its present orbital status.

It seemed as if he knew such people, way back when, in that part of his life that had been so brutally erased. But trying to remember who they were only made his head hurt—and in zero-gravity, every headache was a killer.

So he stopped thinking about these lost memories and dragged his mind back to the matter at hand. A formation of yellow urine bubbles came floating by; the pilot eliminated them with his small handheld vacuum cleaner, and then snidely pretended to blow smoke away from the sucker's barrel.

Down below, was a vast, dark section of the Atlantic Ocean. The water looked like ink; the clouds above it very stormy.

The pilot pulled his collar up further and shook off another deeper chill.

He believed it would be a long time before he saw the sun again.

# Twenty-one

There was only one way to fully comprehend the size of the Great Middle Eastern desert: fly over it.

It went on forever. In every direction, for hundreds of kilometers, there was nothing but sand, mountains, and more sand. The only break in this bleak landscape was the sparkling greenish waters of the Persian Gulf. This sea looked very much out of place, as if it had been forever struggling just to moisten the dry terrain below. The fact that there were literally billions of barrels of oil still sitting beneath this strange piece of Terra made the mix even more bizarre. It was the closest thing one could get to passing over an alien planet.

So Hunter was glad when the big Bear finally left the Arabian desert behind, skirted the top of the Gulf and passed over into Asia. Below them now was the rugged, equally bleak land once known as Persia, and then Iran, and now Persia again.

This was a strange place in itself. The country below looked as it might have thousands of years ago—except its coastline was dotted with supertankers left rusting after an innumerable string of armed conflicts. There was evidence of small wars still going on eight miles beneath the Tu-95; clouds of smoke rising here, a burned-out city there. Village against village, tribe against tribe, the whole place appeared to have reverted back to life as it was centuries before, with the thought of all the oil buried beneath *its* top layer apparently lost in the giant step back-ward.

So while there was evidence of civilization down below, Hunter could see no runways, no highways, not even a clear stretch of flat hard terrain that could be utilized by the shuttle if it chose to set down on an unprepared land-ing strip. This was fine with him; the last thing he wanted was to challenge Viktor in the wilds of modern Persia.

They had flown into early afternoon when they saw a huge mountain range off on the eastern horizon. This, Hunter knew, was the Makrans, the southern terminus of the old Iranian territory. Over these peaks was the coun-try known these days as Greater Pakistan. He brought the big Bear down to thirty thousand feet, below a cloud layer that had wrapped itself around the Makran range. Right behind him, Baldi was working the airplane's rudimen-tary radio, trying to get through to the United American Expeditionary Forces in Vietnam, or even UAAF head-quarters back in Washington. But it had been a futile quest so far for the man from Malta. The Bear's commu-nications set was so underdeveloped Baldi was having a hard time just picking up radio transmissions coming from land directly below the big bomber, never mind con-necting a call halfway around the world. With commend-able patience though, he never stopped trying.

Chloe was sitting in the copilot's seat, fully awake now, still buzzing from their sudden bombing of the runway at Uruk. The importance of their strange mission was growing on her with each passing hour. She was gravely studying the terrain below them, eyes peeled for anything even resembling a runway. Whenever Hunter would glance in her direction, he would feel an odd jolt of pride run through him—this mixed with the usual wave of tes-tosterone that pumped inside him and anyone else any time they looked at her. It was as if she was growing up, maturing right before his eyes.

It was good having another pair of peepers, for the terrain below them changed dramatically after they passed over the Markan range. Most signs of the desert wilderness were gone now—the Markans were simply the beginning of hundreds of miles of high snowcapped mountains, rugged hills and deep valleys. Though rather chilling, Hunter again welcomed the switch in topography. The wild desert terrain could hide just about anything: cities, villages, secret military bases. Everything but a runway of any size. Below them now was nothing but vast, oddly majestic, mountainous desolation. Lifeless. Empty.

Then they came to Karachi.

Hunter knew something was wrong more than one hundred miles out.

He'd felt a vibration start up from deep within him; in seconds it was doing a slow buzz around his brain. Karachi was the capital of Pakistan; had been since the country's birth. But there was a large military base located about five miles from the city that rivaled downtown Karachi in size and scope. The place was known as Ras Muari Rim. It was a large, five-runway installation built by the Americans from which not-so-secret bombing raids could be launched against Soviet troops fighting in Afghanistan in the 1980s. Its landing strips could handle anything from fighter-bombers to B-52s to C-5s and bigger.

But Ras Muari Rim also had another distinction. Its longest runway had been extended in the 1980s, not by the U.S. military, but by NASA of all people. It seemed that Karachi, though thousands of miles from Cape Canaveral, was actually fitted as an emergency landing spot for the American shuttle should it have to come down shortly after launch.

As such, it was more than large enough to handle the Zon.

But as Hunter brought the huge bomber over the city now, to his surprise he couldn't even locate the huge base at Ras Muari Rim. Below they could see miles and miles of houses—hovels really, shacks plopped down anywhere they could fit. This was no surprise, this is what most of Karachi always looked like. But in the area where the Ras Muari Rim was supposed to be, they could see nothing but people—swarms of humans, with numbers in the hundreds of thousands, maybe even more. They were covering the military base like ants, blotting out any evidence of buildings, facilities or the runways themselves.

"This is great!" Baldi exclaimed as he peered down at the patch of humanity covering the air base. "That air strip is more blocked than the last one. Even more fouled than my own in Valletta."

Baldi was right—but Hunter was feeling very uneasy about all this. There were almost a million people huddled below them—and from the looks of it, no one was in the city itself. Were the people living on the base refugees from the capital just five miles away? If so, why had they retreated to the air base, while a much closer commercial airport lay directly on the outskirts of the city, apparently empty?

"I don't like this," he murmured. "It seems so . . . unnatural."

He looked over at Chloe and then at Baldi. The terrified look coming across the Maltan's face said it all. He was just getting over his fear of flying, now he knew Hunter was going to reignite it in him again.

"I think we've got to go down there," Hunter told them. "Something tells me all is not right here . . ."

Five minutes later, Hunter set the big Bear down on Karachi airport's north-south runway.

They ran into no opposition during their sharp descent; no sign of interceptors, no SAM radar indications. Hunter taxied the huge bomber over to the largest terminal, shut down the airplane's four huge engines and then sat there, welcoming the silence after hours of hearing the Bear's quartet of prop-jets.

"There's no one home," Chloe said innocently.

"So we can leave?" Baldi asked hopefully.

Hunter was shaking his head. "Why would there be so many people crowded into the air base just over the hill and no one here?"

"What difference does it make?" Baldi asked him. "The big runway is crowded, the Zon would not set down there. Just crushing the bodies would screw up the spacecraft, no?"

"It would," Hunter replied. "But that won't stop Viktor or his goons. If they have to use that runway, they'll clear those people out of there—and use any means to do it."

Baldi thought about this for a moment, then nodded in grim agreement. "He killed hundreds of my people," he said disgustedly. "Why would he stop at thousands? Or hundreds of thousands?"

"Exactly," Hunter replied grimly.

Baldi took a long look out the plane's nose window. The airport *was* completely empty. No planes, no vehicles, no signs of life at all.

"So what do we do?" he asked.

"We find out why everyone is crowded onto the military base," came the answer—not from Hunter, but from the sweet lips of Chloe.

"That's exactly right," Hunter said with a brief grin.

She *was* learning fast.

They climbed down out of the bomber; Hunter and Baldi armed with M-16s, Chloe carrying a flare pistol.

It was now getting close to midafternoon and the sun was beating down with its worst heat of the day. Baldi had his gun up and ready for anything. But Hunter knew there wasn't anyone around in the immediate area. They walked through the empty terminal and out onto the service road that was once a highway leading in and out of the place. It, too, was deserted.

There was a line of vehicles parked outside the terminal—old-fashioned military jeeps painted yellow and redesigned to serve as taxis. Many of them still had keys in their ignitions and gas in their tanks. It was as if everyone just disappeared from the airport one day, leaving in a rush and never coming back.

Hunter reached into one of these taxis and twisted the key to the right. The engine started immediately.

"I hope my driver's license is still valid," he mused as they climbed in.

Minutes later they were speeding along the empty thoroughfare, heading into the center of Karachi itself. Like the airport, the sprawling city was utterly deserted. There were vehicles still in the streets, the traffic lights were still blinking and the electricity was still on. But there were no people, alive or otherwise.

"This is so strange," Chloe opined. "This place looks okay; why *would* everyone leave?"

They continued through the downtown business district and into the residential area. There was no way to adequately describe these living conditions other than to say they were slums. Blocks and blocks of dilapidated apartment buildings, shacks and covered alleyways. The sun beating down did little to ease the smell rising from these places. All three of them in the jeep found themselves holding their noses. Even the stale air inside the bomber was better than this.

Hunter turned off one particularly crowded backstreet to an avenue that was slightly wider, slightly less congested, and they found the first clue why Karachi was empty.

It was a huge crater sitting right in the middle of the main street. There was water at the bottom of it, covering what looked to be about two dozen skeletal corpses. The hole was at least a hundred feet across and probably half that deep.

"Jessuzz," Baldi gasped. "What the hell is this?"

"Is it from a bomb?" Chloe asked.

Hunter was shaking his head. "Not a bomb," he said, carefully studying the dimensions of the hole, and its slightly irregular shape. "It was caused by a shell, something shot out of a gun."

Chloe's hand went to her mouth. "A gun?" she asked. "What kind of a gun could do this?"

Hunter replied with a grim shrug. "A damn big one," he said.

They steered around the hole—and came to another. It was about a block away and located in the exact same spot on the roadway as the first one. They drove around this one, too, only to find another and another and another. In fact, there were more than a dozen huge craters in the avenue, perfectly lined up as if they'd been dropped with the help of a plumb bob.

"This gun is somewhere in the two hundred fifty maybe even two hundred eighty-millimeter range," Hunter said, not quite believing it himself. The biggest gun he'd ever heard of was the two hundred eighty-millimeter atomic cannon, a weapon built specifically to lob nuclear-tipped artillery shells for distances up to twenty miles. There had been rumors for years that someone here in the approaches to the subcontinent had developed a monster gun, a supergun, that could fire a shell up to one hundred miles.

Did such a gun exist? And was it somewhere in the neighborhood of Karachi?

They finally found their way out of the slums and onto the four-lane highway which headed southwest, and in the direction of the Ras Muari Rim military air base. The roadway was completely clear of any traffic, moving or otherwise. This was no surprise either: there was a neat line of gigantic shell craters running parallel to the raised highway, too.

They came to the top of a hill and Hunter stopped the jeep at the crest. The roadway led into a valley and the Ras Muari Rim air base. Gazing down at it now through the afternoon haze, all three of them felt their jaws drop. The air base was literally crawling with people—thousands upon thousands of them, huddled together in a clump of humanity that stretched from one end of the base to the other.

Chloe especially lost her breath at the sight of it. It looked like a hive of ghastly insects, crawling and unreal, like from a dream. She nearly got sick just looking at it. Baldi too became physically upset.

"People cannot live like this," he said through gritted teeth. "People *should* not live like this."

Hunter dug out a large kerchief and tied it around his mouth and nose. The smell from the slum was bad enough; the odor coming from the air base was close to overwhelming.

They began driving again, and gradually they came to realize that the enormous shell craters spread out from the highway and enveloped three sides of the air base's northern end. From there back, the airstrip was protected on all sides by the high mountains. Things began falling into place now. The empty, somewhat battered city, the crowded air base, the miles of pock-marked landscape.

That's when it hit Hunter. The air base was crowded with the liquid mass of humanity for one reason: it was apparently the only place in the area not in the reach of the mysterious monster gun.

They drove another mile—and then the highway suddenly disappeared. A huge shell crater had severed the artery; several more had destroyed the elevated roadway for the last mile into the air base. It looked like a huge beast had come along and stomped the highway down.

At the abrupt end of the roadway they found an armored vehicle dug into a concrete blast shelter so thick, Hunter imagined it would take nothing less than an atomic shell to take it out. They drove up to this small fortress very carefully, weapons plainly in sight, with their chambers open and empty. Three soldiers were manning the lonely outpost. They were Caucasians; possibly Dutch or Belgian. They stared at the approaching jeep, mouths open in surprise. One of them held up his hands, indicating that the jeep should stop. Hunter immediately complied.

*"Mon ami!"* he called out, hoping the men would understand him. They did.

"What are you doing here?" one of them yelled back, sounding authentically puzzled. "This is a very dangerous area."

Hunter hesitated a moment, pondering the question. He really had no good answer.

"We set down back at the airport," he explained, rolling the jeep to a stop about ten feet away from them. "We're on our way to . . ."

Suddenly he stopped talking. His ears had picked something up. Trouble was on the way. The strange thing was, the soldiers felt it, too. Suddenly they were diving back into their heavily reinforced bunker.

The next thing he knew, Hunter was dragging Chloe out of the jeep and running full sprint with her towards the thick fortification. Baldi was right on their tails. From the swarm of humanity below them they heard a very distinct gasp. Then the air was filled with an awesome whistling noise and a crack that sounded like thunder.

The huge shell hit three seconds later.

It came down less than five hundred feet away from them, kicking up so much dirt and dust that the day suddenly turned to night.

Hunter was thrown about six feet into the air, crashing

into the top of the bunker and coming back down twice as fast as he went up. Luckily he had his bone dome on and he was able to hang onto Chloe. They landed in a heap on top of the soldiers, with Baldi coming down on top of them. They all lay there for a few seconds, dazed, confused and nearly blinded by the clouds of dust thrown up from the blast. Hunter's eyes were the first to clear— when he looked out of the shelter's lone light slit, he saw another shell crater as big, if not bigger than the others, had just swallowed up another chunk of already battered terrain.

"What is happening here?" he asked the soldiers as everyone struggled to their feet. "Who is shooting at you?"

The soldiers almost laughed at him. They *were* Dutch, their country's emblem was very prominent on the left arm of their uniforms.

"Who is shooting at us?" one replied, grimly amused. "Damned if we know . . ."

Ten minutes later, Hunter, Chloe and Baldi were sitting on the turret of the small Dutch tank, slowly making their way down the side of the hill and into the teeming mass of people camped out on the long runway.

After further explaining what they were doing in Karachi, the soldiers, part of a long-forgotten UN peacekeeping force, had agreed to take Hunter and his friends to see their commander. His HQ was located at the far end of the runway; a trip through the huge knot of humanity was required.

They entered the squalor and began slowly driving across the airstrip, the people sullenly parting the way for them. It was like one vast shantytown. The people were living in wooden structures, cardboard boxes or simply laying about on blankets. They had small campfires burning, but obviously there was very little for any of them to eat. Everyone Hunter saw—men, women, children, old people—looked like they were about to keel over from starvation. It was obvious that dysentery was also running rampant through the makeshift slum and that there was no supply of clean water or means of sanitation. The smell they'd encountered at the top of the hill was about one-hundredth of what it was down here.

Hunter had it all figured out by this time. Just as he'd suspected, there was a massive gun hidden up in the mountains to the north. It was probably placed so high and its range so long, that any target came under its range within a hundred miles or so—except the air base and its three-mile long runway. That's why all the people were here—more than eight hundred fifty thousand of them the soldiers said. The entire population remaining in Karachi had fled to Ras Muari Rim, to escape the wrath of the massive, blockbuster shelling.

"It's been like this for months now," the soldier in charge of the small Dutch unit told them. "We can only do our best to keep them fed, and to keep the death rate to a minimum. As it is, more than a thousand die a day. Then again, eight hundred are born a day, too, not that many survive for very long."

Hunter studied the faces of the people they passed. Each set of eyes looked vacant, each belly was horrendously distended. He'd seen many horrible things in his day; untold misery, usually after a particularly nasty battle. But he'd never seen anything like this.

Baldi, too, was simply astonished at the ocean of human misery.

But it was obvious that the whole, almost-surreal scene was affecting Chloe the most.

Hunter stole a glance at her while they slowly moved through the staggering number of refugees, and quickly found himself turning away. Gone was the perpetually bright smile, the sparkling eyes, the glow around her face. Now, instead, Hunter saw tears, running from her eyes, and her lovely smile inverted into the saddest of frowns. It was disturbing seeing her like this; she was someone who should never, ever be made this disheartened. To see her cry was almost as painful as seeing the human anguish all around them.

They finally reached the other end of the long runway, pulling up to a heavily sandbagged enclosure surrounded by both Dutch peacekeepers and Pakistani troops. The soldiers brought them inside and introduced them to the commander of the pitiful outpost. He was a Dutch colonel named Van Dam.

Up until that point, none of the soldiers nor anyone jammed into the instant slum on the runway had recognized Hunter. But Van Dam did right away.

He bolted from behind his battered, teetering desk and heartily shook Hunter's hand. He was a massive man, with rock-hard Dutch features. In his enthusiasm, he nearly crushed Hunter's right hand.

"We have mutual friends!" he boomed. "Sir Neil Asten is a close friend of mine. He'd spoke of you often, and your adventures together."

Hunter retrieved his hand and gave the officer a salute. Sir Neil was the man who'd commanded the towing operation to bring the USS *Saratoga* across the Mediterranean to thwart Viktor's invasion attempt. He was one of the bravest, smartest, toughest guys Hunter had ever run into.

"Please give him my regards when you see him next," Hunter said, casually ending his salute. He then introduced Chloe and Baldi.

Van Dam sat down behind his desk and lit up a massive pipe.

"So what brings the famous Wingman to this horrible place?" he asked.

Hunter took the next ten minutes filling in Van Dam on the expedient points of his latest mission. The Dutch colonel's eyes grew wider with each sentence. He was especially amazed at the description of the events leading up to their bombing of the airstrip near Uruk.

"When we arrived over Karachi and saw the conditions here, we felt compelled to come down and check it out," Hunter concluded. "From what I've seen, I think you are all in very grave danger. You, your troops and the people living here."

Van Dam laughed. "We're shoehorned into an area little bigger than a few soccer fields. There's a huge gun somewhere up in the hills that has kept us trapped here for months. We are all hungry, sick, thirsty, dirty, and tired. I really don't know how it could get much worse."

Hunter just shook his head slowly. "I know this character Viktor," he began. "Or at least, I think I do. Believe me, sir, he will stop at nothing to clear this runway if he has to. Regardless of that gun up there and whoever is firing it at you. He'll send forces against the people hiding here. I believe he'll do anything short of nuking this place if he feels he has to use it to get back down—or more accurately, he'll hire someone to clear it for him."

"Poison gas. Nerve agents. Strafing attacks," Baldi chimed in. "He could move a large force in here in hours and just mow everyone down—and probably take out that big gun, too. Or at least shut it down for a while."

Van Dam's face dropped with each syllable. He'd already had his hands full; this latest information was especially troubling.

He quietly laid his pipe aside and ran his hands over his dirty, tired head.

"My God," he whispered. "What can we possibly do?"

Hunter, too, rubbed his tired brow.

"There's only one thing we *can* do," he said, his voice gaining in strength with each word.

Now everyone in the HQ was looking at him. Suddenly there was a huge explosion outside, the ground rumbled for ten full seconds. Another massive shell had fallen just outside the camp limits.

"And what is that?" Van Dam asked hopefully.

Hunter cocked his head in the direction of the latest explosion.

"We've got to take out that gun ourselves," he said finally.

# Twenty-two

Two hours later, Hunter was back at Karachi Airport, his head buried in yet another aircraft engine.

The abandoned airport was not without its airplanes. There were actually a couple dozen airliners, cargo planes and even some small private craft stuffed away in the various hangars. Trapped there by the conditions surrounding the city, there was simply a lack of fuel and knowledgeable people to fly them out.

All of these planes were also woefully unmaintained, and none of them were airworthy. But this didn't bother Hunter. The plan formulating in his head didn't call for an airplane that was safe to fly. In fact, it called for one that had no engine, no propeller, no way at all to stay airborne on its own.

The plane he'd selected for this odd flight was, by a rather spooky coincidence, a biplane, a reconditioned duffer known as a Gloucester Gnatsnapper. Originally built as one of the first planes to operate from aircraft carriers, this particular model had apparently been part of an aerobatic team in better days. It was covered with Arabic writing, the rough translation of which Hunter believed indicated a Yemeni dialect. The plane was nearly seventy years old, yet its fuselage and wings were still in remarkably good shape.

The fact that it was almost identical to the biplanes of his dream had ceased to amaze him more than an hour ago. He was used to strange things like this happening in his life. Signs and omens popping up and then disappearing only to reappear again at a crucial time—these things were run of the mill to him now. What part of his unconscious, yet highly perceptive mind had foreseen his coming upon this particular airplane and thus transplanted it into his dream? He didn't know—and really didn't want to dwell on it. But his dream—at least this part of it—had indeed come true.

He was in the process of taking the biplane's engine out completely; its small size and relatively light weight made this a fairly easy job. With Baldi's help, they had unlocked the engine mounts and allowed the seized motor to fall to the floor of the work hangar. The propeller, landing carriage and all internal instruments came out next. Hunter even went so far as to yank the control sticks and the seats out of the airplane.

None of this stuff would be of any use to it anymore— not where it was going.

The Gnatsnapper was stripped and unladened by 3:30 P.M. Now came the next part—packing it up again.

Once more with Baldi's help, and that of several Dutch soldiers put at his disposal, Hunter pushed the lightened airplane on a dolly a quarter mile across the empty airport to where the Bear bomber was waiting. Another squad of Dutch peacekeepers had already removed what was left of the bomber's weapons load: two five hundred-pound bombs and a single fifteen hundred-gram package filled with incendiaries. Once Hunter and the others had moved the Gnatsnapper into position under the Bear's right wing, the combined group began carefully loading this ordnance into the cored-out biplane.

Once it was all packed in and taped, Hunter positioned the biplane under the Bear's right wing. Here, between the plane's interior and outboard engines, was a hard-point where huge antiship or cruise missiles could be attached. Now the group grunted and groaned and sweated and spit and gradually lifted the bomb-laden biplane up to this hardpoint. It took some doing, but finally they managed to get the thing mated and wired up. Incredibly, the snout and top wing of the Gloucester just cleared the twin-propeller sweep of the Bear's two huge right-side engines.

Though it wasn't all that apparent to the Dutch soldiers at the moment, what Hunter had created was a flying bomb—a crude glider carrying a one thousand-pound plus warhead. Placing a contact fuse on this strange aircraft would be no problem; the parts from any kind of battery-operated device would do. And there was no doubt in Hunter's mind that the glide-bomb packed enough punch to knock out the monster gun, or at least damage it—if it was hit in the right place, that is.

*That* would be the hard part.

By 4 P.M. Hunter had the wiring for the bomb-laden biplane completed.

He'd set up a crude electrical fusing device plus a way to disengage the glider from the wing of the Bear at just the right moment. All this was hooked up to one of the plane's internal auxiliary batteries. When Hunter ran a series of quick checks, everything worked perfectly.

By 5 P.M. the Bear was fueled up with the last of the gas available at Karachi airport. There were about two more hours of daylight left. Hunter wanted to take advantage of every minute of it. But there was another problem they'd yet to tackle. They knew the general direction of the big gun, but they didn't know which mountain, or even which mountain range, it was hiding in.

Searching for it would take valuable time and fuel—and might end up without result. Hunter asked Van Dam to canvass the huge population of refugees and find out if anyone had any idea where the gun was located.

As if on cue, Van Dam and a security attachment ar-

rived just as Hunter was completing the last of his tests
on the glide-bomb. With them was an old Pakistani man
named Koki. He knew exactly where the big gun was located—or so he claimed.

"It is inside the mountain forty kilometers northeast
of here," the man told them excitedly. "It's huge and
very ominous looking."

Hunter greeted the man's information politely, but
with some dark humor. "I flew over these mountains,"
he told Van Dam. "They all look huge and ominous."

But now Koki was grabbing his sleeve lightly. "But this
one," he was saying. "This one will be easy to find."

Hunter just shrugged. "How?"

Koki tugged him a little closer. "Because it is a mountain that looks like no other. It is a mountain that is
shaped like a monster!"

Hunter did laugh a little now. The old man *was* trying
to be helpful. But . . .

"A monster?" he asked him. "What kind of monster?"

Koki threw his arms dramatically into the air.

"Like a dinosaur!" he roared. "It looks just like a Tyrannosaurus Rex!"

Hunter stared back at the man for a long moment;
suddenly more waves from his dream came back to him.
Then he laughed again.

"The mountain is shaped like a dinosaur?" he asked
Koki to the amusement of the others.

"It is, sir," Koki replied.

Hunter put on his helmet and started strapping up his
flight suit.

"Somehow, I'm not surprised . . ." he said finally.


The late afternoon sun was just waning as the final
preparations for the Bear were completed.

To save fuel, Van Dam's men were making arrangements to have the big bomber towed to the end of the airport's north-south runway. They'd hooked the front of the Tu-95's nosegear to a tandem of two small tanks and began pulling. It took a full minute for the plane to even budge. But finally it began rolling, and slowly, but surely, commenced moving out and towards the runway.

Hunter was inside the airport's long-ago abandoned operations room while all this was going on. He was looking for a map, a chart, anything that would help him navigate once they got airborne. The ops room files were a mess; some were so old they'd actually turned yellow and were near-impossible to read. Though there were some computers on hand, there was no way to switch them on. The wire from their electrical connections had all been chewed away some time ago by rodents.

At the end of fifteen minutes of searching, the only thing Hunter could find was an ancient weather map which showed in rather unsophisticated relief the mountainous areas north of the city. It wasn't much but it was better than nothing. He quickly committed the map to memory, folded it up and put it inside his boot pocket. Then he went back outside.

But right away, he knew something was wrong.

The Bear was about halfway out to the runway; it appeared to be moving fine. The weather was clearing up a bit; this, too, was helpful.

But something was buzzing in his ears, something that indicated big trouble.

Hunter did a long look around and then it hit him: Chloe was nowhere to be seen.

An instant later, he was running. Out to the taxiway, where Van Dam and his men were standing.

"Where is she?" he asked the Dutch colonel anxiously. "Where's Chloe?"

Van Dam was instantly confused. "She's not with you?" he replied, astonished.

A second later, Hunter was jumping into the stolen taxi, revving its engine and jamming it into gear. Baldi was just barely able to jump in with him.

Chloe was not at the airport anymore—Hunter could feel it. So with a screech of tires and a shower of dirt, he tore off towards the only other place she could be: the crowded air base.

If anything, the place looked more crowded once night had fallen.

The smoke from tens of thousands of fires rose above the overcrowded camp, making it look like a dreary brown blanket was hovering a hundred feet overhead. The wildest of thoughts were streaking through Hunter's mind. Who knows what Chloe was up to now, he thought. He could feel his chest tighten up. He'd been so proud of her in the past few hours, slaving under the illusion that he had opened her eyes a bit to what the real world was like. Now, all he could wonder was which group of Dutch soldiers was she servicing? The guys at the entrance to the horrid camp? Or those guarding the headquarters?

Hunter peeled onto the base, scattering those few individuals who had the strength to move. As before, the crowd of starving people parted slowly, weakly, as the taxi passed through. Hunter was trying to look in all directions at once. Maybe Chloe was doing some of the people right here in the camp. Maybe she'd found a young husky buck in the swampy pool of a million people who could muster up enough strength to give it to her good, one last time.

It took them ten long minutes to drive the length of the runway; there had been no sign of Chloe. They reached Van Dam's headquarters, and found a squad of a dozen soldiers standing guard outside. Hunter eyed them angrily; they returned his glare with looks of confusion. Why was he mad at them?

Hunter jumped out of the jeep even before it stopped moving—Baldi had to jam the thing back into the parking gear and engage the brake. By this time, Hunter had dashed past the amazed soldiers and into the HQ itself.

He was expecting to see anything: twelve guys lined up, waiting to take their turn on Chloe. Or maybe she was doing all of them at once. But the place was practically empty. A few hungry soldiers manning the small radio sets, another couple guarding the meager Dutch arsenal.

No orgy. No Chloe.

He went back outside; Baldi was questioning the soldiers standing guard. Not one of them had seen her—or so they claimed.

Hunter was back into the jeep in a second. Once again, Baldi had to make a mighty leap to get onboard before he roared away. Now they were traveling through the crowd again. Hunter's anxiety level was rising like never before. He had to sort through nearly one million people to find her—all while time was running out on his mission schedule. Had it been just about anyone else, he would have probably left her behind.

But she was hardly just anyone else.

He was now heading for a small outpost of Dutch peacekeepers located on the northern end of the runway, close to where the big gun's shells were able to come crashing down. Almost on cue, there was a screech above the refugee camp. Instinctively everyone who was able to move fell to the ground and covered their heads. The shell hit three seconds later. It shook the earth violently for the next half minute. The tremor was so deep, it caused many of the fires to collapse and go out. The weak cries of the refugees rose and mixed with the pall of smoke permanently in place overhead.

But none of this stopped Hunter, even for a moment. He kept driving, slowly but steadily, even as the thousands of people were dropping to the ground all around him. The jeep had kicked once as the shock ran through the moist, disgusting terrain; but Hunter simply downshifted and kept going.

They reached the small outpost—it was two tanks hidden beneath a forest of cut-down trees. There were ten Dutch soldiers on hand, and unlike the others at the HQ, they weren't all that surprised to see Hunter drive up.

Once again he was out of the jeep in a shot. He ran up to the sergeant of the guard, an enormous Nordic type with a face full of scars. Just her type, Hunter thought.

The man couldn't speak English, and Hunter was too agitated to start spewing Dutch. So he stood there and pantomimed Chloe's shape, her hair and her pretty face.

The sergeant got it right away. He smiled, displaying a mouth full of bright white teeth. Yes, one of his men had given her a ride to the camp about an hour ago. Hunter was furious. *Where is she?* he growled at the man. The sergeant shrugged and then pointed in the general direction of the mob. Hunter just shook his head sadly—his first intuition had been right. Chloe was screwing the natives.

He plunged into the crowd, firmly but humanely making his way through the pathetic multitude. The people looked at him like he was from another world. A tall pale stranger dressed all in black, wearing a strange white bowl on his head adorned with yellow thunderbolts. He was suddenly aware of many babies crying at once. Mothers screaming, men weeping. Why all this commotion? Did Chloe have an audience?

He finally moved towards a particularly tight knot of people—this was where all the noise was coming from. In the middle of it, he thought he heard Chloe's distinctly melodic voice.

He was less polite this time as he forced about a dozen of the toothpick people aside and broke inside the circle.

That's when he found her.

She was in the middle of the crowd of people. But she had all her clothes on, her hands were dirty and her hair was actually out of place in spots. She had a small bundle in her arms; she was hugging it tightly. Hunter had to take a closer look before he realized that it was a baby, just born apparently, it was that small.

And then Hunter saw that many of the people around Chloe were crying. He took an even closer look. The baby was not breathing.

He stood there, almost paralyzed, as a man appeared and quickly dug a shallow hole in the debris-strewn ground. With great care, Chloe laid the dead infant into the grave and helped push the dirt back on top.

Then she stood up, hugged the grieving mother and father and turned away. That's when she saw Hunter. Their eyes met. His were downcast with pure, unadulterated shame. Hers were filled with tears. All of a sudden, he felt a million miles away from the frozen dreamland of St. Moritz.

She quickly ran to him, embraced him tightly and cried on his shoulder for two minutes, nonstop.

Then, finally, he led her out of the crowd.

# Twenty-three

The Bear finally took off at eighteen hundred hours—6 P.M. exactly.

The sun was just going down behind the mountains to the west, casting a giant shadow over all of Karachi and the overcrowded air base nearby. But there was still light, way above the tops of the peaks, and this is where Hunter headed as soon as the big bomber's wheels left the ground.

It had been a brief but somber farewell with Van Dam and his men. They agreed that if the big gun was destroyed, they would guide the refugees back home, and once the runway was cleared, they would crater it beyond repair. But no matter what happened, they knew Hunter would not return.

*We'll wave when you go over,* the Dutch colonel told him. Hunter wished them all luck and promised to do everything he could for them.

Now the huge airplane was rising out of the darkened valley, heading towards the last of the sunlight. No one inside the bomber could bear to look back. This was like taking the last plane out of Hell. But they knew that the memories of the horror and degradation they'd seen at Ras Muari Rim would stay with them forever.

Hunter did his best to get his mind back on other things. Despite their steep ascent, the stripped-down bombed-up biplane was still hanging tightly to the right wing. The wash from the two great prop-jets was just passing over the top wing of the Gnatsnapper, actually causing a kind of calm area around the biplane.

*So far, so good,* Hunter thought.

They reached an altitude of fifty-five hundred feet before finding the sun again. As soon as those last dying rays of light hit the huge snout of the airplane, Hunter leveled it off and put the big Bear into a wide orbit. Okay, they had made it up here, intact—but still, they had no time or fuel to screw around. Both Chloe and Baldi had their noses pressed up against the cockpit glass, straining their eyes in the fading light, trying to find any evidence of the big gun.

"If only they fired it, right now," Chloe declared. "The flare from such a monster would guide us right to it."

But the big gun remained silent. Perhaps the people who were using it had seen the Bear take off, or maybe they'd received a report from one of their spies who did. Or maybe the ghostly gun crew was simply eating its supper. Either way, Hunter & Co. would not have their help in finding the big gun.

But as it turned out, they didn't need it.

Hunter turned the huge airplane towards the north and west, following his instinct, the rough trajectory of the shells that had fallen on the city, and the scant information provided to him by the crude weather map.

But it was Baldi who spotted it first.

"I don't believe this . . ." he gasped, his breath fogging up the cockpit window.

Chloe saw it, too. "How strange!" she cried.

Hunter was quickly squirming in his seat, craning his neck in an effort to see what they did.

"What?" he pleaded with them. "What is it?"

Chloe reached over and guided his line of sight down and away from the clutter of controls on the Bear's contact panel.

"Way out there," she told him. "See it? Through all those clouds?"

Finally, Hunter did.

It was a peak about forty-five miles north of the city, bordered on two sides with mountains slightly taller than itself. With their enormous shadows, and the way the light was hitting its top, damn if the peak didn't look like a two-mile high Tyrannosaurus Rex.

Hunter had to blink a couple times. Maybe the fumes inside the shitbucket Russian bomber were getting to him—getting to them all. This thing just didn't look real.

The peak was either rounded off or had been artificially flattened. A crack on its south face perfectly mimicked a dinosaur's mouth, craggy and snarling, with rows of teeth. Long lines of fallen rock formed its small, raptor hands. Its enormous spine stretched to the next mountain over; a small range to the east provided the gigantic, coiled tail. Two smaller mountains at its base looked like its huge feet. It all combined to give the illusion of a huge dinosaur, hunched over, as if ready to strike.

It was one of the damnedest things Hunter had ever seen. Was this a natural formation? Or had someone taken the time to blast out the enormous relief, as a kind of Jurasic Mount Rushmore? It was impossible to tell. If it was man-made, then it could only be described as too ambitious, too bizarre. But if it was artificial, then Nature was certainly playing a grand joke on everyone who lived in the region.

"It's frightening!" Baldi gasped.

"It's art!" Chloe exclaimed.

"Either way, enjoy it while you can," Hunter told them, turning the huge bomber towards the strange formation. "Because it's not going to be around much longer . . ."

* * *

It was pure luck that the small, camouflaged AMX scout car reached the top of the hill just as the huge Bear bomber was beginning its bombing run.

Four mercenaries were crammed inside the scout; they were part of a small army of hired troops approaching Karachi from the north. This force, made up of Afghans, Chechins, and assorted *jihad* warriors, was known in the region as *wazi bugti-kalat*, literally "the raghead warriors." They had been hired by a Persian combat-broker to attack the old Pakistani capital and seize the Ras Muari Rim air base located on its outskirts. Not even the Wazi's officer corps knew why they were being paid to blitz the Paki city and its air facilities. All they'd been told was the city was practically undefended and opposition from un-armed citizens would be nil. This would be an easy job.

The main column of the Wazi army was now moving down the old Dwina highway; they would soon be within forty kilometers of Karachi itself. A mixed infantry/light-armor force, the Wazis specialized in quick response and "clean operations," leaving no survivors or witnesses. This was why they were paid almost double the normal wages for hired guns operating in this part of the world.

The AMX scout car had been sent ahead to check the road to Karachi for any obstacles or mines. In strictest confidence, their commanders had also told them to keep an eye out for a huge gun said to be operating somewhere in the area. Though there was no reliable information on this supposed weapon, the Wazi's intelligence service had heard that another mercenary group, the hated Turkish Star, Inc., was being paid by a group of wealthy Ubekis to pummel Karachi for one hundred days and nights, apparently in return for a long-simmering feud between the two territories. They might be fulfilling their contract by using some kind of huge weapon. Though the owners of Wazi had been intentionally vague about how this big gun might affect their own operation, they assured their command staff that the shelling, if there was any, would not affect the most important part of their job—that was, seizing and clearing the huge Ras Muari Rim air base.

The scout car had reconnoitered the Dwina road all the way down to the approaches of Karachi itself and was returning to report back when its driver pulled up to the top of this hill for one last look-see.

No sooner had they stopped when they heard the ungodly screech coming from above them. It was dusk by now, but the golden sunlight, shining about two thousand feet above them, was enough to illuminate the long thin aircraft high overhead. They immediately shut off the scout vehicle, killing all its electronics and radar systems—the last thing they wanted to do was to present themselves as any kind of target.

They watched in fascination and growing concern as the big bomber began spiraling down towards them. At that moment, a large, fast-moving cloud that had been obscuring their view of the east suddenly cleared out. Now the crew of the scout car could see the awesome and strange mountain formation, too. They were stunned by the sight of it. All four men became very nervous, very quickly. They might be fierce warriors, but they were also very superstitious. Coming to a strange valley to make war was odd enough. Doing so in a place protected by the symbol of such a great creature—well, it got them thinking.

But even stranger, now this huge bomber was falling out of the sky in a manner they didn't think was possible. As they stared, openmouthed, it swooped right over their heads, banked sharply to the left and somehow leveled out. All four caught a glimpse of the strange aircraft the bomber was carrying beneath its right wing. It looked like a biplane, but one without a propeller, an engine, an undercarriage or crew.

With growing astonishment now, the scout crew watched

as the gigantic aircraft turned once again; it was so low now, it was below them. Its nose was pointing right towards the strange mountain. Suddenly they saw the muzzle of an enormous gun poke out of a cave located halfway up the mountain's side, right where the mouth of the great creature was located. There was a tremendous roar. A stream of fire a quarter mile long came spewing out of the gun. Some kind of shell—it looked bigger than the scout car itself—went rocketing away from the mountain, just missing the oncoming airplane and quickly disappearing over the southern horizon.

At that moment, the airplane's engines emitted another terrifying screech. Each belched a storm of smoke and fire as the bomber was suddenly thrown ahead in a violent burst of thrust and power. An instant later, the small aircraft dropped off the bomber's right wing and began gliding along, rising and falling, dipping and jinking in the high winds. It looked very unsteady, almost out of control—yet it flew right into the mouth of the cave. There was a brief moment when everything just seemed to stand still. Then a tremendous explosion shook the valley, the mountains, the air itself. The scout car began swaying in the shock wave. Even their emergency/low-battery powered systems began to blink off, the sudden turbulence was so powerful.

In a heartbeat, the monster mountain was swallowed up in a whirlwind of flame and smoke. A major avalanche rumbled down its south face; it gave the illusion that this great monster himself was shaking, mortally wounded.

The scout car crew was absolutely astonished. Somehow, someway, the pilot of the big bomber had been able to perfectly fling the smaller aircraft—which must have been full of explosives—right into the monster's mouth. The one in a million shot had destroyed the huge gun inside, and presumably most of its crew as well. One moment, it was there—the next it was gone.

After releasing the glider-bomb, the bomber went nearly straight up the side of the burning mountain, its engines chorused in an even higher octave now. It reached a height of about seventy-five hundred feet and then it began to turn over again. This alone was a frightening sight for the men in the scout car. Whoever was flying this beast was handling it as if it were a fighter plane, not a huge bomber.

No one inside the recon vehicle wanted to see what this crazy pilot would do next. They quickly shut all their hatches, put on their helmets and jammed the vehicle in gear. With speed not recommended for such an expensive piece of machinery, the scout car flew off the hill and back onto the Dwina highway.

If they made it back to the main column, they all agreed, they would urge their commanders to call off this job and turn the Wazis back to where they came from.

If any of their superiors balked, they would tell them to go on up ahead, and look for the devastated mountain that once looked like a dinosaur and let them figure out how it suddenly got that way.

# Part Four

Part Four

# Twenty-four

*South China Sea*

The four airplanes appeared out on the northern horizon two hours after sunset.

Two of them were F-20 Tigersharks of the Football City Air Force. The pair of high tech fighters were riding lead for the third aircraft, the C-5 turned flying radar station known as Black Eyes. The fourth aircraft, trailing about a half mile behind the C-5, was the RF-4X super recon fighter owned by Captain Crunch of the Ace Wrecking Company.

The four airplanes were picked up by the small radar sets hidden on Tommy Island and tracked for the final twenty miles of their journey. Rising to meet the airplanes were the two Tornados of the small British force. Now riding shotgun for the small group, they escorted the visitors into the small island's landing pattern, pulling away once the first plane began its final approach. Only then did the barely discernible lights illuminating Tommy Island's single runway blink on.

The C-5 came in first. Tires screeching, its engines thrown suddenly into reverse, the huge radar ship floated down, coming to a stop in less than one thousand feet thanks to the trio of drag chutes deployed from its rear end.

The Tigersharks landed next. They, too, were able to shorten their roll with engine reverses and drag chutes. Coming in last for a slightly noisier, slightly longer landing was the venerable RF-4X. In all, the planes were down in less than forty-five seconds. All the lights went out on Tommy Island again.

The dark ground began moving. Figures dressed in black coveralls were running everywhere. Maintenance vehicles whose engines had been muffled down to nothing began wheeling around. A huge fuel truck was brought up into the night air, emerging from a large underground bunker located nearby. In seconds, a ghostly ground crew was swarming all over the new arrivals.

The fuel truck headed for the C-5 first. Using high-pressure pumps, it quickly gassed up the depleted tanks inside *Black Eyes*. The Tigersharks came next; they topped off both their internal and external drop tanks. Last came the RF-4X. Being older, it took longer for the fuel crew to do its work on her, the pressure pumps were turned down to half power, almost in tribute. Still, the Phantom was filled within ten minutes.

A troop truck appeared on the runway, it, too, materializing out of the underground bunker. Driving past the warming F-20s and the RF-4X, it stopped at the open-nose front door of the C-5. Eight men climbed off the troop truck—they were the Tommy Island communications unit—and onto the huge radar ship. No sooner were they aboard when the massive door closed again.

This done, the C-5's engines suddenly roared to life. Already the F-20s were moving back out onto the runway. With a minimum of flare, they roared off into the early evening, quickly taking up stations high above the island. *Black Eyes* went off next. Its massive bulk rose slowly, majestically into the darkening sky. Once again, bringing up the rear, the X-Phantom was last. It quickly overtook the radar plane and slotted into its place at the head of the aerial column.

There was a brief series of radio checks and a moment of self-diagnosis. All four planes checked out okay. With that, a prearranged signal was given and each pilot reached over and turned off his main and secondary radio units.

This curtain of radio silence in place, the four airplanes turned to the east and streaked away, leaving behind Tommy Island, as dark and as quiet as before.

It was almost as if they'd never been there at all.


The An-124 Antonov Condor was still circling in its holding pattern just off the Filipino Palawan Passages when the F-20s arrived.

The Tigersharks' sudden appearance startled the crew of the heavy-lift ship. One moment their radar screens had been clear; the next, the F-20s were rising out of the low clouds, their weapons systems turned on and maneuvering in a very aggressive manner.

The weary Condor crew stared with bleary eyes out at the spectral airplanes. Who were these guys? Friends or foes? It was hard to tell. The An-124 had been circling like this for nearly a full day now; buoyed by no less than ten aerial refuelings and a handful of radio messages from their Indonesian middleman telling them to hang on, promising triple and even quadruple-pay if they stayed at their position. Each time such a message arrived, the crew voted on whether to bag it or not. Each time, the lure of big money caused them to stay.

Now it appeared as if all that had been a huge mistake. Any chance that these two superfighters might be part of the same operation which brought the Condor here in the first place was dashed when the F-20s cranked up their air-to-air missile power and began painting the huge cargo plane. They were lining up the Condor for a spread of Sidewinder missiles. It was a deadly serious tactic used these days when one aircraft wanted another to open up its radio channels.

The Condor crew had no choice now but to click on their radio sets. The alternative was a long fiery plunge down into the dark, and heavily shark-infested waters below. No paycheck was worth that.

The F-20 pilots were already hailing the Condor, using a low-frequency, wide-band UHF channel that could only be picked up within one thousand feet of its intended receiver. When the Condor crew came on, the F-20 pilots made it brief: Follow us, quietly, or you'll swim with the hammerheads. Again, the Condor crew had no choice but to comply.

So they finally broke their orbital pattern, the whole crew feeling dour and anxious as the airplane finally leveled off and began accelerating to higher than cruising speed. Reluctantly, it fell in between the two F-20s and all three streaked away to the west.

No sooner had they departed when the second half of the flight arrived: the C-5 radar ship and Crunch's RF-4X. The big Galaxy quickly moved into precisely the same circular flight pattern previously flown by the Condor. The C-5 was just a few inches shorter, a few pounds lighter than the grand Condor. On a radar screen, they looked exactly the same.

Once in place, Crunch took his airplane up to thirty-nine angels, and snapped off a three hundred sixty-degree video sweep of the far horizons in every direction. Save for the F-20s and the escorted Condor moving off to the west, the sky was empty.

He sent a live feed from his camera down to *Black Eyes*, where its combined crew viewed it with relief and confidence. No one had seen the switch—this was very good. Even better, between the RF-4X riding sky-high and their own myriad of radar systems, they would be able to see anyone coming from many miles away.

Its own radios now set to the frequency formerly used by the Condor, the C-5 settled into the orbital pattern and reduced its speed to a slowish two hundred ten-knot cruise. High above, Crunch kept top guard.

Together, they would hold this position for the next ten hours.

Ben Wa and JT Toomey were there when the enormous Condor landed on Tommy Island.

Still under the protective eyes of its F-20 escorts, the huge Russian cargo plane bounced in, using the entire length of the substantial runway to come to a stop.

The big plane was surrounded by heavily armed Tommy troops as well as special ops teams from the United American Command even before it stopped rolling. Only then did the Condor crew see the five C-5s lined up in hidden shelters just off the runway. Each plane was painted in a different flashy color scheme; each one had a separate name and design. That's when it dawned on the Condor crew that they'd been hijacked not by some rival mercenary group, but by the United Americans themselves. This deflated their morale even further. It was well known that the Americans didn't make deals when it came to matters like this. They always played it straight and cool. Any last hope of the Condor crew buying their way out of this predicament had just gone up in smoke.

Ben and Toomey were the first people to climb aboard the Condor. The two American pilots casually climbed up the big plane's service ladder and into the cockpit itself. They collected the crew's personal weapons and their flight computer tapes. Then they called for a security detachment to come aboard and take the crew away.

They would be interrogated, the merc crew was told, and held "indefinitely." The hired hands were further unnerved to hear the word "interrogation." These days that could mean anything from a bright light in the eyes to mind-altering, brain-swelling truth drugs. But it was an unnecessary fear. There was no reason to work over the Condor crew; no reason to inflate their brains to get at some secret truth. Ben and JT could tell pretty much what the Condor was up to just by looking at it. The braces on its tops, the reinforced ribbing all throughout its vast cargo bay. It was obvious that the An-124 had been hired to lift something very heavy and deliver it to a spot very far away.

But what was the intended load? And where had the Condor crew been contracted to take it?

These things were not so obvious. But Toomey and Wa were hardly worried. They knew what their eyes could not tell them, the hard disks from the airplane's flight computer certainly could.

They left the big plane by its rear door, meeting six of their UA colleagues. These were the members of NJ104, a former New Jersey National Guard combat engineering unit that had morphed into a special operations group extraordinaire. They had just taken delivery on their new C-5, *NJ104-II;* their first plane had been wrecked upon reaching Vietnam two months before. The new aircraft, painted in bold green camo, was a heavily armed airborne engineering station. These men—Geraci, DeLuso, McCaffery, Cerbasi, Palma, and Matus—were lugging components of the plane's field metal stress test module with them. Using this device the engineers would be able to determine just how much weight the Condor had been configured to take, an important clue in determining just what it was up to.

After helping the NJ guys set up their equipment, Toomey and Ben hustled over to the Tommy ops building. It was now close to 10:30 P.M. local time. From here on, every minute would count.

They took over the Tommy's flight control computer, quickly making copies of the hard disks taken from the Condor and adapting them to the room's Mac. Soon enough they were into the data base, bypassing hundreds of screens containing the maintenance background and manufacturing information for the plane itself. Finally, after a few minutes of searching, they came upon the flight plan the Condor crew filed before leaving for its latest mission.

Just as they'd suspected, moving the An-124 up to the holding point off the Palawans had been just the beginning of the Condor's mission. Once told to move, the plane would have flown to a designated land base, picked up its load and then gotten airborne again as quickly as possible. From there, the plane would head for its faraway delivery point and drop off the package.

Though no specific destinations were given for the plane's pickup and delivery, the estimated mileage to these destinations was on the screen. The pickup point was less than three hundred miles west of Palawan. The delivery point was a whopping thirty-five hundred miles away. By delving deeper into the secret plans, Toomey and Wa discovered that this particular Condor was actually one of five similar heavy-lift airplanes which had been hired out and sent to different parts of the globe. The Palawan Condor had been given the code name "Epic." A similar An-124 code-named *Alpha* was flying around somewhere in the mid-Mediterranean; *Beta* was circling high above the Persian Gulf; *Cosmos* was flying station two hundred miles off the coast of Pakistan; *Delta* was somewhere above western Thailand. These four airplanes had been airborne for at least twenty-four hours, too, all awaiting some kind of a major event within their particular region.

While their potential pickup points were far flung from each other, each plane had the same destination should it be the one selected for the job: a base somewhere deep in Russia.

Toomey and Wa were understandably amazed with what they found. When Geraci, the *NJ104* commander, arrived in the control center they quickly revealed to him what they had learned.

"Let me see if I've got this straight," Geraci said after hearing the whole crazy story. "Someone hired five heavy-lifters to fly in circles for twenty-four hours, hundreds of miles from each other, just waiting for one pickup job?"

Wa and Toomey told him he had it right so far.

"And whenever whatever they were waiting for arrived, the one who was the closest was supposed to go pick it up and fly it into Russia?"

Again Wa and Toomey were nodding their heads.

Geraci pulled on his chin in deep thought. He told them that his preliminary analysis of the Condor said the big plane had definitely been outfitted to carry a large load on its back, something much bigger than a medium-sized bomber or fighter plane.

"It must be some pretty important package," he concluded.

But then Wa told him of yet another bombshell they'd uncovered. It had to do with the so-called *Epic* Condor, the one they'd just hijacked and where *it* was supposed to land.

"It says here they were going to proceed to a pickup point approximately three hundred and ten miles to the west if the package arrived in this area," Wa explained to Geraci. "To an island in the lower South China Sea."

Geraci studied a local map and began looking for any possible landing spot large enough to handle such a big plane like the Condor and its "package." It took only a few seconds for him to put it all together.

"Well, isn't there only one place in the SCS that could possibly handle all this?" he asked.

Wa nodded gravely and then moved his finger the equivalent of three hundred miles across the map.

"I'm afraid there is," he said, finally stopping at the pinpoint in the middle of the vast sea known these days as Lolita Island.

# Twenty-five

It was the middle of the night when the Tu-95 Bear appeared high over the city of Rangoon.

These days, most cities around the world went dark at nighttime. Some were under strict blackout decrees, some couldn't afford to burn electricity both day and night. Others were simply dead, or near-dead.

But not Rangoon.

The sprawling Asian metropolis was lit up to the max. The light rising from the city was so bright, it looked like a gigantic jewel, blazing green and yellow in the middle of the dark night. After the long flight over India and then the Bay of Bengal, the warm glow of the Burmese capital looked almost inviting to Hunter, Chloe and Baldi. They were all growing weary; it seemed like they'd been flying for days.

The mad dive bombing run on the big gun had been a success—but not without its cost. The fuel consumption alone had been very severe; the big bomber was now working on the bottom half of its main tanks. The strain on the engines had done them no good either—the twin-bladed powerplants were older than Hunter and Chloe combined; they didn't need any more abuse. The same was true for the airplane's fuselage. Flailing the big bomb-er all over the sky had been kid's play for Hunter. But the plane's skin was older than its engines. It was now bent and rippled in many places; stretched and weakened in many more.

And then there was the noise.

Because of the bad engines, the holes in the skin and a million other things, it was now horrendously loud inside the Bear—so much so, both Chloe and Baldi had spent most of the last few hours tightly holding their ears.

But the racket inside the cockpit was the least of Hunter's concerns at the moment. Not only was Rangoon glowing in the night, it was bristling with scores of electronic weapons, tracking devices, SAMs and radar-controlled AA guns. There was also evidence of fighter aircraft. Even more worrisome, Hunter needed no fancy contraptions like a FLIR or a NightScope to see this vast collection of weaponry. It was all highly visible, caught in the glare of dozens of spotlights illuminating a huge air base located just outside the city.

Whoever owned this wealth of military hardware wasn't making the slightest attempt to keep any of it hidden. This told Hunter volumes about them. There were two ways to avoid trouble around the world these days; one was to hunker down, stay quiet, dark and safe—and hide just about every major weapons system you had, so as not to reveal your hand to any potential enemies.

The other way was to simply pull down your zipper and show the world what you had. And apparently that was the tactic the people of Rangoon were employing. Taking it all in from fifty-two thousand feet, Hunter had to admit it was an effective way of saying *fuck you* in any language. But it was also a very dangerous, almost adolescent, way to live.

The problem was the air base below was sporting a runway in the fifteen thousand-foot range, long enough to handle the Zon shuttle. If Hunter's master plan was to succeed, this strip would have to be made inoperable somehow.

But this wouldn't be easy; obviously Rangoon was not the retro-primitive desolation of Uruk, the hard-luck valley of Karachi or the defiant fortress of Malta. There could be no sneak bombing run here; no hoodwinking, no victory with mirrors. This would be different. This would have to be done up close and personal.

It was a hard decision to make, but when he saw a swarm of fighters rising up from the city to intercept them, Hunter did not run. To the contrary, he started descending, past fifty thousand feet, down to forty and then thirty-five, making it easier for the fighters to reach them.

Within a minute they were surrounded by a dozen Swedish-built Viggens, odd airplanes to find in this part of the world. Each one was painted in bright garish colors and adorned with highly stylized Burmese characters. There was a frantic round of nav-light blinking, followed by the ominous warning tones caused by all twelve fighters flicking on their missile-guidance radars at once.

But Hunter knew they wouldn't shoot him down. Anyone who displayed military might like the people below didn't have to go around blowing everyone out of the sky—not initially anyway. Rather, he guessed they'd be curious at first, like the beast that sniffs its prey before devouring it. This might give him the time he needed to plan his next move.

So with these thoughts in mind, Hunter began blinking his navigation lights back, telling the Viggen pilots he understood.

Then, slowing his speed and lowering his flaps, he followed the fighters to their base.

They called the place the *Yawdoo Kichi-wan*.

It was an enormous palace-fortress, built of teak, polished mortar and jade. Heavily fortified, and surrounded by guard towers, moats and barbed wire covered with tiger spikes, it looked as if it could have been built anytime within the last several centuries. There was even a white elephant elegantly penned up outside.

The *Kichi-wan* or "Kitchen," as everyone called it, was located just a quarter mile from the air base where Hunter's Bear had been forced to land. Even from this distance, the palace looked gigantic and imposing, lording over the air base and the thousands of plain white but tidy buildings surrounding it. The Kitchen was the center of Rangoon's universe.

The Bear was quickly encircled by at least two hundred troops as soon as it set down and rolled to a stop. Hunter and Baldi climbed out of the airplane first, hands up and smiling. They were quickly disarmed by the soldiers and confronted by the officer in charge.

Just as Hunter had predicted, their captors appeared arrogant, curious, but not outwardly hostile. They were also outfitted very queerly. All were armed with at least one shiny AK-47, but many were carrying two or even three. They were all wearing flashy green camos, with insanely bright-yellow pith helmets and sand-colored Schwarzkopf boots. This was hardly proper combat gear. The officer himself was dressed in a garish red uniform with multiple ammo bandoliers crisscrossing his chest and at least a half dozen pistols and knives hanging from his belt.

Hunter took a closer look at this officer. Small of stature and almost demure, he didn't appear to be any more than fifteen years old. Now Hunter looked into the faces of the soldiers surrounding them. None of them appeared over their mid-teens either.

At that point, Chloe emerged from the front hatch of the Bear, instantly swooning the small army ringing the bomber. This gave Hunter further opportunity to do a quick look around. There was more military equipment packed into this place than he would have thought possible. He could see literally hundreds of AA guns, from big one-hundred-twenty-mms to small, multibarreled twenty-two-mm weapons. There were also dozens of SAM sites, all of them Russian-designed surface-to-air weapons ranging from SA-2s to SA-16s. Combined, there was enough AA here to protect a small country, never mind just a city.

The runway itself was crowded with jet fighters. Viggens and MiG-21 Fishbeds mostly, they were lined up, wingtip-to-wingtip, for nearly the entire length of the fifteen thousand-foot landing strip. Like the ones that had intercepted them, these airplanes were painted in the strangest of colors—bold reds, blues and greens. Some were so brightly adorned, Hunter was sure that when airborne, they could be spotted from twenty to thirty miles away.

The arsenal to feed all these potent weapons was sitting very close by also. Lining the landing strip were dozens of small concrete bunkers, enclosures that undoubtedly contained bombs, bullets, and missiles used by both the impressive air fleet and the air defense forces. This was dangerous planning, Hunter thought. Most military men would have strived to isolate their weapons' magazines as far away from the rest of their components as possible for obvious safety reasons. With the arrangement here at Rangoon, one spark could send the whole place up.

A brand new, bright blue HumVee arrived with a heavily armed motorcycle escort waiting in tow. The officer helped Chloe in, politely sitting her up front, while Hunter and Baldi were put in back. All four doors were then bolted and locked, with the young officer keeping the key. The HumVee's driver seemed to be barely into his teens. He shifted into first gear and began rolling, intentionally going slow as they passed the rows of AA weaponry so prominently displayed around the base.

Each one of these guns was painted in bright, shiny chrome. It was absolutely the worst covering one would want for any kind of operational weaponry. With all these lights, the reflective glare from the guns could be seen from miles away, too.

The driver continued poking along as they passed a strange aircraft storage area located off the main taxiway and behind several layers of barbed wire fencing. It contained no less than thirty-six MiG fighters, most of them highly advanced Fulcrums. Each of these formidable airplanes was sporting a loud, reflective camouflage scheme of some sort, again, as far away as one could get from the typical dull green, blue or gray prescribed for air combat and avoidance.

But this was not the strangest thing about the airplanes. The strangest thing was that the three dozen jet fighters were actually sitting in a huge wooden enclosure filled with sand. There were many shovels and large buckets lying around them, and in several places, what could only be described as sand castles could be seen.

"What's going on there?" Baldi leaned over and whispered to Hunter. "None of this seems real."

Hunter didn't know—and he couldn't fathom a guess. Why in the world would someone keep these airplanes locked up inside what amounted to a gigantic sandbox? Few things were more harmful to an aircraft than sand. One speck in the wrong place could definitely ruin a pilot's day—permanently.

One of the MiGs in particular caught Hunter's eye. It was located at the far end of the holding pen, and unlike the others, it was not up to its tires in sand. This jet was painted all black with hot-rod red trim. Like the seaplane he'd procured back in St. Moritz, this airplane looked like it was going Mach 1 even when it was standing still. It was a MiG-25, an airplane originally built to counter the USAF's B-70 *Valkyrie* bomber way back in the 1960s.

Known as the "Foxbat," the '25 was fast—*very* fast. In fact, it could top Mach 3 without breaking a sweat. Hunter just shook his head again. What was an airplane like this doing in Rangoon?

They finally pulled onto the road leading up to the *Kichi-wan* palace. Oddly enough, it was lined with billboards, exhorting the qualities of everything from Coke, Chevrolet and Burger King, to Esso gas, Lucky cigarettes and Burma Shave. Hunter did a quick study of these large advertisements. They didn't look authentic; rather they were reconstructions, props; as if created by someone building accessories for a large model train set.

The Hummer finally zoomed past the front gate of the Kitchen; by this time they were going so fast, the motorcycle escort was having trouble keeping up. They went right through the enormous front door, through a hallway and into a huge royal chamber, coming to a stop with a mighty screech of the brakes.

Hunter took a long look around this place, too. It was filled with every type of individual one would expect to see in such a regal setting: guards, handmaidens, advisors, slaves, hangers-on, and even a court jester or two. But none of them looked to be much older than thirteen or fourteen. And no one batted an eye when the Hummer drove into their midst. The floor of the place was so clean, it looked like it could be eaten off of. But apparently people drove cars in here all the time.

Two thrones were placed at center stage in this great hall, tons of elaborate ornamentation surrounding them. They appeared to be encrusted in jewels and jade. At the moment, only one of them was occupied. A tiny Asian figure was perched up on the left side chair, trying his best to look imperial.

This, they were soon to learn, was the *swammi-wan,* the aptly nicknamed "Kid King" of modern Burma.

He was no more than fourteen years old and still swaddled in adolescent chubbiness. He was wearing the expected long silken gown, but it was covered with a waist-length leather jacket more suitable for the American 1950s.

Now it was starting to make a little more sense to Hunter. It appeared that by some fluke of royal ascendancy, this young kid was the top dog of Rangoon. This would explain the garish uniforms, the young age of his troops, the brightly colored airplanes, the sandbox full of Fulcrums and and all those shiny AA guns. All of the military might centered in Rangoon looked like it had been put together by a child—wild, imaginative and hopelessly naive. In other words, this boy was actually living out many a kid's dream: playing army with a *real* army.

The Kid King made a gesture for the guards to bring Hunter and the others forward. They were led to the bottom step of the elevated throne platform. The Kid King looked down at them, his pouty face a mask of uncertainty.

"Is that your airplane out there?" he asked them in halting, but understandable English. "The big one, with the strange wings?"

Hunter stepped forward. "It is," he replied.

"What kind of airplane is it?" the boy asked. "I've never seen one like it before."

"It's a Tu-95F Bear high-altitude, long endurance strategic bomber," Hunter told him. "Not many of them left around anymore . . ."

The Kid King's eyes lit up slightly.

"It carries four jet-powered, twin-bladed, propeller-driven engines," Hunter quickly went on. "It can fly half-way around the world without stopping for fuel."

Now the kid's eyes went wider. He'd especially liked that last part.

"How fast can it fly?" he wanted to know.

"Close to five hundred miles an hour," Hunter replied. "Maybe more, if it's done right."

The kid's entire face was beaming now. "With just propellers?" he exclaimed

"Jet-powered propellers," Hunter gently corrected him. "The power taken by the jet engine's propulsion turns a pair of contra-rotating propellers . . ."

"Wow!" the kid yelled.

". . . and that's what makes the Bear able to stay up so long," Hunter went on, intentionally feeding his excitement. "You know, when you fly high enough, it takes a lot less gas to get the job done. Well, these engines are really fuel-efficient . . ."

At this point, Baldi stole a sideways glance at Hunter. Even he knew this was bullshit. But obviously the Wingman was trying to work a vein here.

"I have a lot of airplanes," the Kid King boasted. "Did you see them?"

"Sure did," Hunter told him. "Especially those Fulcrums. They're some of the best machines I've ever encountered."

"I'm collecting them," the kid bragged. "I've got almost forty so far. I'm also getting a MiG-23 swing-wing soon."

"I used to fly an F-111 . . ." Hunter lied.

The Kid King practically leapt from his jewel-enraptured seat.

"No!" he yelled, shaking all over. "An Aardvaak? Really?"

Hunter nodded politely. "It was a real gas to fly."

The kid finally did jump off his throne now, running down several steps until he was at eye level with Hunter.

"What's *your* favorite airplane, Mister?"

Hunter smiled again. "I'm partial to F-16s," he said.

"I love them, too!" the kid proclaimed. "I've been trying to buy one forever—but they are very hard to find."

Hunter kept grinning. "I know," he said. "I've got the last one left in the world.

The kid stared back openmouthed at him now, disbelief distorting his chubby features.

*"You do?"* he asked, amazed. "The last one? What model is it? A 'C' or a 'D'?"

Hunter took a step closer to him.

"Neither," he said in a slight whisper. "My airplane is an F-16XL Cranked Arrow. It's got a seventy-five thousand-pound thrust, GE-606 turbo fan inside that's been uprated to 92.5 It's also got six Vulcan cannons on the nose, and twelve hardpoints under the expanded wing."

The Kid King was simply astounded by now.

*"Awesome . . ."* he whispered. "How fast can you go in it?"

Hunter winked. "That's top secret . . ."

The *swammi-wan* let out a low whistle. "Wow . . ."

Hunter stepped back, looked over at Chloe then Baldi—they seemed to know what he was up to. He'd dealt with many crackpot power characters around the world in his travels. Some admired him, some hated him, some wanted to hire him as their own. He'd bargained with them, cajoled them, and when things went wrong, threatened them. Sometimes the art of survival was all in the words you selected—and how convincingly you could fib. But dealing with a kid, that was another thing. He had to be especially careful about what lies he told.

The kid's eyes were still glued on Hunter.

*"I want one,"* he demanded. "An F-16. I want to add one to my collection."

Hunter took a deep breath. Was it really going to be this easy?

"Well," he told him, "I can let you have mine for a while. For free. To add to your collection."

"You will? How? When?"

"Once I get home," Hunter told him. "I'll fuel it up

and fly back over myself. It'll take me a week, maybe a little more—depending on how long your soldiers want me to stay around here."

The Kid King stood up, hands on his hips.

"Well, you don't have to stay here at all," he declared. "You can go free, right now. Return to your home base and then come back . . ."

"All of us?" Hunter asked.

"Yes, of course, go!" the Kid King was yelling. "Please, I must see this super-airplane as soon as I can . . ."

Hunter took a deep breath. Already he was formulating a plan in his mind. The way the ammo bunkers were lined up so close to the air base's runway, he was sure a few well-placed tracer rounds, fired just as they were taking off, could start a chain reaction that would certainly fuck up Rangoon's airstrip in a major way.

"Go, now!" the kid yelled at them. ". . . and hurry, *please?*"

Hunter gave him a quick salute.

"Sure thing," he said, stepping back with Chloe and Baldi. "I'll bring you some other stuff too. Jackets and a T-shirt . . ."

*"Cool,"* the kid exclaimed.

At that point, Hunter looked over at Chloe who looked to Baldi. Then, they all took a step backwards. No one did anything to stop them. They took another step. Again, there was no resistance.

So they simply turned around and began walking, calmly, but anxiously towards the waiting HumVee. *Would* it really be as easy as this? Hunter wondered.

As it turned out, it wouldn't. Just as they were about to climb into the Hummer for the ride back to the Bear, the hall suddenly reverberated with the sound of one word, a forcefully shouted: *"Halt!"*

Hunter, Chloe and Baldi froze in place. Their guards did the same thing. In fact, everyone in the royal hall dropped to their knees once they heard the echoing command. Hunter gritted his teeth—damn, he'd jinxed himself.

He finally turned around to see a large woman had just taken her place at the top of the throne. One look told him that this was the Kid King's mother. She was as big as a house and her face looked perpetually angry.

She flew down the stairs, pulled the Kid King up by his collar and delivered three hard whacks to his substantial hindquarters. The kid instantly began squealing.

"How . . . many . . . times . . . have . . . I . . . told . . . you . . . not . . . to . . . do . . . things . . . like . . . this?" she screamed at him, punctuating each word with a mighty slap to the kid's rear end. "You are the worst child that's ever been conceived!"

She finally stopped and let him go. The Kid King fled the scene quickly. Nearly all the guards were either looking at the ceiling or rolling their eyes by now. Obviously they'd seen this before.

The big, old mean woman scowled at them—then turned towards Hunter and the others.

*"And you!"* she screeched in the same voice with which she had scolded her son. "You are not going anywhere . . . *ever!*"

Five minutes later, Hunter and Baldi were tossed into a cell located in a tower at the rear of the palace fortress.

The guards were much more forceful with them now. They no longer looked or acted like kids playing guns and dressed in ridiculously bright camos. They were flailing their weapons around threateningly—and actually looking like they knew how to use them. They'd roughly thrown Hunter into the clink, tossing Baldi right in after him and slamming the massive door behind them.

Chloe was led to a cell just two doors down from theirs. Hunter could hear her talking to her guards, asking them sweetly why she and her friends were being locked up.

But the guards were not responsive. Finally they slammed her door shut, too.

Hunter's cell wasn't much, as jails go. It was built of bare teakwood, with two large, barred windows and a skylight over their heads. It smelled like the inside of a sauna, and like everything else in the Kitchen, it had a toylike quality to it. There were no chairs or benches, no place to sit at all. Dog-tired and deflated by this time, Hunter and Baldi slowly slid down the wall to the floor.

Hunter folded his arms on his knees and for the first time in a long time, rested his weary brow.

"I should have booked it while we had the chance," he said, his voice low and uncharacteristically bitter. "Those Vigs can't top fifty-one. We had more than a five-angels buffer. We should have just kept going . . ."

But Baldi was already shaking his head.

"To where, Hawk?" he asked simply. "If we had fled from here, what point would there be in going on? Viktor would simply land here."

Hunter just shrugged. He could have easily slept for a week.

"Yes, but maybe I could have figured out something else," he replied wearily. "I mean, lying to that kid like that—that might have been the biggest mistake I've ever made."

Baldi laughed for a moment.

"Hey, you took a chance," he said. "And the kid almost fell for it. How'd we know his old lady was going to ride in on her broom? Another minute or two we would have been gone."

Hunter just shook his head from side to side and was quiet for a long time.

"Well, I feel bad for you," he told Baldi after a while. "You got a wife, a family. You belong with them, not running halfway around the world with me."

Baldi laughed again, this time more powerfully.

"They would *want* me to be here," he replied. "Believe me, the fact that I'm fighting at the side of the Wingman will give them pride for generations. They know this quest is right, and that nothing will happen to me. So don't worry, my friend. Everything is temporary. This will be, too."

*Everything is temporary. How true that is,* Hunter thought. Freedom. Life. Happiness. All of them last but a pin-prick in the vast fabric of time. And now he was wasting whatever precious amount he had left, getting himself locked up at the very worst moment of his dash along the shuttle's reentry line. He stared up out of the skylight window to the star-filled heavens above. It wouldn't have been that much of a stretch if he saw the Zon suddenly pass overhead right at that moment, gradually getting lower and lower, until finally making contact with the Earth's atmosphere and burning its way back in.

How fucked up would it be if he was still here, inside this cell, and the Zon landed, unadulterated, just a quarter mile away? He had no doubts now that some kind of a deal had been worked out with the Rangoonese for just such a thing to happen—maybe that was another reason the place was so lit up. He shook his head and then sank it lower into his knees. His promise to himself would certainly be fulfilled then: he'd vowed to be on hand when the Zon came down and he would be—it was the being locked-up part that he hadn't foreseen.

And then what would happen? Would it really end here? His psychic innards were telling him probably not. At the very least, he believed Viktor would take them with him in chains when he left. But supposing it *did* turn out this way? Supposing the four walls of this cell were the last things he ever saw? What if this was the last place he would ever be? How long would he last? Would he go insane? Would he pace like a caged animal right to the end?

He considered all this just in the course of a few seconds, but, surprisingly, at the end of it, he wasn't totally disheartened. Why? It was weird, it was even irrational, but deep down Hunter knew that a life sentence here would be bearable for one reason: somewhere down the hall, sitting in her own cell, would be Chloe. And if they were really going to be locked up in the Rangoon tower, for the rest of their lives, then at least he would be close to her over the years, and maybe even see her every once in a while.

As strange as it sounded, *that* would be enough for him to die a happy man.

Out on the runway of the huge base, it was obvious great preparations were taking place.

Though it was early morning now, and just two hours before sunrise, there was a lot of activity. Trucks moving this way, airplanes being towed that way. Every light on every taxi strip was at full illumination; even the backup lights were on, as were the blue runway fog lights and the blinking red lanterns that were lit only in times of great emergencies.

Every pilot in the employ of the royal family of Rangoon was on duty—most had been on site for the past forty-eight hours. the guard at all of the main entrances to the bases had been tripled. Tanks had been stationed at most of these checkpoints. Special K-9 squads were now patrolling the perimeters. All civilian access to the base and the city itself had been blocked off.

Just about the only weapons systems not turned on were the empire's substantial antiaircraft forces. Though the whole region was ringed with SAMs and radar-guided AA guns, none of them were operational at the moment—this, on an order from the Palace Mother herself. There could be no errors—an antiaircraft missile launched by mistake now could prove catastrophic on many levels.

It was no surprise that none of the thousands of Royal Burmese troops or their officers knew what all the activity was about, or what was supposed to happen some time in the near future. They were rarely told what was up as far as the royal family and their activities. They were paid warriors, young, impressionable and for the most part, tight-lipped. They simply carried out orders whenever and wherever they got them.

There was one clue lingering about though, one that many of the soldiers could see. At a juncture of roads which eventually flowed into the main thoroughfare leading to the Kitchen there was a knot of T-72 tanks, backed up by a dozen APCs and another half dozen assorted armed vehicles. All this armor was protecting a rather indistinct-looking truck which was parked at the center of this mobile defense perimeter. This truck, known to all as the *hoochee*, was familiar to the soldiers. It was the same vehicle that showed up any time they got paid—and today was not payday.

The Kingdom of Rangoon was expecting some kind of payment for whatever the hell was going to happen. How large a payment?

Enough for more than twenty-four armed vehicles to be on hand to guard it.

The sound of all this activity wafted up from the huge air base and carried easily over the palace-fortress and into the tower cell currently occupied by Chloe. She was more confused than frightened now. She knew Hunter was close by; she thought Baldi was with him, too. At least they were all together. But what would happen next? Did Hunter have a plan? She couldn't imagine he didn't. But what if she had an opportunity to do something, to get them all out of this safely. Should she take it? No matter what?

She lay on the floor of her cell, looking out the skylight. The stars were very bright tonight—it was not too long ago that she was riding up there among them, Hawk at the controls of the big noisy plane, her nose pressed up against the cockpit window. She thought at that moment that she would like to be up there forever, to be as close to the stars as possible. But then she laughed a little at herself.

There was no way _that_ kind of dream could come true—how could someone stay up high, dancing in the sky, and be close to the stars for the rest of their lives?

The knock on her door came softly.

Chloe rose to her feet and backed herself against the wall. Who would this be? The guards? The Mother?

The door swung open to reveal the Kid King. He was surrounded by heavily armed soldiers, all of them peering in at her. The kid took a step forward, stopped and then began fidgeting.

"Am I . . . disturbing you, ma'am?" he asked in a barely audible whisper.

Chloe shook her head no.

The Kid King took two more steps forward. "Can I . . . I mean, may I talk to you . . . for a moment?"

"Of course," she answered sweetly. His chubby cheeks rose into a smile.

With the snap of his fingers, the guards disappeared. The Kid King pulled the door shut behind him and took two more steps inside.

"What's your name?" he asked her innocently.

"Chloe," she told him. "What's yours?"

He shrugged. "I don't have one," he replied. "Not a real one anyway. Everyone calls me the Swammi-wan. But that's not a real name. Like yours."

He took another tentative step closer. His eyes were now glued on her.

"Why did you come here?" he asked.

She just shrugged and smiled. "It's a long story," she replied. "But I can tell you we didn't come to hurt anybody. Not you, or your family. Or any of your men."

"That guy," the kid said. "The one that knows all about the airplanes. Is he famous or something?"

Chloe laughed. "Everyone seems to think so," she told the kid. "He really would have come back here in his superplane, to show it to you. I know he would have . . ."

The kid's features dropped a mile and a half. "I know," he said. "But my mother. She never lets me do anything."

Chloe studied the boy for a moment, then motioned him even closer.

"But you own all this, don't you?" she asked him. "You're the king, aren't you?"

"I am the Swammi-wan, yes," he told her. "But still, my mother is a big nag. I really can't do much . . ."

Now Chloe took a step towards him.

"I thought kings could do anything they wanted."

The kid shrugged nervously. She was so close to him now he was beginning to tremble. She was still wearing her stunning black jumpsuit. But she had long ago cut off the legs to thigh-high, and unzipped the front to halfway down her cleavage. On Chloe, it actually looked stylish.

"Does she let you see your friends?"

The kid shook his head sadly. "I don't have any friends."

She moved a step closer. "No friends?" she exclaimed. "You mean, you've got no playmates? No *girlfriends*?"

The Kid King actually laughed at this one. "My mother would *never* let me have a girlfriend," he said.

Chloe was right up against him now. She bent forward slightly.

"How old are you?" she asked.

The kid let a tremor go through him. "I don't even know that," he admitted. "I suppose I'm fourteen or so."

She reached over and ran her fingers through his tousled hair.

"Oh, you look twice as old as that," she told him.

The kid was shaking like a leaf now. His breathing became heavy. He was moving like he had ants in his pants.

"Really?" he asked her, jittery.

She put her arm around him. He felt stiff as a board.

"I admire anyone who is a king," she cooed. "I know it must be hard work . . ."

"It is . . ." the kid said, losing his train of thought as Chloe squeezed even closer to him. His eyes were now level with her chest. He was getting an awesome shot of her left one.

"And of course, a king's subjects must do whatever he says, that's right, isn't it?"

"Yes . . ." he gulped.

She reached down and unzipped her suit to just above the navel. "It's so hot in here," she lied—actually it was quite comfortable inside the cell. "I think if you ordered me to take off my top, I would have to do it, wouldn't I?"

The Kid King looked up at her, his face a perfect combination of amazement and fear.

"Really?" he gasped. "Do you think so?"

She nodded and snuggled her near-naked breasts right into his plump little face.

"Yes, I think a king should get anything he wants, no matter what his mother or anyone else says," she told him.

"Me, too," he breathed, his nose now lost in her bosom.

"So you could stop a spacecraft from landing here, if you wanted to, right?"

The kid suddenly withdrew and looked up at her. "A spacecraft? Here?"

She looked down at him, still fondling his pudgy ears. "One is coming, isn't it?"

The kid shrugged—and thought for a moment.

"My mother *has* been talking to some people . . ." he said with some uncertainty. "It's all about a special package or something being brought in here. But I don't know much about it . . ."

Chloe now grabbed the kid so tightly, he nearly lost his breath. She buried his face even deeper into her breasts, and slowly began grinding his little belly with her hips.

"But whatever this thing is, you could prevent it from coming here, couldn't you?" she asked him, her voice dripping with sex.

That's when the Kid King felt his crotch begin to rumble for the first time ever. Finally, he'd caught on.

"I . . . I can do anything," he declared, reaching up and at last boldly grabbing her lovely breasts.

She pulled him even closer still.

"So can I . . ." she whispered softly.

Hunter had almost dozed off when he heard the handle to the cell door begin to turn.

He was on his feet in an instant; Baldi was wide awake now, too. They looked at each other even as the door began to open a crack. What should they do? Jump the guards and attempt an escape? But to where? And what about Chloe?

The massive door did at last swing wide open to reveal a dozen gawky guards outside peering in. They suddenly snapped to attention though, as the dark shadow of another figure fell over them. This person walked into the cell and glowered at Hunter and Baldi.

It was the Kid King's mother. She looked furious.

"Why did you have to come here now?" she asked them through angry, gritted teeth. "At this time . . ."

"We meant no harm, my lady," Baldi tried to explain. "We were just . . ."

But the woman raised her hands over her head and let out such an ungodly shriek, she drowned out Baldi's words. Then, suddenly, tears began to flow down her face.

"I'll never forgive you for what you've done!" she cried.

With that she snapped her fingers and the guards flooded into the room. Three grabbed hold of Hunter; three grabbed hold of Baldi. They had no choice but to go peaceably.

A minute later, they were being hauled into the court of the palace-fortress. The Kid King was there, as well as twice as many armed soldiers. Each one looked more nervous than the next.

As they'd been brought by the main door, Hunter had been able to catch a glimpse of the nearby air base. The runway was filled with the empire's collection of MiG-23s and Viggens. Lined up two by two and stretching off into the haze, they were blocking it off completely. What was this all about? Were the airplanes getting ready to take off and provide an escort for the descending Zon? Or was it something else?

Hunter and Baldi were brought up close to the throne, the kid's mother taking her seat and glaring down at them. The Kid King himself looked almost as confused as before—but oddly, Hunter detected a hint of contentment on his face.

Everything became very quiet. The dozens of soldiers in the hall became absolutely mute. Even the noise from the nearby air base disappeared. Hunter pulled himself up to his full height and stared up at the Mother and Kid team.

The son got to his feet.

"I am letting you go," he said simply. "I want you to return to your home base and come back, in your super-fighter, just as you promised."

The kid stopped to take a deep breath.

"And in that time, I will not let any kind of foreign spacecraft land here, until you return . . ."

Hunter was nearly struck dumb. This was definitely a turn of events he didn't foresee.

"Will you do this?" the kid asked him.

"I'll be glad to . . ." Hunter managed to blurt out, trying his best not to let his astonishment show.

Then he looked over at Baldi. "But what about my friends?"

The Kid King pointed at the Maltese officer. "He may stay or he may go," the kid said. "Either way, it's okay."

Baldi now straightened himself. He couldn't imagine any circumstance in which he would want to stay in this weird, Oedipus-mad world.

Hunter looked back up at the kid. He seemed to have matured a couple of years in just a couple of hours.

"And my other friend?" he asked gravely.

At that moment everyone in the hall turned eyes right—to the door from which the royal family came and went. Standing there, dressed in a tight, sheer, Asian-style silk gown was Chloe.

She looked beautiful.

"She's staying here," the kid declared as Chloe joined him on the throne. "With me."

Hunter felt like someone hit him in the head with an anvil.

"No . . . she can't . . ." he began to say.

"She will," the kid told him forcefully, adding: "Besides, she wants to . . ."

Hunter took a step forward—so did the two hundred soldiers stationed inside the hall.

At that moment, Chloe whispered something to the Kid King. He nodded and allowed Chloe to approach Hunter.

"I'm not letting this happen," Hunter told her before

she could say a word. "I just need a few minutes to figure out how we can all . . ."

She put her fingers to his lips.

"No, he's right," she said. "I *want* to stay . . ."

That's when the second anvil came down on Hunter's head.

He stared at her—he never quite knew what to expect from her. But this?

"Why?" was all he could ask.

"Because, you've got a mission to do, and you can't do it until you get out of here," she said, very authoritatively. "Now, here's my chance to make that happen. My chance to make up for all those terrible things I did to you. You know, back in St. Moritz."

Hunter reached out and clasped her shoulders.

"What terrible things?" He really couldn't remember.

But she didn't answer him. Instead she got closer and whispered in his ear. "Just go," she said. "And don't worry about me."

But Hunter knew that was impossible. If he left without her, that's all he would wind up doing: worrying about her.

"I can't . . ." he said defiantly. "Screw the mission. I'm not letting go. Not this time . . ."

She was right up close to him now, looking deep into his eyes.

"If you really care about me, then you have to go," she said. "Now. While you've got the chance . . ."

Hunter was shaking with anger and frustration—not the usual state of affairs for him.

"But I just *can't* leave you here all alone," he was saying. "Who'll look after you? Who'll protect you if . . ."

"I will . . ." they both heard a strong voice say.

Hunter and Chloe looked over at Baldi.

"I will stay here, with her," the Maltan was saying, tears

almost forming in his eyes. "Nothing will happen to her . . . nothing she doesn't want to happen."

Hunter stared at him, speechless. Then he looked back at Chloe.

She kissed him lightly on the lips and then turned and walked up the steps to the Kid King's throne. She immediately took her place at his feet and began rubbing them provocatively.

Hunter was absolutely crushed. But he had to face the reality of the situation—and think quick. Two seconds later he had the basis for a long-term plan already figured out in his mind.

"Okay, I'll go," he told the Kid King, "but if you want me to come back here with *my* airplane, then there's one thing you must do for me."

Suddenly the innocence returned to the kid's face.

"Like what?" he asked.

Hunter climbed up onto the bottom step of the throne.

"You must let me borrow one of your airplanes . . ." he said.

*In orbit*

The pilot of the Zon space shuttle was in such bad shape now, he didn't know if he was hot or cold.

He'd been tucked inside a pressure suit ever since accomplishing a nerve-wracking yet successful breakaway from the Mir. The problem was the suit, which was two sizes too small for him, and had no heating or cooling capability. Even worse, it had a faulty oxygen valve and its urine venting tube was cracked and frayed around the connecting ring. This was actually the most critical of his problems at the moment. He had to go—badly. But they were now less than one hundred minutes from reentry; at this point every second was precious. For him to climb out of the spacesuit, attach himself to the flight compartment's "pee pack," do his thing, then squeeze back into the suit and back behind the controls of the shuttle would just take too much time. So he would have to hold it as long as he could, and when he couldn't any longer, well, he would have no choice but to go in his pants.

He had already convinced himself that this would be his last flight in the Zon. One way or the other, he felt he would not fly in space like this again. One reason for this gloom: the chances were very high they were all going to be killed on reentry—there were so many things wrong with the spacecraft now, he couldn't imagine it coming down in one piece.

Even if they did somehow make a successful return, the whole question of their landing site could prove problematical.

This was due to their wacky orbital status, the one that had sent them staggering through space rather than zipping through it. The cockeyed course dictated that they could come down only within a very narrow burn corridor. The pilot's original orders had him plotting reentry for a site in the eastern Mediterranean. Then this was changed to somewhere in the Arabian desert. When this was nixed, he had his computers—what was left of them—work on a site on the northwest quadrant of the subcontinent. Then this was scratched in favor of a West Asian strip, somewhere in Burma.

But now, he'd just learned, even *that* option was gone—and therein lay the problem. As far as he knew there was only one possible site left, this one lying further along the burn-line from Burma, a place that was, in the shuttle-speak, a "Grade-Delta receiving plot." In other words, it was a highly unprepared landing strip, probably just recently built, with little or no crash protection or emergency services in place.

Also, according to a report handed up to him by one

of the disgusting passengers below, this landing site was currently graded as being under "dubious security." Translation: it was not yet fully in the hands of people allied with Viktor's Legions.

Oddly, this aspect didn't bother the pilot all that much. Certainly the image of an opposed landing of the Zon was enough to give anyone the shakes—after all, once the shuttle returned to the Earth's atmosphere, it was little more than a big glider; there was nothing it could do if someone was trying to shoot it down. But the pilot didn't think this was a real possibility, simply because Viktor's Legions were so cash-rich he knew they would hire every available mercenary crew in the area to rush to this landing site—wherever the hell it was—and nail it down quickly, no matter what the cost.

No, coming down on an insecure landing strip would be the least of the pilot's concerns, he thought as he began working his computers for the new burn site. Just as long as the place was long enough and hard enough, he could set the Zon onto it.

That is, if there was anything left of the shuttle to land once they began the long burn-down.

# Twenty-six

His name was Donn Kurjan.

He was a colonel, a special operations officer attached to the United American Armed Forces Joint Command Staff. Kurjan was an advance man, the first guy sent into an area that soon might be the site of military action involving the UAAF. He was, in effect, the scout riding ahead of the cavalry column. His eyes were their eyes in the most important part of the battle: the opening minutes.

Kurjan also had a reputation for coming back from the dead. He'd been in many situations in the past when he was literally given up for lost, only to return time and time again. This is why his code name was "Lazarus."

At this moment, he was lying in a deep hole on the east beach of Lolita Island, systematically picking the sand fleas off his hands and face. The cleverly disguised hiding spot, built to the exacting specifications of the old SEAL units, was just about invisible to the naked eye. It was five feet by five feet, covered with netting and papier-mâché the combination of which looked like real beach sand. Inside Kurjan had two rifles, a camera, two radios, a satcom locater, several flash grenades, and a gallon of water. His most important piece of equipment however was his Peeping Tom, a hybrid IR/electronic telescope which allowed him to see as far as twenty miles away in any direction, day or night.

Before him was the vast South China Sea; its oddly

green water stretching far as the eye could see. There was no other land mass of any discernible size within two thousand square miles of this place. Kurjan was literally out in the middle of nowhere.

He'd been on Lolita for twenty-four hours now, dropping in soon after Toomey and Wa returned to Da Nang with the startling news that fake foliage actually covered the island. The speculation about the mysterious Lolita had been running rampant when Kurjan left Da Nang; he couldn't imagine what it was like now.

His own guess was that the island had been converted into a secret, though temporary air base, a place where several squadrons of heavy bombers or dozens of fighters could land, get refueled and then go on to a primary objective. Where would all these airplanes be going? An attack on South Vietnam was the best possibility. Perhaps the thugs of CAPCOM were able to hire a massive bombing strike on the already battered country as an attempt to reignite the war they'd just recently lost.

But Kurjan knew there were problems with this scenario, the first thing being that Lolita was still hundreds of miles away from the Vietnamese mainland. There were many other islands just as isolated, that could serve as a disposable landing strip, and be closer to their targets. Plus, besides being a huge concrete slab out in the middle of nowhere, there was nothing else on Lolita—no set ups for fuel tanks, pumps, generators or anything essential for a refueling base, temporary as it may be.

So why did someone go through all the trouble of laying a huge concrete slab on such an out-of-the-way speck in the sea? No one in the UA command had any firm idea—yet.

But as it turned out, Donn Kurjan, would be the first one to find out.

* * *

The battleship appeared out on the eastern horizon just after noontime.

Kurjan had seen its smoke trail even before it appeared out on the sea line. He'd crawled deeper into his observation post even before the ship's stacks broke the azimuth, pulling his sand netting up and over his head and settling down into invisibility.

He had his PeepScope warmed up by the time the battleship was ten miles away. The ship's appearance was not unexpected—that the Asian Mercenary Cult might be behind the activities on Lolita would come as a surprise to no one. The trouble was that the Cult was still a formidable force in the Pacific and beyond. The United Americans had sunk nearly a dozen of their battleships over the past year. The Cult still had up to thirty of them left. This in addition to more than five hundred thousand men under arms and a substantial sea invasion capability. The guns on their battleships alone could hurl a shell the size of a small automobile more than twenty-five miles. Moreover, the Cult was cash-rich; they were capable of hiring any number of mercenary outfits around the world, whether they be airborne, seaborne or strictly ground units.

The cold truth was, far from home, their lines of communications stretched to the limits, the United American Expeditionary Forces were outnumbered by the Cult more than ten to one.

Kurjan studied the battleship as it sailed quickly towards the island. It was moving at all out flank speed, its stacks were belching huge amounts of black smoke into the otherwise pristine sky. This told Kurjan that not only was the battleship in a hurry, but that the people running it didn't care who saw them doing it.

The ship finally slowed to one third speed about a half mile offshore. Kurjan was taking pictures of it now. It was gray and black like most of the Cult battlewagons, but this one also had red trim and only two sixteen-inch gun turrets, both in front. This told Kurjan the ship was actually a converted battlewagon, one that was equipped to carry and launch troop-landing craft.

Sure enough, no sooner had the huge ship dropped anchor when a half dozen landing craft were lowered over the side, filled with troops and pushed off towards the island's north beach.

Kurjan had two radios with him—a VHF field set and a backup UHF. But he could not make a radio call now. He was sure the enemy ship had an electronic interception capability and making any squawk on the airwaves would undoubtedly give away his position. But he did have the sat-com locator, a device that could serve as a beeper system, tied into a receiving station back at Da Nang. He now began pounding out Morse code on its send button. He was confident that someone back at Da Nang was picking him up and getting at least a rudimentary message that something was happening on Lolita.

By this time the first of the six Cult landing crafts had pulled up onto the north beach. It contained a dozen soldiers which were the closest thing the Cult had to marines. They were about a half of klick from Kurjan's hidden position—and even from that distance he could hear them yelling and bellowing at each other. The sound of their voices had a definite edge to it; they seemed to be in an immense hurry.

Now the rest of the landing craft arrived, and soon there were sixty Cult troops charging up the beach and into the *faux*-jungle. The most interesting thing about these guys was they were all armed with the same weapon: flamethrowers.

No sooner did they reach the fake jungle line when they activated these torches and began sending streams of flame all over the edge of the plastic foliage. Kurjan was amazed how quickly the imitation greenery went up.

It ignited like magician's flash paper—one touch of flame and an entire tree or bush would suddenly disappear in a ball of harsh, bluish smoke.

Kurjan dug down a little deeper into his hole. More troops came up from the shore, they, too, were carrying flamethrowers, they, too, plunged into burning the plastic forest with absolute abandon. Kurjan began getting the notion that maybe he should have put his hiding place a little closer to the water. The heat rising around him was getting so intense, he imagined all the sand on the beach would soon turn to glass.

It was a wild thought, but he began punching his satt-com device again anyway. In minutes, half the island was engulfed in flames—and the other half was melting before the raging conflagration. At this combustible rate, the whole five-mile-square spit of land would be cleared in a matter of minutes. Then what would happen?

Again, Kurjan couldn't even hazard a guess.

All he knew was that someone in Da Nang better be getting his message—and start thinking about sending someone down to Lolita damned fast.

It was twelve-thirty hours when every bell and whistle went off inside the airborne radar ship known as *Black Eyes*.

The huge early warning craft had been holding its circling pattern off the Palawan Passages for hours now. Crunch's RF-4X was still flying a couple miles above the big C-5, sending a live video feed of the skies one hundred twenty miles around down to the Galaxy radar plane.

They were just beginning the one hundred first orbit of this repetitive pattern when every primary and secondary warning light blinked on aboard *Black Eyes*. At first the small army of technicians manning the radar ship thought their equipment was malfunctioning. A patch of radar indications—*swarm* would be a better word—had suddenly shown up in their northeast quadrant. They'd materialized so rapidly, it actually seemed like the airplane's major screens had experienced a simultaneous glitch-out, possibly due to a power surge.

But when all the breakers were checked and the whole system purged and self-diagnosed and everything came back on line, the swarm of blips was still there. At this point, the crew went on high alert; its myriad of systems were slaved up to the main screen located above the plane's central console. As the two dozen techs watched, the primary radar arm made its first sweep. Sixteen blips were revealed, their size and profile matching that of medium-sized jet fighters. The next sweep revealed twelve more. In the next sweep, twenty more. In the next, twenty-two more.

Oddly the techs thought once again that this was some kind of equipment failure, a catastrophic one at that. Surely seventy fighter aircraft were not heading towards them—were they?

Just as they were asking themselves this rather heart-stopping question, another swarm of blips appeared in the southeast quadrant. These bogies were bigger and moving much slower than the first set, fitting the profile of midsized cargo planes, medium-sized bombers or possibly both. The techs did another diagnostic, but they knew these babies were the real items. There were five groups of them, each one containing six aircraft. Like the bogies up north, they were heading west.

Their alarm increasing with each passing second, the techs were about to call up to Crunch to tell him all this when he called down to them instead.

All concern about radio protocol gone, the UA pilot was practically shouting into his radio mic: "Jessuz! Can you guys see all this?"

The techs hastily assured Crunch that yes, they did, and then asked him to zero in his long range video camera on the incoming aircraft.

*"Which ones?"* was his equally hasty reply.

Somehow, someone decided they should look at the oncoming fighters first. Crunch turned over and was soon aiming his ultra-long distance cameras at the large group of fighters approaching from the northeast.

They were flying in a tight formation now, seven lines of ten airplanes apiece. Crunch felt his breath catch in his throat as the camera focused on the first wave of these airplanes, now but seventy-five miles away. Somewhere in the back of his head he'd expected to see a row of mismatched, broken-down or barely flying airplanes. These days quantity often meant little quality. The more planes one side threw at another the more likely those planes were ancient machines; Starfighters, Voodoos, even older stuff like Sabres and Starfires, anything that could get airborne and carry a gun.

But this wave of fighters was no less than Panavia Tornados, high tech, ultrasophisticated, air interdiction/ground attack planes. There couldn't be more than fifty of these aircraft left in the world. But now Crunch and the crew of *Black Eyes* were looking at ten of them.

The next wave was only a little less frightening. It consisted of ten Jaguars, pesky little warplanes that could fight in the air or serve in ground attack. Behind them were two lines of Nanchang Q-5s, Chinese-built rip-offs of the ancient MiG-19 design. Behind them, two lines of Hawk 200s. Bringing up the rear were ten A-4K Skyhawk buddy-tankers, small in-flight refuelers that were carrying extra gas for this aerial force.

"Jessuzz, whose party are these guys going to?" Crunch exclaimed.

He turned over and was now zooming in on the flight of larger airplanes approaching from the southeast.

Once again, Crunch felt a bad feeling in the pit of his stomach as the camera focused in on the vanguard of this flight. At first glance, these planes actually looked rather innocuous. They were a flight of C-23 Sherpas, midsized, prop-driven, two-engine cargo handlers famous for lugging big loads over medium distances. These thirty airplanes, obviously a merc group, had broken up into a very loose formation, a sure sign that they were expecting to go into action soon and were trying to avoid radar detection.

The difference between these planes and the seventy fighters approaching from the north was that Crunch knew who was flying the Sherpas. They were the Island Rats, Inc., a short-lift paratroop brigade out of the Marshall Islands. Their forte was island invasion; they'd made a small fortune attacking their way up and down the thousands of atolls stretching throughout the South Pacific.

The trouble was, there weren't many islands beyond the Palawan Passages in the South China Sea. So what the hell were the Rats doing way out here?

Crunch turned back towards the oncoming storm of jet fighters. They were now fifty-five miles away and flying due west, at about three hundred knots, typical precombat cruising speeds. He had to guess that they were a conglomeration of several fighter merc groups in the area. The Jags and Hawks and the Q-5s were troublesome enough—it was the ten Tornados that had him worried. The Tornado came in two flavors: the GR.1, which was a ground attack airplane whose specialty was coming in low, fast, undetected and hitting a target right on the nose with the first pass. Then there was the F.3, the interceptor version of the Tornado. This plane was especially good at knocking big planes, like bombers, out of the sky from as far as fifty miles away.

Unfortunately, these days, some mercs adapted their

Tornados to do *both* roles, adding on a few options, such as sea strike capability as well.

Either way, the Tornados meant major trouble.

Crunch could tell the guys down in *Black Eyes* were getting nervous. The two separate flights were obviously in league with each other; there might even be plans to eventually link up. The cold truth was the big C-5 radar plane was flying right in their way.

Actually, Crunch had seen enough. Large fighter group approaching from the north; island invasion group coming out of the south. Both oncoming flights were obviously going to the same place with a list of possible destinations being a short one.

In Crunch's mind then, he and *Black Eyes* had fulfilled their mission. There really wasn't any reason to hang around here.

He punched his microphone button and called back down to the radar plane.

*Peel off*, he told them. *Head back to Tommy. I'll watch the rear.*

Word of the two, large mercenary flights approaching from the east reached United American Expeditionary Force headquarters at Da Nang five minutes later.

The call from Crunch had to be coded, decoded, re-coded and then decoded again, this through six satellite scramble bursts that bounced his message as far away as the skies high above Afghanistan. Through all these twists and turns, Crunch's message arrived fairly intact. Basically it said two multiple-aircraft attack columns had been detected and were coming on fast. By their direction and speed, they could be heading for Tommy Island, Crunch reported, or for an attack on the Vietnam mainland itself.

Or they could be heading for Lolita.

Either way, Crunch was strongly advising that the UA

get as many of its airplanes in the air as quickly as possible and be ready to go into action.

It was a suggestion that the UA high command had to take. Whoever made up the two airborne forces, there was a good chance they would have to go into action against them. And at the very least, the UA could not be caught on the ground should some kind of an attack be coming their way.

Within a minute of receiving Crunch's message then, the scramble horns began blaring at Da Nang.

There was an explosion of thrust and power as nearly sixty jet airplanes lit their engines at once. Two squadrons of UAAF C-5 Galaxys were currently active at Da Nang. Of these thirty-two airplanes, fifteen were outfitted as either gunships or missile carriers, two were armed navigation ships, one was a radar ship, seven were troop ships, and seven were refuelers. Within five minutes each one was loaded, engines hot and rolling out to the base's myriad of runways.

There were also three squadrons of fighter jets at Da Nang. One of these was the famous Football City Air Force's F-20 Tigershark squadron. The other two units were comprised of a hodge-podge of jet models, from the ubiquitous A-7F Strikefighters, (ten in all), to several T-28 armed trainers and one, ancient F-106 Delta Dart. All of these airplanes and their pilots were veterans of the wars in America. All of them were outfitted for both air defense and ground attack.

They were also experts in getting off ground in a hurry. No sooner had the warning klaxons around the base died down when the first of the F-20 fighters were lifting off. Climbing high into the midday light, they quickly went into a protective circle around the huge UAEF facility. Four F-20s were already airborne, patrolling the local coasts; they'd arrived back over Da Nang by this time and took up station with their brother Tigersharks.

It took but six minutes and change for all of the fighters to get airborne. Now it was time for the C-5s. With
remarkable, almost scary precision, the huge air beasts
rolled down the runways and clawed their way into the
air, one right after another, nonstop for three and a half
minutes. As soon as each one became airborne, it flew
to a preassigned spot at a preassigned height above Da
Nang and stayed there until the whole group was in the
air.

Then, on one call, the C-5s formed up into combat
profile: six waves of six planes each, the missile ships
guarding the fronts and rear, the gunships holding the
flanks while the troop transports, the refuelers and the
support planes stayed huddled in the middle.

Surrounding this formation were the fighters: F-20s at
the front and back, the older airplanes mixed in on the
sides and down below. It was an amazing choreography,
close to sixty airplanes big and small, falling in behind
one another as if they'd done it every day for the past
years, which in reality, they had, between alerts and training sessions.

Leaving a small contingent of F-5s back at Da Nang for
defense, the United American aerial group turned towards the south just as they received word that the two
mercenary groups heading east had indeed linked up and
were flying in one, large loose formation, too.

Like two naval fleets, anticipating a battle on the high
seas, the two great air armadas were now heading at the
same speed for roughly the same spot over the South
China Sea.

If everything continued as it was, they would collide
over Lolita Island in less than an hour.


Lazarus was hot. *Very* hot.

The heat generated by the immolation of the fake foliage on Lolita Island had been so intense, it had hardened some of the sand on top of his hiding place, causing it to break off and fall in on him, a few torturous chunks at a time. At one point, the flames had come so close, there'd been a real danger that his hiding spot would collapse in on itself, exposing his position or worse, burying him alive.

But luckily the fires eventually retreated and the heat began draining away. It was still extremely hot inside the hole, but for the time being, he was confident the walls would stay intact.

Kurjan still had a peephole to the outside world—his sliver-thin imaging scope was still poking out of his sweaty, precarious position, looking this way and that. Truth was though, he hardly needed the scope's enhancements to see what was going on.

Lolita was now a huge flat slab of white, coarse, rock-hard cement. The Cult landing force had managed to burn away every bit of the fake jungle that had covered the island for the past two months. Only now could Kurjan appreciate the scope of the strange construction project that had been carried out on the anonymous little atoll.

The amount of cement alone needed to flatten the place must have been in the millions of cubic feet, he figured; just getting such a mortar to mix with seawater must have been a major challenge in itself. Though the engineering looked fairly elementary—the island was covered by a squared-off slab that appeared to be sound enough to serve as . . . well, as what? An airport? A troop staging area? A jump-off spot for some further, larger action? Something else completely?

Once again, Kurjan just didn't know.

As soon as the entire island had been uncovered, the Cult troops had laid aside their flamethrowers and had commenced another odd little enterprise. Landing craft coming in from the battleship offshore had been dropping off dozens of six-foot rolls of a bright orange material, possibly plastic or fiberglass, some of it not fifty yards away from Kurjan's position. Teams of Cult soldiers were grabbing one roll between them and scampering off the beach and back up on to the slab. A small group of officers overseeing the operation were mercilessly driving these men to get the bolts of material into what were apparently preassigned positions all along the width of the concrete island. Once in place, the soldiers stood at attention, waiting in the broiling sun for their next command.

Finally, on an officer's radio call, they began unfurling the lengths of orange material. Then, as Kurjan watched with some amazement, they began marching across the huge slab, some traveling east to west, others north to south, dragging the long lines of orange behind them.

It took a few minutes for Kurjan to figure out exactly what they were doing. But then, slowly, it became clear.

The Cult soldiers were laying out the orange material into the shape of a huge arrow stretching along in the center of the slab. And at the end of this gigantic marker they were similarly laying out a gigantic cross.

Well, at least one of Kurjan's questions had been answered. The Cult was undoubtedly preparing the island slab as a landing strip; the large arrow and the huge cross were obviously meant to help pilots spot the place and land on it. But if this was the case, then the runway they'd outlined was nearly three miles long and more than a half mile wide.

*Christ,* Kurjan thought as he began hitting the button on his sat-com device again. *What the hell kind of airplane are these guys expecting to land here?*

# Twenty-seven

Crunch spotted the incoming missile first.

It was about twenty minutes after he and *Black Eyes* abandoned their station off of Palawan. He was flying at forty thousand, covering the rear of the unarmed radar plane now just five thousand feet below him.

He'd left all of his airborne detection going during this hasty tactical retreat, still painting the combined force of the seventy fighters and the thirty troop carrying planes belonging to Island Rats, Inc.

One of the fighters had fired the long-range missile at *Black Eyes;* most likely a Matra Super 730 antiaircraft missile off the wing of one of the Tornados. Crunch's weapons warning buzzer went off when the missile was still thirty-two miles away. He quickly called down to *Black Eyes,* who acquired the MSAAM just moments later.

There was no doubt the radar ship was the missile's target. The fighters had probably expected to find the heavy-lift An-124 Condor waiting at the Palawan station. When they found nothing and turned up their long-range radars, they'd obviously detected the fleeing C-5. Whether they mistook it for the Condor, bugging out on its contract, or something else, they'd launched a missile at it—and that missile would probably hit it sometime within the next forty seconds.

The crew of *Black Eyes* began broadcasting a Mayday call back to Da Nang immediately—but this was just procedure, a quick emergency call to give last position and location before disaster hit. They were still two hundred fifty miles from the mainland. There was no way the C-5 could outrun the long-range "smart" missile or attempt any radical maneuvering to throw it off course. There were four enormous engines burning bright under the monsterous cargo plane's wings and the MSAAM was a heat-seeker. The chances were very good that it would search for the big plane all over the sky, and when found, it would kill it.

But Crunch couldn't let that happen.

So he, too, made a very hasty report back to Da Nang, then switched over to a local frequency and called down to the *Black Eyes*.

"Get down to the deck and stay there, no matter what," he told the pilots.

With that, he turned his RF-4X around and began heading right for the oncoming missile.

The crew of *Black Eyes* obeyed Crunch's order immediately.

No sooner had the Phantom pilot signed off when the pilot of the huge radar ship pushed his steering column practically down to the floor and put the big plane into a heartstopping dive.

Down they went, nearly straight down, through thirty-five thousand feet, thirty. Twenty-seven. Twenty-five.

Their evasion maneuver was so sharp and so steep, the crew inside the C-5 became momentarily weightless—just like on the old astronaut-training airplanes known as Vomit Comets. Only after the big cargo plane went down past twelve thousand feet did the pilots begin trying to get it back. With hundreds of tons of plummeting airplane on their hands, it took all their strength to pull the Galaxy out of its murderous dive. They did finally level her off around eight hundred fifty feet. They'd been going close to three hundred twenty knots on the way down—another few seconds and they would have plowed into the sea.

But no sooner did they straighten out when they realized they had stumbled into yet another precarious position, one that quickly became much more dangerous than the pursuing antiaircraft missile.

Incredibly, they had come down practically on top of a formation of airplanes that had so far escaped their detection, but who were obviously heading for the same rendezvous point as the oncoming fighters and paradrop planes.

This third formation was made up of six C-123 "Providers," two-engine cargo planes from the first Vietnam era. Looking like a smaller brother to the more famous, four-engine C-130 Hercules, these six particular Providers were not in the business of carrying cargo. They'd been reconditioned into gunships, the latest fad among many former cargo-fliers these days. Each airplane had three Vulcan cannons sticking out of the left-wing side, with a swing gun poking out of its right.

It was obvious that these airplanes had been listening in on the attempted attack of the C-5. In fact, they'd been waiting down here just a few feet above the sea for it to appear.

Now that it had, they pounced. Two of the gunships banked inward and positioned themselves about fifty feet off the C-5's right wing. Immediately both planes opened up with cannon fire—six individual streams of tracers leapt out at the radar plane, scoring many direct hits in the blink of an eye. The C-5 crew frantically began rocking its wings—but at this low altitude the big airplane had no power for any evasive maneuvering. After having lost all its energy in the maddening dive, the C-5 was just barely crawling along now, lucky to be making one hundred fifty knots. This was perfect for the relatively-speedy, stripped-down C-123s. Boldly, their guns still blazing, they moved in even closer to the flailing C-5. Now more than half their rounds were tearing into the side of the big plane.

Then two more Providers moved in off *Black Eyes'* left wing. Though they were only able to fire their single right-side swing gun, these two were slightly above and slightly ahead of the struggling Galaxy, directing their cannons down onto of the C-5's flight deck itself.

Now the two remaining gunships decided to join the action. They took up positions below and behind the Galaxy's left tail and began pouring fire into the big plane's starboard engines.

Throughout all this, a kind of controlled panic was taking place inside the C-5. Those crewmen not already dead or wounded were hastily shutting down all unnecessary systems even as barrage after barrage of cannon fire ripped through the airplane's hull. Many were climbing into survival suits and grabbing their parachutes, though they knew bailing out was hardly an option. They were so close to the top of the water now, there was no way they could expect a parachute to open quickly enough to save them.

In the end, they had no more choices, other than to cover themselves and await the end.

So onward the C-5 flew, not two hundred fifty feet above the sea, the six airplanes surrounding it, guns blazing, and slowly but surely moving in for the kill.

Meanwhile, Crunch had doubled back and was now tracking the oncoming antiaircraft missile with his long-range optical weapons detection system.

Having no way of knowing whether the C-5 had managed to get down to the bottom fast enough to lose the deadly MSAAM, he had to assume that they hadn't.

This meant he would have to try and destroy the missile himself.

Trying to shoot a missile out of the air was not an exacting science. But Crunch had learned a few tricks in his years of air combat. He knew that the MSAAM, while sophisticated, was nevertheless no better than its "smart" guidance system and its heat-seeker. To wit, any kind of warm target would do, whether it be the hot engines on a C-5 or on a Phantom.

He picked up the missile visually at about ten miles out. It was clipping along at two hundred fifty knots, its nose wavering a bit as it flew, as if it were trying to sniff out the big C-5. Crunch immediately put his Phantom into a steep dive, crossing in front of the missile's path at about five miles out. The MSAAM's warhead reacted exactly as he'd hoped—it abandoned the scent for the C-5 and locked onto his own engine exhaust instead.

Crunch kept diving. Every warning light in his cockpit went off at once, screaming that he had a deadly missile on his tail. He hastily made it down to eleven thousand feet where he pushed the control column to the left and twisted his air truck off at a very sharp angle.

The missile turned with him, but lost about half its energy doing so, again just as he'd hoped. The MSAAM was still in hot pursuit, still hungry for a kill—but doing so at half speed.

Crunch turned over again and put the Phantom into an all-out power climb, twisting a half dozen times as he zoomed back up through twenty-five angels. The missile adjusted and climbed with him, but it was now down to forty percent power. Still deadly, it was also fading fast.

Crunch reached thirty-two thousand, then tipped the big Phantom over for a third time. The MSAAM adjusted at around twenty-nine, but by this time, it was almost out of gas. Crunch simply went flaps-down, drastically slowing his speed and ripping seven gs throughout his body. He blacked out—but only momentarily. When he came to, the MSAAM was about two thousand yards off his nose, and barely making sixty knots.

Calmly, coolly, Crunch let go one of his four Sidewinders. The missile caught the last residues of the MSAAM's expended engine heat, zeroed in on it and hit it. There was a quick explosion—and then nothing but a ball of flame and smoke. When that cleared, all that remained was the microscopic debris of both missiles.

But Crunch would not have even a moment to celebrate. For no sooner had his missile destroyed the MSAAM when the Phantom's cockpit warning lights began blinking again. He twisted around in his seat to see that two of the oncoming Tornados had pulled ahead of the main group and were now bearing down on him. Suddenly the sky was filled with long orange streaks of cannon fire. Crunch felt the rear of his big Phantom shudder once, twice, three times—reactions to long-range but direct cannon hits. He quickly began losing fuel and electrical power. A few seconds later, the Phantom became very hard to steer. He turned again to see the speedy Tornados pulling to within a mile of his suddenly crippled plane.

That's when Crunch felt his heart sink to his boots.

Unlike the MSAAM, he knew it would impossible to lose these two guys.

Twenty-five thousand feet below and fifteen miles to the west, the C-5 named *Black Eyes* was still being battered by the C-123 gunships.

The radar plane's starboard outer engine was now on fire; the inner right one was smoking heavily. The C-5's cockpit was in a state of total confusion as many instruments had sparked out, causing acrid fumes to fill the compartment. Three crewmen were already dead, seven more were seriously injured. Most of the remaining crew was now huddled just below the flight deck, watching as barrage after barrage of heavy-duty rounds tore into their high tech airplane, and grimly awaiting the end. The ruthless attack was like trying to kill a whale with shotguns—it might take a long time, but eventually something vital would be hit and the airplane would crash into the sea.

Throughout all this, the pilots were madly sending out SOS calls to anyone in the area who could help them— but they knew any kind of assistance was just too far away. The C-5 was still struggling at around one hundred forty knots, having neither the power nor the altitude to break away from its attackers. If anything, the gunships became bolder, flying even closer to the dying giant, each one foolishly greedy in its effort to deliver the killing blow.

One particularly accurate barrage suddenly ripped through the cockpit, killing the copilot and the flight engineer. Now one of the C-123s was riding just above the nose of the C-5, tipped to the left and firing its three side guns directly into the flight deck. The C-5 shook once, lost about fifty feet in altitude in three seconds and began scraping its rear end along the top of the water. Only through herculian effort was the pilot able to pull the giant airplane back up to a relatively safe seventy-five feet.

But that's when the inner left-side engine suddenly blew up, causing a deathly tremor to ring throughout the airplane. The gunships were closing in for the *coup de grace* now. The smoke was so thick inside the cockpit, those still alive could barely see anything out the windows.

In that moment, all of them believed a dark, violent, watery death was just seconds away.

How odd it was for them when all the firing stopped. The next thing the pilot knew, he was yanking the huge airplane to the left in order to avoid colliding with one of the C-123 gunships which was suddenly going down in

front of them, totally engulfed in flames. The quick reaction from the C-5 pilot saved them from a midair col-
lision. The C-123 hit the water so hard an instant later,
it simply disintegrated on impact.

*What happened?* No one on the C-5 knew. One moment
the gunship was pounding them from above—the next it
was on fire and plummeting into the sea. Not a second
later, another of the gunships went into the water about
five hundred feet off their starboard; it, too, was in flames.
Then another exploded in midair just off their smoking
right wing. It was so noisy inside the battered C-5 now it
was almost impossible for those onboard to realize that
no one was firing at them anymore.

Those who were able, dragged themselves up to the
cockpit windows and tried looking out. But all they could
see was smoke, water—and a fourth gunship going down
in flames just below them.

"Jessuzz, what's going on?" someone shouted as yet another gunship exploded close by, splattering them with
thick, oily debris and further clouding their vision.
Smartly, the pilot had pushed forward on all working
throttles and the C-5 was able to gain another one hundred feet of precious altitude. Those looking out the windows saw the last C-123 trying to dash off to the east, its
tail and right wing smoking wildly. It was suddenly engulfed in a cloud of red streaks—hundreds of points of
tracer fire were perforating every square inch of its airframe. Then it, too, just blew up.

When the smoke from this cleared, there was hardly
any wreckage of any size to fall into the water. The last
gunship had been simply vaporized; only a few wisps of
smoke remained.

Still flying practically blind, still dealing with massive
damage to its fuselage, wings, engines and control systems, the C-5 nevertheless was able to gain another one
hundred fifty feet and level itself out. No one onboard

had any idea what happened—it had all gone by that quickly. But at least for the first time in nearly two hellish minutes, no one was trying to shoot them down.

Struggling for more altitude in the empty sky, they found themselves suddenly alone. Someone had shot down the six gunships—and it was certainly not Crunch's Phantom.

So who was it then?

It would still be some time before they found out the answer to that question.

Crunch was dying.

The cockpit of his beloved RF-4X was shattered. Nearly all his controls had been shot away, and those that were still working were blinking out one at a time. His radios were kaput, his oxygen supply was gone, his electrical power was draining away. The control surfaces on his left wing had been torn to pieces; his starboard engine had long ago flamed out. There was a hole the size of a fist in his canopy; the cannon shell that had created it was now lodged in Crunch's right shoulder. There was blood everywhere. He was numb on the entire right side of his body.

He'd been tangling with the pair of Tornados for nearly five minutes now, probably four-and-a-half minutes longer than it should have taken for them to shoot him down. They were, in effect, playing with him. Like cats taunting a mouse before finally killing it, the Tornados were making long sweeping passes at him, firing off short bursts from their massive nose cannons, picking off the important parts of his airplane, one at a time.

Crunch had tried every evasive maneuver in the book for the first couple of minutes—climbing, diving, twisting, turning. But in the end, none of them made any difference. The Tornados were generations ahead of the venerable Phantom. With their powerful engines, and their high tech, variable sweep wings, they could literally fly circles around the old Rhino. Crunch had somewhat pathetically fired off his three remaining Sidewinders at them; he actually saw one of the pilots laugh at him as he streaked by after nimbly avoiding one of the failed missiles.

Now Crunch was defenseless, horribly wounded, and his airplane was but seconds from being shot down over the unforgiving South China Sea. Odd the thoughts that passed through his mind as he felt his spirit struggling to get out of his body. His wife and kids were first and foremost; his friends in the UA were a close second. Just like they said it would, events from his life flashed before his eyes: the many air combat sessions, the many long-range recon jobs and all the planning and plotting in between.

The Tornados went by again, tearing away his extended nose and destroying more than ten million dollars in recon equipment with one pass. The left-side engine bucked once—drenched now in oil, hydraulic fluid and fuel, it didn't have much left in it. Through blood-soaked eyes, Crunch peered out at the sea below and wondered if he'd be dead before he hit the water or not.

The Tornados came back again. It was becoming clear they were getting bored with this game now. Crunch knew they would soon finish him off. Again his thoughts went back to the long, adventurous life he'd led, back to when there were two people and two airplanes in the Ace Wrecking Company. It had been a gas back then—exciting, fast-paced, and hugely rewarding on the financial end. Those had been the best times, he thought, coughing up a sickly amount of blood. Strange then that though he held these memories the closest to him, he could not for the life of him remember the name of his long-lost partner. In fact, he could just barely picture his face in his increasingly hazy mind's eye.

All he could remember about the man was his strangely curled lip and the beyond-regulations sideburns.

*What* was *his name?*

The Tornados were suddenly in front of him again. This would be their last pass—they had more pressing things to do than taunt this old geezer any longer. Both jets started about five thousand feet off his left wing and began a vicious, high-energy dive. He saw the twin streaks of their cannons coming down to meet him. He tried to nudge his control column one way or another, but this did him no good. His plane was beyond any hope of maneuvering now; he had no choice but to sit there and take it.

But then, through bloody eyes, he saw a great flash of light—it happened so quickly, he thought his own airplane had blown up. Somehow, he was able to make out the pair of Tornados, now just one thousand feet off his left wing. Incredibly, both were on fire and breaking up, with the pieces of individual wreckage comingling in the middle of a ball of smoke and flame.

*What the hell had happened?* Had the two Tornados collided? Had they run into each other in their vigor to be the one to actually kill him and shoot him down? It was the only rational explanation for the totally irrational event.

But then, out of the corner of his eye, he saw something that even further defied reality.

It was just a streak of light at first; a flash of silver bright enough to blind him a little bit more. Some kind of airplane went right over his head—it was huge and powerful, with two great engines, two great tailfins and a shape that looked like it was traveling at Mach 5. Suddenly his plane began vibrating tremendously—not from all the damage it had incurred, but from a shock wave emanating from somewhere outside. This concussion was so violent, it served to lift Crunch's dying airplane up several hundred feet in altitude. Somehow, someway, because of this added elevation, he was able to look off to the west horizon and miraculously, spot a thin strip of land just over the horizon.

He twisted around in his cockpit, gravely disoriented, searching for the mysterious airplane he'd seen just for a fraction of a second. But all that was left in evidence of it now was a thick white contrail that rose straight up, as if it were pointing towards Heaven.

Confused, close to going into shock, Crunch summoned up every last ounce of strength in his depleted body. With all his might, he pulled the Phantom's control column to the right—and somehow, the Rhino had enough left in her to respond. Sputtering, smoking and bleeding, the plane nevertheless began heading towards that almost dreamlike piece of *terra firma* off in the distance. Was it an island? Or the coast of Vietnam? There was no way for him to tell. It was still a long way away.

Would he actually make it? He didn't know this either. But he sure as hell was going to try . . .

# Twenty-eight

*Lolita Island*

It was thirteen hundred hours when Kurjan first spotted the C-23 Sherpas belonging to the Island Rats, Inc.

They were coming out of the east; at least thirty of them, lined up in a long, single file flight pattern and heading right for him.

It was very warm inside Kurjan's hiding place, so much so he was down to his skivvies and his gun belt. The activity around Lolita had not stopped one bit. Another Cult battleship had appeared and anchored about a half mile out; more Cult troops had flowed out of it and come ashore. Most of these soldiers, along with the first contingent to arrive, were now in the process of securing the huge arrow and cross they'd made with the bright orange materials. In some cases, these men were hammering portions of the huge marker into the concrete slab with the aid of sledgehammers and spikes. Others were going up and down the three-mile-long landing strip, painting what looked to be a centerline, dividing the huge slab in two.

Still others were setting up mobile communications stations and sections of temporary scaffolding. One of the radio units was just one hundred fifty feet away from Kurjan's position. It was so close, he was worried that the sat-com messages he'd been sending back to Da Nang nonstop since the first Cult soldiers arrived were somehow being glitzed. If that was true, then he might be the only guy on the good side to be invited to this party.

The Sherpas came roaring off the water, their noisy engines rising to a crescendo as all thirty of them went into a long orbit about three thousand feet above the island. Kurjan was familiar with the Island Rats, familiar with their take-no-prisoners method of operation. He, too, was surprised to see them way the hell out here in the South China Sea, especially when their usual field of operations was hundreds of miles to the east.

*Must be some big job for these guys to be here,* he thought, as they continued circling the island.

But their unexpected appearance only served to confuse the issue even further. True, the Island Rats were paratroopers. But if given the option, they would always take the choice of landing their airplanes and disembarking rather than jumping out of them. Why then weren't they setting down on the huge, brightly lined runway? Furthermore, the Rats were experts at depositing large numbers of troops on the tiniest, unmarked locations. Why then had the Cult soldiers laid out the huge cross and the miles-long orange arrow? After all, Lolita Island was a five-mile-square slab of cement in the middle of the sea. A battalion of blind men would be hard pressed to miss it.

This told Kurjan one thing that might have seemed obvious to an outside observer: the large arrow and cross were not for the Island Rats.

They had been laid out for someone—or something—else.

The Sherpas had been circling for about five minutes when another development took place.

Off on the eastern horizon now, Kurjan could see a mass of airplanes that was so large, they looked like a swarm of killer bees. The man they called Lazarus directed his high-powered peepscope in their direction. He was astounded. There were at least five dozen fighter aircraft heading for Lolita Island.

Kurjan clicked his scope up to full-power, and was just able to make out the first line of these airplanes. They were Tornados—high tech attack planes that he knew were not in the inventory of any force friendly to the United Americans, not in this quantity anyway. Behind them were lines of Jaguars and other fighter-attack craft. Kurjan felt his heart sink into the sweaty sand all around him.

This massive air fleet was undoubtedly in league with the Cult and the Island Rats. But something was telling him that the huge landing strip laid out on Lolita Island was not for their use either.

The roar of the Sherpas got louder. Kurjan adjusted himself so that he was now staring straight up through his peephole. Not unexpectedly, the first trio of C-23s was flying over the center of the island, their back doors open and disgorging paratroopers. At the same time, the first wave of fighter jets had arrived high overhead. They began taking up wide orbits around the slab of an island. Paratroopers, a vast number of air cover jets, huge arrows and crosses—still Kurjan just couldn't make heads or tails of any of it.

Three more Sherpas went over—they, too, let loose with twenty paratroopers apiece. Kurjan watched them slowly drift down, most of them landing with a painful scrape and thud on the rough, cement airstrip. As soon as they were down, each Island Rat gathered up his chute, stored it away and then almost casually walked to preassigned positions around the enormous airstrip, totally ignoring the Cult soldiers, as they did them.

Three more Sherpas turned towards the island and began emptying out the back. These paratroopers were landing at the far end of the island, down near the beginning of the big arrow. Three more Sherpas appeared to let go their human cargos over the center of the slab. Kurjan had to admit the Rats were good. They were landing with pinpoint accuracy and slowly but surely forming a mighty protective ring around the island. All this time, the massive sixty-plus air armada continued to circle high above the tiny, cement—clogged atoll.

The sixth set of Sherpas began turning off the beach, roaring right over Kurjan's head and dropping troops not five hundred yards from his position. He heard a completely different noise—one that cut through the clumsy racket of the Sherpas and the high tech squeal of the five dozen jets overhead. This sound, faint but growing louder, had more of a *whooshing* quality to it.

*Damn,* Kurjan thought, *it almost sounds like a . . .*

A second later, he saw it. It was a missile—a Phoenix antiaircraft missile, known for its distinctive hollowing cry usually heard before its arrival. The thing was streaking in from the northwest, diving out of the sky with a shriek now reaching banshee-status. In a heartbeat, it impacted on the third-in-line Sherpa, simply obliterating the two-engine cargo carrier and incinerating everyone inside.

Kurjan was stunned, as was everyone on the island. The missile had come out of nowhere, literally.

Now, even as the bare pieces of wreckage came floating down, Kurjan heard another whooshing sound. An instant later, a second Phoenix appeared, it, too, coming out of the northwest. It caught the tail of the first Sherpa, the one that had already jumped its troops, spinning the airplane around helplessly in the sky before it went up in a ball of flame.

Everyone on the ground was scattering now as two more missiles came in. One went right over Kurjan's head and kept on going; the second one hit something way up at the other end of the airstrip. Suddenly a Jaguar fighter simply fell out of the sky, its fuselage engulfed in flames from the wings back. It hit just to the left of the huge orange cross, its pilot burning to death, still strapped into his cockpit.

Now more and more missiles came screeching in. Overhead the Sherpas began to scatter; way up high, the aerial carousel of fighters began breaking up, too. But for three of them, it was too late. Two more Jags and a Hawk came plummeting out of the clouds, all three crashing into the massive coral reefs which ringed Lolita on three sides.

Suddenly everything was madness. Kurjan looked up to see the jet fighters and Sherpa transports flinging themselves this way and that, trying to find some flying room and get the hell out of the way of the incoming Pheonix missiles. But for three more of them, this was a useless effort. A trio of missiles arrived and took down another Sherpa, another Jag and, surprisingly, a Tornado. All three crashed into the sea about a mile offshore.

Kurjan had his peepscope drilled out on the northwest horizon now. There was only entity in this part of the world that possessed Phoenix missiles and the knowledge to shoot them so accurately: the United American Expeditionary Forces. So was it true? Had his messages gotten through to them?

He strained his eyes and prayed for some kind of vision to feed the greenish tinge of his scope. A few seconds later, that vision appeared. Way out on the horizon, flying incredibly low, he saw the six C-5 gunships of the UAAF bearing down on Lolita Island.

The cavalry was on its way.


The lead C-5 approaching Lolita Island had a very unlikely pilot behind its controls.

Ben Wa was a fighter jock; he'd flown the massive Galaxy barely a half dozen times before, and all those during transit or shakedown missions.

But now here he was, pressed into service, driving one of the gigantic airplanes right into the teeth of combat over the unlikely battlefield of Lolita Island.

That the climax to all the events over the last few days would come here, to this isolated speck of land in the middle of the South China Sea, was not all that surprising. It was the speed at which things had come to a head that was rather mind-boggling to Wa. One moment, he'd been deciphering the flight plan of the captured An-124 Condor; the next he was flying back to Da Nang with this encryption; the next he was hearing the warning call from Crunch and the crew of *Black Eyes* about oncoming mercenary forces, the next he was lifting off from the UA base, riding the wheel of the C-5 known as *Nozo*, arguably the most powerful of all the Galaxy gunships, and serving as the UA's flight leader.

It was on his orders that the two missile ships on his flanks first located and then targeted the paratroop planes circling above Lolita Island. These airplanes launched a spread of Phoenix missiles from thirty-three miles out—indications were that all but one had hit a target. But Wa could see both on his forward-looking radar screen and with his own eyes, that there were dozens of airplanes orbiting Lolita, some scattered up high above the island; others skirting the sea all around it, hoping that altitude alone would protect them from the near-infallible Phoenix missiles.

That all these airplanes, and the men within them, were now enemies of the United American cause was simply a matter of economics. The Cult was involved in the bizarre activities on Lolita, and anyone in their employ became an enemy of the United Americans. Wa could not help but feel some pity for the mercs who had thrown in with the ruthless Cult. That was the trouble with being a paycheck soldier—it really didn't make any difference which side you were on.

"Hope you all got paid in advance," he muttered.

The vanguard of his C-5 force was now about twenty-two miles out from Lolita. The standard formation had changed slightly since they'd left Da Nang. The gunships and missile planes were up front, the troopers, nav planes and refuelers were hanging back. Everyone was flying way down on the deck—Wa's C-5 was barely seven hundred fifty feet off the top of the waves. The missile ships were actually fifty feet below and behind him.

At twenty miles out, one of the other shooters launched another spread of Phoenix missiles. Six of them left the underwing on the missile ship on Wa's left, each one trailing a trademark cloud of orange-white smoke in its wake. Not thirty seconds later, Wa could see six nearly simultaneous puffs of flame explode over the barren, oddly flat Lolita Island. Six more kills, all of them right on the money.

But this meant there were still some fifty-odd enemy airplanes to deal with.

At nineteen miles out, the air weapons warning buzzer went off in Wa's cockpit—being unfamiliar with the C-5's layout, it took him a few moments to figure out what was happening. But then it became very clear: some of the fighters that had been circling Lolita had finally wised up. They'd broken away from their suicidal orbital pattern and were now heading right for the oncoming force of C-5s. Warplanes like Tornados, Jaguars and Q-5s would normally make short work of the relatively slow, leviathan Galaxys—and the sight of thirty of them heading towards Lolita must have made for an inviting sight, a "target-rich environment" in military speak.

But of course, that was the whole idea.

* * *

Flying two and a half miles above the lead C-5s, JT Toomey was also squirming in his seat.

He, too, had been quickly rushed into service just moments after landing in Da Nang from the code-cracking trip to Tommy Island. While Wa had run to one of the C-5s as soon as the alert was sounded, Toomey had headed for the part of Da Nang field that housed the UAAF's fighter squadrons. But unlike the Galaxy units, which were always in need of a pilot or two, just about all the fighters were claimed by the time JT arrived on the scene. As a result, he found himself strapping into the last of the UA's current auxiliaries, the ancient triangle-winged curiosity known as the F-106 Delta Dart.

To say the '106 was old was like saying the South China Sea was a pond. This model, dredged from an air museum somewhere in South America, was more elderly than Toomey's father. It was big, heavy, lopsided to a factor of five degrees and ran damn hot at altitude. But it was a jet fighter nevertheless, with a full cannon load in its nose and two racks of unguided missiles under its wings. Toomey had gone into battle with much less.

Flying in chevrons of three each all around him were the UA's most potent air unit—the famous F-20 Tigersharks of the Football City Air Force. As far as firepower, maneuverability, endurance and just pure speed, it would be hard to beat an F-20. Trouble was, there were only twelve of them, and the hodge-podge of secondary UA warplanes only numbered a dozen and a half more.

According to JT's rudimentary air defense radar, there were more than fifty enemy airplanes coming right at the combined United American force, putting the UA at a clear two-to-one disadvantage as far as the fighters went. Troublesome if not impossible odds.

But there was little Toomey or anyone else could do about that now. They were just a minute or two away from a battle royale. He reached down and began clicking on his weapons systems even as the first line of Tornados began diving onto the advancing C-5s.

Toomey took in two long breaths of oxygen and then on his signal dove out of the sun along with five of the Tigersharks.

"*This* will be very interesting," he murmured to himself.

The first wave of Tornados hit the C-5s just as the F-20s appeared out of the sun.

Ben Wa was too busy grappling with the controls of the big Galazy gunship to breathe a sigh of relief when the Tigersharks showed up—suckering in the enemy warplanes was one thing; actually avoiding them until the F-20s could spring their surprise was another.

The plan was for the C-5 gunships to break through the furball enveloping the F-20s and the opposing fighters and get in close to Lolita. But the scene in front of them almost defied description. The sky was literally filled with jet fighters, twisting, turning, diving, climbing. Anyone who had a cannon was firing it—there were so many tracers crisscrossing in front of Wa's eyes, their hypnotic effect disoriented him for a few moments. He shook away this illusion and jammed his airplane's throttles ahead to full max power.

A Tornado flashed right past his nose, its cannon sending streams of fire towards the gunship off to Wa's right. A Q-5 appeared just below him, its pilot pulling out of a murderous power dive, his sights set on the same Galaxy. Wa immediately screamed into his intercom, and not two seconds later, the twenty-one massive GE GAU-8/A thirty-mm cannons in his gunship's hold came alive in full mechanical computer-controlled power. They simply vaporized both enemy airplanes, sending out an incredible eleven-thousand cannon rounds in a two-second burst.

Now Wa and his line of gunships pressed on, through the sky raining smoking airplanes, wreckage and, in some cases, horribly falling bodies. It took all of thirty seconds to finally clear the incredible dogfight—the longest half minute of Wa's life. But when it was over, he was still in one piece and so were the other six gunships.

Lolita was just five miles away from them now—the slab of an island was cloaked in smoke and flames; no less than eighteen aircraft lay burning on its hard surface or in the shallow waters offshore. There were many troops in evidence on the island, too; Cult soldiers, Rat mercs scrambling around, looking for cover in a place that had virtually none. Wa did a quick sweep of the land mass with his weapons detection system looking for any substantial AA threat—there was none. One of the other gunships did the same for the pair of Cult battleships anchored offshore. They did have Sea Dart antiaircraft systems onboard, but none of them had gone red—at least, not yet.

Three miles out now, and Wa gave the call back to his gun crews to get ready. Of the twenty-one guns sticking out of the left side of the massive gunship, each one was capable of spitting out four thousand rounds a minute; the computer-controlled firing system for all this took as much power as two of the Galaxy's engines. The ammunition belts alone for the twenty-one guns were literally miles long. A five-second burst could cover an area equal to three football fields with at least one cannon round exploding every six inches.

Two miles out and Wa got the call from the back that all systems were green. Through the left side of his headphones he heard one of the other gunship commanders call out that the Sea Dart AA missiles on the two Cult battleships were warming up to yellow, the next step away from going red and being able to fire. Ben couldn't worry about the naval AA threat at the moment. He had other things to do.

One mile out now. He could see the troops on Lolita diving wildly for defensive positions—they'd spotted the oncoming six pack of gunships and Wa could almost feel the terror gripping the enemy troops. They knew of the huge United American C-5 gunships; they knew what utter destruction they could deliver. And here they were, on a five square mile concrete island with no place to run, no place to hide.

At a half mile out, Wa sent a message back to the five other gunships, and as one, they began rising in altitude. His was the first one over the beach, making landfall above the island's northwestern tip just as he reached the preordained firing altitude of thirty-five hundred feet. There was absolute panic below him now—there were probably two hundred fifty troops scrambling around, many were heading to the southern beaches, others were jumping into the shallows off to the east. Again, Wa could not help but feel a pang of conscience for these paid warriors; they'd simply signed on with the wrong side. Now they had to pay the price.

He called back to his gunmasters and told them to commence firing. A few seconds later, the flight compartment was filled with the strangely muted sound of the gunship's weapons computers ordering the twenty-one individual cannons to fire. An instant later the whole airplane began shuddering, again a strangely muzzled vibration as the massive weapons began spitting out thousands of uranium-tipped cannon rounds.

There was nothing but smoke at first—probably the worst vantage point to see *Nozo's* guns in action was up on the flight deck. The five-second burst seemed to last forever, but finally, the whirring sound stopped and the smoke cleared away. Wa craned his neck to the left—below him he could see several dozen enemy soldiers, lying broken and bloody on the hot concrete close by the huge orange cross; they were all dead, literally perforated by the cannon rounds. There were never any wounded soldiers after a gunship attack like this. Anyone caught within the firing zone died in the first few seconds of the surgical multicannon burst.

Wa pulled the C-5 back to level flight and increased throttle just as the second-in-line gunship opened up on an area south of the one *Nozo* had just pulverized. Wa pulled hard right, pressing the C-5's nose back to the northwest. The gigantic dogfight was now stretched from one horizon to another. Wa's mouth dropped open—it looked like something from a dream. Planes were streaking all across the sky, some firing their weapons, others in flames themselves. The contrails left by their smoking wreckage now crisscrossed the sky like a canvas from a madman's fever.

But who was winning?

It was impossible for him to tell. Wa's headphones were filled with a cacophony of sounds—excited radio calls between the outnumbered UA pilots, telling each other to watch out here, look out there, bogies closing from twelve o'clock, others coming out of the six . . . He heard screams, whoops, yelps of both pain and joy. Nearly one hundred jet airplanes were mixing it up—that had to be some kind of record. But numbers alone said the enemy still had the advantage over the United American aerial force. In the sounds bouncing around in his ears, Wa could hear a desperate edge in the intonations of the UA pilots.

Yet in among this chatter, mixed way down in this symphony of terror and men dying, Wa thought he heard another voice. A familiar one, echoing way off in the distance.

*"Hang on!"* this ghostly voice was saying. "I'm on my way . . ."

Flailing wildly all over the crowded sky in his antique F-106, Toomey had heard the strange, disembodied voice, too, somehow discerning the six words in the racket pouring out of his headphones.

"Hang on. I'm on the way . . ."

*Who the hell is that?* he wondered as he climbed on to the tail of an enemy Jaguar.

Just like every other time he'd been inside an ACM, this dogfight was passing before Toomey's eyes in ultraslow motion. All types of warplanes were falling out of the sky around him. Tornados, Jags, F-20s, C-5s. Of all the aircraft involved in this titanic battle, the poor, stubby A-7s and the underpowered Q-9s were probably the worst suited; more of them were going down than anyone else.

The furball was so chaotic, so confusing, Toomey had no idea how many enemy planes he'd downed. He'd nailed at least two Tornados—they weren't the best air combat fighters in close—and two Jags, the latest one now plummeting away from him, minus its tail and left wing. His F-106, heavy and sluggish, had taken about a dozen direct hits, mostly on its wingtips and tailcone. One advantage of tooling around in this ancient beast was that back in the fifties, when the Dart was born, they really knew how to screw the bolts on tight. The plane was nothing if not rugged—in fact, Toomey swore that in at least two cannon runs taken at him by a Tornado, the rounds actually bounced off his airplane's thick skin.

Or at least it seemed that way.

A pair of F-20s went streaking by him now—to his dismay, both were heavily damaged and smoking, though they were still in the fight. Above him, he saw a UA Corsair simply evaporate in a combined barrage from three Tornados; below him, one of the C-5 missile shooters, caught in the middle of the knifefight without much leeway to fire its AA-weapons, had its left wing blown away by two Jags. It was going over, slowly, but irretrievably. A few seconds later the big plane impacted with a mighty crash into the already wreckage strewn sea, taking seventeen men down with it.

Toomey gritted his teeth and went after the Jags that had iced the big shooter, but deep in his gut, he could feel the tide was turning in favor of the enemy pilots simply because they had more airplanes.

Suddenly, things got a lot worse.

It came in a call from one of the C-5 early warning ships, a cousin to *Black Eyes* hiding way in the back. Its pilot was reporting yet another large aerial force heading for the battle out of the southwest. Preliminary indications showed at least four dozen fighter-size aircraft. They appeared to be one type of airplane—a sure indication of a merc force—and were cruising at three hundred fifty knots, a typical precombat speed.

As word of this new development flashed to all the UA aircraft, Toomey tried and failed to get the large aerial group on his dinky air defense radar set. But he didn't need to see these newcomers to know that if they were indeed heading for this battle to fight on the side of the Cult and their allies, then the United American force *was* doomed—it was as simple as that.

At that precise moment, he heard those six words again: *Hang on. I'm on the way.*

Whose voice was that?

Toomey couldn't even hazard a guess at this point.

But whoever the hell it was, he was now praying that he'd get there, damn soon.

*On Lolita*

Donn Kurjan was not sweating anymore.

In fact, he'd grown quite chilly in the past few minutes, due to the cold sweat running through him as he lay huddled in his hiding place, watching the titanic battle unfold before his eyes.

He'd seen his share of combat over the years, from quick-strike covert actions to large-scale battles. But he'd never seen anything like this.

He'd witnessed the attack by the six C-5 gunships from a perspective no one in the UA should ever experience—close to the receiving end. It astonished and sickened him. He'd seen dozens of troops, Cult and Island Rats alike, simply evaporate before the thousands of cannon shells unleashed by the big UA jets. The noise alone was enough to drive a weaker man mad. A combination of mechanical firing and the sound of the huge, depleted-uranium rounds puncturing soft flesh—it was too much even for a veteran like Lazarus to take. He found his hands on his ears and his mouth wide open and screaming in an effort to block out that awful sound—but he didn't even come close to doing so. He began praying instead, beseeching the cosmos to make it stop, to end the carnage.

Finally, it did.

Only after the sixth gunship had passed over was Kurjan able to turn his scope towards the runway where most of the enemy troops had been shot down. He saw little more than collections of cracked bones and smears of runny blood. No uniforms, no weapons, no boots. Nothing—but blood and broken skeletons.

That's when he began sweating ice cubes.

Off in the distance, the massive dogfight was still going on—the sky was now filled with contrails so thick, there was no longer any bright blue sky along the horizon. Just in the course of one minute, he saw at least twelve planes drop into the sea, most of them on fire, or in pieces; most of them providing metal coffins for the pilots within.

It was madness. Man-made, uncontrollable madness all

around him. And he was part of it, for this was the business he'd chosen for himself.

Now his attention was turned towards the east, where the two Cult battleships were anchored. He'd checked them about a half minute before the gunships arrived overhead and saw their crews lined up against the railings, foolishly exposing themselves as they watched the unfolding battle.

Now both ships had their warning klaxons wailing and their crews scampering about the decks. At first Kurjan wasn't sure why the ships' masters were suddenly swinging into action. A glint of light off to his left answered that question. Moving faster than he thought was possible for a surface ship, he spotted two destroyers under full steam, heading right for the battleships. They were the tin cans operated by the secret unit based on Tommy Island. At last, the Brits had decided to come out of their self-imposed cocoon and join the bedlam of combat. Though they were still miles apart, the destroyers opened up on the battleships, sending a stream of seventy-six-millimeter shells into their midst. Kurjan could see both battlewagons turn their massive turrets towards the destroyers, but the smaller, speedier ships, using the north tail of the island for cover, were moving way too fast to get a bead on.

His attention was directed back towards the center of the island. The sky overhead was once again dark with aircraft—but these were not the C-5 gunships returning, nor the enemy fighters swooping in to provide air cover for the troops on the ground. Rather, they were the Sherpa paratroop planes, those few that were left.

Unbelievably, they were coming in low, engines whining, totaling fifteen in all. Kurjan's jaw dropped to his chest when he saw the back ramps of the Sherpas open and lines of paratroopers begin to stream out.

Now *this* was real insanity. The Island Rats were dropping the rest of their airborne force onto the burning, smoking, bloody cement island. Whether they'd been offered more money, or they felt they had no choice in the matter, they were coming down like huge brown raindrops.

The closest ones were landing just a stone's throw from Kurjan's position. They were all trying their best to hit the ground running and scramble for cover, with niceties like gathering up their chutes and forming up into viable units long forgotten.

Another deep rumble drew his attention away from falling para-mercs and back to the skies. He saw then what the recently dropped Island Rats had seen: up high, maybe at fifty-five hundred feet or so, two chevrons of C-5s, a total of six in all. The Island Rats, having seen what happened to the first of their group to be dropped to the island, assumed these planes were the gunships returning to strafe them as well.

But they were wrong—these particular C-5s weren't flying gun platforms. They were the UA troopships; bigger, more powerful than the dinky Sherpas, but carrying the same cargo: paratroopers. As Kurjan watched, his mouth open so wide he was literally swallowing sand, UA parachutists began falling out of the backs of the big Galaxys as well.

He couldn't believe it. Was this really happening? A paradrop *on top of* a paradrop?

It was. The UA command had apparently decided that the one way to take prevent the Cult and its paid allies from taking Lolita Island was to take it themselves.

Kurjan began climbing back into his combat utilities. With this small war—on land, sea and in the air—raging all around him, he knew he was not long to stay inside his hiding hole. All the while he watched as the UA paratroopers dropped swiftly down, some of them catching up with the last of the falling Island Rats. Incredibly, firefights broke out between these rival troops even before they reached the ground. Streams of tracer fire were being traded back and forth even as the two sides drifted down to the hard landing on the cement slab.

Kurjan's head was spinning now. Maybe he was hallucinating all of this—after all, he'd been on the island for nearly forty-eight hours, without sleep, or food and just the barest amount of water. He found his eyes fluttering rapidly—as if some internal mechanism was trying to wake him from this bizarre self-induced dream.

But there would be no easy way out of this one.

He would never know why he suddenly turned his peepscope to the south. In the pandemonium happening all around him, this direction had been relatively quiet. But now, he saw a long dark line, scoring the southern horizon.

What could this be? Another aerial force approaching the fight?

His heart sank lower as he focused in on this new development. These were not friendly aircraft—this was obvious by the direction from which they were approaching. And there were so many of them, it was almost impossible to count them all or identify their aircraft type right away.

But perhaps the strangest thing was the color of this new, oncoming force. Either Kurjan's eyes were going on him or something was wrong with the long-range lens in the peepscope.

Because to him, these airplanes appeared to be painted in the most unlikely color of pink.


They were called the Red Lanterns.

Headquartered out of what was once known as Singapore, the Lanterns were known in aerial mercenary circles for three things: their high contract price, which was three to four times more than typical fighter-pilots-for hire; their absolutely ruthless, win-at-all-costs tactics, which included strafing parachuting pilots or adversaries who survived once they'd hit the ground; and the color of their airplanes, which was actually more pink than red.

The Lanterns flew the Su-27 Flanker exclusively. This big, maneuverable Russian-designed fighter was especially deadly in the hands of an experienced pilot, and that was another trait for which the Lanterns were famous. Their pilots, drawn from pirate air forces all over the world, were among the most combat-hardened in the high-fly merc game. There was an almost Zen-like quality to them: they were more experienced because they lived longer; they lived longer because they never gave their adversaries an even break.

There were now forty-eight of them heading for the fight over Lolita Island, a massive reserve force sent in by Viktor's moneymen to secure the victory once the lower-order combatants had killed each other off. Just like the fliers fighting in the massive dogfight or scrambling around on the ground on the disputed island itself, none of the Lanterns' pilots knew why they'd been paid to fight here, in the middle of the South China Sea, nor did they care. It was just another job to them—a high-priced contract with a large financial pot waiting for them at the end of the day.

The lead flight of Lantern Flankers were equipped with the most advanced, long-range radar sets and had picked up the action over Lolita about twenty-two miles out. The situation looked chaotic and confusing. On one hand they could see the massive dogfight going on just off the island's northern beaches. Then there was the sight of the huge C-5 gunships circling above Lolita, plastering troops on the ground with massive firepower. Close by the eastern shore was the small but continuing battle between the two Cult battleships and a pair of swift-moving destroyers.

Even by the Lanterns' own janissary standards, this was

a wild scene. But their mission was clear. They simply had to shoot down as many of the large C-5s as possible, rout their fighter escorts, sink the destroyers and then provide air cover for the Cult troops already established on the concrete island.

If everything went as they hoped, they'd have the whole thing wrapped up in less than thirty minutes.

Maybe even less.

Exactly what Kurjan and the others saw next would be a matter of intense debate for some time to come.

Not that anyone disputed what happened—it was just *how* it happened and how long it took.

Everyone agreed that the line of pink Su-27 Flankers appearing out on the southern horizon was so thick, they looked at first like a solid entity, as if a huge prehistoric bird was heading for Lolita Island to swallow up anyone still left alive.

Only when the mercenary air fleet broke up into its preattack formations did this frightening vision fade to be replaced by an even more startling one.

The Lanterns split into four waves of twelve. Two dozen maintained an altitude of about eighty-five hundred feet, and turned directly towards the massive dogfight still going on five miles north of Lolita. The second contingent, also containing twenty-four aircraft, swooped down to wavetop level, approximately the same altitude as the rotating C-5 Galaxys.

Right away this brought up twin visions of horror for Kurjan. For the huge C-5s, the gunships, the missiles shooters and the depleted troop carriers, the two dozen Flankers represented an unbeatable foe. Even now, the missile ships were struggling for height and distance from which they could launch their remaining Sidewinders at the oncoming Flankers. But while the C-5s strove for altitude, the Flankers simply went even lower, cutting down the chances of their being hit by any of the C-5 missiles.

As for the pink Su-27s heading for the dogfight, it was all too clear that once they linked up with the surviving Tornados, Jags and Q-9s, they would make mincemeat out of the remaining United American airplanes, depleted of fuel and ammunition as they were.

So, like the legions of Pithicus Augustus, marching on to the field of Galdo in 56 B.C., just in time to rescue his brother-in-law Titucus, the sudden arrival of the Red Lanterns and their high tech warplanes appeared to seal the fate of the United Americans.

But once again, appearances could be deceiving.

It would never really be clear just who saw the strange airplane first, those still battling in the never-ending dogfight or those involved directly in the action on Lolita itself. Everyone agreed on two things though: the airplane was painted all black with a hot red trim, and it came out of the northwest. It was huge for a fighter, long of snout, thick of wing, with a pair of high-rising tailfins. It tore through the air so swiftly, it seemed to be intentionally laying down a constant barrage of sonic booms, deafening the ears of friend and foe alike.

From the beginning there was no doubt whose side the mysterious airplane was on. As soon as it was first spotted, it ripped into those forces allied with the Cult with almost unbelievable abandon. By this time, many of those who saw it realized the airplane was actually a MiG-25 Foxbat, probably the fastest combat aircraft ever built. This would later be used to explain, at least in some small part, how the airplane was reported seen in two places at the same time.

The all-black airplane went spinning through the dogfight, the huge nose cannon firing in such a way that every single round spewing from it not only found a target in one of the enemy airplanes, but managed to hit a place critical to the operation of that aircraft. Many in the depleted UA force saw Tornados, Jags and Q-9s start to drop out of the sky after being hit with just one cannon round, usually placed directly into the airplane's cockpit and killing the pilot, or hitting the airplane's main fuel tank, causing it to explode.

Oddly, the big, black Foxbat saved the worst of its surrealistic venom for the newly arrived warplanes of the Red Lanterns, many of which never even made it into the dogfight. The Flanker was a highly maneuverable airplane that had a reputation for being able to fire-on-the-run, that is, light off its cannon no matter what its position and altitude. But none of this helped the Lantern pilots as the Foxbat picked them out of the crowded sky and ruthlessly hunted them down, delivering a burst of three or four cannon rounds to their cockpits, as if to make sure that the pilot not only died, but died of massive head wounds, thus eliminating any possibility of survival after impact with the already bloody South China Sea.

This aerial brutality, coming so swiftly, so unexpectedly, put the Red Lanterns in a position they'd rarely experienced before: the possibility they would actually have to withdraw from the field of battle; in other words, bug-out on their contract. But even this was not allowed by the mysterious Foxbat.

Thirteen of the Flankers had been destroyed by the rampaging MiG-25 in the span of ninety seconds; in this time two others fell to the guns of the remaining F-20s, and two more had crashed on the shoals a mile offshore from Lolita. The seven remaining Flankers all turned as one and began to run, back towards the south, from whence they came.

Not one of them made it though—each was shot down, seemingly by an air-to-air missile, specifically an AA-6 Acrid IR homing weapon. The problem was the MiG-25 had storage points on its wings for only *four* such AA missiles.

Yet the many witnesses swear they saw a *barrage* of Acrids leave the Foxbat, traveling at incredible speeds towards the fleeing Flankers and picking them off one at a time. Whether other missiles were fired at the cowardly Lanterns—from UA fighters or perhaps from one of the C-5 shooters—was a possibility, thereby giving the illusion that the Foxbat fired all seven missiles. But this would never really be determined.

All that was certain was the seven Flankers were blown out of the sky and not one of their pilots survived.

And with that, the massive dogfight came to a very abrupt end. Any mercenary pilots left alive from the Tornado group quickly left the scene, escaping towards the east, though many of them had hardly enough fuel to stay aloft more than twenty minutes or so. Some of the survivors of the United American force—one third had been shot down, including three F-20s—withdrew about twenty miles north of the battle, where the C-5 refueling planes had been waiting. Those that could took on more fuel, and of those, the ones that still had any significant ammunition left, headed back towards Lolita Island.

It was here that the time element of this bizarre engagement would become the most confused and debated. For even as they saw and heard the Flankers and other enemy airplanes dropping out of the sky from the dogfight offshore, the UA paratroopers that had landed on Lolita itself, swore that the mysterious black jet was over their heads, battling the second contingent of Red Lanterns, the ones that had dropped down to perform ground attack duties even as the dogfight was still going on.

There were at least two hundred UA paratroopers on the southern end of the island fighting both the Cult troops and those of the Island Rats when the pink Flankers suddenly appeared. The ground fighting, centered at first around the base of the gigantic orange arrow, had been fierce and close at hand, so much so that the six C-5 gunships had to back off for fear their intense firing would kill some of the UA soldiers.

The ground-attack Flankers felt no such restriction. They came in, single-file, low and fast, their cannons opened wide, their rounds exploding around UA soldiers, Cult troops and Island Rats alike. They made one unopposed pass and killed more of their nominal allies than UA personnel. But it was as the two dozen airplanes banked up and around for a second run, that the black MiG appeared. As with the raging dogfight, it simply tore into the enemy airplanes, its cannon firing wildly yet with frightening accuracy. And just like the dogfight, Flankers began dropping from the sky like rain. The MiG's performance was so ethereal, fighting on the ground actually stopped as soldiers on both sides couldn't help but look up in awe at the huge fighter's performance. What kind of flying devil was this? To twist and turn through the sky, not more than one hundred feet above them, firing in every direction at once, each shot so unbelievably accurate—a shorn-off wing here, an exploded fuel tank there—that the high tech Flankers appeared to be crashing on purpose, as if just to get out of the MiG's way.

Some on the UA side said the whole thing lasted but a minute; others put the time at just a little longer, perhaps two minutes or more. However long it took, the results were the same. When the smoke cleared, and the noise of the speeding Foxbat finally eased, all twenty-four ground-attack Flankers were gone—dropped into the sea or augered into the hard concrete of Lolita Island.

Of the entire force of Red Lanterns, not one pilot, not one plane survived.

Still in his hole, still gazing out at it all through his peepscope, Donn Kurjan still could not shake the feeling that he was actually in the middle of some kind of extended waking nightmare.

To witness an airplane in the act of crashing was a traumatic event. Seeing tons of metal and machine slam into the ground, even at the height of battle, was such an unnatural thing, it could leave an emotional scar on one's consciousness that just might turn out to be permanent.

Kurjan had witnessed no less than forty-two such crashes in the past quarter hour. Starting with the Sherpas knocked down by the C-5's long-range Phoenix missiles to the rain of Flankers which had recently come down at the hand of the black MiG-25, flying machines had spiraled in all around him, each one hitting with an ungodly shriek that sounded so human, Kurjan still had his hands up against his ears even though all was nearly quiet on the island.

The only noise now was the exchange of long-range shells between the Cult battleships and the pair of Tommy destroyers; this, and the mild roar in the background coming from the engines of the remaining UA warplanes circling nearby.

Through his peepscope, he could see fighting was still going on between the UA paratroopers and the combined Rats/Cult forces at the far end of the island. Just as the battle in the air had subsided, this ground action was heating up. Devoid now of any kind of air support, the two sides were back to hammering each other with small arms, grenade launchers and in many cases, pistols and bayonets. Kurjan felt yet another chill go through him. Despite all the other action, the battle for Lolita would really come down to who won this nasty little fight.

Again, the question came back to him: what the hell was this all about anyway? A battle that rivaled Iwo Jima or Saipan in intensity, all for a chunk of concrete out in the middle of the South China Sea, a place so isolated that even the sea birds didn't come here?

It seemed like most of the island was on fire anyway. Between the plane crashes, the gunship barrages and the battle still raging at the other end of the slab, all he could see was smoke and flame, and all he could smell was spent gunpowder, scorched metal, melted rubber and fuel, and the unmistakable stink of death.

And for what?

He just didn't know.

But something inside him told him to look up, to the northwest, past the circling UA fighters, through the contrails left by the mysterious black Foxbat, through the thin clouds which now blanketed the island. Way up, into the stratosphere. That's when he saw it: a speck of light, surrounded by its own halo of smoke and flames. A speck that was growing larger and going as fast as a meteorite hitting the Earth's atmosphere.

It was so strange, and moving so quickly, to Kurjan's tired, battered eyes, it almost looked like it was coming from outer space itself.

*Forty-two miles above the Earth*

It was now rattling so violently inside the flight deck of the Zon shuttle, the pilot didn't know if he was peeing his pants or not.

All around him was fire, scorching the cracked windows, burning the out-of-joint nose, melting the shaky wings. The build-up of heat was so intense, the control panels, the CRTs, even the steering column itself was hot to the touch. Acrid fumes—from smoldering wires, unvented fuel and a million other things—were filling his nostrils, right through the piece-of-shit spacesuit, suffocating him even as he imagined himself being cooked to death.

They were heading for the so-called "Grade Delta"

landing site, a place he had only just learned from those below was a barely prepared spit of land in the middle of the South China Sea. It had taken him nearly forty minutes to input the new reentry commands into his balky flight computer; usually such a program would have taken about five minutes to perform, but this time the navigation and guidance links fought him the whole way.

He wasn't even sure if he'd gotten all the numbers right and in the proper sequence—but this didn't bother him. He was certain now that his premonition back up in orbit would prove correct—that this would be his last flight in the Zon. He would be killed during reentry, either in this frightening burn-in or by impacting with the Earth. So who cared if the burn numbers were correct or not?

*Death* . . . would it be all that bad? the pilot wondered as his teeth began rattling and the tips of his fingers began to ignite. Life was not such a bargain for someone like him. The captivity was bad enough—it was not knowing who he was, where he came from, who his friends were, that was killing him.

A flaming death might even prove beneficial. There was comfort in the fact that this infernal space machine would go down with him, leaving Viktor rather high and dry. At least if he was dead, someone in the afterlife might actually tell him who he was.

He was just barely able to raise his head now for one last glance at the instruments. The shuttle was coming down much faster and at a much steeper angle than ever before—the pilot couldn't imagine it holding together another moment longer. And even if it did, what then? His navigation and control computers had been working all this time on an error-factor of thirty-percent. This meant that even if the Zon did survive the fiery plunge of reentry, the chances that he would be able to direct it to the small patch of land in the South China Sea was only seventy-percent. There was a three-in-ten-chance then that he would wind up in the sea.

Death by fire or water? What was his choice? This thought went through his addled brain even as he felt the tips of his space boots began to spark, so hot it was now inside the cabin. If he'd had his druthers, he'd pick a quick burning death. Suck that fire right into his lungs and explode like a star. He'd been shot down over water already—two years before, when he was captured and this long, hellish imprisonment had begun. He really didn't want to go through all that again.

Somehow, he managed another glimpse at the smoking control panel. They were still thirty-five miles up and dropping like a rock. Yet to his mortification, it was actually getting cooler on the flight deck. He let out a long, shaky sigh and wet his pants again. The Zon was apparently going to survive the hell of reentry. It looked like it was the water for him again.

He stayed like this for another minute, hoping he would hear the intense rattling turn into a grave crackling sound indicating the spacecraft was breaking up—but that noise never came. Instead, several bells began ringing on his control panel. He looked up to see that, damn it, the shuttle had successfully reentered the atmosphere and now the cockeyed flight computer was steering it to its landing spot—or at least somewhere in the vicinity of it.

The Zon pilot had no choice now but to sit up and start pushing the buttons that would allow him to bring the spacecraft in for a landing. The first thing he activated was his primary guidance computer; this was the baby that would tell him where he was and how far off the mark they were. He pushed the read-out button and his eyes nearly popped from his head.

Not only were they running right on the money, he could actually see the computer outline of their landing spot taking up the center of his read-out screen. He sat up further, looked out the front window and damn if he didn't see it. An island lay dead ahead, not thirty miles away, with a big arrow pointing to a huge cross laid out on its surface.

The pilot began working frantically now—something deep inside him was saying, no, this was *not* his time to die; this was actually his time to do something else. With movements quicker than he'd mustered up in two years, he began pushing buttons, throwing levers and wiping computer read-outs, all the necessities needed before he could take manual control of the Zon.

They were still falling like a brick though, and the Zon's imperfect snout was causing them to buffet violently. The pilot began flipping more switches, pushing more buttons, and entering more commands into his pri-fly computer than it could absorb. Ahead of him, the island was growing larger by the second—the giant arrow and cross almost looking comical from this height.

It dawned on him that what he at first believed were clouds surrounding the place, were actually columns of smoke rising from all over the tiny island. Another kind of tremor ran through him—*was* this place really secured? Hadn't Viktor's henchmen arranged for it to be in their hands before they came down? He didn't know.

They were suddenly only twenty miles from the place and dropping so fast, the pilot imagined his fingertips were burning up again. He could see fires now, and burning wreckage both offshore and on the island itself, some of it very close to the huge arrow that he would have to follow in. It looked like a small war had been fought on the island. But between who? And to what outcome? Another series of shakes went through him. He really couldn't take much more of this—he was not a well man. He took another look at the island, now filling the windshield very quickly as they closed within seventeen miles.

Who the hell was waiting for them down there?

The next twenty seconds were filled with more button pushing, more lever throwing, more computer overrides. When he looked up again, he was at seventeen thousand feet, traveling at five hundred knots and about fourteen miles from set-down. The island looked like a little chunk of Gehenna at this point—smoke, flames, burning machines, all over the place. A stray mad thought filled the pilot's head: maybe he *was* dead, and this was his introduction to Hell.

More computer-killing, more systems to be shut down. His hands gripped the melting control column tightly now. Somehow his attention was drawn to the outside, a glint of metal off to his left. He nearly wet himself again—there was an airplane out there, riding right beside him. It was so close he could see the pilot looking in at him.

Back to the computer screen. He was now at eleven thousand feet, trying like crazy to reduce his speed and coming almost straight down. Though he shouldn't have, he looked out the window again—damn, there were two airplanes out there now, both pilots were looking right at him. He was too far removed from reality to know what kind of airplanes they were flying, but he could see that they had the strangest emblems on their sides.

What the hell were they? They looked like little footballs . .

Suddenly he was at five thousand feet, still riding at four hundred fifty knots and barely seven miles away from the burning, smoking island. He was going much too fast for a safe landing—but what the hell could he do? He looked back out at the airplanes chasing him. The pilots were motioning to him frantically. They seemed to realize his problem. Suddenly one of them lowered his landing gear, violently jerking his plane back and off to the side as he did so.

The Zon pilot had to think a moment—why would an airplane's pilot do that? Then it hit him. He leaped for the button which controlled his own landing gear and pushed it hard. He felt a violent kick and saw a row of red lights pop onto his control panel. His gear was lowering way too early for a normal landing—but it was also serving to slow the Zon down dramatically.

He looked at his guidance computer again. Just four miles away now, altitude at thirty-one hundred. Speed was down to two hundred ninety and still dropping.

He chanced another look out the window and was startled to see a huge airplane pulling up along his portside. It was painted like a circus train and had a thousand guns sticking out of it. So, he'd been right! He *was* descending into Hell. This thing couldn't possibly be real.

Just two and a half miles out now—he was close enough to see all the wreckage burning on the island was demolished airplanes. Yes, it was making sense now. This wasn't a landing spot—it was a place where aircraft of all types and sizes came to crash.

Now he was just a mile and a half away. He could see the big arrow was just some kind of an orange stripe and the huge cross was, too. He could see bodies everywhere, broken and bloody.

He shook his head and laughed—all this time he thought Viktor was the devil; he certainly looked the part. But now the pilot was sure he'd be meeting the real item very, very shortly.

A half mile out now, and only one thousand feet in height. Another strange airplane with the little football painted on its side came up beside him, stayed a few seconds then peeled off. The smoke was clouding his windscreen now. He killed the computer completely and yanked the control column back towards him. All he could see were flames, rising up to meet him. He imagined he could feel their heat, and not just on his fingers and toes, but all over. He was insane. He was dead, and landing the shuttle here in Hell was just a matter of procedure.

Suddenly every single light on his panel lit up. He reached out and pulled the lever that released the Zon's enormous drag chute. Bells were ringing in his ears but by rote alone he pushed the control column forward. The shuttle's nose rose instead of falling, then fell when it should have climbed. The chute caught, but the Zon pilot imagined it would quickly burst into flames. He was, after all, landing in Hell.

There was another huge bang, the Zon shuddered from nose to ass and back again. Now the bells got louder and the lights on the control panel got brighter, and oddly, he felt heavy again. Another jolt, another bounce, this one so hard he bit his tongue, causing it to bleed. Another bang, and then a strange dragging sound. Suddenly he felt his feet pressing hard on something just below the control column. Were those the brakes? He didn't know.

He looked out the window, near terrified now. He was speeding along, oscillating between the ground and the cushion of air beneath the mighty Zon. He was passing rows of airplanes, some with little footballs on them, others the gigantic kind with the strange paint jobs. And he could see soldiers, lined up along the strip, firing their guns in the air and pointing at him.

Finally, with what he believed was the last effort left inside the last sane part of his body, he pushed down on the control column again. He immediately felt a mighty thump, then a second one, then a third, and then, at last, the sound of the shuttle's tires finally catching hold of the ground and staying there.

He was down.

The shuttle seemed to roll on forever, careening this way and that, the sounds of the tires burning up and brakes locking filling the flight compartment. But gradually, it began slowing down and now the lines of airplanes and men outside weren't so much of a blur. These aircraft—they seemed somewhat familiar to the Zon pilot, especially the ones with the little footballs painted on their sides. Something way back in his memory, something that was not completely erased from his mind-washing nightmare was telling him that not only had he seen these airplanes before, but that he might actually know the men who flew them.

The shuttle finally rolled to a stop, ironically right in the middle of the huge orange cross—he couldn't have made a better landing if he had tried. He began shutting down all primary and secondary systems, making sure to click the fire extinguishers to ready should something happen now that they were down.

Through the window he could see at least a couple hundred soldiers gathered at the side of the runway. Some were armed and looked as if they'd just gone through a terrible fight; others were sitting on the hard concrete, hands tied behind their backs.

A squad of the armed soldiers began pushing a shaky-looking piece of scaffolding over to the side of the shuttle—this would be his disembarking ramp, the Zon pilot supposed. He stared out at these soldiers, watching them as they worked feverishly to move the scaffolding into position alongside the shuttle. The pilot disengaged the pressurization cap and soon the flight compartment was flooded with the warm, smoky air of the outside. Down below, he could hear some rumbling from the passengers he'd carried back with him, but there were no signs that they wanted to get off the shuttle in any kind of hurry.

Did they know something he didn't?

The Zon pilot took one more long look out the window. Of all the airplanes parked helter-skelter at the end of the rough, concrete runway, one stuck out. It was a huge, black jet with red trim, and two high tailfins. It was an odd-looking aircraft, frightening in a way. *What kind of pilot would fly that?* the Zon pilot wondered wearily.

He yanked off his helmet, unstrapped from his seat and

then walked to the side door and commenced to unbolt it. Outside he could hear the scaffolding being placed next to the hatch. He took a deep breath, gloomily wondering exactly what awaited him on the other side of the door.

Then he finally twisted the dog-lock, pulled back the lever, and swung the door open.

He was immediately hit with a blast of hot smelly air. He looked down to see two hundred faces looking up at him. Who were all these guys? Mercenaries hired by Viktor to secure this place? Or were they representing somebody else?

He'd expected a dozen of them to come charging up the steps towards him, but now only a single man was approaching. The Zon pilot looked hard at this man— that face, the hair, the thin angular body. He almost looked . . . familiar.

The man had an M-16 up and pointing at him, but as soon as he reached the top of the platform, the man nearly dropped the gun in disbelief. They stared at each other for what seemed like a very long time. The Zon pilot felt many things suddenly begin to click way back in that part of his memory which had been robbed from him two years before.

Wait a second, he thought, I know this guy—and he looks like he knows me.

The Zon pilot took one step out onto the platform, his jaw hanging open, astounded by the man in front of him.

Then it all came flooding back. All the times before he'd been shot down over the Pacific; fighting in America, working with a guy named Crunch O'Malley and a company called Ace Wrecking. A thrill went through him. Those memories hadn't been stolen—just hidden.

"Jessuzz . . . Hunter?" he asked. "Is that really you?"

Hunter's jaw dropped to his chest, too.

"Elvis?" he gasped. "Is that really *you?*"

# Twenty-nine

*Three days later*

The huge CH-53 Sea Stallion helicopter orbited the tiny island twice before finally setting down on its long luxurious beach.

Sticking out of the white sand, just a few feet from the receding water line, was the charred, battered wreckage of a jet fighter. Its tail was twisted horribly, its wings shot through with holes. The damage was so severe, it was hard to tell at first exactly what model jet aircraft it was.

Three men alighted from the helicopter, weapons ready but not cocked. They slogged over to the wreckage and examined it briefly. Finally one turned to the others and nodded.

"This is it," he said. "At least he made it this far."

The three men climbed off the beach and contemplated the heavy jungle before them. This island was part of the Paracels, a handful of atolls located a couple hundred miles off the coast of Vietnam. Ironically enough, this one's name was Money Island.

They reached the foliage line and, as one, bent down to feel the leaves on the byucus trees. They were real, all three decided at once. Not plastic, not fake.

Guns raised midlevel now, they walked carefully into the jungle, looking in very direction, ready for just about anything. Not thirty seconds later, they came to a clearing, in the middle of which was a row of thatched huts. They immediately came to a halt; they could hear people talking, the high, sing-songy cadence of *trang* Vietnamese, a dialect spoken by the very few people who inhabited these remote islands.

But in among these voices, they heard one that was lower, deeper, almost raspy. Its owner was laughing.

They finally walked into the clearing to find most of the commotion was coming from the center hut. Three young girls were sitting out on its bamboo porch, preparing a meal. They were topless. Three more females could be seen just inside the door to the hut. They appeared to be bathing a fourth person.

The three soldiers greeted the girls on the porch as peacefully as they could. The females were startled at first but calmed down right away when they saw the American flag patch on the left shoulder of the soldiers' uniforms.

"We are looking for one of our men," one soldier said. "His plane is down on the beach. Do you know where he is?"

The young girls couldn't speak English but they understood the men anyway. They began nodding and laughing and then pointed inside the hut. The soldiers lowered their weapons, walked up onto the porch and went inside.

The hut was a communal bath house. There was a huge wooden tub in the middle, and in the middle of the tub, covered with suds, was Captain Crunch O'Malley.

He looked first surprised, then relieved, and then embarrassed to see the three soldiers. He didn't know any of them personally, but he recognized their uniforms as being part of the United Americans' Search and Rescue team.

"Doctor Livingston, I presume?" he asked them with a smile, which quickly turned to a grimace and back to a smile again. His right shoulder was heavily bandaged and coated with a slimy substance the rescue soldiers believed was akin to aloe.

"We're glad to see you alive, Captain," one soldier said. "We've been looking for you for three days."

Crunch tried to sit up a little, but his wound prevented him from moving very much.

"I appreciate that, guys," he said. "But I've been in good hands here."

The soldiers eyed the trio of topless Asian beauties and then exchanged knowing glances.

Crunch readjusted himself once again.

"What happened?" he finally gasped.

The soldiers nearly laughed out loud at the question.

"The short story?" one said. "We won . . ."

They gave Crunch an abbreviated version of events since he'd crashed on the island. The fight for Lolita. The sudden appearance of Hunter in the strange MiG-25. The turning of the tide. The arrival of the Zon space shuttle.

Crunch listened to it all with his mouth open so wide, the soapy water was leaking in.

"Viktor has a shuttle?" he asked incredulously.

*"Had* a shuttle," one of the soldiers corrected him. "It's been appropriated by us, you could say. In fact, Hunter and the guys flew the big SEXX Condor into Lolita yesterday morning, somehow loaded the shuttle onboard and flew it out. Majors Wa and Toomey are hopscotching it back home, to the old Cape Canaveral."

Crunch's eyes were now wider than ever. "And where the hell is that devil Viktor now?"

The three soldiers shifted uneasily at this point.

"Still up there," one said, pointing straight up. "When his guys got word that they were running out of landing sites, he transferred aboard the Mir space station."

Crunch nearly leapt out of the tub—but his wound forced him back down.

"Well, we've got to get him," he began ranting. "Someone's got to . . ."

One of the soldiers held his hand up and gently interrupted Crunch.

"They're working on that right now," he said.

Crunch sank back down into the tub. The three girls began soothing his wounds again.

"How many guys did we lose?" he asked softly.

"One hundred and fifteen," was the somber reply. "Sixteen airplanes shot down, including three C-5s. A dozen more heavily damaged, not counting yours. You'll be glad to know *Black Eyes* made it back though."

Crunch smiled at that.

"And there's something else you should know," another soldier said.

He pulled a photograph from his pocket and handed it to Crunch.

"Do you recognize this guy? He was at the controls of the Zon when it came down."

Crunch looked at the photo and once again nearly stood up in the tub.

"My God, is this some kind of a joke?"

The three soldiers shook their heads in unison. "No joke," one said. "That guy is flesh and bones and he says he's a friend of yours . . ."

Crunch stared at the photo. The face, older, with more wrinkles and without the long sideburns, nevertheless looked very familiar.

It was his old partner, Elvis Q, the guy who'd made up the second half of the Ace Wrecking Company.

"How the hell did he . . ."

One of the soldiers held up his hand again.

"That's an even longer story," he said. "Just know that he's alive and well and you guys can get together as soon as we get you out of here."

Crunch sank back down into the warm water again, a

look of contentment replacing the pain and amazement on his face.

"And when will that be?" he asked the three men.

"Whenever you want," one answered. "Right now, if you can make it."

Crunch looked at them, then at the three girls and then down at his wound.

"How about tomorrow?" he asked them, sinking even deeper into the water. "Can you come back then?"

The three soldiers smiled and then saluted him.

"Whatever you say, sir . . ." one told him. "Early morning okay?"

Crunch looked at the three girls once again and then back at the men.

"Make it the afternoon," he said with a soapy grin. *"Late* afternoon."

# Thirty

*One week later*

It was just an hour after sunset when the strange airplane appeared high over Rangoon.

To the legions of radar operators manning dozens of early warning stations around the city, it seemed as if the aircraft had suddenly materialized out of thin air. One moment, their screens were clear; the next, this mysterious blip appeared. Most of the radar techs thought something was wrong with their sets. But several rounds of hasty radio calls to other stations confirmed what their systems were telling them.

The high-flying craft had somehow entered their air space, flashing in at fifty-five thousand feet from somewhere in the east.

What's more, it was heading down towards the city.

By the time the scramble planes at Rangoon's main air base were able to taxi out to their runways, the mysterious airplane was already coming in for a landing. A security detail, a mix of armed jeeps and small tanks, roared out to the landing strip, their soldiers nervous. Nothing like this had ever happened before.

The men inside the advance vehicle of this detail were the first to see the strange airplane up close. Though these soldiers had been around air bases and aircraft for several years now, they had no idea what kind of an airplane was rolling towards them.

The wings were in a delta shape, its nose was long, thin and agile. It had more weapons draped beneath it than the security troops could count. Its tail, high and wildly curved, was also adorned with a number of strange, stiletto like protrusions. Most unusual was the airplane's color scheme. Though the security troops had gotten used to the childish colors of their own air force, this plane's covering almost looked as if it had been burned on. It was bright red and blue on the wings and tail; the rest was almost luminescently white.

The airplane stopped right in front of the lead security truck, and to the surprise of the heavily armed soldiers, its canopy suddenly popped open. The pilot stood up, removed his helmet and rubbed the tangles from his hair.

Then he looked down at the security troops and said: "Please take me to your *swammi-wan* . . . I believe he's expecting me."


Ten minutes later, Hunter was being escorted into the main hall of the Kitchen Palace.

There were three times as many guards on hand as before, but now they stared at him as if he was a ghost. Obviously, word had gotten around about his rather sudden appearance over Rangoon.

Both the Kid King and his mother were waiting on the throne for him. The mother looked angry and bitched-out as always; the kid looked . . . well, he looked worn-out.

Hunter bowed deeply and then took to the first step of the royal platform.

"I have returned as I promised," he told them. "I have kept my word to you. My airplane is at the airport; you may go and see it, touch it, and even keep it in your collection for a while."

The mother snorted a few words of grudgingly disbelief.

"You do me no favors by returning," she huffed. "I'd have been just as happy if you'd stayed away forever."

Hunter took another step up closer to them.

"We had an agreement," he explained, "I kept my end of it. And you kept yours . . ."

They all stared at each other for a long time.

Finally Hunter took a deep breath and asked the big question: "Where is she?"

The Kid King stirred uneasily. He looked down at Hunter, a mixture of emotions spreading across his face. He appeared older, more mature, with wisps of a mustache now sprouting beneath his nose. But one look into his eyes and the Wingman knew something was wrong.

"Where is she?" he demanded again.

But the Kid King did not answer. Instead he looked at his feet.

Hunter took another step closer to him.

*"Where is she?"* he asked a third time, a great fear rising inside him.

But the kid continued staring at his feet.

"She . . . she is not here," he whispered finally. "She stayed with me, as she said she would . . . but only for a little while. I just couldn't take it anymore . . . she was just too . . . too much."

Hunter climbed two more steps. He was furious and the Kid King knew it.

"If anything has happened to her, I will . . ."

"She is safe," the mother huffed again. "In fact, she's in a lot better hands now than when she was flying around the world with you . . ."

Hunter was now level with both of them. The kid still

refused to meet his eyes. The mother, on the other hand, looked like she wanted to take a bite out of him.

"Tell me where she is," he said to both of them.

The mother laughed a little, even as the kid sank lower into his seat. He looked like he was about to cry—a feeling Hunter could relate to.

"By her own choice, she is far away," the mother said finally. "Too far for you to ever find her."

Hunter felt his face turn bright red. He'd been through a lot in the past ten days. Securing the victory on Lolita. Getting the Zon shuttle back to America. Reuniting with his UA comrades to discuss his most recent mission and to plan the next one. But in all that time, Chloe had not once left his thoughts.

"I will go to the ends of the Earth to find her," he told them forcefully.

Now the mother laughed again; this time it was louder and more demonic.

"Oh, you'll have to do that," she told him with a cruel smile. "And more . . ."


*Downtown Rangoon*

The bar was dark and dingy and smelled of burnt coffee, spilled liquor, cheap perfume, and body sweat.

Hunter took a few moments to allow his eyes to get used to the dim light. There was a time in Rangoon's past where consumption of alcohol would have been strictly forbidden. From the looks of the crowded bar, those days were long gone.

He finally stepped in and began walking past the dilapidated tables and booths. They were filled with either gangs of foreign mercenaries or the young soldiers of the Kid King's army. Everyone seemed drunk, the poison of choice being a sweet red rice wine known locally as *pyapon*.

Hunter moved past the bar and the booths to a table far removed from everything and everybody.

This is where he found Baldi.

There were several empty *pyapon* bottles in front of him, and his table was sticky with pools of spilled wine. But Baldi was not drunk. He was beyond intoxication.

Hunter casually sat down, laying his M-16 across the table. The Maltese fighter looked up and gasped slightly. Then tears formed in the corners of his eyes.

"I'm sorry, my old friend," he told Hunter, sinking into his seat. "I fear I let you down."

Hunter picked up a bottle that had just a bit of *pyapon* left in it. He allowed a few drops of the sickly-sweet alcohol to run out onto his finger and then he put it to his tongue. It tasted even worse than it looked.

"They told you where she was?" Baldi asked him, eyes still downcast.

Hunter nodded. "Yes . . ."

"I could not stop her," Baldi told him. "I tried, but she . . . she wanted to go."

"I know," Hunter replied.

Baldi sniffed once and then looked up at him.

"And you are going to try to find her?"

Again Hunter nodded. "I have to."

Baldi's eyes brightened ever so slightly. "Then why have you come here?" he asked.

Hunter put the sticky *pyapon* bottle down then handed Baldi his cap.

"I came, my old friend, to ask you to help me," he said finally.

And so they set out.

First by hired car, up the Taungup highway to Mandalay. From there they crossed over to a ferry which brought them up the Irrawaddy River to Mawu, then Hopin, then Kamiang.

From there, they hired a four-tracked vehicle and headed northwest, towards the highlands of the Kumon Range. Upon reaching the outpost of Kumawang, they traded in the four-track for three llamas and a team of pack hands. They trekked through the hills of Gawai until they reached the Diphu Pass, close to the convergence of the borders of Burma, China and Tibet.

Here was the mountain they called Ch'ayu.

The pack hands left them at this point, leaving one llama and enough food for three days. Hunter and Baldi continued on, walking up the steep, narrow roads, and when they disappeared, the snowy, icy paths which led to the top of the 15,225-foot mountain.

The llama died at about eleven thousand feet.

Night was falling when they reached a way station located at the 14,450-foot mark.

Through the gathering darkness and gloom, Hunter and Baldi could just barely see the spires of a building located on an outcrop of rock near the top of the mountain. The faintest of lights were shining from the top of one tower, one was blandly yellow, the other deep red. Through his knowledge of the local religion, Hunter knew the pair of lights meant visitors could come forth, but only if they promised to descend the mountain after being made faithful.

It was here Baldi decided to stop. He was sore, weary and not predisposed to become "faithful" any time soon. He promised to wait here.

Taking the last of their water, and a cracker tin of food, Hunter continued up the mountain without him.

It was almost midnight when he reached the summit.

The temple was ablaze with lights now, some red, most the bare yellow. Oddly they did not blot out the illumination of the billions of stars stretched overhead. Even in all his travels, Hunter had never seen the stars so bright, so close to the Earth. His eyes were filled with the illusion that he could simply reach out and touch them.

A Be'hei monk was standing by the front door of the temple, solemnly ringing a cast-iron bell every fifteen seconds or so. He looked neither surprised nor concerned when he spotted Hunter approaching. Rather he smiled slightly, displaying a set of crooked, yellowed teeth.

Hunter didn't have to say a word to him; the monk knew why he was here. He simply made a series of hand gestures which directed Hunter around the north side of the temple, to a smaller building located at the very edge of the three-mile precipice. It looked to be an exact recreation of the larger temple, but at about one-tenth the size.

Sitting at its main door, wrapped in saphron and ringing a smaller, brighter bell was Chloe.

Hunter suddenly felt numb from his head to his feet. The long journey, the hard climb, the thinning air, none of it had adequately prepared him for this moment.

Like the monk, she didn't appear surprised to see him.

"You look . . . beautiful," he gulped—it was a stupid thing to say because she *always* looked beautiful.

She simply laughed though and rang her bell once.

He took a step closer. He could smell her fragrance on the wind.

"This is a long way from St. Moritz," he told her.

She laughed again. "It is and it isn't," she replied sweetly. "I've only been here a short while, and yet it feels like forever."

Another step closer. "What's the attraction?"

Another laugh, another ring of the bell. She swept her hand over her head.

"Look at the stars," she said. "They look as close as when we were up in the airplane."

Hunter nodded slowly. "I'll give you that."

"This is my dream come true," she said, her eyes still gazing upwards. "I wanted to be as close to the stars as possible. And now here I am . . ."

Hunter took two more steps towards her. "They tell me that the people up here practice a very—how shall I say it?—'clean' kind of lifestyle. Is it all it's made out to be?"

She laughed again and rang the bell twice. "The word is 'chaste,' Hawk," she said. "And yes, so far, it is . . ."

She pulled her eyes away from the stars and centered them squarely on his.

"Did you come up here to ask me to return with you?"

Hunter just shrugged. "I'm not sure . . ." he said. "Do you want to leave?"

She shrugged right back. "I don't know—yet."

She returned her gaze to the stars. Hunter took two more steps towards her—and the next thing he knew, she was in his arms and he was kissing her, a first.

His heart was pounding, his breath became short. What was happening to him? He had more things to do in other parts of the globe than ever. Yet he didn't want to leave her, ever again.

"Maybe I should stay," he surprised himself by saying.

She looked deeply into his eyes and then slowly shook her head.

"No . . ." she said. "This isn't the place for you. Not now. You wouldn't be happy. And then neither would I."

He kissed her again—and then backed away.

"Will you ever want to leave?" he asked, again with an audible gulp.

She looked at him again.

"Maybe . . ." she said, tears forming in her eyes and rolling down her cheeks. "If you came back. In a year. Maybe I will."

Hunter's next few words had a hard time getting out. Never had anyone affected him this way. He felt a knot tighten in his chest; a lump suddenly grew in his throat.

"I'll come back," he heard himself say. "In a year. Maybe less."

She, too, was beyond words now. She simply looked at him, tears flowing, her face revealing all the time they'd spent together, everything they'd done. Suddenly she looked very much like she did the first time he saw her, swimming in the cold deep lake back in Switzerland. She had changed so much in that short time—and yet she had remained exactly the same.

"I love you, Hawk . . ." she finally managed to say.

Hunter felt like a giant hand had grabbed him around the throat and was squeezing him unmercifully.

"Me, too," he finally coughed out.

They stood and looked at each other for the longest time. Then Hunter pulled up the collar of his flight jacket and adjusted his cap on his head. He pointed up at the stars and smiled.

"I'm going to be a little closer to them very soon," he told her. "Keep an eye out for me, will you?"

She instantly knew what he meant. She wiped away the tears and managed a smile. They'd only known each other a short time, but it seemed like forever.

"I'll wave as you go over," she said.

And with that, Hunter turned around and quickly walked away.

# Thirty-one

*Cape Canaveral*
*One month later*

The dawn broke hot and hazy over the everglade marshes surrounding Launch Pad 37.

Glistening in the early morning sun, being laughed at by squadrons of seagulls, a huge spacecraft stood poised on the rusted platform. It looked very strange at first glance. A huge orange tank, filled with liquid hydrogen, was at its center, flanked by two thinner rockets filled with solid fuel. Attached to these multistoried firecrackers was the refurbished Zon space shuttle.

Clouds of steam were now pouring out of vents in both the Zon and its enormous main fuel tank. A scattering of launch workers—they were not yet experienced enough to be called technicians—were attending to last-minute affairs. Two miles away, inside the main control building, a small but harried group of men were checking a long laundry list of items, making sure that everything was flowing smoothly.

The resurrection of Cape Canaveral and its space facilities had been accomplished in what could only be described as "miraculous time." Actually it had taken ninety-six hours of straight work by a small core of experts, men who'd been space workers before the Big War, just to get the essential computers up and running again.

From there the launch pad had to be cleaned up and made workable, the fuel tanks and solid boosters filled and tested and a billion other details attended to. The Zon itself had spent most of this time inside the massive VAB, the vehicle assembly building, getting flight-worthy again.

Like everything else pertaining to the anticipated launch, it was a question of omission rather than addition. Anything nonessential—from extra safety chutes to redundant toilet flush lines—had been eliminated from the shuttle. This philosophy, that less was more, had transformed the creaky Russian spacecraft into a lean, mean machine, one that would run almost entirely by computer once it left the pad.

*If* it left the pad, that is.

Though security around the space center was extremely tight—no less than a division of UA troops had cordoned off the area, with a squadron of UA fighters patrolling the skies all around—word of the impending launch had spread far and wide. Just like the old days when NASA used to do this on a monthly basis, crowds of civilians had encamped on the beaches and along the roadsides nearest the cape. While they'd all come to see if the United Americans were really going to attempt to put a shuttle into space, most just didn't believe it was possible. Not five years before, America was in ruins, the government nonexistent and daily life in shambles. To be reaching for the stars again, so soon, seemed almost too good to be true.

All through the long hot day, the preparations continued for the launch. At 3 P.M., a small bus-like vehicle left the main control center and began a long, slow journey out to the pad. A small contingent of workers was waiting for it. Gingerly, they helped six spacesuit-clad men out of the transporter and into the elevator and then rode with them to the top of the launch platform.

Moving very slowly, very carefully, the six crew members were loaded inside the Zon, each person taking as long as fifteen minutes to get into place and hooked up for launch.

Then, the preliminary countdown began.

Dusk came as quickly as the dawn had, and soon the long shadows around the cape faded and were replaced by a slight breeze and some bare mists. Activity around the launch pad was oddly muted now. All workers were gone, only the rockets, the shuttle and the crew within remained. On the beaches surrounding the platform and on the roads leading to the space center, vigilant troops and anxious citizens stood together, jackets and hats up against the chill, counting down the minutes to the early evening launch.

By 6 P.M., the secondary countdown was completed—all systems were go. The main computer program was working perfectly, all backup systems were, too. Only about forty-percent of the activity that would have been performed in a typical NASA launch had been initiated this day. If there was one thing the UA had proved, it was that launching the shuttle could be as complicated as its controllers wanted it to be—or as simple.

The sun finally went down for good at 7:01. Two minutes later the final countdown began in earnest.

It was cramped inside the flight compartment of the Zon.

One of the most radical modifications to the spacecraft was the placement of all the blast-off seats up in the flight compartment itself, rather than scattered around the interior of the ship as originally designed.

Two seats were positioned in front of the controls. Two more were located directly behind these, with the third pair facing each other, just inches away. Sitting in these two rear jump seats were Ben Wa and JT Toomey. Like the rest of the crew, both men were stuffed into Russian-style spacesuits that had been thoroughly deloused since being used by the members of the Zon's last flight in space.

Strapped into the middle two seats were the spacecraft's "flight engineers," Colonel Frank Geraci of the NJ104 and Captain Jim Cook of the JAWS team. Both men had had a crash course in Zon operations during the past thirty days.

Sitting in the right-hand front seat, serving as the shuttle's copilot was none other than Elvis Q, fully rehabilitated and anxious now to get back up into space, despite his previous vow never to return.

Sitting in the left-hand seat, and serving as pilot and overall flight commander, was Hawk Hunter himself.

At 7:05, the sixty-second countdown began. Hunter found the strangest thoughts running through his head. Their mission to gain orbit, rendezvous with the Mir and take Viktor by force was oddly removed from his mind at the moment. Rather, he was thinking about his father, ten years gone now, and what he would have thought of him at this moment, poised to either leap into space or die trying. He was sure his old man would have wanted him to at least try, as dangerous as this whole enterprise was.

In the shrinking countdown, Hunter's thoughts also drifted to friends once close to him who had passed on. Mike Fitzgerald, "Bull" Dozer, General Seth Jones. Hundreds of others who had died to regain America's freedom from the clutches of scum like Viktor. This was their day, too.

Thirty seconds to go. Though he tried to avoid it, Hunter then felt his thoughts coming around to Dominique, his long-lost girlfriend, who, as far as he knew, was still living at his farm, *Skyfire,* on Cape Cod. He had not tried to contact her since returning from Southeast Asia, simply because he didn't know what he could say to her. She was used to him being gone for long periods of time—*too* used to it, that was the problem. He knew that even a trip into space would not make confronting her any easier; rather, it would simply delay it.

Down to fifteen seconds now and his mind was vibrating slightly at the irony of it all. If someone had told him a year before that he'd be in this position, ready to go into space, he would have replied that they were crazy. And if they had told him that someone other than Dominique would be on his mind as the seconds ticked down to lift-off, he would have probably suggested mental therapy for them.

But here he was, just moments away from the massive rockets being lit, and the one face that was flooding his consciousness was Chloe's.

Life was very strange.

*Ten seconds,* he heard Crunch's unmistakable drawl tell him through his headphones. Repaired and rejuvenated, the Crunch-man was serving now as launch director.

Eight . . . seven . . . six . . .

Hunter readjusted himself in his seat and took a deep breath. What was Chloe doing right now? Right at that very moment? he wondered. Did she know he was thinking about her? Was she thinking about him? Did she even remember him?

Five . . . four . . . three . . .

His heart began racing. He felt Elvis reach over and tap his arm twice for good luck.

*Dreams do come true,* Hunter thought as the entire world began shuddering with unbelievable violence. They just don't come true in the way you think they will.

Two . . . one . . . *zero!*

There was a strange pause, just a heartbeat or two, and then the rumbling increased, and the noise exploded, and the flight compartment began shaking, and the glow of flames filled the windscreens and the cockpit and the controls. And then it felt like a giant lined him up and gave him the swiftest kick in the pants imaginable.

The Zon began to rise, lighting up the landscape for hundreds of miles around, reflecting on the faces of the security troops and the launch workers and the civilians who'd come to watch, and scaring the gulls who'd been mocking it with their cries all day long.

The Zon cleared the tower with a roar that sounded like a million people cheering at once. Up it went into the darkening sky, the flame from its engines and solid-rocket boosters looking as bright as a comet, making the night turn into day. Up it went, past its own exhaust and smoke, past the thin cloud layer, past the heat of the day.

It quickly turned over just as it should have and began building momentum and velocity. The solid boosters commenced bucking and then separated perfectly. The message was flashed from below that the Zon was go for throttle up—the computer responded and pushed the engines to one hundred ten-percent. Very quickly the miles began passing by like they were feet. Soon the Zon was moving down range at Mach 3, then Mach 4, then Mach 5. Mach 10. Mach 20. Five sonic booms, right in a row, exploded across the empty sky and echoed all the way back to the cape. The crowds roared again; the shuttle streaked up and nearly out of sight until it was a bare light, racing to meet the stars.

Within minutes it would achieve escape velocity of eighteen thousand, five hundred miles per hour—seven miles a second—and break free of the Earth's atmosphere and into that eternal region beyond.

And only then did anyone who cared to finally realize that what seemed impossible just a few months before was now a reality.

Hawk Hunter, the Wingman, was at last, going into space.

*Six hours later*

On the edge of the cliff at the top of the mountain called Ch'ayu, Chloe pulled her robes closer to her face and shook off the dark, early morning chill.

High above, the stars seemed to be twinkling with extra luminescence tonight. The wind was whipping through the valley below, causing a sprinkling of pure crystal snow to rise up and wash across her face. Through these sparklings, she saw a bright light pass overhead, speeding across the sky, leaving a faint trail mixed in among the stars.

She watched it sadly, a single tear rolling down her cheek. Then she raised her hand and waved to it as it raced over, watching until it passed out of sight to the east.

Then she gathered up her robes again and walked back to the temple.

## INFORMATIVE—
## COMPELLING—
## SCINTILLATING—
## NON-FICTION FROM PINNACLE TELLS THE TRUTH: